DURAJAN

BOOK ONE OF THE DURAJAN SERIES

A. H. LEWIS

For information, contact:
Alania Press
www.alaniapress.com

First edition.
Cover design and interior formatting by A. H. Lewis.

ISBN: 979-8-9988458-4-0

Printed in the United States of America

THE CHRONICLES OF DURAJAN

BOOK ONE OF THE DURAJAN SERIES

A. H. LEWIS

ALANIA PRESS

Foreword

This is a story I've carried with me for a long time. Before there were names or timelines, before I knew what shape the world would take, I felt the need to build something rooted in memory, resilience, and the quiet strength of those who refuse to be forgotten. *Chronicles of Durajan* began as notes and fragments written in the spaces between everything else. Over time, they grew into a story I could no longer keep to myself.

This book is a love letter to the kinds of tales that shaped me, and a reflection of the ideas I hold close: that strength can be quiet, that identity can be reclaimed, and that even in isolation, there is power in remembering who you are.

I didn't set out to write a fantasy novel that follows a trend or fits neatly into a genre. I wrote to explore something deeper and something personal. *Durajan* is a world built from questions I've asked my whole life. About belonging, faith, and about what survives when everything else is taken from you.

And maybe most of all, this book is a way of honoring the creative spark that's been with me since childhood, the one that never left, even when time, love, and responsibility set it aside. It's the fulfillment of a promise I made to myself.

If you've picked this up, I hope you feel what I felt while writing it: that there's meaning in the attempt, that story matters, that imagination, when given space, can shape something lasting.

— A. H. Lewis

A Journey Shared

This story would not exist without the creative partnership, encouragement, and foundational world-building work shared with my wife and better half, Anne. Her insight, imagination, and dedication helped shape this novel from the very beginning.

CONTENTS

What was lost.

The world has lingered in silence. The world has forgotten. The world has awakened.

What has risen.

Nine nations, shards of memory and faith, where border wars are common, trust is rare, and peace is a pause, not a promise.

What is feared.

The forgotten lands beyond the Nine, that none dare enter, lest they be claimed by silence, weakness, and forgetting.

A Land between Nations

In the space between conflict and war, faith and fear, gods and creed, lies the land between nations, The Durajan.

None come to the Durajan of free will. They are sent.

Every nation touches its borders: Càrnoth, Skarn, Tharios, Marukh, and Shadura to the west, Khadar and Xeyath to the south, and to the east, Jhandai, and Vordos.

It was born as the result of a truce between the Nine, where oath breakers, rebels, dissidents, and criminals were sent to be forgotten by their people as punishment.

It was where thanes, warlords, kings, and emperors buried their mistakes and discarded their unwanted. A place to dispose of political rivals, silence revolutionaries, and remove those who stood in the way of power.

The Durajan is erasure. A land of the banished, where the condemned are not merely sent to die, but to be unwritten.

PROLOGUE

Beneath the setting wolfsun, mirewings soar above a blood-soaked battlefield, circling, waiting, and descending only once the cries of the wounded and dying fade and the smoke rises. But it is not a battlefield that lies at the borders of nations. It is within the heart of one.

Tharios. North and south. Aguran and Agustus. Brothers and kings, locked in a years-long civil war.

At the field's edge, soldiers light pitch-soaked torches one against another, flames leaping from hand to hand. They stand spent, their victory a weight, not a relief. Spears are pulled from racks as they set out to seek those who remain. Some survivors will be kept for convergence, others for servitude; the fortunate will be slain.

With the battle won, the weary spearmen watch as their commander takes his leave and rides south, carried swiftly by his steed. But there is no pride in him, only purpose. The battle was won, and Aguran, their king, has more pressing matters to tend to.

A long tree-lined road leads to a hilltop manor, where, beneath aged arches and worn pillars, house guards watch their king approach. A stable hand takes his reins, a servant, his gloves and cloak. Both leave in silence.

Inside, Aguran walks through halls and past walls upon which rest weapons, shields, book-lined shelves, and scrolls of all nations.

His path continues up to a chamber where a woman rises from a long table attended by servants. She is fair, calm and statuesque. Her silver hair is worn high and bound, and she is dressed in a gray gown, adorned with simple bands of gold about her arms.

She is Laevina, wife of Aguran.

"How went the battle?" she asks.

"We won," he responds and steps past. "Another victory."

"Does he still resist?" Laevina probes.

"He will always resist. He is no different than the rest. They fell, and so will he."

Aguran sits at the long table. Laevina joins opposite him. Between them, the space is filled by far more than distance.

They share a meal in silence, and while the food is cleared, she watches him, seeking his eyes, admiring his dark hair, his youth, his strength. But he is elsewhere.

Breaking the silence, Laevina asks. "Are there survivors worthy of convergence?"

"I will know by morning."

She knows that is all she will be given.

Her silence softens him. Rising from his place, Aguran walks to stand behind her, placing his hands on her shoulders. Laevina's jeweled hand, aged and frail, touches his. She begins to look away, but Aguran lifts her chin.

When their eyes meet, she hopes that he still sees what rests within her, but he studies her like one seeking to remember but only seeing something that is no longer there.

He bends, and their lips meet briefly before he steps away, leaving the chamber.

Past a grand hall, a girl sits reading within a temple lined with scrolls and books. Priests and scribes work in quiet diligence, transcribing texts from the lands and languages of the Nine.

Under their tutelage, the child studies, her every need tended to, and awaits her daily lesson in the sacred scriptures of the Hollow as written by the First Ones.

The rhythmic echo and rising volume of boots striking stone mark King Aguran's arrival. Holy men and scholars rise as their king enters. As he approaches, the girl smiles at him and he at her, warmth rising in his expression.

Aguran sits alongside her and takes her in. Her skin is dark, warm and rich, with hair as black as night and storm gray eyes that are as beautiful as they are intelligent. For a moment, he is captivated.

"You are beautiful, my dear." His voice is fatherly, yet there is more between his words.

"Are you ready for your studies?" He asks with a soft smile.

She nods and sits closer, alongside him.

The highscribe retrieves a leather-bound tome, accented with umbrasteel and gold. He brings it to their table and sets it before them with reverence. With precise and ceremonial movements, he positions it before his king and the girl, opens it to a specific page, and steps away. Within the book, its sacred scriptures are written in a single language woven of many, the Alltongue.

Aguran's fingers brush the cover as he admires all that has gone into its creation. The king and child share a smile. After a moment, he begins to read the chapters and verses that guide the path upon which he and his house walk in faith. As he begins, his voice is clear and calm. Beside him, her eyes follow the words written.

THE BOOK OF AWAKENING

Chapter 1

1. No one knows how long the Silence lingered but all know what it left behind. Memory was stolen, gods and their monuments lost their meaning, cities collapsed into ruin, language splintered, and knowledge of the very world itself was lost. But life finds a way.

2. The Awakened wandered, discovering places of safety and lands that must not and could not be crossed, for many who went into these lands did not return. Those who did spoke of whispered rituals that could be heard in the ruins of the world before. Fear settled in the hearts of the Awakened, until fear gave way to the sounds of prayer.

3. Belief began to take form as faith reemerged, giving rise to the remembrance of the last of the false gods - Mother, Mountain, Wolf, and Maw.

4. Tribes were formed, led by the faithful and strong. The believers, shamans, and priests, and those who possessed a connection to the gods and the spirits of a world wishing to be remembered.

5. Whether by the hearts of their followers, or by the unseen hands of the false gods, those of deepest belief were rewarded, bringing about the rise of those capable of miracles; sorcerers, sorcerer-priests, and the rare few who carried the authority of the gods themselves: The god speakers.

6. Tribes claimed territories, territories became nations, each one named after their first leaders. Nations became wary and fell into conflict and war.

7. Amidst the conflict, there rose one who began to see its futility. One who believed the only path to peace was a return to silence. One remembered only by the name, Nakarra.

The child listened as she had done many times before. And as he had done each time, he paused here, kissing the top of her head before continuing.

THE BOOK OF NAKARRA

Chapter 1

1. Nakarra walked in places both feared and forbidden, and dreamt of a time before time and thought, beneath hunger and life, and beyond the conflicts that ravaged the Awakened Lands.

2. Emptied of all things, Nakarra found not revelation, but something more profound: a perfect stillness and peace. A place that Nakarra named the Hollow.

3. Nakarra saw that life always ended in sorrow and death. Beasts preyed upon man, and man preyed upon their own kind in an endless cycle of both hunger and savagery.

4. Nations rose with pride and resistance to others. A pride that would lead to bloodshed. There was only peace in the stillness Before. Peace in letting go of what drove all to such senseless cruelty.

5. And so Nakarra wandered, shared, and sought to unite people in the abandonment of these things and to seek stillness in forgetting and surrendering. In time, across the Nine, he found those of like minds.

6. Followers grew, as the Path of Nakarra found fertile soil within the silent places at the edge of nations.

Chapter 2

1. But all things pass. Nakarra died, leaving behind those who felt his work was not yet complete, for change had not yet come to the Nine.

2. These new disciples sought to achieve more than those who walked before. They looked past the teachings of Nakarra and sought to not just observe but to reach into the Hollow itself.

3. And so the Hollow stirred, offered, and waited.

4. Within the silence and stillness, they surrendered themselves wholly. In sacrifice, the disciples sank into the Hollow and like empty vessels, allowed themselves to be filled.

5. Through their sacrifice, the First Ones rose and among them, the first of the Hollowborn, blessed with the power to humble the proud, weaken the strong, cleanse the Awakened World of arrogance, passion, pride and greed, and allow all to be filled with the stillness and silence of the Hollow.

6. From this, the path to the Before became clear. If the Awakened World could not see for themselves, they would be made to. And so the Nakarran Crusade was born and the Hollow Creed was written.

Aguran paused once again and flipped through the book, stopping at a passage.

"The First Ones wrote this, Samike," he said to the child. Then he asked, "Can you read it for me?"

He touched her hair as she sat beside him. She tilted her head, her gray eyes scanning the page, and read the passage before her.

"Pride is pestilence.
Love is loss.

Voice is vanity.
Borders are barriers.

The path has become our purpose,
and from the forgotten to the awakened,
our reach will extend.

We walk forward to the time Before,
where silence is sacred,
where many are made one,
and where the Hollow is holy."

Samike's voice was sweet, and her mind was sharp. Aguran could see she was not merely repeating, but thinking, and he was sure never to interrupt her thoughts. After a moment, she looked at him, and then he pressed his lips to her forehead.

"Well done," he said with warmth and love as the highscribe approached and waited.

"Sleep well, dear child."

Laevina stood nearby, watching beneath the doorway. Aguran noticed his wife, tensing momentarily, but Samike made him smile once again. As she was led away, hand in hand by the highscribe, she waved to Aguran. He smiled and waved in return.

Scribe and child passed by Laevina, who watched her husband for a moment longer before stepping away, leaving her footfalls to echo through the silence.

She who remembers

When the first prayers were whispered in the Time After, she lived and believed.

As wife, shield maiden, warrior, and priest of the Mountain, she rose to stand against the Hollow Creed when it was still forming, and had just begun its spread at the dawn of its crusade.

But she would fall.

She watched her kin surrender their names.

She watched their temples crumble.

She fought against the ruin.

When her people fell, she wandered.

The world forgot her.

She forgot the world.

But she never forgot the Hollow One.

And she never forgot the Mountain, the one God who did not move, even as all things unraveled.

She died with no name.

But something remained.

A breath. A vow. A divine love.

And memory that could not be silenced.

He who endures

"I was born Russom Balewa of the nation of Marukh in the southwest of the Awakened Lands, north of Shadur and south of Tharios. There, the air was warm and the land fertile. My father was a man of declining wealth and waning influence, and I was the firstborn of his three wives, living my days cleaning a shop with too few customers or hawking their wares to passersby.

Marukh and Shadur had suffered enough bloodshed on their borders and had settled into a fragile peace for some time. War would come again, but the truce had held for now. As for Khadar, theirs was a nation of many tribes spread across the southern sands, each led by a Khandar. As a people, they lived in harmony with the land and were peaceful toward neighboring nations and one another—unless provoked.

But to the north, Tharios was not so fortunate, for north of Tharios was Skarnvald, and the Skarn knew little of peace. They were a warrior nation in constant conflict with Càrnoth, along their northern borders, and were forced to endlessly face the never-ending cycle of the Càrnothi Tide.

To the Càrnothi, war was breath, and blood was proof of strength, so as a result, Tharios suffered the wrath of the Skarn, who raided them in the hopes of balancing the losses to their northern foes.

And so it went, on the western ridge of the Awakened World. Conflict and its ripples echoed and flowed southward, affecting all within its wake, but weakening as it ebbed. Càrnothi bled Skarn, and Skarn raided Tharios, but Tharios did not seek outright war with Marukh.

It was common to see Thariosian lords ride through the streets astride steeds born of the savannah herds, clad in their gleaming breastplates, layered battle skirts, and armored sandals. Thariosians considered themselves above the brutality of their northern neighbors and didn't wish to bring blood to Marukh, directly. Instead, they offered gold. Primarily for goods and supplies, but in desperate times, they asked for more.

When I was thirteen years old, one such lord visited my father. His guards' eyes lingered on me as they spoke in hushed words. In the end, a coin-filled coffer was placed on the table. My mother cried, and my father comforted, but both carried on their faces a look of mourning.

On that day, I was sold to Thariosian hands, my body given to King Agustus. All houses of Tharios, loyal to him, had a quota to fill for their wars against the Skarnvald.

My father told me to be strong. He told me I *was* strong. I was angry, but something within me couldn't blame them, for that coin meant life for those my father loved and cared for, so I left without struggle or protest.

Over the years that followed, and in lands far from home, I was made to train, to fight, and to serve, but my will remained my own. Blood and battle became my new mother and father, and I quickly realized the brutal balance of life and death on fields I felt I would not long survive. But I also learned what I could of the languages, peoples, and cultures I encountered.

The Steppelands between Tharios and Skarn were a land of warcamps, fortifications, and fragile peace. There, I rested alongside other warriors, weary of the fighting and grateful for the brief respite that the talks provided, as together we all watched as commanders of our opposing forces held negotiations that decided our fates.

Here, the drawing of blades was forbidden, and to defy meant the brand, so we all obeyed. Oftentimes, in these peace talks, amidst seas of tents and campfires, slavers entered to trade their wares.

It was surprising how many made their living in this manner, hunting down and capturing defectors, escaped slaves and those who had managed to slip free of the grasp of one of the Nine, before receiving the brand and being left to the Durajan.

The most well-known of the slavers were the Xeyathi of the south. They were known for their ability to capture anyone, and hunted like sand hounds.

Skarn brought slaves of their own. Those won in conflicts with Càrnoth and Tharios often discussed the release of Skarn slaves as part of negotiations.

As I sat, I watched, listened, and learned.

As the years came and went, I rose, fighting for survival in wars that I wished to have no part of. I was meant to die, but I fought to prove, even if only to myself, that I was more than a piece of flesh to be bartered for, broken, and abandoned on some distant battlefield.

I was good and became more than just a survivor. Lord Agustus's little boy gave me a name, *Dothemides*. It meant *He who has proven mighty* in the tongue of the Thariosians. To please his son, Agustus ordered that I be referred to by this name, from that day forward.

In time, my birth name no longer felt like it was mine. The thunder of the charge, the roar of the battlefield, and the clash of sword on shield became my breath and heartbeat. I did not revel in victory, but taking the lives of those who sought to take mine was preferable to brutal death. So as I rose and my reputation grew, I learned that with victory came privilege.

King Agustus and his wife, Queen Photini, told me plainly that I would never see my home again. I was a warrior of too much value to their house and the morale of their soldiers. Aside from that, their son liked me and wanted me to stay. And when King Agustus was called to council with allied Thariosian houses, I was brought to his Queen. The darkness of my skin, the strength of my body, she found them pleasing, and I was made to serve in whatever ways she deemed necessary.

It went this way for years, until at twenty-five, I fell.

The battle did not go our way. Legatus Gaius, whose banner I fought under, was slain. The Antonian line had fallen, and the Skarn descended like a storm upon those of us who remained.

The chaos of the field became quiet, and my focus was on survival as battle cries bellowed and blood spilled amidst the collision of opposing forces. In the chaos, I emerged into a clearing and checked to see if I was whole. I thanked the gods, but the space closed in quickly.

To my right, my hammer turned the knee of a warrior inward, cracking it from the side like a broken branch. To my left, it caved in the helm of a shieldmaiden whose face I never saw. Above me, the haft rose to deflect the blow of an axe aimed for my head. My shoulder met his chest, and he stumbled, tripped, and fell over backwards. Beneath me, I saw his face, eyes wide beneath a mask of filth, and then I felt the spray as his head ruptured beneath my hammer.

The strike that nearly took my life was sudden.

Breath left my body, air rushed from my lungs, my strength followed, and my weapon fell. Looking down, a bloody spearhead had suddenly appeared, as if it had somehow grown out from my chest like a thorn from the stem of a rose. For a moment, it was part of me. Then the glinting steel vanished as it was pulled free. I collapsed beneath a haze of pain and the copper taste of blood. As she ran past, spear in hand, axe tucked in her belt, she paused as I lay staring at the sky.

She retrieved my hammer and placed it in my hands.

"The Mountain will judge you," she said.

"And the Far Sky will embrace you."

Hair of flame fell about her face. Eyes blue as the sky above her. I thought, as she left, swallowed by the battle, that she was beautiful.

As the battle ebbed, the field grew still, and I waited.

The soldiers of Skarn roamed, checking the fallen, sinking spears and swords into Thariosian soldiers that I imagined were too far gone, or not of any worth. A soldier found me and glanced down at my wound. He raised his spear, pressed it to my chest, but someone called for him to stop.

With a gesture, my life was spared. Then the world went dark.

I was taken to the home of a woman and learned that her name was Friela—a priestess of the Mother. Friela and others of her faith lived apart from their clan. The Skarnvald prayed to the Mountain and Wolf, but in times of war, the Mother's blessings were looked to, for none knew the ways of life, loss, pleasure, and pain as they did.

I recovered under her care, and she took me before her Thane. Others who were fortunate enough to have survived were gathered as well, each of us bound for a life of servitude. But Friela requested to keep me, stating to her leader that she saw the Mountain's spirit in me: enduring, immovable, and defiant. But more importantly, to her, she saw the Mother's in me as well.

She was granted her wish, and under her touch and teaching, I learned of the Mother's wisdom through devotion and ritual. Where war had taught me pain and loss, the Mother taught me pleasure and life. I abandoned the ways of the blade for the ways of the divine.

For years, I lived and learned with her on the eastern border of Skarn, where the forests gave way to the Durajan, and it was the first time in a long time that I felt the joy and hope of peace and freedom.

In my seventh year by her side, Friela fell ill. A slow, creeping sickness that caused her mind, grace, and beauty to wither and fade. I was allowed to stay by her, to help keep her comfortable, but nothing could be done.

I stood near as the shamans and priests placed her dagger in her hands and prayed for her before she took her last breath. When she died, I watched the flames of her pyre rise and listened to hymns of the Mother, Mountain, and Far Sky.

And as the weeks passed, I realized that I no longer had a place among them. I left and traveled for weeks, making the long journey south to Marukh. When I arrived at the Bulwark of Tharios, the great wall that encircled the nation, I didn't enter. Instead, I followed the wall west, then turned south towards Marukh, all the while wondering what I would do when I arrived.

Soon the Bulwark was behind me and the beauty of Lake Anrhema stretched ahead, the lands of my people. But I didn't continue. Marukh no longer felt like home. The Season of the Mother had come and gone nineteen times since I was sold. Part of me was afraid of seeing my family. Part of me didn't want to. I wondered, were they alive? Were they dead? Had they forgotten about me? I didn't want to face the answers to any of those questions. So I traveled to Tharios and made my way to the southern side ruled by King Aguran where I found peace and purpose working as a woodwright—building homes, and fixing carts and wagon wheels.

My shop was small and simple, and I convinced myself that I could live this way. That I could be content. But I came to understand that the gods move mortals the way winds sweep sand.

I lived a quiet life. But at forty years old, in a market square, I witnessed an injustice.

I don't remember the name of the man who suffered that day, beaten and left to bleed for the amusement of those who held power. I do remember how his eyes pleaded and searched for someone to care.

I was that someone.

Beneath my hand and simple hammer, his three attackers fell. For a brief moment, I reveled in their broken bones and bludgeoned bodies. They weren't soldiers forced to war; they were cruel and corrupt. It was justice, and it was deserved.

Then Aguran guards overwhelmed me. Shackles, beatings, and mock trials followed. My sentence was absolute, and with hot steel, I was branded with the mark that would bar me from all nations.

I was thrown into a cage meant to be my end, and like rotted refuse, I was carted miles southeast into the lands of the Durajan, where I've been left to be scorched by the Wolfsun and die of thirst.

It has been days. So many days. Waiting to die.

They left me with my journal.

But the well has run dry.

The quill is worn and dulled.

These are my last words.

I will perish here on these sands..."

Book of Dothemides, Wolf's Blood 57

Part I

BLOOD

Chapter One

THREADS

Year 1

STILLNESS AND DECISION

The Khadari Desert, Wolf's Blood 59

She had heard the story many times. A story described as fate and purpose. A story defined as destiny. The Nakarrans and their promise of peace, silence, and unity. Between study and duty, King Aguran always spoke of how, without the Nakarrans, he would never have found her. The story was always the same.

Visitors from the forgotten lands to the west, the Nakarrans came bearing no banner. They rode in, seeking an audience with the rival houses of King Aguran and King Agustus, promising a path that would lead to the end of the pride that separated them.

They felt that Tharios had suffered too long and promised a path to unify them beneath one way, one path, one creed. Aguran welcomed the idea. Agustus wished nothing of it.

That was how it began, when Samike was just a child.

To prove his loyalty, worth, and devotion, Aguran was sent to raid one of the Marukhan merchant houses along the shore of Lake Anrhema to the south. It was an unprovoked attack against unsuspecting people.

With their victory came a prize. Slaves were taken, goods seized, and among those found was a girl, one who caught the eye of King Aguran. Considered a blessing, she would remain his until she came of age to serve. Her name was Samike.

Born of Shaduran and Marukhan blood, Samike grew into a stunning beauty. Rich dark skin, pale gray eyes, black hair that fell in waves about her face and shoulders.

By the time she reached eighteen, Samike had become a priceless treasure to Aguran. She possessed a form as alluring as it was elegant, and a mind that was keen and observant. She was raised in the ways of the Creed and taught to please and pleasure the mind and body of her King.

In return, Aguran lavished her with gifts, provided for her every need, granting a life of comfort and education within his palace. She was his obsession. A jewel that Laevina, his wife of many years, tolerated. But when Samike gave birth to twins born of her union with Aguran, it was her end.

Not days after their births, while Aguran was out on another raid, Samike was torn from her quarters and dragged into the depths of the palace. There, she was met by the amber glow of the brand of banishment. Then followed the sting and stench of seared flesh, and the merciless glare of a vengeful wife.

Now, within the tight confines of a sweltering iron cage, Samike sat bent, burned, and bruised. For days, she had been taken southeast, through the Valley of Tharioc, and further east into the Khadari desert region known as Sifur's Breath. As the journey stretched on, her memories ebbed and flowed with the slow sway of the wagon beneath her, dreams of a life now lost.

The wagon stopped, stirring her awake. Her hands reached for the bars and she peered out past the edge of the open cart at the lines left in the sand by its passing. They stretched on for miles. Her eyes lowered. Her heart sank. She would not survive this.

Voices. Discussion. Laughter. Footsteps and the clatter and clink of armor. The doors creaked open. If she could shrink back into the cage, she would have. If she felt there was any use to begging, she would have, but she knew the hearts of these soldiers.

The guards of House Aguran seized her. Rough hands dragged her forward, the heat rising from the pale sand bit into her skin as she stumbled. A satchel and waterskin were thrown at her feet, and a horse, days from death, was left for her.

The soldiers mounted the wagon without another glance. The remaining horse pulled and the wagon wheeled, turned, and rumbled away, growing smaller and smaller until it disappeared beyond the distant dunes.

Samike was left alone, with nothing but wind and horizon.

She wandered for days. Her radiant beauty was dulled by the grime of suffering, yet her spirit remained as unbroken as it had always been.

Samike soon came upon a man who clung to life within the cramped confines of a cruel cage, meant to be his tomb. Studying him, she saw that his body bore the scars of a life spent fighting. His strength was evident, and even in torment, his presence was undeniable, and so she approached with caution.

To free him would be a risk. To let him die would be a cruelty. He was beaten, branded, injured, and dying. If she aided him, she stood the chance of gaining a protector. But what would his expectations be? What would it cost? Her mind filled with both hope and fear, but she was alone. She needed him to survive.

Ignoring the risks, she dismounted, searched and found a stone. From within the cage, she saw his eyes open. Cracked lips parted, his throat too dry to speak. His arm raised, daring to hope.

Samike stood with the stone held above her head. Arms trembling beneath its weight. Their eyes met, and she could see in him both a plea and a promise. She nearly faltered at the sight of him in that moment.

Doubt filled him as she paused. His fate was held in her hands. A tear rolled down his cheek, and in his silence, his eyes revealed acceptance and understanding. Nodding, he rasped.

"I... understand... It's alright."

The sight of him broke something within her. Here was this man, facing his end. Yet he did not beg, he did not rage.

He nodded again, and his eyes closed, freeing her from the fear she held of him. His head fell forward, his body slumped, and he pitched. Samike felt her tears fall as her fears left her.

As his body fell, so too did her heart. She brought down the stone, her chest heaving. She brought it down again, her arms weakening. She brought it down a third time, her voice screaming.

The stone split. The lock shattered. His near lifeless form fell forward, the cage swinging open beneath his weight. She sank by him and brought her waterskin to his lips, pouring what little remained, and prayed.

Dreams. Dreams of the Mother. Her hands raised. Her thunder. Her cry. Her tears. Her touch.

As he opened his eyes, she was there. Not the Mother but his savior. Sitting. Watching him in the light of the morning.

He knew that fate had both found and freed him. He could not speak, he could barely move, but from that moment, he vowed to never let harm come to her.

She reached next to him and placed something on his chest. It was his journal. Left in his cage as a cruelty so that he might write his last words and die without hope of being found. Upon seeing it, he held it and closed his eyes, gripping it tightly.

She watched as he moved to speak, but she calmed him and encouraged him to rest.

By day, Samike searched for water, and by night she sat by his side. As his strength began to return, their bond deepened with each passing moment.

His eyes followed her, and she felt the gentle, welcome weight of his stare. She knew the hearts of men, but he was unlike any she had met, for never once had he asked anything of her. Never once expecting. All she saw and all she felt was his gratitude.

Each day, he watched her and thanked her. She could have left him to die. Yet she risked everything to free him. She was the most beautiful woman he had ever seen and carried about her a gentle mystery that lured him. She was silence, grace, and peace.

One day, when his strength had finally fully returned, he spoke.

"Please know..." She felt his words fall as if he were frightened that she would flee, "...that I will never harm you," he continued.

She stopped and turned. He was sitting up. His black locks fell about his dark shoulders, and his amber eyes shimmered like embers beneath his brow.

"All I will ever do...is protect you."

Samike knew he spoke the truth. She bowed and smiled. She didn't know what to say. She almost felt as if she were held in place by his gaze.

"Thank you..." her voice was soft, serene, and beautiful to him.

He studied her for a moment more. "My name is Dothemides,"

With the campfire between them, she responded. "Samike."

That evening, she returned from finding liferoot and sourgrass and saw that he was gone. She searched, eyes scanning, then heard him return. He stepped into their small camp bearing tinder and scraps of wood and approached. Each movement made to instill trust. She watched him kneel by the fire, offer his finds to its flame, and move back away from her, watchful and respectful.

That night as he slept, Samike crept close and watched him for a time, trying not to make a sound, listening to his breath. Then, there, alongside the crackling fire, she lay alongside him and rested her head and palm against his chest.

Her presence stirred him awake, and upon feeling her weight against him, he did nothing but hold her.

She listened to the rhythm of his breath, slow and deep, and felt the quiet thrum of his heart beneath her cheek. In that stillness, she wondered what kind of man he had been before the cage, and what kind of man he would become now. He hadn't asked for her body and hadn't asked for her name. He had given her no reason to fear him, only reasons to remain.

"I will never harm you...All I will ever do...is protect you."

His words echoed in her mind as she felt his arm wrap around her, and for the first time in years, she let herself be still. Not as a servant. Not as a prize. Just as herself.

Something passed between them in the hush of that night. It wasn't a promise, nor was it love, but something akin to it. Something that asked to be built.

Together, they left their camp. Samike's steed had grown too weak to ride, and fell to sickness and thirst. They continued north towards the hopeful shade of the canyonlands, and in that time, they fought for one another and survived together.

Both had heard and now were experiencing the perils of the Durajan firsthand. It was a brutal, unforgiving land filled with grim scenes. The corpses of branded soldiers who had fallen against one another's blades. Huddled forms of husbands and wives, having succumbed to poisons cloaked in tempting fruit. Half-eaten nobles, their bloated bodies exposing gnawed bones and ravaged limbs. Each of them dying and knowing that no one would remember them.

The Nations banished people from all walks of life. Many of the branded were unfit to survive and many perished. Respect was paid to the dead. But to survive, Dothemides and Samike claimed and put to use the possessions of the fallen—weapons, armor and whatever they could find and put to use, to aid them. Predators were killed, small prey, trapped and hunted, and on the darkest of days, others who were banished were slain.

They were not enemies. Many were not soldiers. They were people who once had families. Sons and daughters, fathers and mothers, each one made wild and feral, driven by fear and famine. Dothemides was no stranger to taking the lives of enemies, but the Durajani were not enemies; they were merely people who were lost, abandoned, frightened, and alone. Samike accepted this as something that must be, in order for them to survive, but for Dothemides, each life taken took its toll.

One morning, Samike chose to share her story. She spoke of the fall of her parents, her captivity as a slave, and the education and luxuries that had shaped her life before banishment. When Dothemides asked about her captors, she said only that she had served in a Thariosian noble house—never daring to speak of Aguran and Laevina, their names, their influence, or their devotion to the Hollow Creed.

She spoke of an initial loathing, however, and the eventual understanding of a master who lived in a loveless home and was married to a bitter and vengeful woman.

She went on to say that she grew to even accept her master's care and eventual love for her. A love that led to the birth of two children, the promise of a place of permanence, and her eventual banishment by his embittered wife.

Dothemides listened not with pity, but with respect. When he told her of the lives he had lived, his age, and the path that led him to the cage, it only reinforced all she had felt for him. Their shared tales brought them closer.

But as they traveled, Dothemides remained plagued by the fate of those left to the Durajan. He began to wonder, to hope, and dream of a way to bring others together, as they had been, and a way to turn the lives of the forgotten into something greater.

Their journey led them to the lush lands further east along the river, where the canyons gave way to jungle and the air was thick with the scent of life. In that fertile riverbed, the seeds of hope were sown, and as their humble camp grew into a home, their struggles shaped their bond and became the cornerstone of their love for one another.

Dothemides soon confided in Samike his dream of forging a sanctuary of order amidst the chaos of the Durajan. She listened and committed, but only did so with half of her heart. She had her protector, friend, and lover, and wasn't sure they needed more. But as the weeks passed, his dream lingered.

It began with her waking to see him gone, only for him to return with word of camps spotted, or torches shimmering in the darkness before sunrise. He was loving, kind, gentle, and passionate, but he was also determined.

It wasn't until he returned one evening, calling out from the forest's edge, that things began to change.

She knew his tone and call. The subtle shifts in pitch and cadence—distant to assure safety, higher to signal danger, quick when he was eager, and low when he desired her.

But this evening was different, and when she opened the gates of the small walls that surrounded their home, she saw that he wasn't alone. He returned with two men and a woman. Each was thin, hungry, skittish, and as she watched, he encouraged them to follow.

Upon seeing Samike, he paused as if awaiting judgment, a look of hope behind his eyes. Samike hesitated, smiled, and stepped forward, pushing the gate open in welcome. Relieved and overjoyed, he smiled in return.

From that day, he channeled his efforts towards convincing the weary, and while some came willingly and others refused, Samike watched with a veiled weariness as the simple life of silence and peace she sought began to change.

And far from the river where dreams took root, fate stirred in the hearts of two children, each bound to the threads of the Durajan's fate.

To the southwest, amidst the Sands of Sifur's Breath, a two-year-old girl named Umaru toddled through her village. Born the daughter of parents banished from the nation of Khadar, her small tribe lived as wanderers of the deserts and canyonlands within the Durajani borders, and were attuned to the rhythms of survival, and the traditions of The Maw.

Even at such a young age, Umaru's fiery nature shone through as she fearlessly mimicked both the hunters and beasts that she observed each day. She was quick, perceptive, and possessed a will that defied her slight frame and few years. The elders of her tribe watched with knowing eyes, sensing that the child who played among the shifting dunes would one day carve a path unlike any before her.

Far to the north, a new life was beginning. On the icy cliffs and shores of Càrn Valloch, a child was born amidst the rising tide and crashing waves of the Sea of Souls. Svirva came into the world on a night when winds howled and storms split the skies. Arican clutched her newborn daughter with silent pride as the firelight flickered upon the infant's black hair and amethyst eyes, rare among her people.

The days that followed saw whispers spread through the Càrn that the Mountain had marked her for something greater. Some called her a blessing, others a curse. But her father merely grunted, calling her *a raven born beneath the storm*.

Chapter Two

FOUNDATIONS

Year 2

LABOR'S YIELDS

"The Nine Nations branded and banished those they sought to forget. It was a greater punishment to live with that understanding than to die beneath an executioner's blade. Whatever you were in life dictated what you were given when sent into the Durajan.

Warriors were left with dulled blades, hunters with fragile bows, merchants with scant goods, and tradesfolk with meager tools. If you were a slave, you were sent with nothing. I was left only with my journal, and I thank the Mother for it.

The fight for survival is our only certainty. That, and the brutal cycle that consumes most of the Durajani we encounter. I hope for a place of safety. A fortification where the fractured and forgotten could rebuild their lives, and where strength, unity, and purpose would replace chaos and despair.

Now, fertile banks promise food and water, while the nearby cliffs and canyons offer natural defenses. I believe the Mother guided us here.

This land is a gift, and we have made it our home."

Book of Dothemides, Mother's Breath 12

"We spend our days searching or working and our nights tending to the sick and mending the wounds suffered during hunts or construction. There is a craftsman of Marukh, two warriors of Shadur, and a hunter of Khadar. Each one bears the brand for reasons they do not speak of. Perhaps it's better this way.

Language is another barrier that keeps them apart, but Samike is our great interpreter. I know some, but not nearly as much. Together, we work to maintain the fragile peace by doing what we can to ease tensions when they rise.

It's not easy, but I hope that in time they will see that there is unity in purpose and hope in belonging."

Book of Dothemides, Mother's Hand 50

Despite the challenges they faced, Dothemides, Samike, and their settlers continued. Trees were felled, thatch woven, and bricks of clay and grass left to dry. Beasts were hunted, croplands were carved, and burdens were shared. Sound traveled far up the river, and the rising smoke of their numerous campfires drew more attention than they sometimes wanted.

As more came and humble homes were built, protective walls rose along the east and west ends of their growing settlement. It had become a fortress, not of size or might, but of spirit and promise. Promise of what it represented and the hope of what it could become.

With the passing of the seasons of the Wolf and Maw, Dothemides proposed an ambitious plan to Samike.

Friela of Skarn had spared his life years ago, and Samike's freed him from his cage, but he believed that it was the Mother who had set him on this path and allowed him to see the balance of things and the reasons behind them. That without their pain and loss, they would not have found one another, these people, or the life and abundance that they all stood to share.

While such thoughts felt strange to her, Samike saw a truth to them and in him. So when Dothemides finally expressed his desire to build a temple to honor the Mother, she could do little else but accept, believing that with it, the Mother might indeed continue to bless their efforts and bind their people under a shared belief.

The temple was constructed, and within it, guided by the teachings of an earlier life, Dothemides led them towards the understanding of the Mother's dual nature.

By the end of the season of the Mountain, carvings and simple paintings honoring the mother adorned the humble sanctum. The scenes depicted were of workers planting seeds and picking fruit, builders felling trees and raising walls, hunters killing prey and drying meat, and lovers entwined in passion. There were images of children being born and of flaming pyres sending the fallen to the Far Sky. The open space, lit by flickering candles, was filled with simple kneeling mats, woven rugs, benches, and furs, and became a space to reflect on their struggles and unity.

Dothemides oversaw the temple's rituals, Samike by his side, her presence lending an air of grace. Though not as much a believer, Samike respected the goddess's influence on their survival and acknowledged the temple's unifying power within their growing community.

“The settlement has grown and the temple is complete. There are fewer conflicts, more trust, and while this is only our second year, there is a growing feeling that something lasting may be born of our efforts.

The proof of that came just this morning when one of the fishermen wondered why people had stopped coming and why we had stopped searching. Samike and I knew that he meant no harm, but I told him that we may have stopped but we have not forgotten. That now, with the Mother honored as she should be, we will begin again. When my eyes fell on Samike I knew she believed as I did.”

Book of Dothemides, Mountain’s Trial 33

Efforts shifted to the lands beyond the settlement's walls. The southern regions were rife with fragmented tribes, and each was a potential adversary or ally.

Each tribe and campsite was approached with an offer of stability. Samike’s knowledge of various cultures and her ability to speak many languages proved invaluable. Her words, coupled with Dothemides’ growing reputation, convinced more to join his cause.

However, not all tribes welcomed them. Violent clashes were as common as the blessed rains, but whenever possible, Dothemides offered peace.

By the year’s end, The Obsidian Fortress, named by his followers to honor the strength and skin of its leader, stood as a testament to hope, resilience, and determination. Beside it, the Temple of the Mother had become the spiritual center of their growing community.

On the last eve of Mountain's Silence, a day that marked the end of things, a time of transition, judgment, and reflection, Dothemides stood with Samike on the fortress walls, watching the sun dip beneath the horizon. Below, the river flowed steadily, its waters a reminder of the life they were building.

He took her hand in his. "This is just the beginning," he said, with a voice filled with hope.

Samike placed her hand atop his, her gray eyes catching the last rays of the sun.

"And it is a beginning, blessed with promise."

Chapter Three

The Way of the Mother

Year 3

TIDES

Amid the harsh realities of life within the Durajan, Dothemides and Samike welcomed their first child into the world. They named her Kaelani. Her birth marked a moment of joy within the walls of the still-developing Obsidian Fortress. Samike bore their daughter in the season of the Wolf, surrounded by the sounds of construction and the scent of stone dust—a reflection of the unfinished world into which Kaelani entered.

Kaelani's amber eyes, inherited from Dothemides, seemed to blaze with his determination, while her soft features spoke of Samike's quiet resilience and beauty.

One was not expected to live long, once banished, let alone bear children. And although Kaelani was born without the brand, she was branded by birth nonetheless. As they watched her, they wondered if perhaps she was the first child born to the Durajan amidst a blended people and relative peace and safety.

Most Durajani kept to themselves. Many lingered near their home nations, clinging to hope, only to face being driven away from their walls and borders, but settlers did speak of children born amidst struggle.

Some parents attempted to leave their children at the gates of their home nations, others dared to send their eldest into the nations to fetch goods, steal, and find what they could. However, each story ended much the same—grim, unspeakable, and unforgiving.

Opposite to those who clung to their homelands were those who clung to their own. They were the People of the Sands, born of Khadar, Howlers of the savannah born of Marukh, slavers of the jungles born from the banished of Xeyath, and coastal settlements of the Jhandai and Vordan.

The great tribes of southern Durajan were more heard of than seen, and the lands north of the canyons remained a mystery to the southlanders. Though many still fought one another as smaller versions of their former nations, closed off and often cruel, Dothemides still saw them as people of shared pasts.

But in Kaelani, the people of the Obsidian Fortress didn't just see hope, they saw a future. The Mother had blessed them with life, shelter, and safety. Surely more would be born here among them, and Dothemides determined that children of the Obsidian Fortress would be taught to take pride in the people that would one day emerge from this place of refuge and unity.

Some settlers began to call Kaelani, Princess and Firstborn. Titles that cemented Dothemides and Samike's rising authority. They were no longer just leaders in hope, defiance, and faith; they were founders of what some dared to dream would one day be a kingdom. Kaelani was the first, and many felt the Mother would bless them with more.

Kaelani was just months old, but had already become a symbol of what life within the Obsidian Fortress could offer. With the rise of the temple and the falling away of language barriers, a desire for life spread amongst the settlers.

Life and new beginnings became more valuable than the bonds of marriage. There were pairings, but Dothemides believed they should be pairings of the heart, not bindings of the body. He believed they had no place here. Not in a land where life could be so fleeting.

Friela taught him that it was the way of the Mother to ensure the continuation of life in a world defined by war. Lives were often lost, and The Way of the Mother ensured that in her temples, all boundaries and bonds were left at the altar so that all could embrace the passion-fueled fires that brought with them the promise of new life.

Dothemides first witnessed a ritual of the Mother after a battle in which several warriors had not returned. Led by Priests of the Mother, villagers assembled, shed their clothes, pride, and bonds. It was sacred and it was beautiful.

He decided to initiate the same here. At first, many seemed shy and reluctant, but in time and with guidance, their feelings changed, and the rituals were embraced by all.

On one such eve, as the fortresses' defenders fell into one another's arms, a Vordan woman, new to the Obsidian Fortress, caught Dothemides' eye. Her gaze lingered upon him as the temple ebbed and flowed rhythmically around them.

A glance across the room revealed Samike in the arms of another. She, too, was uncertain at first but had learned to lose herself in the rituals as well. When he looked back, the woman of Vordos was before him. Her striking black hair and piercing dark eyes captivated him, and together, they sank into the tides that filled the room.

Celebrations of several births marked the year's end. Among them was a child who would be named Amubira, the daughter of Dothemides and the gentle woman of Vordos, Loreiaka.

Amubira was born in the Season of the Mountain. A daughter whose presence would forever tie Loreiaka to the burgeoning settlement and its leaders. And while she was not taken as a wife according to Marukhan traditions, Loreiaka held her place through the grace and warm embrace of Samike and the gentle protection of Dothemides.

Amubira, half-sister to Kaelani Firstborn, was blessed with her mother's grace and her father's indomitable spirit. She became a curiosity and symbol of unity within the community, embodying the complexities of their growing society. Where Kaelani stood as a promise, Amubira was proof that even fractured beginnings could forge unity.

Chapter Four

The Blade Not Drawn

Year 4

FAVORED BONDS

There are years that change everything, and others that allow things to take root. Year four was the latter. The walls of the Obsidian Fortress rose higher, its people grew in number, and amidst the shore and soil, new lives were nurtured. Children took their first steps on dust-packed roads. The voices of many tongues learned languages they never thought they would speak. Samike, now twenty-two, held her daughter with quiet strength and led their people with grace, while Loreiaka moved without fear, walking freely among settlers who once eyed her with suspicion. It was a year where craft folk carved toys of wood, mothers and fathers sang lullabies, and all learned to smile more easily.

For Dothemides, fatherhood deepened his purpose. Each breath drawn by Kaelani and Amubira seemed to reaffirm what the fortress had become, not just a place of survival, but one where new life could take root and flourish.

And still, he carried the weight of its future. He felt it in his bones when he walked alone, in the silence after temple gatherings and rituals, and in the dreams that returned with ever more urgency.

It was in this quiet season, a year of growth and nurture, that he made a decision to leave the fortress and venture into the unknown lands to the east alone.

The Xeyathi Jungles. Several miles east of the Obsidian Fortress.

The eastern jungles. A rain-soaked region claimed and fiercely protected by those branded and banished from the southern island nation of Xeyath. Dothemides searched for days. The rain fell in heavy sheets, drenching the jungle in a rhythmic whisper of droplets against leaves and earth.

He had barely taken another step before the blade flashed through the downpour, a silver arc aimed at his throat.

Instinct saved him. Dothemides twisted, his sword rising just in time to meet the strike. The rising storm muffled the clang of steel. His attacker was quick and relentless. A second strike followed, testing his defense, slicing the air too close to his ribs. Whoever she was, she meant to kill him.

He took a step back, studying her. Black hair, jade eyes, full lips curled in defiance. Rain traced the contours of her form, lithe, strong, a coiled spring of intense beauty, strength, and intent. But beneath the sharp skill, her eyes flickered with something else. Fear.

Dothemides held his blade steady but did not press forward. He had seen her kind before, in the lulls between campaigns for his former Thariosian masters. She was of the Jhandai—seafarers, traders, and warriors from the eastern nation. But here, alone and ragged, she bore the brand. A fate he knew all too well.

His grip loosened. A stayed blade. A raised hand. A chance.

"We need not be enemies," he said, hoping and praying she understood his crude attempts at the language of her people.

She understood him. Yet still, there was wariness and distrust. The distance between them was more than a blade's length. It was the chasm born of banishment and of different pasts.

But she didn't strike again.

Dothemides sheathed his sword, tapped his chest gently. "My name is Dothemides."

For a moment, only the sound of the rain. Then, finally, her lips parted. "Bianzhi."

Her eyes swept over him. Assessing. Considering. Her breath slowed, the tension in her limbs unwinding just enough for another kind of tension to form between them. A wariness that did not deny curiosity.

But the barrier remained. Words. Trust. A reason.

He reached into his satchel, fingers brushing the worn pages of the journal given to him by Friela long ago. In it, he kept notes, observations, plans, flipping past maps, and sketches of landscapes, until he found the sketch of the fortress. His dream. The future he was building. He turned the book toward Bianzhi, tapping the inked outline of the half-built stronghold.

"Bianzhi...this is where I, and many others, live." He said with hope and warmth. "Are you alone? If so, you need not be."

Her jade eyes flicked between the drawing and his face. He could see the questions in them. Why should she believe him? Why should she trust him?

"I can be trusted." His eyes held hers. It was an invitation to a better life.

Then came the screams.

A chorus of war cries, cutting through the rain like sharpened steel.

Xeyathi.

Sword Clans and slavers of the eastern forests, always hunting lone Durajani for bloodsport, bondage or trade. They emerged from the shadows, faces painted in deep green and brown, sigils of the hunt. Their leader wore the head of a longtooth as a helm, its paws decorated his pauldrons, and its hide formed a cloak. Their blades were thirsty, but it was their nets the pair feared. They circled them like hunters circling prey. Ready. Waiting.

The net soared, whirling through the rain towards Bianzhi. Time slowed. Through its coarse mesh, she saw him briefly before she rolled away, a bronze-skinned, black-haired hunter. As she stood, he was already upon her. Her curved blade met his fighting sticks in a series of rapid deflections. Her movements were effortless, deadly, poetic. Dothemides was soon at her side, and together they fought as though their lives depended on it.

The Xeyathi were fast, relentless, and merciless. It was clear they wanted Bianzhi captured alive and Dothemides dead.

One blade found his side, and fire shot through his ribs. Bianzhi was struck from behind. A blunt blow that knocked her off balance and sent her sprawling into the mud. He was on her immediately.

She struggled, but her blade was pinned.

Dothemides roared. Through the agony in his side, he lunged, his sword cutting through flesh, spraying red into the downpour. The attacker fell, and he reached down, grabbing Bianzhi's hand and pulling her back to her feet.

More were coming. Too many. Another fell beneath the arc of Bianzhi's blade. She exhaled, staggering. Dothemides barely stayed upright. His vision blurred, his body screaming.

"It is not safe here," he rasped, each word drenched in agony.

Through the downpour, his journal lay in the mud, pages smeared and torn. He reached down, fingers unsteady, and picked it up. His hand, slick with blood, pressed against the fort's image. A mark. A promise.

Bianzhi looked at him. Then the journal. Understanding flickered in her jade eyes. Not complete trust, but something close.

She nodded once.

And without another word, they vanished into the jungle.

Chapter Five

The Beginning of Memory

Year 5

LIFE'S TAPESTRY

"My weathered journal's last page. Since it was given to me by Friela, I've filled its pages with all that has gone before. All the lives I've lived thus far.

It was she who first told me that in me she saw a man the world must remember. That the Mother had told her so.

It has been five years since the cage was broken by Samike, and the seed planted by my dream has finally broken the surface of the soil.

Through these pages, I remember who I am. This journal means everything to me because it means that I have lived. The words in these pages are anchors that defy the silence imposed by banishment.

Wouldn't it be a beautiful thing to give all who settle here such a gift?

I think I will. And with it, a promise and path to remembrance.

If the world beyond chooses to forget us, then I will ensure that here, within our walls, all will be remembered."

Book of Dothemides, Mother's Breath 7

Weeks passed as stone continued to rise at the heart of their settlement, shaped by calloused hands and quiet will. Fires burned through the long nights, and the people worked not by order, but by choice. Dothemides moved and worked among them, steady and grounded, providing direction, not demands. What they were building was far more than walls.

Dothemides spoke to Samike of his plan for the journals and the beauty of their meaning. To her, it was a wonderful idea, and the thought of it brought a smile to her lips and warmth to her heart. She promised to keep his efforts secret until he was ready to reveal his gifts.

He worked in the evenings when the noise of construction gave way to silence. Bark sheets, scraps of parchment, and pressed hide were shaped into simple books. Soot, water, and oils were crushed into ink. Reeds and feathers, whittled and shaped into quills.

The first came from his own hands.

Dothemides gave them out, one by one. Not in speeches or rituals. Just a quiet handoff accompanied by a nod, a touch of the shoulder, a heartfelt gaze, and words that let them know that they need not be forgotten. He told them with sincerity that they could be remembered in their writings and that each of them, no matter their past, possessed a voice that was sacred.

The bindings were rough at first, but they held. Their covers were as bare as their pages, for what mattered was what went inside. It wasn't long before others stepped forward to lend their craft and offer their help.

At first, only a few wrote. Sitting by their fires, scratching out short thoughts and brief notes of the day. Some didn't know how, so those who could write began to teach.

Names were spelled out with patience, as hands were guided. Letters were practiced until they held meaning, and at night, as torches burned low and fires crackled, the silence of a people lost in reflection began to fall over the settlement.

At the end of each day, people gathered in corners, in humble homes, near the walls, or by their bunks. They wrote what they saw, what they felt, and what they remembered. Not all words were perfect. Some pages were marked with tears. Others with sketches, pressed leaves, strands of hair, or bits of twine or cloth.

They became the books of the remembered, and soon it became ritual.

The Obsidian Fortress had become a place where memory was held, lives were named, and silence gave way to story. And every night, as the wind crossed the river valley, pages turned, revealing quiet proof that they were still here, and still worth remembering.

"An interesting thing happened tonight in the temple just after the ritual. We were all preparing to return to our homes when a voice rose and a man stepped forward.

Like each of us, he held his journal in his hand.

He could have been born of Marukh or Khadar, but by his accent, he was Marukhan, and by his look, he was a recent arrival. He stood straight but humble, and spoke his name with a calm strength. Koba.

He was a tall, rugged man of dark brown skin, short black hair, and a coarse beard. He stood slender, strong, and bore several scars.

He addressed Dothemides as *Great King.* Dothemides smiled, embarrassed by the title, and humbly asked him to call him by name.

When he was encouraged to continue, Koba stated that they had embraced the gift given—the right to remember, to write, and be seen. The right to live in *Dothemia*.

Dothemia, it was the first time our settlement had been given a name. I could see that my love was as surprised and touched as I. The people had named it after him. It was beautiful. I wondered how many had been using the name and how far the name had traveled.

Koba stated that he loved the gift, and then asked.

But when do we begin?

Not in history's terms, or by the years agreed upon by the Nine, but by Dothemia's terms. Dothemia's history.

He wanted to know when *our* story, *this* story, truly began.

It was a question that neither Dothemides nor I had considered, and it sparked discussion across the room.

Another voice rose above the rest. Stepping forward, she stated that her name was Haphira and that she hailed from Tharios. She was pretty but shy, with shoulder-length hair like the sun and eyes like the open sky.

She stood beside Koba and said she had heard that it had been five years since Dothemides and I met in the desert. Five years since I freed my husband from the cage. Five years since his dream began to take shape.

She first spoke with reticence and timidity, but then with conviction, and hope that perhaps the day the cage was broken, should mark the beginning of our time. The day all should view as their beginning.

Koba looked at her, and there was an understanding between them. Then he spoke again, adding to her thoughts. He said with passion and agreement that if we chose that day, we could cast off the timekeeping of the Nine and that in doing so, we and all Durajani could begin a new era.

Dothemides looked at me, and when I looked at him, I saw both pride and humility in his eyes. I took his hand and nodded. He did as well.

There was no vote or great proclamation, just a quiet agreement, shared in glances, words, and small smiles. Some embraced one another. Some wept, but we all felt it.

So tonight, in my journal, I still honor the gods, seasons, and cycles, but we begin again, grounded and sure."

Book of Samike, Mother's Hand 29, Year 5

"Koba and Haphira. A newcomer from Marukh, and a young woman of Tharios. Their questions and words brought great pride to the hearts of the people.

Koba reminded me of home, and Haphira reminded me of the people I was made to serve.

It made me think of my years in service to King Agustus, of the city of Tharios, of the time I lived under King Aguran, and of the Skarnvald Steppes beyond its eastern walls, where the Skarn sent those they banished.

Surely there are people of Skarn who now wander alone. Or perhaps tribes willing to build bridges. If Dothemia is to grow, its future is to be more than survival. If others are to believe and understand they are not forgotten, we need to find them, ally with them, and through them, learn of what lies beyond.

But between us and the Steppes lies the canyonlands. Steep, treacherous, and miles long.

If this dream is to be realized, we must find a way through."

Book of Dothemides, Mother's Hand 40, Year 5

"He does not wish to be called King, but I believe he is more of a king than the king I once served in Tharios. Aguran is a madman, and Agustus resists, but their war is leading the nation to ruin.

I knew what my refusal to fight would lead to, and I refused anyway. I think I am better for it. At least here I have something to fight for. Something I believe in."

Book of Haphira, Mother's Hand 45, Year 5

"Exploration has become part of our daily rhythm. Some days, Samike remains home with Kaelani. On others, she joins us. When she does, I always ask Bianzhi to stay close to her. Protect her.

I was grateful Samike was not with us on our last journey.

We traveled northeast for days, and journeyed miles from home, yet still we found only the unbroken expanse and jagged stone of the canyons, and no visible passage.

We considered scaling the cliffs, but the risk was too great. So we turned back and once home, we shared the news.

Later, around the hearthfire, newcomers spoke of a passage seen far to the northeast, somewhere north of the Woundwood.

I left to rest, while stories were still being shared. I kissed Samike, and she handed me Kaelani, who smiled but quickly drifted to sleep as I walked back home. Clearly, she was as tired as I was.

Tomorrow is another day, and plans for a journey northeast can begin then.

But for now, it's time for me to stop writing and for both of us to get some rest."

Book of Dothemides, Mother's Hand 50, Year 5

"Last night, when Dothemides went to rest, he may have missed the best tale of the evening.

It came from a man named Bakhuran, a Durajani born of Khadar.

Bakhuran was an elder who claimed to have wandered the canyons in his youth and warned us of *Hollowed Ground*.

According to him, they were *places of forgetting with land that quakes beneath your feet, and where those who enter are never seen again.*

*Go not into those hills and canyon*s, he told us.

To me, he was just a long-lived shaman, preparing to ascend the Mountain for the last time, and just wished to share some tall tale.

I laughed. Perhaps too hard. Definitely too loud.

I walked back with Samike, and before we parted ways, she touched my hand and said that all voices should be heard and all warnings heeded. She did it in her way, with strength and calm. Sometimes I feel the steel gray of her eyes matches the steel of her spirit. It was not a reprimand, just a reminder.

Earlier this morning, Dothemides pulled me aside and told me to prepare. I guess Samike retold Bakhuran's story, and it struck a chord with him.

I suppose we'll soon see if there is any truth to them."

Book of Bianzhi, Mother's Hand 51, Year 5

"We followed the rumors and traced the loose sketches drawn up by Bakhuran. At first, it looked like any other canyon. Worn rock, weathered stone.

I could feel the disappointment in our group.

Then something shifted. Not around us, but beneath us. A deep rumble. A low, almost living sound. It made the hairs rise on the backs of our necks. On either side of the canyon along the eastern and western walls, gaping holes sat in the cliffsides. It was a bad sign.

Then, something came from the western cave. First, a hand. If you could call it that. Clubbed fingers crumbled the stone where they gripped, high in the cave entrance. Then the head emerged, carved like a sculpture. It was weathered and massive, eyes glowing like embers beneath a cracked brow. Horns swept back from its skull, like those of a great ram.

The creature that stepped out before us was ancient. A thing born of stone. We all thought of Bakhuran's warning. I cursed myself for not taking him seriously.

Massive arms rested on the ground like rooted trees and its legs were like stone stumps. Then the thing just stood, stooped, towering, unmoving, and watching.

Dothemides voiced what we all knew. Our weapons would shatter against its hide and our armor would be crushed with us inside it. This was not a fight we could win. And it wasn't a thing to be reasoned with.

There was no argument when he ordered the retreat, and we pulled back without hesitation.

As we made our way home, Dothemides rode beside Samike, silent in thought. The rest of us traded nervous laughter, trying to turn fear into something smaller than it was.

Gods help us. What else are we going to find out here?"

Book of Bianzhi, Mother's Womb 58, Year 5

"Tonight, following the ritual of the Mother, the tale of their encounter in the Northwest Passage was retold. Dothemides has been asked to retell it many times in the days since their return.

Everyone wanted to hear of the Living Mountain—of the stone that walked, watched, and waited. They listened with both fear and awe.

But as our king spoke, I found my eyes drifting to Samike. She was beautiful. I felt my mind wander to places it should not. Sights I had glimpsed during rituals to the Mother. Of becoming one of her favored, but then her eyes found mine, and I froze as she held them.

All listened as Bianzhi joined in the telling again, and laughed as she spoke about her initial disbelief, pausing to bow to Bakhuran, who sat wordlessly at the edge of the gathering.

But Samike glanced across the room, with a slight widening of her eyes and subtle tilt of her head. Still half-frozen, I followed her gaze and at the end of it was Haphira. Sitting there beneath the dim light of the temple candles. And she was looking straight at me.

Haphira's cheeks darkened, and she looked away as if she had been caught doing something secret. Something stolen. Just like me moments ago.

I glanced back at Samike, who smiled laughed gently, then raised her cup to me and Haphira. I looked back to Haphira and felt a quickening in my chest as I felt her lingering stare. It spoke of invitation. I smiled at her and she smiled back at me.

Somehow, I think Samike knew this path before Haphira and I did.

It is morning now, and Haphira stirs beneath the furs we shared last night. She smiles at me as I write and summons me to her side with a pat of her hand and a sweet laugh.

Lady Samike, Mother bless her.

She is the speaker of tongues and a knower of passions."

Book of Koba, Mother's Womb 65, Year 5

"I received a gift today. At first, I was unwilling to accept, but Samike encouraged me to embrace the gifts given by those who come to live among us.

The gift came in the form of a steed, presented by a man of failing health who hailed from the nation of Shadura. He introduced himself as Rahandi.

He bowed as he approached, and his voice was gentle, with eyes lined with both pride and sorrow. He told me the horse's name was Cepharion.

Over the years, our explorations had taken us southwest to the Savannah, where we found young foals, injured mares, or young stallions who had been ousted from a herd. It was not without risk that we claimed them. They served us well in our expeditions, but this one. Cepharion was something entirely different.

According to Rahandi, Cepharion was a storied steed. He was won in a duel between a Shaduran swordsman named Sajiram and a Marukhan warrior named Tumasheq, who had bested a Thariosian officer named Cassion in a wrestling match, earning Sajiram Cepharion's reins. That

Thariosian officer claimed to have ridden Cepharion into numerous battles against the Skarn.

When I asked how Rahandi came to own the horse, he stated that his son was Sajiram, the Shaduran swordsman who bested the Marukhan warrior.

When I asked where his Sajiram was, Rahandi stated that his son remained home with his mother, Tavindra, and that Rahandi took the brand in his son's stead, believing that the sickness he bore would claim him soon anyway and that his mother would need his son's strength and protection more than his failing health.

Heartbroken, Rahandi's son gave him the steed to carry him northeast, across the savannah, towards the rumors of a rising safe haven—Dothemia.

When Rahandi gave the steed to me, he said that Cepharion belonged more to a warrior and king than to an old man.

I thanked him, embraced him, and welcomed him. We all did. And in return for his gift, he was given a home and a journal so that his tale and the story of his beloved wife Tavindra, his brave son Sajiram, Cassion, the warrior of Tharios, and Tumasheq of Marukh would be remembered.

It saddens me that Rahandi's end is nearing, but I am glad to know he will spend them here in comfort and peace."

Book of Dothemides, Mother's Womb 72, Year 5

Mother's Womb 73

With the northeast passage blocked by the Living Mountain, Dothemides called for volunteers to seek a new way north through the canyons. Several stepped forward, new faces, eager and ready, and among them, two familiar ones—Koba and Haphira.

Dothemides, Samike, and Bianzhi rode on horseback, while Koba, Haphira, and four others traveled on foot.

Steeds remained scarce in the Durajan and difficult to come by. The southwestern nations had long looked to the savannah herds, and as Durajani, they did the same. But the herds were dangerous, and success was rare. What little horses they gained were pulled from the weak, lost, or injured. Most were fit only to serve as beasts of burden, and the rare few that were strong enough were prized and granted to those whose roles demanded reach and speed.

They moved northeast through narrow ravines, then bent westward, following the canyon's spine. For days, they traveled. Their feet were worn and spirits pressed by the long, winding ascent. The path wound until they crested atop a plateau.

Canyon walls reached high on either side, and at its center, surrounded by jagged stone, stood a crumbled altar. Weathered. Ruined.

Samike froze at the sight of it. She knew this kind of altar and had tried and failed to forget the kinds of rituals once performed around them.

"We should turn back." Samike's voice faltered. She could not explain and she didn't wish to. She only knew that something was wrong.

Dothemides had never seen her look so unnerved, but beyond the altar, on the far end of the canyon, the land sloped away and the canyons gave way to the open plain and sky of the steppelands. It was the path they had sought for weeks.

Dothemides paused, considering her words and weighing the risks.

"We've come too far and searched too long. We are too close."

He felt it too. Something did not sit right with him. With this place.

"We can't turn back, my love. Just a little further."

His eyes met hers and again she saw the look of hope within them, and his lingering promise of protection and love, no matter the cost.

The others waited as their leaders decided. Samike nodded reluctantly, and Dothemides held her hand firmly for a moment. Then with a gesture to the others, they moved forward carefully.

Bakhuran's warnings echoed in their minds as unease shifted into a quiet dread. They all felt it. First, an unsettling chill, then thoughts growing unclear, followed by an ache born not from exertion, but from something deeper.

Dothemides was grateful for Cepharion's calm, but the others were not so fortunate. Their steeds stamped and tossed their heads, eyes wide, muscles tense, nostrils flared.

"First the Living Mountain, now this." Bianzhi cursed as she steadied hers.

"These canyons are cursed." Haphira drew her blade and readied her shield, stepping closer to Koba, who said nothing but only watched, tense and ready.

Then came the movement. Figures stirred in the shadows and emerged from both ahead and behind. They were clad in leather armor, wore heavy fur cloaks, boots, and bracers. Their skin was fair, hair braided, their faces were blue streaked, painted for war, and they bore swords, axes, spears, and shields.

"Skarnvald," Dothemides spoke the word with certainty.

"We mean no harm," He called, gesturing to the others to lay down their weapons.

"We only seek passage through to the steppelands."

No response.

"They may have been Skarnvald once, my love, but they are no longer." Samike's words hung in the air.

Then they began to see the signs—the cracks in shields, chipped axes, and broken swords. The faded warpaint, disheveled and unkempt hair, the filth and poor condition of armor that hung too large against gaunt, worn bodies, as if their skin were stretched too tight across their bones.

They neither spoke nor gestured. They only watched the group in silence—dozens of men and women.

Dothemides called out, rallying the group to draw close. Bianzhi moved to shield Samike. Koba and Haphira flanked him, and the remaining volunteers stood nearby. Their armor was humble, their weapons simple. But their strength lay in one another.

Then the stillness shattered. The guardians of the pass surged.

Dothemides held Cepharion's reins and drew his blade. Samike and Bianzhi readied their bows. Koba's spear lowered, and Haphira stepped forward, sword and shield raised as the volunteers readied their bows and spears.

The circle tightened.

The battle began.

Arrows were loosed and found their targets. Striking but not slowing. Bianzhi's arrow struck the throat of one, Samike's the heart of another. Still, they came, closing the distance. They did not cry out. They did not roar. They came without sound but with deadly purpose. Aside from the impact of arrows, all that was heard was the shuffling of their footfalls, the rustling of their armor, the commands of Dothemides, and the steady breath of Bianzhi, Koba, and Haphira alongside the remainder of the Dothemian volunteers.

They were too close now. Dothemides struck first. His blade descended, splitting the brittle shield of the warrior before him, cleaving the arm with it, yet still the Skarn's axe raised and swung. Dothemides deflected the blade and kicked, sending the man sprawling back.

Ducking beneath a strike, Haphira severed a leg at the knee, sending her attacker crashing down, but still he crawled, clawing forward. Samike loosed an arrow into the thigh of another, but he remained upright, dragging his foot as he advanced.

Dothemides claimed another arm. Haphira's blade found the throat of a woman who stumbled, bled, and still came forward.

A jagged spearhead caught Haphira's arm. Blood flowed, and as she staggered back, Koba thrust his spear into her attacker's belly, pulled it free, and struck again. Both attacks should have killed, yet they didn't.

These dark Skarn felt no pain and would not fall. Dothemides shouted for them to press north, to push through. Bianzhi hesitated.

"We should retreat!" she called.

"We've come too far!" Dothemides replied.

They fought through moving together. As they drew closer to the altar a weight dragged at their limbs, something not seen made their thoughts slow.

They pushed through and gained ground, fighting past the altar. Their minds cleared as the distance grew and their silent attackers fell. Together, they pressed north, and soon the footsteps behind them ceased. When they looked back, the guardians did not follow. They simply stopped and remained. Silent, still, and watching.

Dothemides looked around and remained near Samike, ensuring her safety. Bianzhi remained near her as well. Koba, Haphira, and others suffered wounds but lived.

That night, they camped, tending to the wounded.

"Bakhuran warned us," said Haphira, catching her breath as Koba bandaged her wounded arm.

"*Hollowed Ground...places of forgetting with land that quakes beneath your feet, and where those who enter are never seen again,*" Dothemides repeated Bakhuran's words.

"Yes, we were warned," he continued. "Clearly, there are things we know little about, but we made it through. We carry our wounds, but we live. It's not the first warning, and it won't be the last. But we cannot let words hold us back, no matter how well meant."

Haphira fell silent. Dothemides regretted his tone, but he glanced out and saw an open sky filled with stars atop the steppeland expanse beneath.

"You fought well and each of us will have much to write in our journals tonight," he concluded with warmth and a touch to Haphira's shoulder and a press of his forehead to hers.

Dothemides' words raised morale as he moved among them, checking on each in turn, offering quiet thanks. No one was overlooked.

Samike was sitting, reflecting on what they had just survived, when Dothemides approached and sat alongside her. She composed herself and smiled at him. She knew how to hide and mask. Dothemides took comfort in her smile and kissed her, lingering. She leaned into him and drew a deep breath as he held her close.

The air still carried the taste of that place. In the silence of morning, they named it. Not for the dead, but for the dread that lingered long after they passed through it—Hollowwind.

"Most days, I go unnoticed. And I do not mind.

The young pass me by with the pride of youth. Their strides filled with a strength, grace, and a beauty that they do not yet know they possess. I watch them, as I once watched my own reflection long ago. Even now, in a place shaped by remembrance, they forget. They forget those who came before.

I do not blame them. This is the way of things, of the Mountain, of breath, of memory passed between the old and the young. Mother, Wolf, Maw, and Mountain. The rhythm of life's seasons never changes.

Few truly listen.

But Dothemides does, in his own way.

He listens because he does not yet know. And in his not-knowing, there is wisdom.

His young queen is different. She listens as well, but with a knowing, as if something speaks to her from beyond the world, whispering truths too old to teach. There are secrets between them. And secrets between this land and those who walk it.

I only pray the path to learning such truths does not come at the same cost I once paid.

My time is approaching. The last climb before the silence at the pinnacle before judgement.

I must leave behind, in this book, all that I have learned, for Dothemides, our young king, and them, the followers of his dream.

Perhaps, in the little pages my story has left, they will find what I could not give them in life."

Book of Bakhuran, Mother's Tears 80, Year 5

"When he said he had lived through one hundred seasons of the Mother, most doubted him. Some called him mad. He said he was branded when he was a child. Banished for asking questions, for insisting he saw the crimson gaze of the Pale Spirit, watching him. Whatever his past, none could deny that Bakhuran had endured longer than most, longer than any I have known.

He was Khadari by blood, but Durajani by heart. I believe he loved and learned more about these lands than Khadar. He said he had wandered the sands and canyons for countless years, driven by the Maw's hunger, but today, his time was ending. We gathered beside his tent: the elders, the young, the faithful. We lit the oils and whispered his name as he lay still, with thin breath and clouded eyes.

He beckoned me forward and when I knelt beside him, he took my hand.

"You know now," he said, "that I was never mad."

He smiled like a man watching his final sunrise. "There are still secrets in those canyons. Secrets that the branded were never meant to return from. But you. You might, young king."

I asked him what he meant. What secrets?

He spoke of the Pale Spirit, a name known amongst his people and one I had never heard before.

"The Pale Spirit remembers what the world has tried to forget: ancient rites, silent stones, places of power carved in the Time Before. Where emptiness opens like a mouth and the brave and knowing may step through."

He gripped my hand with what little strength he had left.

"If you find them... You may learn to pass across this land through faith and miracle. But such gifts come at a cost."

His voice faltered. He spoke of why the branded are cast into the Durajan. Not simply to be erased. Not to rot.

"To be consumed," he said. "By the Hollow. By what sleeps here, waiting."

I felt the weight of his words settle in my chest.

Then, softer, his final breath a whisper, I heard, "Do not give up your dream, Dothemides."

He reached weakly toward his journal and pressed it to my chest. His eyes found mine, then closed. And he was gone.

I write his words as they were spoken to honor and remember him.

Bakhuran had no children. He said his husband was lost to the canyons many years ago, taken by winds that do not return what they steal.

Bakhuran left no heir. Only pages and a path.

I carry both now.

His words haunt me.

And they guide me."

Book of Dothemides, Mother Tears 90, Year 5

"I am far from my homeland now, both in body and within my heart, but I do not miss Vordos. Not the hunger behind its courtesies. Not the cold politeness of my family. Not the lands touched by a thing I dread yet cannot explain.

Dothemia is more than a fort or village. It is becoming a symbol, blessed in many ways and welcoming to all who come with an open heart and willingness to work.

I am happy to be here, to witness this. To see the beginning of memory and the spread of hope, despite fear.

My king seeks new lands, and I serve my queen as our children, Kaelani and Amubira, play as sisters should. I watch them chase one another as I sit alongside our beloved queen, who is radiant once more with the promise of motherhood. It suits her.

They are my king and queen. Words I feel more than speak. Their humility will not allow it. But I see it in them. We all do. We speak of it when they wander, roam, and discover. Sometimes, I envy them and wish to explore and fight alongside them. I feel I owe them more than what I give. But they know that a warrior's heart does not beat in my chest. They love me as I am, and I them.

I have a new family now. I give thanks to the Mother each day in quiet prayer, for Dothemides, for Samike, for my home here among them."

Book of Loreiaka, Wolf's Wake 12, Year 5

"The rituals continue, filled with passion and reverence, and I offer my part as best as I can, by attending and observing but not participating, for our child will come soon.

Dothemides remained at my side, not wishing to participate without me, but I encouraged him to be with our people, just as I had before Kaelani's birth. He leaves my side each time with reluctance, but the ritual's rhythms are impossible to resist.

The ways of the Mother are no longer foreign to me, and I understand their purpose. In the Durajan, lives are lost every day, but these rituals are an act of defiance and preservation, ensuring life amidst the suffering, and the deepening of bonds and friendship among the settlers.

What I wonder, what I still do not know, is whether my acceptance of it is true and born of faith, or is it a desire for peace, and a reflex of survival.

I love Dothemides and he loves me, of that I have no doubt. Two years ago, I embraced Loreiaka, but now Bianzhi lingers near him and is the first to approach him during recent rituals. I wonder how Loreiaka feels.

Dothemides and I have been through so much. Many have sought me. It would be simple to choose. To name one, as he has named others. I feel many eyes upon me during each ritual and as I walk the roads of our village, but they do not interest me.

But still I wonder. Is this what comes with power? Will I, in time, do as my love does? Will someone catch my eye, as Loreiaka and Bianzhi have caught his?"

Book of Samike, Maw's Feast 38, Entry Year 5

"The Mother has blessed us with balance and with life. Samike's labor was short, and as I held her hand, and the midwives and healers encouraged her to bear down, she did not scream, she did not cry, she was silent just as she had been with Kaelani.

Soon, not one, but two were brought into the world. I could not believe my eyes. I could not believe her strength. We named our daughters Tananda, who emerged first, and Kanike.

The celebrations have now come and gone, Samike rests, and each morning I return to work alongside our people, where I bear witness to toil, reward, hardship, endurance, those who lack strength, and those with strength enough to willingly carry them.

The hardships, challenges, and trials we endure shape our resilience and have helped forge the bonds we now treasure. I hope and pray that they remain paths to freedom, release, and understanding, and never be turned into cages, tools of power, or twisted into manipulation and corruption.

As Durajani, we come from the Nine Nations. Each with their ways and walls. Each one having shed themselves of us. But in our banishment, we have been given freedom and a chance to shed ourselves of their traditions, and build something new.

We all bear the brand, yet still we remain, flourish, and grow. Perhaps it is time that this mark of shame be changed into a symbol of unity. Perhaps it is time for our brand to become our banner."

Book of Dothemides, Mountain's Rise 20, Year 5

"It must have been raised in the darkness of night while Dothemia slept.

But there it was, fluttering in the river breeze beneath the light of the morning sun.

Everyone gathered and just stood in silence. It was a strange thing to see, and it brought back so much. Too much almost.

The terror, the pain, the rage, the hopelessness.

But then I saw it in everyone's eyes, I saw it in my memory, felt it on my skin, and felt it rise in my chest as we understood its meaning.

I felt the tears fall, felt my chest rise with pride, and heard my voice cry out, soon to be joined by others. We screamed, roared, cried, and laughed. We understood. We understood."

Book of Bianzhi, Mountain's Silence 1, Year 5

Chapter Six

BRIDGES OF FIRE AND BLOOD

Year 6

FOOTHOLD

"What began as calling Kaelani Princess has evolved into those we lead calling us King and Queen. Dothemia grows, and followers flock. Days are spent working beneath the sun, cooled by the river breeze.

A deepening desire to expand our family has become an unspoken longing that draws Dothemides and I even closer. It is a dance we both enjoy.

I watch him work alongside the settlers. Building beneath our newly raised banner. I watch him build walls, lending his strength and sharp mind. He always seems to find me doing so, and when our eyes meet, I lure him. He smiles each time with adoration and love. It is a love returned, in all ways.

Tonight, in the golden glow of the temple, we offered prayers to the Mother, seeking her blessing before we sank into one another's pleasures.

Now I watch them sleep as I write. Dothemides rests silently on his back, Kaelani asleep on his chest, his hand resting on her tiny form. Our little ones, Tananda and Kanike, sleep in their cribs.

When Laevina took my children from me and cast me out to die in the Durajan, I never imagined I would one day have a family, a man that I loved, and this kind of peace. I love him more than he knows... more than I allow myself to tell him."

Book of Samike, Mother's Breath 1, Year 6

Books of the Remembered

"The Season of the Mother is a time for hands in the earth and sweat on the brow. We plant. We mend. We build. The air feels gentler during this season. My sister led the blessing at sunrise, beneath the banner, and afterward we shared bread and drink along the western wall. There will be a naming soon, another child born under Mother's Breath."

Book of Aruna, Mother's Breath 9, Year 6

"I saw the queen today. She was seated in the shade with an elder I'd not seen before. They sat near the planting stones speaking in quiet conversation. Queen Samike's hands were resting in her lap, in that calm, silent way she has.

I've seen queens before, once in Marukh. She was from Tharios and had come to see one of the Queenwives of our King. I felt that queens never listened to their people. But ours does.

I could see it in the way she nodded when the elder spoke, and in the way she asked questions and smiled, not for show, but because she meant it. Some of us are beginning to believe we might follow her as we do him."

Book of Envas, Mother's Breath 20, Year 6

"I passed King Dothemides by the north quarry. His shirt was off. Dirt clung to his skin. Hammer in hand. He was not giving orders, just working. Like any of us. A man building a wall and a home, not the kingdom that we all felt in our hearts, was rising. I don't think the younger ones realize what he's carrying. But I do, and I believe he carries it well."

Book of Daien, Mother's Hand 27 Year 6

"Newcomers whisper about what was seen years ago in the Northeast Passage. A creature three times the height of a horse and the marks its hands left on the canyon walls, as if it clawed its way through stone. One of the scouts said the air shifted as they passed near, with a silence deeper than death. Stone-licking fool. He's lucky to have returned."

Book of Tamira, Mother's Hand 35 Year 6

"The Ritual of the Mother's Womb is only days away. I've cleaned my best tunic, the green one with gold stitching on the sleeves. I am no warrior. But I have labored well. Perhaps Queen Samike will notice me. Perhaps her hand will reach for mine. To be chosen, even once, by the queen would mean that I was seen."

Book of Oren, Mother's Hand 47, Year 6

"My sons, Hrinda and Balad, said they wanted to join the king's explorers and have the threads of our family name forever woven into the tapestry of Dothemia.

They said they would brave the dreaded Hollowwind to prove themselves. They begged me to say nothing, but I feared that I would never see them again.

That was four nights ago.

I dared not approach King Dothemides or Queen Samike. A reluctance born of shame, not fear. But I gathered the courage to tell Bianzhi. Better the king hears it from one of his chosen than from me. I saw her frustration and anger as she left me there.

She took it upon herself to lead a search party and rode out this morning. I pray they will be brought back. I pray the Mother is watching over them."

Book of Mandavi, Mother's Tears 77, Year 6

"Bakhuran's words stay with me. I've read his journal twice now. His mind was clear and his hand steady, even near the end. No rambling. No madness. Just record.

He mapped what he saw—stone circles, standing columns, places he believed held power from the Time Before the Silence and Awakening.

One passage refuses to leave my thoughts. Bakhuran writes of a man who entered one of those caves alone. A branded wanderer, without blade or guide, who stood in prayer, and then vanished.

Bakhuran says he watched from a distance, waiting in that chamber for two days. Then the wanderer returned, walking out of the cave as he had entered.

He never learned where the man had gone. He only knew what he saw.

Bakhuran wrote: "If you find them… you may pass across this world through faith and miracle. But such gifts come at a cost."

I do not know what waits in those places. Whether they are remnants of the Time Before or echoes of the Hollow. I do not pretend to understand what faith can open.

But I believe Bakhuran.

And when the time comes… I will find that cave."

Book of Dothemides Wolf's Hunt 48, Year 6

Wolf's Blood 68

Between Hollowwind Pass and the Northeast Passage, the choice had become clear. The Northeast Passage was sealed by the Living Mountain. But Hollowwind offered a way forward. It was the path they knew they could cross, and so it was the one they took.

Skirmishes against the *Hollowed* continued, but Dothemides and his people learned their rhythms and weaknesses. They took wounds, but in time the pass was cleared. When the last of them fell, they were given proper burials. Pyres were lit. Hymns were sung. Prayers to the Mother were offered.

Dothemides made certain that tokens were kept—fragments of armor, carved bone, pendants—for he knew these had once belonged to sons and daughters, mothers and fathers, and brothers and sisters. He hoped that one day, returning these to the families of the fallen might bring them peace.

But although they were victorious, the curse endured.

They knew the altar at the heart of the pass was its source, but destroying it was not an option. Approaching it remained too great a risk. So Dothemides ordered that warnings be carved into the canyon stone, marking a safe boundary, a ring far enough to not suffer the effects of the Hollowed Ground.

The result was a circle of prayers, etched in the known tongues of Dothemia: Marukhan, Thariosian, Shaduran, Khadari, Jhandai, Vordan, and, from Dothemides' time learning under Friela, the tongue of Skarn.

Hollowwind.
Hollowed ground.

Here, memory trembles and feet forget their way.
It is a place of unmaking.

To pass is to remember.
To enter is to forget the silence that fell,
the Hollowed who rose,
the dread that clung to breath and bone.

Let it be known: it was Dothemia and its people
who carved a path through shadow,
who faced men and women made hollow.

When the Hollowed fell,
we gave them fire,
we gave them song,
we gave them peace.

Let this be a warning to all, that none should pass lightly.

Do not stray near the altar.
It is not stone. It is a wound.
To cross this ring is to risk being trapped within.

Heed these words,
and may the Mother guide your steps.

Wolf's Howl 85. Hollowwind Pass

Hollowwind Pass had become a near-sacred place. Braziers of wrought iron bearing the likeness of the Mother were placed at the edges of the circle and the paths that led to Dothemia were being cleared and widened for easier passage.

Dothemides and Samike kissed their daughters and left them in the care of Loreiaka. Together they left with Bianzhi, Koba, and Haphira to set out and explore the steppelands beyond Hollowwind.

Along the way, workers on the roads bowed and bid their king and queen, and their protector and soldiers, farewell. Beneath the blessings and prayers of their people, Dothemides felt humbled.

"I am still not used to being called King," he said, as he rode astride Cepharion.

"Nor I, Queen, my love. But it is how we are seen. It is what we have become." She rode to his right, taking his hand in hers, adding. "Did you think it would be any other way, with all that has been done?"

He caressed her hand, knowing there was truth to her words. "I suppose I just never saw myself as one."

Bianzhi listened and rode to Samike's right as Koba and Haphira walked behind them, accepting the gifts of bread, fruit, and dried meats for their journey that were offered by the people. These were added to packs and saddlebags already filled with goods meant for trade in their encounters—each item shaped by the diverse hands and heritages of Dothemia's people.

"That is what makes you one of worth," said Bianzhi finally with a smile, wink, and bow of her head.

"When I met you two years ago and we fought together against the Xeyathi, something told me that I should trust you, Dothemides. That I should follow you out of that jungle to wherever it was that you were leading me, and I am glad that I did."

"I am glad you did too. And I am also glad that you didn't kill me." Dothemides replied with a heartfelt smile as he rocked in his saddle.

Bianzhi returned the smile and slowed her steed, falling back to allow her King and Queen to ride ahead together. She liked to see them side by side. Their bond and love were something she felt protective of.

As Bianzhi watched Koba and Haphira collect the offerings, she felt eyes fall on her as she rode. Eyes that held respect and pride. The smile she returned to the onlookers was uncomfortable but kind.

Since she returned with Hrinda and Balad, the sons of Mandavi, the people began to look at her differently. They began to see her as a leader and protector. Was she ready to be looked to in that way? The thought made her shift in her saddle, so she turned her focus to what lay ahead.

Before them, the canyonlands gave way to the broad sweep of the Skarnvald Steppes, where they found grasslands, rolling hills, a sky that seemed impossibly wide, winds that tore across open plains, above nomadic camps and larger settlements. Farther beyond, miles away, mountains clawed at the sky.

Their travels took them to many villages. Some welcomed them with cautious respect, others with suspicion or rejection. They encountered mostly small, weary, and watchful settlements, protected by low stone walls, with homes built of wood, stone, and hide. They were occasionally welcomed to rest, eat, and trade in half-sunken, thatch-roofed halls dug into the earth, and to warm themselves by ever-burning fire pits.

Trade was often offered, but always tested. Visitors were measured not only by word or wealth, but by strength and spirit.

Preparations for the next day of travel began before the sun cleared the ridgeline of the horizon to the east. Bianzhi watched the mountains as she tightened the cinch on her saddle, then moved to Samike's steed. "I'll take care of it," she said. "How are you faring?"

Samike hesitated, brushing a loose strand of hair from her face, bringing her cloak around her shoulders to protect against the cold morning air. She watched as smoke rose from the crackling campfire and the winds licked the tall grasses.

"Alright," Samike thanked Bianzhi with a smile. "Aside from being cold."

Bianzhi laughed with understanding and looked back out across the Steppes. Samike followed Bianzhi's gaze towards the eastern mountain ridge, across northern forests, and to the distant mountain range beyond them.

"I miss home," Samike continued. "But I know how important this is for us. For him."

Samike glanced towards Dothemides, who was kneeling alongside Koba and Haphira. The couple looked worn, but were smiling at something he said.

"He tries to keep spirits high, but I wonder how much it takes from him."

Bianzhi listened and finished preparing Samike's saddle. She studied her queen and sensed her fatigue.

"I hope this is the last day of our expedition. We all could use some rest." Bianzhi offered. Samike gave another soft smile of gratitude.

Dothemides' eyes found Samike's as they always did. He stood. His expression warm, loving, and kind. Bianzhi and her queen shared another glance before Samike stepped away.

As his beloved approached, Dothemides sensed her thoughtfulness and fell into stride alongside her. As the two stepped away, Bianzhi joined Koba and Haphira.

“One more day, my love,” Dothemides promised. “Then we return home.”

Winds surged again. He brought her close against him, wrapping his cloak about her. They shared a kiss and stood silently.

Samike looked out across the steppes and to the mountains beyond. “Do you truly seek to explore … all of this?”

Samike leaned against his chest. He felt her warmth, took in her scent, and kissed the top of her head. His heart felt suddenly heavier beneath the weight of his hopes and the depth of her question. But he thought of those back home, how their lives were made better, and of all they had built together. He thought of Kaelani, Tananda, Kanike, and Amubira and of the children born to others, and of the future he believed this work promised them. He held Samike closer to him.

“I do…”

He waited.

She closed her eyes, wanting to feel only him, beneath this calling.

An echo of memory rose; a passage taught to her years ago. Words she once considered holy. The chapter and verse had faded, but the scripture danced in her mind.

The Hollow cares not for what we do.
It waits, as ages wander through.
It watched before the world awakened.
A hush beneath the stars unshaken.
Before the pride of kings laid claim,
And nations spilled their blood for flame.

Dothemides felt her fatigue, heard her silence, and understood her needs.

“One more day, my love,” he whispered.

Samike looked up at him and smiled again. They shared another kiss and lingered in their embrace. She nodded and touched his face. Kissing his cheek, before parting from him.

"There is a weight to her step," said Koba, watching.

"We are all weary, Ko," Haphira replied.

As the two began to douse the flames of the campfire, Bianzhi watched Samike approaching. Her Queen's head lowered in thought. Dothemides watched her with concern.

As the steps grew between them, Bianzhi thought to herself. "None of us is as weary as they are."

The sun was at its peak, and with it came warmth as the Dothemian explorers rode north beneath the vast sky.

"I've seen the Steppes before," Haphira said, partially lost in thought and memory as she scanned the horizon. "From the Bulwark of Tharios. I had a patrol along the eastern wall."

"But Tharios does not send its branded into the Steppes. They send them down the barren descent of the Valley of Tharioc, and into the sands of Sifur's Breath," she continued.

Dothemides listened. "A cruel and deliberate choice. The fertile steppelands would offer hope. The sands offer death."

"But death did not come for either of you," Koba said with a smile.

"I, for one, and ... selfishly so ... am glad you both made that walk, and that you broke that cage, my queen." Together they smiled and continued on.

Drawing her horse to a stop, Bianzhi broke the moment of reflection. The group followed her gaze.

In the distance was a village, larger than any they had encountered. Its rooftops silhouetted against a low ridge, smoke rising from its many chimneys.

"What do we think?" Dothemides asked, scanning the distant outline.

Samike peered ahead. "If we can see them, they can certainly see us. And no horn has been sounded. That's something." Her voice was calm and certain.

Bianzhi tilted her head, her belly rumbling. "If there's a warm bed and food in there, I say it's worth the attempt." She trusted Samike's instincts.

Koba and Haphira studied their leaders, awaiting their decision.

Dothemides exhaled slowly and dismounted. "The Skarnvald are not cruel, and we are few. We pose no threat. I'll head up alone."

Bianzhi scoffed. "As if I'd allow you to do that," she said, swinging down from her horse.

"If you think I'm letting you walk up to that gate by yourself, you're mad."

He smiled and nodded. "Very well."

Dothemides handed the reins of his steed to Haphira, while Bianzhi passed hers to Koba. Samike watched her husband and remained confident. A confidence she passed to Dothemides through her eyes.

She leaned down, and their lips met with passion, then he kissed her hand. The wind swept a strand of black hair across her delicate features as he took her in. He raised his hand and brushed it away from her face with tenderness. They shared another smile before he turned towards Bianzhi, and together, they walked toward the village.

The gate loomed tall, and high walls of wood, stone, and mortar surrounded the village. Guards clad in fur and hardened leather watched from the ramparts above, hands on spears, eyes tracking every step.

“Friendly lot,” Bianzhi muttered.

Dothemides and Bianzhi stopped near the gate, making themselves seen and their presence known. There was no response. They watched and listened as one watchman called over another. The second approached, their eyes never leaving the wanderers at the gate. Together they studied, inspected, and exchanged words, calling over a third who loomed over those who summoned him.

“No shortage of words either,” Bianzhi added.

“That must be their captain,” said Dothemides.

A few more moments were spent watching the discussion unfold until Dothemides decided to step forward.

“Perhaps I can answer your questions.” The guards fell silent when they heard the stranger speak in their native tongue, but the captain responded, unimpressed.

“You are better off stating which clan has given you coin to spy on us so we can send you back with your lives and a message. Was it that thornprick Rolki? Or perhaps that arrogant, clutchless bastard, Vulfgar.”

Bianzhi’s tensions rose, but Dothemides calmed her with a glance.

“We are not mercenaries or spies. We come from Dothemia, a settlement to the south, past the canyons,” said Dothemides.

“Not possible,” the captain interrupted and continued.

“The canyons are cursed. We learned long ago to stop sending our people there. No one returns from them.”

“And we understand why,” Dothemides then began to explain.

“Bakhuran, an elder among our people, said there are parts of the canyons that steal strength and memory. Places that make men Hollow. We saw it firsthand.”

The Skarn captain fell silent. His guards began murmuring.

“It must have been scouts and warriors from your village that we encountered there,” Bianzhi added, sensing a shift in the conversation.

"They were dressed and armed as you, but gaunt, worn. Blue war paints and sigils. They protected an altar and fought to defend it." Dothemides hoped his words would build some trust among them.

"Now we know you lie," The captain scoffed. "The season of the Wolf has come and gone many times since we last sent scouts there. One of the last sent was my wife."

"I am sorry for your loss," Dothemides said respectfully before continuing. "But...we have every reason to believe that by the time the last of them fell, they'd long forgotten who they were. They fought only to defend that place."

More silence from the captain and quiet words from his guards. He held up his hand to quiet them as he watched the movement below.

Dothemides reached into the satchel slung over his shoulder, revealed a hand filled with the items taken from the fallen, and held them high.

"These were taken to remember those who fell in the pass. Those we laid to rest. We did so with respect. Sending them to the Far Sky with weapons in hand, but we took these before lighting the pyres that sent them to the Mother and Mountain."

Dothemides' words seemed to soften them.

The captain spoke and gestured. The gates swung open, pushed by the guards below as he disappeared behind the wall, followed by his guards.

Back on the ridge, Haphira's hand went to her blade, and Koba stepped forward, spear in hand.

"No horn," Samike said calmly, eyes fixed on the unfolding scene. "They're still safe."

A few moments passed, and the Skarn captain, along with his guards, emerged and approached.

The captain was a heavy-set man with gray eyes, and hair and beard the color of dry grass. Much of his body was enveloped by a heavy, weathered cloak of blue wool and thick fur that fell about his shoulders. Three etched copper pendants hung about his neck. A sword could be seen sheathed on his left hip alongside a hand axe tucked in his belt. Standing before them, he stood the height of Dothemides and bore several scars.

Dothemides began to question his earlier assumptions about this man being a mere captain.

The captain glanced at Dothemides and Bianzhi. Neither flinched, but Bianzhi's right hand reached across her waist to rest on the hilt of the long, curved blade, sheathed on her left hip.

The captain took notice as Dothemides' glance caused her hand to lower. He then gestured, wanting to inspect the items this visitor held. Dothemides placed them back into the satchel and handed it to him.

The captain studied the contents, eyes narrowing on a particular item held within. Dothemides and Bianzhi watched his reaction. There was emotion in his eyes. Pain. Memory. The captain closed the bag and handed it to the guard to his right.

A slightly shorter man with sandy hair, sky-blue eyes, and a short beard. He, like the other, held a bow. Full quivers rested on their backs, adorned with colorful beads, swords, and knives at their waists.

Dothemides watched as the items were inspected by the two guards and decided to attempt to garner more trust.

"Our people gave that passage a name—Hollowwind. Since its cleansing, we have etched prayers of warning around the altar. If you seek more proof, please send scouts. You will see that we speak the truth."

Bianzhi shifted with impatience. The captain raised a brow towards her, but she held his gaze. The woman to the captain's left spat at the ground near Bianzhi's feet and chuckled at Bianzhi's fire. A dismissal. A challenge. One that Bianzhi did not take lightly and one that would, under different circumstances, be met with eagerness. Instead, she smiled back at the woman and remained calm, deciding to not take the bait.

The captain shook his head. "Forgive my sister. She is not overly fond of strangers, and we do not get many. Our village is well protected, and our reputation runs far and wide."

"What is it that you seek here?" he continued, now visibly intrigued; his guard lessened.

Dothemides paused to choose his words carefully. "To know the other peoples of the Durajan, to form bonds and build something between us and them."

Dothemides gestured as he spoke. "I was cast out from Marukh. Bianzhi, from Jhandai. My wife was born of Shadura and Marukh, yet hails from Tharios. In our village, we have people from across much of the southern lands."

Bianzhi watched him as he searched within himself. She felt his hope and burden as he continued.

"The nations brand our flesh... cast us out... They send us here to forget us. Erase us. It's something I cannot accept as our end ... our fates. So I seek to change that."

The captain listened. His tensions fading. "How?"

"By trying," He continued.

"By searching for others. By sharing the idea that the lives of the Durajani are not forgotten. That we are worth remembering. Not just within our walls,"

Dothemides glanced up at the ramparts, then back to the captain.

"...but beyond them."

The captain and his guards listened before he spoke.

"You speak like one who leads."

"That is because he is our King," said Bianzhi with pride.

Dothemides smiled at her with warmth and continued.

"Remembrance. Life. Worth. Lesson learned from a woman of your people. A priestess of the Mother, who saved my life after I fell in battle against the nation of Skarn, while I was in service of Tharios. Her name was Friela.

She died years ago, but I still carry her words in my heart."

Again, the captain considered.

With rising respect in his voice, the captain spoke.

"Your words are worth hearing. Please, bring your people forward."

"Thank you," Dothemides waved Samike, Haphira, and Koba down the slope.

As they drew near, he shared a smile with Samike. "This is my beloved Queen Samike," She nodded, greeting Llothvik with a soft smile, noting that Dothemides had embraced his station as King by announcing her as queen.

"And these are dear friends and soldiers of Dothemia, Koba, Haphira, and you have already met Bianzhi."

Bianzhi moved to Samike's side. Koba and Haphira nodded but remained slow to trust. Samike's stillness calmed them as she smiled at the Skarn captain's guards.

The captain welcomed them, finding Samike fair. He bowed to her and the others, then gestured to those alongside him. "This is Thornsten, husband to my sister, Brynvi," He gestured to the huntress.

"And I am Llothvik. Thane of this village."

Dothemides understood. Now it made sense. He smiled and chuckled. A smile that Llothvik returned, Thane to King.

"And what are you called?" asked Thane Llothvik.

"My name is Dothemides."

"Dothemides of Dothemia." Llothvik smiled and paused.

"Your words carry weight and purpose. And your dream is bold. Still, I will need more before you are welcomed behind our walls. I trust you understand."

Dothemides nodded.

Llothvik leaned over to Brynvi.

“Bryn, Thorn, ride to ... Hollowwind, and return with word of what you find.”

Thornsten and Brynvi looked to one another, stepped away, and quickly returned on the backs of two steppeland steeds.

“You Dothemians had best be telling the truth,” Brynvi said with a smirk as Thornsten looked on. “I would hate to have to show you what happens to liars here.”

Bianzhi spat at the ground near the hooves of Brynvi’s steed.

“When you return, with proof of our word, I promise to show you what happens to those who make such threats and spit at the feet of guests who come in peace.”

“I look forward to it, Bianzhi of Dothemia.” With a kick, Brynvi and Thornsten urged their steeds into a gallop.

Wolf’s Howl 92

The next morning, camped outside the walls of Clan Llothvik, Haphira, the last to take watch, was the first to see Llothvik’s riders returning. Koba and Bianzhi stood and joined her. Samike and Dothemides dressed and emerged from their tent shortly after. As the riders approached, the gates groaned open and closed slowly behind them as they passed.

“How do we know they will not attack us...attack Dothemia using the path we bled to clear?” Haphira's mistrust lingered.

Dothemides responded reassuringly, “If they meant us harm, we would be dead already. Don’t worry. We’re safe.”

“Do you think they found Hollowwind?” asked Koba.

“We will know soon enough.” Samike touched his shoulder.

Dawn gave way beneath heavy clouds that covered the sky as they sat and waited. Then the gates opened once again. Thane Llothvik emerged, flanked by ten guards. Brynvi and Thornsten walked close to him.

Koba and Haphira tensed. Bianzhi looked to Dothemides, stepping towards Samike defensively. Dothemides held out a hand to ease everyone, as Llothvik approached the Dothemian campsite. Llothvik studied them for a moment, then spoke.

"Welcome. Please. Come inside." His voice was warm and sincere.

"Tonight, we will hold a feast in your honor and in honor of those made hollow by that cursed place."

The music that rose from Llothvik's hall was loud, rhythmic, and percussive. It echoed over the mudgrass roads and paths, filtered through walls and windows, flowed over the ramparts and out into the steppeland night.

The Dothemians learned quickly that earning a place of honor among the Skarnfolk carried with it tremendous privilege and recognition. Word spread about their deeds in Hollowwind, their etched altar, and the honor with which they laid their kin to rest. As they entered the hall, all eyes fell on them.

Within Llothvik's high hall, the Dothemians were brought to sit at their hosts' longtable and were arranged in positions of station. Llothvik sat at the head. To his right sat Dothemides, Bianzhi, Koba, and Haphira, and to his left Samike, Brynvi, and Thornsten. Between them all, the table was filled with more food than the Dothemians could consume in a day.

Samike and Dothemides exchanged smiles as their hands met across the table, and for a moment, the room fell silent between them. Seeing their affection, Llothvik smiled and admired them.

"You know, when my wife lived, my eyes met hers the way yours meet one another's." His voice was low, sincere, and spoken from his heart.

"The Mother has blessed me in many ways." Dothemides' eyes remained fixed on Samike's.

"Blessed *us,* my love," she replied, her voice carrying despite the music.

Dothemides bowed in agreement, then spoke with a softened tone. "Llothvik...I am sorry again for the loss of your wife." He paused and met his eyes as his hand squeezed Samike's gently. "I couldn't imagine the pain." His eyes went to Samike's, and for a moment, his heart filled with dread at the very idea of it. He looked back to Llothvik.

"I imagine Vasira fell with a weapon in hand," Llothvik said solemnly. "She feared nothing and loved the people of our clan. I know she rests in the Far Sky now."

Down the table, Bianzhi sat and ate, taking in the sights and sounds. Her eyes traveled to Koba and Haphira, who sat close and quiet, laughing and smiling at a crude question asked of them by Thornsten about size, girth, and frequency. She was happy to see them relax, but she couldn't. Brynvi's eyes had not left hers in some time, and her patience was wearing thin.

At the head of the table, Samike spoke. "Thane Llothvik," Llothvik turned.

"Of the precious items we returned, did any of them ... belong to her? To Vasira?"

He reached beneath his tunic and tugged on a leather strap, pulling free a carved ivory pendant, depicting a wolf, standing atop a mountain. It was beautiful, intricate, and, to him, it was clearly priceless.

"This was hers," He said to Samike, beneath the laughter and revelry around them.

"The Wolf and Mountain guided Vasira's every step. To hunt and to endure, that was her calling and path. She was my mountain and my wolf. Not a night passes that I don't see her in my dreams."

Llothvik paused, taking in the pendant. His mind momentarily adrift with unspoken memories.

"I never thought I would see this again. But thanks to you," He kissed the pendant and tucked it back into his tunic and smiled at them. "I have a piece of her with me now."

Dothemides and Samike said nothing. No word could express the joy they felt for him, and for a moment, the three shared a simple silence that spoke volumes.

A sudden commotion down the table caused their attentions to shift as Thornsten's laughter filled the air. Bianzhi and Brynvi stood facing one another, Bianzhi smiling and Brynvi drenched with wine, clearly from Bianzhi's cup.

As Brynvi strode away from the table, Koba and Haphira looked towards their king and queen, then back towards Bianzhi, who had stepped free of the bench and followed Brynvi. Soon, tables were being moved, and a ring of cheering voices was forming amidst the sounds of rhythmic stomping that all the Skarn, from child to elder, were taking part in.

Llothvik clapped his hands and rose to his feet.

"Finally!" He looked to Dothemides and Samike. "I must say, I have been waiting for this!" He stepped out from his place at the head of the table and walked out, urging them to follow.

Dothemides and Samike stood and followed, watching the two circle one another in the ring of chants, cheers, and stomping feet. Bianzhi's path took her close to him. As he spoke, her eyes never left Brynvi's.

"Bianzhi, the why and how of it is known and clear," Dothemides called. "Just... be careful... Promise me..." he added with a smile.

Overhearing Dothemides' words, Thornsten laughed. "Afraid for your fighter?"

"No... I am afraid for yours..." Thornsten paused, noting Dothemides' confidence.

As Dothemides and Samike shared a smile, Koba and Haphira joined in on the cheers and jeers, and fell in line with the room's rhythms, adding their feet to the rising thunderous energy.

With a glance, Samike caught the attention of Thane Llothvik. He leaned down to hear her speak.

"You had best make this Circle of the Wolf, Bloodless, Great Thane. For your sister's sake..." Her voice was low. Low enough for only Llothvik to hear.

The Dothemian queen was alluring and beautiful. Though respectful, his eyes could not help but wander. Eyes, lips, slender neck, deep skin, the fullness of her chest, and the darkness between, revealed by the low cut of her bodice.

He cleared his throat. His eyes had lingered too long. Samike took notice and smiled.

She was disarming, but her words gave him pause. She knew their customs and ways, she'd named them clearly, and she was too confident in their fighter.

He stood up and stepped out into the circle as Samike stepped close to Dothemides to hold his arm. They shared a kiss and watched. Llothvik's voice boomed.

"Let no blood spill in the Wolf's Circle," he warned.

"And let this... felt, yet unspoken feud be settled between my warm sister Brynvi and Bianzhi of Dothemia." The crowd laughed. Brynvi was known as anything but warm. He then exited the circle and called for the fight to begin.

"Now then. Fight!"

Brynvi stood with shortsword in hand and a bronze bossed buckler of stout wood strapped to her arm. Bianzhi held her curved blade out before her. Brynvi struck her blade against the shield, smiled, and waited.

Bianzhi had no such intention.

Bianzhi's blade rose, poised near her ear, its tip facing her opponent. Her steps began again, tracing lines across the dust-covered floor. Llothvik tilted his head, Brynvi paused, taking in her opponent's soft footwork and sideways motion before carefully closing the distance.

Three steps in, Bianzhi feinted left and thrust forward with a stomp, dust rose at her feet as the tension broke within the room.

Brynvi lifted her blade to deflect, Bianzhi coiled, withdrew, and spun backward, stepping deep into Brynvi's defense. With her stance low and wide, Bianzhi's elbow sank into Brynvi's belly, bending her opponent forward and sending the air rushing from her chest.

Bianzhi didn't wait; her knee touched the ground as she continued to spin around Brynvi's bent body, then she stood, her blade held in her right hand as her left gripped Brynvi's neck, and forced her down into a rising knee that slammed into her cheek.

Brynvi's head snapped back, and her body stumbled out to the circle's edge.

The silence erupted, cheers rose, music and stomping followed.

Brynvi was in the fight now. Bianzhi smiled.

Brynvi shook her head, willing the two blurred images of Bianzhi to become one. Her footing returned, and she smiled through the ringing, dull pain echoing across the left side of her face. That would not happen again.

Shoved back into the fray by the cheering crowd and egged on by her husband, Brynvi charged, shield held close, blade held high. But her thrust was deflected, her shield strike sidestepped, her upward sword slash slipped, and her downward arc parried.

Bianzhi smiled. "Slow. Predictable. Who taught you how to swing a sword?"

Her eyes then fell on Brynvi's swelling cheek.

"Your brother said no blood," she taunted. "Consider yourself lucky. I would hate to leave a scar on that pretty face."

Dothemides smiled and laughed, and soon both he and Samike found themselves cheering.

Bianzhi went on the attack again. Her knee rose. Brynvi flinched. Bianzhi took advantage of the opening, stepped behind her with one leg, her foot landing with a stomp placed for both drama and purpose. Brynvi felt her balance giving way already.

She tried to step past, over, away, anything to avoid what was coming, but Bianzhi's hand pressed against her chest, shoving her back, up and over her leg.

Brynvi's world spun, and she landed hard, coughing beneath the cloud of dirt and dust that floated in the air above her.

The music, stomping, and cheering stopped.

Gasping, Brynvi moved to rise, and was met with the tip of Bianzhi's blade to her chest. Bianzhi remained serious, tilted her head, and held Brynvi's gaze, then spat at her feet. Brynvi considered, but knew she was outmatched, and after a brief but tense pause, laughed and conceded defeat with a nod.

Bianzhi sheathed her blade and offered her opponent a hand up. When they clasped, the room erupted once again. Dothemides, Samike, Koba, and Haphira surrounded Bianzhi.

"Well done," Said Samike with a smile that showed she knew the match's outcome before it began.

Dothemides put his arm around Bianzhi and laughed. "You took it easy on her,"

"You noticed?" Bianzhi replied with a wink.

Llothvik approached, flanked by Brynvi and Thornsten and took in Bianzhi with surprise. "Well done, Wolf of Dothemia. Well done indeed." Bianzhi smiled, Brynvi reached out, the two shook hands and were quickly swallowed by the applauding crowd.

"Well, that was a night to remember. More like a day, and a night, and a morning to remember. After the fight, things got a bit touchy. Gods, how can I put this?

Wild? Unexpected? It was so loud. Singing. Dancing. Feasting. So much food. So much, everything.

Koba and Haphira were off in a corner. Brynvi and Thornsten, I think, were on a table. The gods only knew what else was happening around the room.

I looked for Dothemides and Samike, and I found them. More like I heard them. They slipped away, and judging by the sounds, it wasn't a good time to knock. I stood by the door. Stopped others from entering or wandering in. They needed that time alone. REALLY needed that time alone...

When things finally fell silent between them, I went out for some air. I just needed a bit of quiet. The last thing I expected to see when I turned to head back inside was Brynvi and Thornsten stumbling out of the hall into the night air, half-dressed, arm in arm and laughing.

They asked me to join them. It was clear what they meant and wanted, but I thanked them, declined, and watched them stumble off together.

When I came back, I noticed Thane Llothvik. He had been watching me since we approached the gates, through the evening, during the fight, and after.

That was the strangest moment of the night, needing to tell Llothvik that I wouldn't sleep with him. He is a good man. He wanted company. Someone to hold. I helped him to bed and he toppled into it like a felled tree.

Before he fell asleep, he called me Vasira.

The sun is rising now, and my head feels like a smith's anvil.

I should sleep. I think most of us will sleep this day away, but it was definitely a night to remember."

Book of Bianzhi, Wolf's Howl 93, Year 6

Evening, Wolf's Howl 93

The next day saw the people of Llothvik and their Dothemian guests rise exhausted, but in good spirits. Clearly, they were unaccustomed to the manner in which the Skarnfolk celebrated. By mid-afternoon, Koba and Haphira wandered through the village together hand in hand. Dothemides and Samike were shown around by Thane Llothvik as Bianzhi walked just behind, watchful as always and deflecting the open flirtations directed at her by others in the village.

By nightfall, another feast blazed to life, and as the Dothemians entered once again, many eyes followed.

The mood was quieter as Bianzhi was pulled away to drink with Brynvi and Thornsten, their laughter already rising in newfound kinship, while Haphira and Koba were welcomed to a soldier's table to share tales.

Village women led Samike away, and she later returned in robes of the Steppes, adorned with delicate threads, intricate woven patterns, glinting beads, and precious stones. She bowed playfully to her husband across the room, and Dothemides smiled, entranced.

Llothvik raised a cup to get Dothemides' attention, beckoning him forward to sit.

The evening stretched on as Llothvik began to tell Dothemides of the fractured steppe clans, of undying rivalries and feuds as old as stone. He laughed about raids, retaliations, and the endless blood debts that only bred new ones. All the while, Dothemides listened and learned.

When Dothemides questioned the purpose of the endless conflicts, Llothvik responded. "We do not unite easily. It is our way." His tone made it clear that it was not a matter to press.

Following the exchange, Dothemides and Llothvik said little as they watched the room with mutual pride.

"I see bonds forming amongst our people...A good sign," Llothvik said.

"This is what I hoped for when we set out." Dothemides' words were sincere. "Thank you for giving us a chance."

Llothvik filled Dothemides' cup.

"Knowing you," he paused and looked out at the Dothemians as they mingled with his people. "Knowing your people...I can very much say the same."

Llothvik then paused before speaking.

"Dothemides... It is not a Marukhan name."

Dothemides drew a deep breath. "It's not. It was a name given to me by the young son of a Thariosian king whom I served years ago."

Llothvik paused again, but couldn't resist asking. "Then...what is your real name, and why do you keep this one?"

"I ask myself that often," His eyes were distant.

"I was sold by my father, his name was Rhadur Balewa. He had three wives: Leatah, Udae, and my mother, Imali. She was his most beloved, and I was her only son.

There were several other children, my siblings from Leatah and Udura, a failing shop, too many mouths to feed. To be a poor merchant in Marukh is to live a life of shame.

I was the oldest, and King Agustus of Tharios offered enough coin to my father and mother to help them not only survive, but recover and thrive.

I still remember the coffer on the table. It was...sizable."

Llothvik listened.

"As a boy, I was trained, and as a young man, I fought to help defend the northern borders of Tharios against Skarn raids. I fought and I survived for years, and in time, was named *Dothemides—He who has proven mighty,* by his son."

Dothemides paused again and chuckled at the ridiculousness of it. Llothvik raised a brow, and Dothemides nodded knowingly in silent agreement.

"I suppose... Russom Balewa was forgotten along with the life he once lived." Dothemides said, finally.

Llothvik looked into his cup, then back to Dothemides.

"Russom Balewa... Dothemides... They are both men of strength and duty. Men who place the needs of others above their own. They are good men, my friend."

Llothvik placed his hand on Dothemides' shoulder. "Good men."

Though he could find no words, Dothemides' gratitude was clear.

Wolf's Howl 95

Llothvik invited his Dothemian guests to stay for as long as they wished. Each day since their arrival was filled with exchanges of information and plans for trade between them.

On the third day, Brynvi and Thornsten returned with word of trouble. A rival clan was on the move. When Thane Llothvik asked which one, laughter filled the hall when they responded with the name "Rolki."

Still, things grew serious. Llothvik explained to his guests that the feud with the Rolki clan had existed for years and that Rolki had borne the brunt and backside of the battles since they first began. They were angry, shamed, and sought revenge, so much so that he felt they would rather break themselves against Llothvik's shields than lose face amongst the clans of the steppes.

As the riders continued to approach, Llothvik met Dothemides in private.

"This is not your fight," he said. "If it comes to blood, stay here and see to your own, my friend." He gripped Dothemides' shoulder firmly and settled his eyes on his to drive home the weight of his words. Then he left to meet the threat.

As the door closed behind Llothvik, a glance was passed between Dothemides, Samike, and the others. As they sat in the hall, each nodded in agreement and understanding—if this led to conflict, they would aid Llothvik and his people.

Outside, hooves rumbled from the west and came to a stop before the high walls. Llothvik strode, accompanied by soldiers, armed and ready. Ascending the stairs of the ramparts, he stopped at their edge and called out to the riders below.

"So the Rolki have come again." He turned to his people. "We have guests," he turned back. "This can wait for another day."

"Guests?" the rival leader scoffed. "Who?"

Llothvik waved him off. "None of your concern, cub. Now, go home."

"You know why we are here, Llothvik Oldstone." The young rider continued, and the riders who accompanied him urged their steeds a step closer. "The Wolf has awakened, hunted, and now it howls for blood."

Llothvik sighed, eyes narrowing with recognition. The boy shouldn't be here.

"My patience for your pestering is waning, boy. When will you learn? The Rolki have a history of defeat at our hands..." Llothvik said coldly. "Unless you wish your clan's name wiped from the steppes, ride back to it while you still can. You'll not be warned a second time."

The rider laughed.

"You speak of names wiped from the steppes..." He steadied his steed,

"When you've not a child to call your own. No sons. No daughters...Just a dead wife."

He laughed again and looked to his men, who smiled in support of him. Llothvik bristled. The venomous insult was heard inside. It was a grave mistake.

"Speak of Vasira again...and another thane will stand with no heirs to his name."

It was a promise. Not a threat.

Inside the Dothemians heard the tensions rise. Dothemides stood. Bianzhi, Samike, Koba, and Haphira heard it as well. They opened the door and watched. Waiting.

"Leave now, or fall where you stand." Llothvik's voice trembled. Reason fading as his enemy stubbornly remained.

"Leave!"

Nothing.

Rolki came for a fight and would not leave without blood debts being paid.

Inside, the Dothemians watched as Llothvik descended the ramparts. Thornsten and Brynvi took their orders and returned to the wall. A shield and helm were brought to Llothvik. Soldiers fell in line behind him. They assembled before the gate. Llothvik drew his blade.

As Dothemides, Bianzhi, Koba, and Haphira prepared, Samike moved to join them, but Dothemides asked her to stay. There was a fear in his eyes. Perhaps it was the tale of Vasira that haunted him. Samike understood, took hold of his arm, and kissed him.

As they emerged, Llothvik's defenders glanced at the Dothemians with surprise, then with understanding as they walked to the front and stood alongside Llothvik.

"I told you to stay inside," Llothvik said, his eyes fixed on the soon-to-be-opened gate. But when Dothemides didn't respond, Llothvik knew his allies would not stand down.

With Dothemides and Bianzhi to his left, Haphira and Koba to his right, and his soldiers behind them, Blades were drawn, the gate opened, and the Rolki charged.

Thornsten and Brynvi remained atop the walls, their arrows taking down three riders before the opposing blades crossed. Samike stepped up alongside them, heart racing and bow in hand, to lend aid.

Dothemides led his people with sword and shield. He fought close to Llothvik, his eyes constantly moving to him and across the field, reading the chaos as it unfolded. Where he pointed, the Dothemians followed. His command of his people did not go unnoticed by Llothvik.

Samike's silent gaze swept across the field like a shadow, her arrows precise and unrelenting. Bianzhi, with her curved blade, flowed like water and wind, slipping around attacks and striking with power and precision. She was both the shield and the blade of her king.

Haphira fought with her Thariosian shortblade and shield in hand, side by side with Koba, whose spear struck high and clean, upending charging raiders from their steeds. Both were fierce and fearless.

Llothvik's defenders fought hard, holding their ground, and the thane knew that this was not a fight that the Rolki would win.

In the end, the charge was broken. Llothvik scanned the field, his chest heaving beneath his cloak and armor. One of the Rolki stood bloodied, stunned, frozen. Llothvik followed his gaze and saw the Dothemians standing alongside his people. He saw Dothemides. Then he saw the body that lay at his feet. He called to Brynvi and pointed; she obeyed, fired, but it was too late. The rider had mounted and fled, already disappearing over the western hills.

What remained of the Rolki clan was captured and, by tradition, made slaves of Llothvik.

Llothvik watched the rider fade into the distance as the Dothemians joined him. Thornsten, Brynvi, and Samike descended the walls, exited the gates, and joined the soldiers on the field.

"Should we give chase?" Brynvi asked.

Llothvik shook his head. "There is no chance of catching him. Tend to the wounded and get the Rolki inside. See that they are mended and fed."

Thornsten nodded and left. Brynvi remained by her brother.

Llothvik turned to Dothemides and those around him and nodded, extending his hand in thanks. They shook hands—a warrior's grasp.

No words were necessary. As Llothvik strode past, the Dothemians fell in behind him and were soon joined by others.

Evening. Wolf's Howl 96. Llothvik's Hall

"You were warned, yet still you stood with us," Llothvik said as he rose to his feet in the crowded hall. He placed a gentle hand on Samike's shoulder, then firmly upon the shoulder of Dothemides.

"The Mountain," he continued, "lives in you and your people, and you fight like wolves. I have seen it. We have all seen it." Voices rose in agreement.

"But know that the Steppes remember. It remembers the blood of allies and it remembers the blood of enemies."

His voice came quieter now. Loud enough to be heard, but it carried meaning and promise as he spoke.

"You've stepped into something ancient, brother." His gray eyes settled on the amber of Dothemides'.

"Tonight, as Rolki licks its wounds, the Wolf howls for my clan and yours."

"To Llothvik and Dothemia!"

With that declaration, voices, music and song rose throughout the hall and lasted through the night.

"Koba and I had hoped to be together before our long ride home, and finally we had some time alone. We'd had enough feasting, drinking, and fighting.

I pressed him into our bed furs, and he smiled. I straddled him, coaxed his hands onto my body, felt his want within me, and he felt mine envelop him. This was going to be a morning to remember. Then the flap of our tent opened.

Bianzhi's timing leaves something to be desired. Sometimes I think she does it on purpose. Feigning innocence, laughing with that tease in her eyes.

Well fought, she said. Then she just lingered. Waiting. She knew what she was doing.

You both showed courage in the battle. she said.

All we could manage was an awkward thank you.

Then again, she paused and just waited.

Finally she looked at us and said *Well ... carry on.* That smirk and smile. I'm sure she will tell that story to everyone. We'll never live it down.

Koba called her a menace and smiled up at me. I think he wondered if she wanted to join us. I silenced him with a kiss and did as commanded."

Book of Haphira, Wolf's Howl 97, Year 6

Sunrise. Wolf's Howl 98

Bianzhi, Haphira, Koba, and the people of Llothvik were saying their goodbyes and admiring the goods they had traded. Dothemian pottery, medicines, canyon herbs, and jungle furs were traded for steppeland fabrics, dyes, weapons, jewelry, as well as vibrant tunics and dresses of red, green, and blue.

Nearby, Dothemides and Samike shared a lingering kiss. They had earned an ally in Llothvik and learned much of the Steppes. But in their shared gaze, they both thought on his words.

Llothvik approached, his expression warm despite his scarred visage.

"Ride well, Dothemides and Samike of Dothemia." He smiled at them, considered, then called for Thornsten and Brynvi, who approached immediately. Brynvi was shoving Thornsten about something spoken between, but unheard.

"Bryn, Thorn, go south with our new allies. See their settlement and fortress. Live among them. Speak of us and represent our clan well." he paused. "That is, if this arrangement works with you." Llothvik turned to Dothemides and Samike, awaiting their decision.

Together, Dothemides and Samike nodded with gratitude and acceptance before Samike responded. "We would be honored, Thane Llothvik."

Brynvi and Thornsten shared glances and accepted as well. Bianzhi winked at Brynvi, and she returned a sly glance. Llothvik laughed, hugged his sister, then patted his brother-in-law on the shoulder before the two scouts left to pack their belongings.

As they left, he called after them. "And bring around the horses. The fallen of Rolki won't be needing them."

Two horses were brought to Haphira and Koba, who accepted them with gratitude and humility.

Llothvik continued and looked to Dothemides. "Take them, my friend, and ride well."

"Thank you, Llothvik". Dothemides said.

"Yes, thank you, Thane Llothvik." Samike followed.

The people of Dothemia departed for home with new allies and the eyes of the Steppes now watching.

Books of the Remembered

"I've learned their names, Brynvi and Thornsten. As they walked beside King Dothemides and Queen Samike, I couldn't help but watch them with measured eyes, for no matter how warm the words were that were rumored to have been spoken by the steppeland Thane, it is in shared fire and labor that trust is truly forged."

Book of Havia, Maw's Hunger 21, Year 6

"It was another cool day along Market Row, and it had been days since their arrival. These steppe-born seemed true enough. There were no great acts or bold gestures, just small moments. If this is who they truly are, those small things will gather meaning over time.

That Brynvi is a restless one though. Keen to learn the layout of the roads, the names of the builders, and the direction of the wind before dusk. She's asked me my name twice already, just to be sure she remembered.

Her husband Thornsten is observant too. Doing more watching than speaking, but never absent in labor or duty. He stands guard when others rest, observes the flow of water channels during the rains, and he's even begun marking routes through the Woundwood with his own signs."

Book of Vali, Maw's Feast 39, Year 6

"The rains of the Maw came later than expected, but they came all the same. Soft at first, then steady. They softened the soil, cooled the stone, and reminded us that nothing lasts forever, not even drought.

It was not a season of bounty, but of balance. We measured grain and counted our stock. The storerooms were not full, but they were not empty either. We moved with purpose, checking roofs, sharpening tools, walking the perimeter in pairs.

And in the quiet of the evening, as most put pen to their journals, I wondered, not about what had been earned, but what it might cost to keep it."

Book of Okali, Mountain's Vigil 70, Year 6

"The season of the Mountain will soon come to an end. And it has been ten days since Dothemides left for the north. If all has gone well, he should be there now.

Before he left, he expressed his regret with desire. But I saw in him a distance and an uneasiness.

I watched him and the others leave until I could no longer see them, but I was comforted by Loreiaka and those around me.

Kaelani cried, and Amubira comforted her. Neither likes to see their father leave."

Book of Samike, Mountain's Silence 90, Year 6

CHAPTER SEVEN

FOUNDATIONS OF DOMINION

YEAR 7

RISE

Part I

"We've returned north, following the trails further. Bianzhi, Brynvi, Thornsten, Haphira, and Koba are with me. We've made camp in a narrow valley, near the northern edge of the steppes, where the air is colder and pines crest the hills.

Thane Llothvik's maps have helped guide us this far, but something about this pass doesn't sit right with me. I've asked Brynvi and Thornsten to scout the ridges, as they know this land better than the rest of us. They agreed and left moments ago.

It's been a long road, and there's more ahead. We cross into the Càrnothi Highlands tomorrow."

Book of Dothemides, Mother's Breath 4, Year 7

Mother's Breath 5.
Border of the Skarnvald Steppes and Càrnothi Highlands

For days, the hunters watched, followed, and kept their distance. Covered in earth, mud, and fallen branches, they lay low in the underbrush of the forest's edge and waited for Brynvi and Thornsten to leave.

With them gone, their leader, a mountain of a woman, stood still as stone. Her pack did not speak, but they were near. Each one watching her as she waited for the right time. Her chin lifted, and around the camp the earth moved as they obeyed her silent command.

One year ago.

In the dim firelight of the thane's chamber, the cool morning air had settled into the room as two figures slept beneath heavy furs and wool sheets.

She was tired, but she felt her husband's want press against her, as it did each day. She stirred beneath the warmth of his wandering hands and felt the chill as the furs were drawn away.

Pulled up by her hips, her legs spread by his knees, she smiled then laughed, resting her face on the furs as his hands gripped her waist and his fingers sank into her flesh. The room was cold, but soon she was warm and wanting, as her husband's breathing deepened behind her in steady, increasing rhythm.

Then the door flew open, the pleasure ceased, and her hand went to the blade that sat by the bedside at all times. Her husband raged but immediately fell silent upon seeing the bloodied warrior standing in their doorway.

Her husband pulled away and walked towards the warrior, and asked what had happened. With bed sheets draped across her, she approached.

Time slowed as he told his tale, and her heart sank into the dread rising within her chest.

A foolish ride against Clan Llothvik.
An insult against Llothvik's dead wife.
Allies from the lands south of the cursed canyons.
Marukh, Shadura, Jhandai, Tharios.

Blades drawn.
Her son, slain not by Llothvik but by another.
Black locks, dark skin, leader of the southlanders.

She screamed, the blade in her hand rose with intent to kill the survivor for not dying in place of her son.

Her husband struggled against her, soothed her, and promised vengeance. Promised blood.

And as her blade fell, she wept and prayed.

The memory of that night had lingered for a year. She prayed for this moment, and the Wolf had finally answered.

As she watched from above, her tear-filled eyes narrowed with anticipation. The time for promised blood and vengeance had come.

From lips trembling with rage, her war cry split the air, shattering the morning silence. Clad in wolf hide and fur, her pack surged, each one rushing down the hill in a frenzy.

She watched and smiled, her expression a mix of pain and rage, as beneath them, their prey scrambled.

Below, chaos ensued as the silence was broken.

Dothemides turned, shaken from his writing by the screams, and reached for his blade as Bianzhi entered his tent. Her expression revealed all that was needed. Together they stepped out, as Haphira and Koba moved to draw in closer.

Dothemides studied their attackers, picking up what details he could—steppeland hides and wolf furs, crimson warpaint and red wool cloaks. A dozen soldiers, their leader descending slowly behind their frenzied advance.

"Clan Rolki." His voice was low and grim.

"Three to one…we won't win this fight," fear rose in the hearts of those he loved as their eyes darted between wild faces of the descending warriors.

Haphira and Koba sprinted to close ranks, but she was the faster of the two, and as distance grew between the pair, the opportunity was seized by the descending pack. Weighted nets flew through the darkness, and Haphira fell beneath one, her limbs entangled before her blade could be fully drawn. Bianzhi rushed to her aid only to be caught beneath another.

Part of the pack split, leapt down, then rushed towards Dothemides and Koba, separating them from Haphira, Bianzhi, and one another.

The hunters of Rolki tightened the circles around Dothemides and Koba as they closed in around each of them. Raised nets swung in slow circles above their heads, and sharp spears formed a deadly barrier on all sides as they taunted, feinted, and threatened. Daring them to draw a blade. Hoping they would resist.

Bianzhi and Haphira struggled until the sharp ends of pointed spears held by three warriors of Rolki halted their efforts with the only warning that would be given.

The battle cries rose. The howls of the hunters filled the forest. Just outside the circles, their leader stalked, savoring the moment. This will be a glorious day. There would be no escape.

Her hand lifted, the nets soared, and Dothemides and Koba were caught beneath them. The hunters planted their spears and quickly moved as one, drawing close together, each one gripping ropes attached to the nets. A second signal was given, and together, each pack heaved. Eyes wide with fear and confusion, Dothemides and Koba lost their footing and fell. Bianzhi and

Haphira screamed. The hunters continued to pull, dragging them further apart as they struggled.

Again, they paused, and again she savored. Her steps were slow and deliberate as the cries of victory continued to fill the air. A third signal was given. Crude clubs were drawn from their belts. The hunters rushed in, like winterwolves around wounded stags, and began to batter and pummel their prey.

Koba attempted to rise but fell to his knees. A blow to the temple dazed him, another to his jaw dropped him, and his world went black.

Beaten, bloodied, and barely clinging to consciousness, Dothemides rose to his knees beneath the net and lifted his hands. He understood the Rolki were not here to slay them. If that were their goal, they would have been pierced with spears and left to bleed out onto the forest floor.

The woman loomed. Dothemides met her gaze. Her mud-caked features were further hidden by a heavy hood. She bent to crouch before him.

"You murdered my son." She said coldly.

"I should kill you here, southlander." Her voice was coarse, heavy, fitting for a woman of such size and girth.

She stood and walked to Koba's limp body, kicking it over easily with her foot. She tilted her head, studying him, and looked back to Dothemides.

"Marukhan, yes?" Dothemides remained silent.

The pack parted as she turned to walk towards Bianzhi and Haphira, stopping near them.

Reaching through the net, she lifted Bianzhi's chin roughly. "Jhandai..." Bianzhi tried to turn away but could not move. The woman's grip and strength were too great.

"Move again...and I break your neck," Bianzhi obeyed, despite her rage.

After inspection, she shoved Bianzhi's face away, discarding it like half-eaten fruit, and stepped to Haphira and wrenched her head back by her hair. Wincing and unable to move, Haphira met her gaze.

"Tharios... I hate... Thariosians." She shoved Haphira away.

Bianzhi's and Dothemides locked eyes. There was nothing either of them could do.

Hearing the distant fighting, Brynvi and Thornsten returned and crouched low as they crested the hill unseen. What they found filled them with dread.

Below, Rolki's hunters circled the four captives and rummaged through their possessions.

Neither Thornsten nor Brynvi dared to speak. They knew the Rolki clan. They were ambushers and pack hunters—masters of these lands and attuned to its sounds and scents. Even a whisper could risk discovery.

Leading them was Thrala, wife of Thane Rolki. She stood with a girth and strength that they would recognize anywhere.

Helplessly, Brynvi and Thornsten watched as warriors began to pile the Dothemian possessions. Nearby, others surrounded Bianzhi and Haphira, their eyes lecherous as they made crude remarks and spoke of their carnal plans.

Dothemides scanned the ridgeline, praying, searching. Then he spotted Thornsten.

Their eyes met. A subtle shake of the head. Thornsten nodded, then crouched back low, under the cover of the ridge.

Brynvi's hand hovered near her bow. "We should strike now!" she whispered through clenched teeth.

Below, a hunter turned, paused, and dismissed the sound.

"No," Thornsten replied. "We go to Llothvik. It is their only chance."

Brynvi nodded with reluctance, not daring to speak another word. She peered over the ridge one last time. Bianzhi was unharmed, and Haphira as well. "Give them strength," she prayed to the Wolf and Mountain, and slipped off silently alongside her husband towards their steeds.

Dothemides' relief was short-lived. All he could do was watch as, around the camp, their journals were discovered and pulled from their tents. He shifted his attention to the woman, and as she drew back her hood, he studied the details that defined their captor.

She was tall, thickly framed, stout, and strong. She wiped her face with a coarse, worn cloth, pulled from her belt, leaving streaks of mud and red warpaint in its wake. Her thick hair was dark brown, almost black, and fell about a round, full, pale face with ruddy cheeks, red, full lips, and large pale-green eyes. She was stern and carried a hatred in her eyes that ran deep.

Her men scurried, obeying her commands and rounding up the food, equipment, weapons, and horses of their captives. One of her soldiers approached and presented her with the found journals as she stood by the edge of the campfire. She gestured for him to burn them.

Dothemides shouted in desperation, earning a vicious blow to the back of his head. A new trickle of warmth flowed down his back, but he remained conscious.

"Wait," she said.

The woman called for the man to stop and gestured for one of the books. Her thick arm emerged from beneath her cloak. She took hold of the journal with a coarse hand, blackened with soil and ink and armored with a bracer of fur and leather. She reached for the twine that bound one of the humble tomes as her eyes rose to study the deep concern and fear of her captives.

Opening the journal, her pale eyes scanned its pages and recognized immediately that there was knowledge here worth keeping.

"We take these to my husband."

"Yes, Lady Thrala."

The hunter nodded to his commander, journals in hand, and left.

Thrala looked back to the captives. "And we bring him our spoils."

Morning. Mother's Breath 7

Bound and forced to remain silent, Dothemides, Bianzhi, Koba, and Haphira were taken east where they began a descent down a path that ran along a steep hillside. Thane Rolki's settlement soon came into view as low horns sounded from within.

The village was broken and rested within the gray bed of the valley like a starved beast in a shallow grave. It was clear they had suffered from their years-long feud with Clan Llothvik. They rode past farmers as they worked failing fields, planting seeds within stony soil.

Gates swung open on rusted, weakened hinges. Throughout the village were homes of stone, timber, and thatch, and the trodden earth between smelled of piss and dung. Worn and weary eyes watched from every window and doorway as the hunters returned with their quarry. Gathering in silent groups, they stared as the Dothemians were led to a longhouse where stone steps rose to meet rough-hewn beams of brown and gray wood.

The doors were pushed open, and they entered a hall that was dim and quiet. A small fire burned in a smoldering hearth. Torches rested in sconces hung from beams that rose to support a sagging roof that stood in a state of disrepair and neglect.

"What do we do?" whispered Haphira.

"We hope and pray," said Koba. "Stay close to me." Their eyes met in shared fear.

"Quiet," Bianzhi hissed back to them.

The hall echoed with low voices, heavy footsteps, and the clink and clatter of a table being cleared.

Beneath the noise, Dothemides whispered. "Thornsten and Brynvi saw us. I told them to flee...they will come for us. I know it."

Servants, soldiers, and elders moved about the hall as their eyes turned towards the entering party.

Ahead of them sat a gaunt, aging man with sunken cheeks, thinning hair, and a downturned mouth locked in a fixed grimace. Thane Rolki.

As they were brought in, words were exchanged, and there was recognition in the eyes of Rolki as the hunter spoke. Thrala approached him and they shared a smile and passionate kiss as he gripped her broad backside and she tugged at his short beard. She moved then to stand alongside him and sat, crossing her stout legs as she assessed their prisoners.

"Didn't see that coming," Bianzhi whispers.

"My love," Thrala's eyes fell on the prisoners with contempt. "These are the southland dogs. The allies of Llothvik. The murderers of our son."

Thane Rolki sat back in his throne and called over a tall, scarred, one-handed man who hurried to his thane's side.

Dothemides and the others watched as a question was asked and hastily answered. The man pointed towards Dothemides, and Rolki nodded. Guards seized the man and took him away.

"So...it was you." Rolki's deep-set eyes fell on Dothemides, who said nothing but did not cower. Rolki smiled.

Thrala gestured. One of her pack, hurried over, retrieved a satchel, and handed it to her husband.

"They had these, husband. Books carried by each."

Rolki's hands reached in and pulled the journals free.

Thrala continued. "These books have value...they contain secrets about their people, their customs, histories, battles, their land ... safe routes through the canyons and of Llothvik's trade routes. Routes he shares with them."

Rolki's eyes narrowed as he flipped through the pages. Some words he could not read, others he could. His hand rose to call someone to him.

A woman approached, stepping out from her place to stand alongside the thrones. She took the journals and began to read, knowing the languages of each.

Her pale, shaved head was crowned only by a single white braid from its crest, and her silver eyes were masked with red warpaint. She was dressed in an ashen and blue wool skirt, fur boots, and the hides of numerous steppeland beasts. Her left breast lay bare and covered in crimson runic war paints and skarn sigils. Slender, ink-stained hands held the journal as she scanned silently.

The shaman soon spoke, and the room fell silent as her voice carried. She stepped down with one journal in hand and began to walk amongst the kneeling captives. Behind her, another man of weak and meek stature followed, holding the remaining books.

"This one carries the tale of a woman of Tharios. It must be you." She looked to Haphira, lingering, and looked back to the book, flipping through its pages.

"The words speak of a lover born of Marukh. Quiet. Protective. Dreams of children one day." Haphira's jaws clenched as her journal was read. The shaman's feeble aide exchanged one book for the next.

"But it is not you," She looked to Dothemides as she scanned the next journal. "It is you," she said, looking to Koba. "They fight as one, one heart, one love between them. It says... *I would die, without her, and she, without me.*" The shaman's face wore a look of disgust.

"This one contains the writings of a warrior of the nation of Jhandai," She continued to scan, and her brow raised as she laughed mockingly. "You," she says to Bianzhi, "have *many* hidden feelings for someone, it seems. Feelings...unspoken."

Dothemides looked to Bianzhi. Their eyes met, and she looked away.

The shaman approached Dothemides, while Rolki and Thrala listened, enjoying the moment.

"That means you," the shaman pressed, her aide remaining close. "You must be the one written of in this passage..." She glanced at the journal and continued to read. Bianzhi's head remained lowered as the shaman's voice echoed across the hall.

I have always felt that fate has a sense of humor. The one man I love just happens to be the one man I know that I can never have. He is my king.

So I serve him with my blade. Protect my queen with my life, and long for his touch and kiss when our rituals to the Mother descend in the temple.

I feel I will love him for all my days.

Bianzhi and Dothemides' eyes met again, but this time she did not break away.

Rolki laughed and clapped his hands. Thrala smiled, entertained.

"That ... was touching..." The shaman grinned.

"Do these journals bear their names?" Thane Rolki asked.

"Yes, my thane." She walked by each, gesturing as they were named. "Haphira, Koba, Bianzhi and their king, Dothemides ... or as his name was before his parents sold him...Russom Balewa." She glanced at him with contempt and disgust.

"Little more than a slave with a lie masked as a dream..." Her words fell with a tone void of emotion or care. She looked back to Thane Rolki. "Their city to the south is named Dothemia. Apparently, he has a wife and four children."

The shaman strode proudly as she continued to speak.

"A busy man, aren't you?...King Dothemides of Dothemia."

The shaman's aide took the last book and placed each one carefully on the side table near the thrones. Thane Rolki then stood, his eyes grave with intention.

With a gesture from their thane, the soldiers drew their clubs and descended on Dothemides and Koba. The impacts, grunts, and groans of pain filled the halls as their captors enjoyed the spectacle.

Thrala smiled as she watched, and her eyes floated between Dothemides and Koba, trying to determine which one would be her slave when this was done.

As the last strikes fell, Haphira was dragged away, screaming Koba's name and led into Rolki's quarters. Bianzhi's tears flowed as she was roughly lifted and saw Dothemides beaten, rendered unconscious, and dragged away.

They were taken down a narrow hall past iron gates to two cells opposite one another. Bianzhi was placed in one. Dothemides dropped into another. Koba shoved in after him.

As day turned to evening and the three sat in their cells, Haphira's cries filled the halls, confirming their worst fears.

Morning. Mother's Breath 8

Dothemides awoke to the quiet and distant sounds of the longhouse coming to life and the deep ache of a battered body. Pushing away from the stone floor, he looked across the corridor to where Bianzhi sat alone in her cell. She stood and walked slowly to the bars that caged her. Their eyes met. As he struggled to his feet, her tears flowed once again as she saw his condition. She could barely recognize him as he stood—one eye was swollen shut and covered in his own dried blood. Dothemides shook his head and offered her what hope he could.

Behind him, Koba stood staring through the slit of a narrow window at the crowd gathering in front of the longhall.

"We will not see the end of this day, my King," Koba said with resignation.

Dothemides looked back over his shoulder, pulled between offering comfort to Bianzhi and hope to Koba.

At that moment, sounds of struggle rose. The voice belonged to Haphira. Rolki, laying cruel claim to his chosen one once again. Dothemides shut his eyes. Bianzhi lowered her head and slipped back into the darkness of her cell. She leaned against the damp, cold stone of the wall, slid down, and sat, crouched and filled with rage.

"We still have a chance, Koba." Dothemides knew his words offered little comfort.

Koba watched the crowd, his expression blank and empty. Ravens perched on the wall as if they were waiting.

Footsteps approached, and the cell doors rattled open. Soldiers of the Rolki clan entered and seized their captives, dragging them out and down the hall, spears at their backs.

The longhouse doors opened, and the Dothemians were met with the morning light of a cloudless sky and the utter silence of the people of Clan Rolki, as they watched the southland allies of Llothvik positioned and put on display, side by side.

Moments of tense silence passed as they watched the crowd. Then a hand rose and a fistful of filth was hurled, and struck Dothemides across the cheek. Another was flung and landed on Bianzhi's shoulder, as Koba was struck across the eye. The silence was then broken by a frenzy, leaving Dothemides, Bianzhi, and Koba powerless as they were pummeled and spat upon by the mob.

In time, the deluge ended, and the people once again fell silent with anticipation.

Dothemides heard the footfalls first. They were distant but grew louder as the moments passed. Then Thane Rolki emerged from the longhouse arm in arm with Thrala. Their footsteps, the only sounds heard.

A guard's warning glance turned Dothemides' head forward to face the crowd.

Rolki and Thrala inspected their captives, making a show of it as Rolki paused near Bianzhi. “Tonight, it will be you instead of your Thariosian friend.”

He was unimpressed with her defiant stare and smiled as Thrala stood behind him, large and looming.

Rolki stopped in front of Dothemides, holding a journal. His journal. He leaned close to Dothemides’ ear. “You die today, King of Dothemia.”

Rolki then turned towards his people and lifted the book before them. Nearby stood his shaman. Her silver eyes fell upon the captives as if she had walked their dreams the night before. Rolki’s speech flowed like a sermon.

“We have suffered. We have fought. We have bled. All at the hands of Llothvik. They have taken our wives and husbands, brothers and sisters, sons and daughters. They see us as weak, broken, and forsaken by the Mountain and Wolf. And I see in your faces, and know in my heart that you share that belief.

“But the Wolf and Mountain have not forsaken us! They have not! They have given us a gift.” Rolki gestured to the Dothemian captives.”

“My beloved Thrala, guided by her faith and vengeance, tracked, defeated, and captured the murderers of our son. Murderers who are allies of Llothvik and are led by this man. The man who struck the blow that felled him.”

Rolki’s eyes turned from the crowd back to Dothemides with disgust, hate, and loathing.

“This dog’s name is Dothemides, and he has been crowned king of a rising city called Dothemia.” With the journal thrust high, he continued.

“Proof of its existence is here, written in this and other books carried by each of them. Books that reveal much about their people.”

“This would-be ruler of the lowlands is a builder of temples, not of worship, but of lust. A spinner of tales, promises, and platitudes. They come with smiles and soft words, but they are masks that cloak the manipulation of his people.”

"He seeks to claim all things under his name. He would have those who follow him forget themselves, forget their struggles, their blood and kin, and begin their histories anew, in ink that glorifies his might, his ambition, and his greed! All masked beneath what he dares call... a dream."

Here, Rolki paused and paced before them, allowing the moment to build as Thrala watched her husband with love and pride.

"He is no king. I believe that he and his people ... are agents of the Hollow."

Rolki's words stirred those gathered, then the crowd began to murmur and question, as tensions rose.

"They have already put a leash upon Thane Llothvik, who, in his blindness, has given them maps and routes that lead to each known clan and village, as well as the roads that lead north to blackpines of the Càrnothi."

"I cannot allow this! We cannot allow this! If left alive, this king and his kind will spread across the Durajan, like rot through roots, changing and erasing *everything* we are... stealing what little we have left!"

Dothemides listened to the twisting of his dream, to the voices of the gathered, rising in anger, rage, and the calls for retribution, torture, and death. He looked to Bianzhi and Koba, who looked to him as they saw their end approaching.

"So I will end this." Rolki continued.

"I will kill him, kill his warrior, and his women will serve our great hall as slaves beneath our roof and rule. And when he is dead, we will ride south through the pass they call *Hollowwind*. There, we will raze Dothemia, enslave his queen and their children, capture its people, and claim their riches!"

Cheers rolled through the crowd as fists were held high, and chants cried for the spilling of Dothemian blood.

Rolki, seeing the passion of his people, roared.

"Let none say we were weak! Let none say we were fooled! And let this day be remembered!"

Haphira was brought out into the chaos of the crowd. She was quiet, her eyes low, her steps small and reluctant. A bruise colored her cheek. She had suffered, and Dothemides, Koba, and Bianzhi could see it.

Haphira was made to stand beside Rolki, her shoulders stiff, her gaze fixed somewhere far beyond the crowd as if she could not bear to meet the eyes of her love, her captain, and her king.

Dothemides' heart broke. He looked at her and felt the weight of failure press into his chest like a rusted blade. He could not move. He could not speak. His breath caught as rage and sorrow churned beneath his bruised ribs.

Bianzhi wept, not with fear, but with fury. Her hands shook as she was held, rough hands gripping her arms to keep her in place. Her jaw clenched as she stared at Haphira, then to Rolki, then to the faces of the gathered, these people who would watch and call it justice. Her mind raced, contemplating what fate awaited her among them, and the role they would carve for her in this place of rot and ruin.

Koba was dragged to a stump of wood. Haphira screamed. Dothemides struggled. Koba fought, but he was weak and outnumbered. A knee in his back forced him forward. His arms were held tight. His chest heaved with breathless fury. They pushed him down. His neck was forced toward an aged and bloodstained stump.

Koba's face was pressed into the wood, and his eyes sought Haphira's. At first, she could not bear to watch, but he called her name. His voice was calm as the blade in Rolki's hand was lifted. Finally, she met his gaze. Both cried as their love was exchanged through their eyes.

His arms were pulled painfully back, and as the steel caught the morning light, Koba's breath stilled.

Then from the ridge...a whistle.

One of the wall watchers collapsed, an arrow lodged deep in his throat. Another fell, clutching at his chest.

An alarm sounded as shouts rang out from the perimeter walls. A guard stepped backward, pointing wildly toward the distant rise, screaming, "Llothvik!"

Warriors scrambled, villagers scattered. The rhythm of the execution was broken. In the confusion, Dothemides surged forward, wrists still bound, but his body was filled with fury. He slammed his shoulder into a guard as the pain of broken ribs ripped through his chest. As the guard fell back, Dothemides pulled the sword from his scabbard and soon felt the warm spray of a neck, sliced open.

Bianzhi wasted no time. She lunged for the fallen guard and pulled the axe from his belt. Her eyes fixed on Thrala, who drew her sword and axe, as two guards rushed to defend her.

Rolki would not be denied, and so he brought his blade down on Koba's neck only to have it deflected by Dothemides' sword. The two met eye to eye as Koba rose to his feet.

Llothvik's soldiers hurled torches and pitch-filled canisters over the walls that landed on rooftops and spread smoke and flame throughout the village, leaving its scattered people caught between defending the walls or watching their homes burn.

Two more guards were felled by arrows, clearing a space for breach ladders to be hurled, hooked, and climbed. The first over the wall was Thornsten, followed by Brynvi, who ducked low amidst the smoke and flame and made their way to the gates, felling charging warriors before they could close the distance.

Below, Bianzhi stepped forward and sent her heel into the knee of the rushing guard, cracking it backward as the guard collapsed in pain. The second guard was shoved forward by Thrala and collided with Bianzhi, who lifted her knee between his thighs. A crushing blow that buckled his legs on impact.

As he fell writhing, she took hold of his dropped sword, only to feel the impact of Thrala's fist against her jaw, but the only expression Thrala was met with was Bianzhi's vengeful smile.

Nearby, Dothemides and Rolki remain locked, but the aging thane began to lose ground to Dothemides' strength, and with a surge, Dothemides pinned Rolki's arms against his body, twisted and sent his elbow into Rolki's jaw, shattering it beneath the blow and sending him spinning backward.

Clutching his jaw and half blinded by pain, Rolki's eyes fell on Dothemides, as Koba emerged from behind him, hand in hand with Haphira.

The sword held by Dothemides was handed to Koba, who gave it to his love. Rolki's heart was filled with the understanding that his end was near, but he would not go quietly. His voice rose past the numbing pain of cracked bones and he charged the trio, only to be met by Haphira's blade, driven to the hilt within his belly. With eyes locked on his, she pushed, teeth bared, tears flowing, face trembling with vengeance, until the blade pushed fully through him and exited his back.

Haphira's arm wrapped around Rolki and gripped him in a close, fatal embrace as her eyes closed with the memory of his cruelty. The thane stumbled. Her hand twisted. He choked on his breath and collapsed to his knees. She let go of the blade, leaving it sheathed within his flesh as blood poured from his gaping mouth.

Across the square, Thrala roared at the sight of her husband's death. Her eyes locked onto Bianzhi, venomous and wild. She crashed into her like a hammer. Her blow landed against Bianzhi's ribs. Pain from the impact bloomed white-hot. The world faded for a breath. Sound became distant. Movement slowed. But she did not fall.

Bianzhi gritted her teeth, pushed up from the dirt, jade eyes blazing. They circled each other now, bloodied and breathless.

Thrala lunged again. This time, Bianzhi's blade found its mark. It sliced clean across Thrala's side, cutting deep. The Thane's wife stumbled, gasped, and dropped to her knees. Bianzhi finished her, sinking her blade down through Thrala's shoulder until it met her heart.

Thornsten and Brynvi reached the gate amidst the spreading flames. Together, they heaved against the wooden beams, lifted the heavy crossbar and threw the gates wide.

Llothvik rode through.

His warriors followed, thundering into the settlement like a storm of steel. The battle surged until the last of Rolki's were surrounded. Those who surrendered were taken. Those who resisted were cut down. Clan Rolki was no more, and when the victors searched for the shaman, she was gone.

In the aftermath, they gathered around Haphira. No words were needed. She was comforted by Bianzhi, by Thornsten, by Brynvi, and lastly by Koba, whose arms wrapped around her protectively and lovingly.

Dothemides broke away.

He moved through the bodies, through blood and churned mud, until he found Llothvik.

Face to face, amid the ruin of Rolki's hall, Dothemides met his friend and ally.

"I owe you a debt," he said. "And I will repay it."

Together they stood in momentary silence until a warrior approached. One of Llothvik's men. In his arms, wrapped in cloth and bound tight, were the Dothemian journals.

He offered them to his thane.

Llothvik took them, then turned and placed them in Dothemides' hands.

Dothemides accepted them, his fingers curling around the worn leather, and nodded with gratitude. Llothvik placed a heavy hand on his shoulder and the two embraced.

"It is over, my friend." Llothvik's voice was filled with sorrow for the condition of Dothemides and for the torment that he and his people had suffered.

"Go," he said. "Your people need their king."

Dothemides said nothing more. His eyes fell to the journals, as tears welled within them. His mind raced, filled with the horror of what they had endured and the realization of what was nearly lost. For a moment, he was unable to move. Then he turned and carried the journals back to his people as Llothvik watched.

With the battle won, Llothvik claimed the survivors of the conflict. As was the way of the Steppes. They now belonged to him, in sword and name.

"There were celebrations. There were feasts. There was time to heal. I watched as King Dothemides reunited with his Queen, his family. Watched as Samike's tears flowed upon seeing his condition.

Theirs is a love that holds their people together. That now binds me to them as much as I am bound to Llothvik. Thornsten and I were given journals so now we write, wait, and hope that the peace lingers."

Book of Brynvi, Wolf's Wake 6, Year 7

"We thought the fire ended with Rolki, but we were wrong. We would learn that Llothvik's victory, and his standing beside Dothemides, had drawn the eyes of the steppeland wolves. Thane Vulfgar, Rolki's brother, had taken notice.

Rolki's death was a blow struck that Vulfgar could not bear and one that could not go unanswered.

Now we hear that he moves. Not just to avenge blood, but to cut down any chance Llothvik has to rise. To smother him and our Dothemian alliance before it can further take root.

Vulfgar will come and it won't be a raid. It will be warcamps, banners, and fire in the eyes of every Thane who thinks the south seeks to remake the north in its image.

I feel that Dothemia rises on the winds of a storm it did not start.

But I will rise with it, and I will ride with him."

Book of Thornsten, Wolf's Wake 17, Year 7

“I haven't written in some time. I don’t write as often as others. But recent events, recent bloodshed calls for it.

It’s been months and tensions have lingered. My husband and I have traveled to and from Clan Llothvik. We exchanged what we could in trade and brought back ever-darkening news of the tensions on the steppes.

I brought news that Vulfgar and the escaped remnants and lesser allies of Rolki had declared war and that Llothvik was calling on Dothemia to hold true to its oath.

Queen Samike was against it. But she did not plead, and she did not beg. She warned.

Warned her husband that no matter the outcome, all would lose this war. But Dothemides is a man of honor and true to his word.

We have since returned north, and tomorrow I will once again stand on Llothvik’s walls alongside our allies of Dothemia, to face Vulfgar’s forces and what remains of the Rolki.”

Book of Brynvi Wolf’s Blood 53, Year 7

“The steppelands are red with the blood of the fallen. This fight has gone on for weeks and today the plan is to face them at Highsun in what many feel will be this war’s final battle.

King Dothemides requested that all be given a moment to write what may be our last words. I wonder if these will be mine.

I remember standing in the tent. Dothemides, beside Llothvik, speaking with weight in his voice. He looked tired, not from fear, but from the weight of what was coming. Both my beautiful Bryn and I felt it as we watched.

In a futile attempt, Dothemides said that the battles had escalated too far. He begged Llothvik to consider peace and tried to convince him that this would be the end of the three clans. That the blood already shed was enough.

But he didn't know the ways of our people. At least, he didn't accept them. He didn't understand what it meant to be raised in the ways of the Skarnvald. He didn't know that sometimes reason bends to honor, and honor does not yield.

Llothvik looked at him and told him that the Mountain does not move because the wolves and winds howl, and that neither he nor Vulfgar would ever give ground.

Then he placed his hand on Dothemides' shoulder and said calmly. "If I fall, my friend... let me and my Vasira... my people... be remembered in your pages."

And with that, Llothvik left the tent to prepare. I saw the surrender in Dothemides' eyes before he stepped out after him.

Now the sun is climbing. And soon, I will close this book and step into ruin."

Book of Thornsten Wolf's Blood 54, Year 7

"Battle. Broken armies. Hewn bodies. What have we become?

Thane Llothvik fell.

Thane Vulfgar killed him.

And then Vulfgar turned to face Dothemides, bleeding and worn. Dothemides gave him a chance. Even then, he tried to speak, to find some other path. But Vulfgar would not hear it.

Vulfgar spoke of the Far Sky and of The Mountain. I saw in Dothemides a sorrow that I felt would consume him whole.

And then, Thane Vulfgar charged, and Dothemides killed him.

Across the field, Koba lay dead, his body pierced and slashed by many blades.

Four of Vulfgar's warriors lay around him. Two were run clean through. Koba's shattered spear protruding from the chest of a third, the jagged wooden shaft embedded into the neck of the last.

I didn't see it happen, but the aftermath told the tale.

Haphira was bent over him, shaking, sobbing. Her voice broken, her fingers clenched and gripping his hair and clothes as if she could hold him to this world.

I stood beside Dothemides. I didn't say a word. I don't think either of us could. We both felt it, the weight of it all.

This was not a victory. It wasn't even survival. It was just the silence that comes when there's no one left to fight and you are the last ones standing.

Around us, survivors stood in the setting sun. Three clans—Llothvik, the defeated Vulfgar, and the last remnants of Rolki. All shattered. Their leaders dead. Their futures uncertain.

And still... They looked to him. To Dothemides.

Among them, many stepped forward. Swords lowered. Blades pressed into the blood-soaked grass, trampled flat with battle. And one by one, they knelt.

Dothemides didn't understand.

He turned to me, eyes unfocused, and then to those who knelt before him.

Brynvi approached and said to him that it was their way. That he had endured, and like the Mountain, he remains. Thornsten let him know that those who knelt looked to him now.

I watched as those who didn't kneel walked away, and I could see in their eyes that they hated us. One man spat at Dothemides' feet. Another cursed him, and had to be held back by kin.

Then I saw it in my king's eyes. This was not what he wanted. This was not the dream."

Book of Bianzhi, Wolf's Blood 54, Year 7

"We lit the pyre before dawn. The winds were gentle, as if even the steppes had gone quiet to watch. We stood in silence. Just smoke rising.

Haphira stayed closest to the flame. She hadn't spoken since Koba's fall. She wept without sound. Her fingers still held his journal. I could not speak to her. What words could I give?

I watched the fire catch. I watched it climb. I whispered the Mother's words, as I remembered them.

In smoke and prayer,
let the remembered rise.
Let the soul walk free,
carried by those who loved him.
Carried to the Far Sky.

We named this place for him.

Fort Koba.

So we will remember."

Book of Dothemides, Mother's Wolf's Blood 55, Year 7

"The journey home was long. Bianzhi, Haphira, and I rode in silence. Thornsten and Brynvi remained behind for now, until a new commander could be chosen to lead our link to our new northern foothold.

I embraced Samike and kissed my children. It was good to see them.

I called for a gathering at dawn in our temple, to honor Koba, to mourn so much loss.

We hung his name on the temple wall to let all know the names of those who bled and died for this dream.

The fire burned low. We stayed until it died.

Then we went back to work. That's what he would have done."

Book of Dothemides, Wolf's Blood 70, Year 7

"Dothemides had been gone for so long.

I dreamt of him again last night. He stood in silence, covered in blood, not his own, eyes hollow, hands trembling. And when I called to him, he did not speak, he only turned away.

When my husband returned, a part of him did not.

There is glory in what they did. A foothold gained. An alliance forged. Honor upheld. But glory does not fill the bed we share. A bed now empty more often than not. Glory does not kiss my hands or whisper to me about our children, or laugh as they play.

I see the way he walks now. It's heavier.

I fear that every time he returns, less of him remains. Not because he is weak, but because he is enduring. And that is what frightens me most. Endurance, after a time, becomes silence. And silence, too long held, becomes forgetting.

I pray the Mother takes his pain. But I know she will not. She asks us to carry it.

So I do, for now."

Book of Samike, Maw's Hunger 1, Year 7

"Vulfgar, once a hub of the steppes, is now in ruin. I watch from a distance, what was once a place of fire and voice, and of moot and shield. And how it now lies quiet.

But from its ashes, a seed has been planted, a seed of bitterness and resentment.

Those who have remained here and traveled to and from their broken moots speak of the southland king, Dothemides, and they do not all speak kindly.

Word spreads. Tales twist. The story that reaches the edges of the steppes is no longer of alliance or survival. It is of infiltration. Of a usurper from the south who seeks to extend his reach, take lands that were never his, and wrap them in the silk of unity only to bind them in chains.

The steppes are cleaved in two. There are those who reject him. Who speak his name with disgust and fear. But there are others, fewer in number, who watched him bleed, watched him burn our dead alongside his, and who now raise the Dothemian black sun banner willingly.

Fort Koba rises not from conquest, but from duty. From honor. We lead it not because we claimed it, but because no one else remained.

Dothemides wonders, sometimes aloud, if this is the Mother's will. To bring life and rebirth to a land soaked in old, useless feuds and vendettas. To shape peace not from treaties, but from scars.

Brynvi and I were given charge of the fort. To lead it in Dothemia's name. We agreed and remain. Determined to do so until a new leader could be chosen, but we wish to be in Dothemia. To stand by him.

We do not fight for him for glory. We fight for him because we were there. We saw what was lost. And what might still be built.

Vulfgar is broken, hungry, and angry. They will raid. They will rebuild in blood.

Some clans, closer to the heart of the steppes, are too far gone. They will fall. But others? They will watch, hold moots, and choose to halt their feuds and raise their walls. To see what will come next.

I do not blame them."

Book of Thornsten, Maw's Hunger 12, Year 7

"Haphira still mourns Koba's fall. The Mountain within her crumbles beneath its weight. I can see it. She trains and fights but she no longer writes. Sometimes I feel as if her story has ended with Koba's."

Book of Bianzhi, Maw's Hunger 17, Year 7

Part II

Maw's Hunger 20. Northwest Region of the Durajan

Crashing waves collide with a weathered dock.
A cliffside settlement rises against jagged shores.

Wooden huts crouch beside black cliffs, their thatch soaked with sea spray and brine. Pines reach into the mist, rising from rock, like claws reaching for the sky. Stone chimneys belch smoke into the gray, while seal skins and fish hang drying on woven lines.

A ship approaches. Ropes are thrown and tethered. A weary crew clad in fur, leather, hide, and plated steel disembarks and walks down the docks. All eyes settle on them, watchful, weathered, and weary.

They are inspected by armed guards. Their leathers and armor were pulled aside to expose the left breast of both men and women. Each one bears the blistered brand of the Durajani. There is a grim welcome. They are placed in a wagon, the cage is shut, and they are ridden southeast through small coastal settlement roads, bordered by the sea to the west and tall pines to the east.

Cresting the ridge trail, they reach a fortress village carved into the snow-veiled cliffs. Stone foundations groan beneath massive longhalls, their roofs heavy with snow and ice, smoke curling skyward through iron vents. The scent of pine tar and ash lingers beneath the cold. Palisades and watchtowers ring the settlement like teeth. Every wall bears claw marks, some from beasts, others from men.

The people are dark-haired and weathered—men and women of considerable size and strength. No one here is without scars. No weapon is without wear. No glance without warning.

The caged wagon comes to a stop. The branded are pulled out. There are eight of them. Guards escort them through the gates and into a hall of wood, stone and bone. A man enters, accompanied by guards and sits on a wooden throne adorned with fur, ivory, and weapons, held together and bound by coarse rope and iron nails. Totems rise on either side of it, carved with motifs of highland beasts, standing above crashing waves and beneath mountain peaks. Fires crackle and smoke fills the room. A circular window behind the throne allows daylight to pierce the darkness, illuminating the rolling haze with its soft beam.

The man on the throne watches as the group is brought to a halt before him. When he stands, he is a head higher than his guards and is draped in a long coat of longtooth hide and mammoth fur. He wears heavy necklaces of bone and ivory—the teeth and tusks of countless hunts. His beard is full, his black hair is tied in a topknot bound by coarse leather, and two streaks of blacksap warpaint run the length of the left side of his face from forehead to chin.

The guards meet his gaze.

"Warchief."

The warchief nodded to them, respect in his eyes. He looks to the branded, and the respect vanishes.

One of the them speaks. "So you are Valloch."

"And ...what gave that away?"

"How many ships did the sea claim?" Valloch asks.

As he awaits an answer, he moves aside the armor of one of the men, inspecting his brand. Valloch walks down the line, approaching a woman and moves to do the same. He pauses, eyes rising. She is rough and weathered but fair. She catches his wrist in her grip before he can expose her. He smiles, raising his hands in amusement, surrender, and promise, eyes lingering on hers and hers on his as if daring him. He moves along down the line, knowing she finds him handsome, and that she is merely playing the game that must be played for now.

"What ... defiance earned your shame?" asks Valloch.

They stand without fear, their weapons are not taken. They do not kneel. Such a thing doesn't seem to be expected. Each of their eyes locks onto Valloch's as he passes.

Finally, one speaks.

"Two other ships were lost, Warchief Valloch. None aboard survived."

"As for our shame? We bear no shame. We were mouths to feed in a year of thin hunt and harvest. Names were chosen. We were the unlucky ones."

Valloch takes them in.

"You will hunt." He gestures, "The wilds will be your home. Until you hunt enough to sustain you," Guards approach them, they look a bit taken aback as they are given crude bows and arrows.

"And build enough to shelter you." He paces away, back to the newcomers and turns back to face them. "There is plenty of wood among the Blackpines and prey enough for those who possess the teeth to take them down."

Guards return with simple tools. Axes, saws, skinning knives, picks. All are dropped at their feet. The halls fill with silence.

Valloch gestures again towards the door.

"This is what you get from me, until you prove yourselves worthy of more. Càrn Valloch has no use for dead weight. But we honor those who fight to remain standing."

The branded look towards each other, resigned. Each bends to pick up the tools. They look around, but nothing else comes. They walk towards the doors of the hall and step out. Valloch turns around and heads back to his throne as the doors close behind him.

From a distance atop the southwestern wall, two guards watch the new arrivals as they walk towards the edge of the village. The forest beyond is dense and dark.

"So... what do you think of them? Think they'll make it?

The second studies them.

"They've made it this far. The Sea of Souls didn't claim them. They have a chance."

"One can only hope." The first nods.

Two guards approach, and one calls out. "Larastus! Agatir! You're relieved!"

They descend and clasp hands with the two guards, who replace them on the wall.

As they walk side by side, they are regarded warmly by the villagers. The roads and paths are slick with mud and snow as people mill about, carrying out their various duties. Smiths, carpenters, hunters, weavers, and farmers cross their paths, leaving tracks through the snow, mud, and trampled needles that coat the roads. They wave from darkened stalls and work in dim workshops with both duty and purpose.

Larastus walks with pride and boast in his stride. His wild hair is pulled back, held by strands and strips of leather that bind braids that fall about his broad shoulders. Agatir is hairless other than his short beard, and walks alongside his friend, smiling more than his companion. He is the larger of the two and is carried by steps that are sure and strong.

They reach the end of the narrow road, where on the other side of a path that intersects it are two cabins side by side. Agatir pauses as horses pull a cart past them, the driver offering each a nod.

"How is he?" Asks Larastus, concern in his voice.

"Not well. He holds on. Though I wish to the Mountain that the Far Sky would claim him already."

"Sorry you have to return to that each night, brother." Larastus places a hand on Agatir's shoulder.

"I just hope they haven't been at one another's throats again today," Agatir responds.

Curses and swears rise from within one of the cabins. Larastus offers a smile, part pity, part amusement, but upon hearing the continued, anger-filled scream of the child within, his expression grows somber.

"It sounds bad today."

Something shatters inside the cabin.

Agatir looks to his home and sighs. "It gets worse as the seasons pass. I'd better get in there."

Larastus nods, and as Agatir hurries across the road, he cannot help but hope for his friend and for the little one they both protect.

The door opens, and light streams into the cabin. A central hearthfire, pots at its base, a kettle of stew, dark wood walls with hung furs, trophies of the hunt, blades, axes. Spilled stew from a discarded bowl, bread lay caked with dirt from the floor.

An aging, scarred man, with a gray beard, thinning hair, and a once muscular frame, sits on a bed. His bare feet rest at the bedside, naked other than the furs and blankets that cover him. Fading tattoos sit on weathered skin. Across from him stands a young girl with black hair, amethyst eyes, and a wooden tray in her hands. She is angry. The aging man looks at her, angry as well.

Both stare up at Agatir. The girl slams the wooden tray on the ground and rushes out the door past him.

"Svirva..." Agatir's words do not slow her.

"You and I will speak later..." He says to the man and heads out, shutting the door. Villagers look on as if this is a common occurrence. Agatir catches up to the girl and grips her arm.

"Svirva..." She wrestles away, attempting to break free.

"Svirva... please... please!" She calms and looks up at him. His skin is fair, and her skin is olive. His beard is brown. Her hair is as black as night. His eyes are green and hers are amethyst. Even as a child, she possesses a beauty unlike any in the village. He kneels and she watches him. Eyes never leaving his.

"I wish he would just... die already. He never liked me!"

"Never will." She is past hurt. Her voice is laced with a hate that should not be in a heart that has lived for only seven turns of the seasons.

"His time will come." Agatir soothes as others pass by, taking in the scene with stares and whispers.

"Then it will be just you and me..." He comforts her.

"With Larastus nearby." He adds, and she smiles a little, cheeks blushing a bit.

Agatir sighs. "I'll clean up. Go say hello to Larastus. It's time for your practice anyway. I'll come by after I've dealt with father."

Svirva calms and nods, looking back over Agatir's shoulder. Her eyes narrow. Agatir stares back at their father, who stands at the threshold of their cabin.

"Go..." he says to his little sister. "I'll be over soon."

Agatir stands, watching her amethyst eyes drift back toward the cabin. There is no love in them, only the kind of silence that carries memory and wounds.

He sees it, and his own eyes flicker with worry and sorrow. Then, without a word, she turns and walks toward Larastus' home.

Returning to the cabin, Agatir enters, stepping past his father, who enters behind him, now draped in a simple robe and fur cloak. Rocked by a fit of coughing, he stumbles. Agatir catches him, softening with a sigh. Anger fading in the face of his father's condition. He helps him sit back on the bed and begins to clean up.

Moments pass and Agatir breaks the silence. "Will you go to your death, resenting her?"

"I should have cast that child out with her mother."

Agatir's father, Haegun, had once been a warchief in Càrnoth, a hard man forged in ice and blood, born of war-torn lineage and duty. He ruled not only a house but a tribe, one of the oldest bloodlines on the eastern cliffs. His first wife, Merron, Agatir's mother, had stood beside him in battle and bore him his son beneath the smoke of conquest. She died many years ago, honored, mourned, and remembered.

In time, loneliness grew within the chieftain. That was when Haegun noticed her.

A younger woman. A rare beauty among the salt-hardened snows, dark of eye, skin, and hair, and light of foot. She did not speak much, and never spoke first. She was not of noble blood, nor was she seasoned by war. But she was the brightest flame he had ever seen, and he wanted her. Her name was Arican.

Perhaps it was loneliness. Perhaps pride. Perhaps something more primitive. Whatever the reason, Haegun sought her hand and, with her agreement, took her as his wife.

But her heart remained far from his hall. She slept beside him, but never turned to him. She bore his name, but never wore it with pride. And over time, his desire turned bitter. What began as affection soured into jealousy, and his jealousy into suspicion. She had secrets in her silence, and he hated her for it.

Meanwhile, Haegun's hold on power faltered. Younger warriors questioned his judgment. Rivals whispered of his weakness...of how his blade no longer gleamed, how his beautiful wife never smiled. When the challenge came, it came with ceremony, but not with mercy.

He fell in combat, wounded but alive. As was custom, he and his kin were branded and banished, sent across the Sea of Souls, where the cold meets the horizon, and honor is drowned beneath the tide.

The càrn had just crowned a new Warchief—Valloch. Younger. Sharper. He showed a measure of mercy, but not without its price.

Intoxicated by her beauty, Valloch claimed Arican as his own. The price for acceptance to the càrn. Her beauty stirred him, and he took her as his bride. But he left the broken chieftain and his son alive, shadows of a tribe that had already forgotten them.

Years passed. Haegun and Agatir built a cabin beyond the edge of the village. They hunted and cut timber, repaired tools, and remained tolerated. But they were not honored. They were a reminder.

Then came the child.

Valloch's new wife bore a daughter, black of hair with eyes like witchfire. Born on a night of storm and tossed seas. A child who bore no likeness to him. Arican named her Svirva - *Survivor* in the old tongue of Càrnoth.

Valloch knew that Svirva was no child of his. He had always known. But pride, perhaps, or guilt, stayed his hand.

He declared that Svirva would be raised by Arican in his halls, but when she came of age, when she could survive the mountain cold and speak the tongue of warriors, she would be sent to live with Haegun and his son Agatir, those who brought Arican and her ghosts, to these lands.

That day came, but Valloch did not accompany her. Instead, soldiers brought Svirva, silent and wide-eyed, across the village. Arican said nothing.

The child of two outcasts and one betrayal was placed at the threshold of a home that barely knew how to receive her.

To Haegun, the girl was a symbol. A symbol of his weakness, his loneliness, his fall, and banishment.

Love for the child never took root, and Agatir knew it never would.

"Home again. The events that have transpired. The spilled blood and lost lives. We have much to be grateful for. More to question. For now, we rest and recover. The weather is turning. The season of The Maw is rising.

Hunger and feast. Withering and Silence. We have much to reflect on.

This morning. Tananda and Kanike took their first steps, and Kaelani was proud of them. And Samike. She still stands by me.

May the Mountain bless her for her grace and her understanding."

Book of Dothemides, Maw's Feast 26, Year 7

"Dothemides now works with the north and contends with occasional attacks on Fort Koba. He is sure to return home frequently, and I go with him and Bianzhi when I can, but it is not often, especially since I am with child once again. When I told him, tears filled his eyes. He called for a celebration. The people call us blessed by the Mother. It is a light in the season of The Maw."

Book of Samike, Maw's Feast 40, Year 7

"It's been months since the battles that many have come to call the Three Thanes War, and the rise of Dothemia's foothold in the north. I still can't shake the sight of Haphira holding Koba's body.

The scattered remnants of Rolki and Vulfgar have attacked our supply caravans. In response, I've led attacks on the Ruins of Vulfgar and settlements where the Rolki are said to remain. Only some were sanctioned by Dothemides.

We don't attack to kill but to warn and to remind—Dothemia has become a presence on the Steppes. After the last, Dothemides took me aside and asked me to put an end to them. He is my king, my friend, and in my heart. So I listen. But still, I hold no love for the Steppes."

Book of Bianzhi, Maw's Wither 50, Year 7

"Things have settled since the Three Thanes War. Dothemides sets his sights even further north, to the Càrnothi Highlands. We have already endured a great deal, and although there is concern, there is agreement.

Three days ago, scouts were sent from Fort Koba into the Càrnothi territories. I tell myself that I understand why. Yet sometimes I still question."

Book of Samike, Maw's Wither 60, Year 7

"Last night, our scouts returned from the highlands. Their report spoke of a land of few settlements. Of tall pines and trails that wind through endless forests. A harsh, cold, and unforgiving land of whitewolves, greatsabers, cave bears, and mammoths.

They said they followed the trails and saw a city far to the Northwest and gathered from talks with tribes scattered on its outskirts, that it is ruled by a Warchief named Valloch.

I have sent riders south to bear the report to Dothemia. We will see what Dothemides says. But with the season of the Mountain rising, we will either be going soon or waiting until the season of the Mother returns. I just hope that when we do go, this Valloch will be open to speak."

Book of Brynvi, Maw's Silence 78, Year 7

"Dothemides has been quiet. Reflective. He is guided by his heart and his faith. He believes the Mother guides his actions and that the Mountain aids her in helping Dothemia and its territories endure.

With the news from Brynvi, he has decided not to wait and prepares to lead an expedition to the northwest in search of Warchief Valloch.

With all they have experienced, he says that he will encourage everyone to leave their journals behind. By his plan, they will go heavily armed and with a sizable force.

He prays that things will go well. He will not allow fear or threat of violence to halt his dream. Lives have been lost because of it. And because of that, he will never give up on it.

He is not a man of pride or vanity. But when does a dream for one thing become ambition for another?

I cannot let such thoughts linger, lest they be filled by the Hollow."

Book of Samike, Maw's Silence 90, Year 7

Maw's Silence 95. Càrn Valloch

Rain falls across the Blackpine. Horses carry lumber from the forests. Wagons carry fish from the sea. Frost flows from the lips of bone carvers, shamans, priests, and merchants who wander, whisper, pray, and parade their wares of spirit and coin in gray and mist-veiled movement.

The warriors, Nelah and Sunh, walk side by side and enter a darkened longhall. Nelah is the older of the two, but not by much. Her wide mammoth-fur cloak conceals her form and shields her from the Maw's chilled air. Hair, both braided and loose, falls about their shoulders in similar styles. Nelah's brown contrasting with the warm honeyed strands of Sunh.

Sunh wears a cloak of saber fur. Both are as strong as they are fair and carry a presence that draws the attention of the men of the càrn who watch them walk with minds that wander as much as their eyes.

Such behavior is commonplace, but as warriors, they are respected as much as they are desired. They handle themselves well and take their place at the table as Skarnvald slaves fill their cups.

At the head of the hall, Arican sits silently alongside Valloch, her eyes watching them. As they take their seats, a faint smile is offered. The pair's blue eyes meet those of Valloch's wife as they nod in return.

Runners enter and approach Valloch, speaking of a contingent of warriors seen riding across the steppes. Valloch tells soldiers to double the watches on the walls to the southwest and southeast.

Nelah and Sunh share a glance, watch the scouts leave, and continue their drink.

Mountain's Rise 10. Càrn Valloch. Southwestern wall

A few days pass, and Nelah and Sunh watch the return of the runners. They are cold, wet, and breathless, with eyes wide with urgency.

"They'll be upon us before Highsun," one pants, his voice ragged.

Valloch steps forward as the sun rises over the ridge, casting long shadows down the wall.

Nelah dismisses the runners as Valloch approaches, and together they watch.

Before long, the contingent is spotted. Nelah studies them. They are armed but seem to come in peace, bearing weapons more for the wilds than war.

Nelah recommends speaking to them, but Valloch would have nothing of it. He studies the man at the head, noting his dark skin, black locks, and those who follow him— southlanders and people from the steppeland tribes.

Skarnvald slaves had spoken of the southland king. He knows this must be him and sees this as a chance to strengthen his name.

Looking to Nelah, he ponders then speaks. “Nelah, prepare.” Valloch’s eyes remain fixed on the advancing group.

“Warchief,” Nelah responds with a glance to the sky and back to Valloch.

“It is Highsun. Mists of the Blackpine have long since rolled away. No one attacks without the benefit of concealment.”

He listens, but seems unmoved.

Sunh adds her voice in support and concern. “Nelah is right...No war cries, no thundering hooves, no calls of challenge...Perhaps they come in peace.”

Valloch’s arms cross as soldiers within earshot feel their warchief’s patience thin.

“Or perhaps, as the rumors claim, they are servants of the Hollow.” Valloch turns towards Nelah, as she was the first to speak. “You see the wolves of the Skarnfolk with them. You’ve heard as much as I about the Three Thanes War.”

He studies the Dothemians. “The Skarn...following a southlander? Something is not right. Tell me, Nelah, how is this possible?” His gaze returns to the approaching foreigners. “I’ll not fall as those fools have.”

“Let them know that they are not welcome here. Nelah. You lead the attack. Sunh, you remain on the wall.” His decision and words are as much a punishment as they are an order.

Nelah and Suhn share a glance, then clasp hands in the warriors’ way. Both know they have pushed as far as they will be allowed. Nelah turns and descends the ramparts stairs, each step carrying her towards a conflict she feels should be avoided.

Her hand raises, signaling soldiers to fall into ranks behind her, but her eyes do not meet theirs.

On the field, Nelah stands in command of a contingent of warriors. Weapons rise from the rows and ranks as she waits. In the distance, she takes note of these visitors again. At their head, a man who must be their leader sat astride a warhorse. Alongside him rode people from many nations. A woman of the Jhandai, a man and woman of the Steppelands, a woman of Tharios and more. They were not few, but they were clearly no army.

Her eyes narrow. She hopes they will retreat. Glancing back to Valloch, she sees his mind is set. Sunh offers a grim nod, begging her not to defy their warchief and incur his wrath.

Nelah's eyes move back to the foreigners and with a deep breath, she begins to trot forward, the feet of those behind her start as well. As their voices rise, her heart sinks as she sees the faces of those before her fill with confusion. Then she is filled with dread when they draw their weapons.

Warriors race past Nelah, eager to prove themselves in the eyes of Valloch. Among the foreigners, only a handful are on horseback. Only the leader, the woman of the Jhandai, the woman of Tharios, and two of the Skarnvald. A clear advantage they discard when they dismount, close ranks and stand together. Nelah wonders if this is honor or a show of their reluctance to engage. But it's too late.

She remains focused on the southland leader as he takes command. He calls his people to brace and prepare. In him, she sees rage, sorrow, regret, and warning.

The young and brash warriors break away from the line, lose discipline, and race to close on him. Nelah calls to the remaining Valloch line, commanding them to drive the opposing forces back, not to kill. It is all she can do. The Càrnothi, once unleashed, cannot be easily contained.

She calls to those racing ahead, ordering them to hold. Some do not listen and pay the price with their lives. There is no time for the southland commander to ready his shield, but his blade proves enough.

Nelah sees two rush towards him. The southland ruler's movements are quick, his feet steady. The placement of their blades is read by him, the look in their eyes understood by him. Something within him no longer hesitates. His fist arcs, his blade strikes down, tip first, sinking inches into the neck of his first attacker. The blade is withdrawn as the warrior that remains attacks with a slash meant for his throat. The attempt is deflected, and Nelah watches as he returns it in kind. Two fools fall seeking glory. Nelah knows their mothers and knows they will mourn the deaths of their sons.

The woman of the Jhandai wounds two others as Nelah crosses blades with the man of the steppes. He is skilled but lacks the discipline of his commander. The quiver on his back tells her that he does not belong on this field. That he didn't fire upon them proves they did not come for a fight. Still, orders must be followed. Nelah wounds his leg with mercy. Enough to remove him from the battle. He goes down and is pulled away by a woman. Another marksman. Perhaps he is hers. It doesn't matter.

Why don't they retreat?

Nelah notices a woman approaching. She is too young for this field. Too fair of face and frame, and for a moment, she fears the look in the woman's blue eyes. A hollowness, but there is no silence. She is not like what they have been taught to fear. This woman has lost something, someone, and views Nelah as a path to an end, a path to peace and stillness.

The woman glances towards their commander, and for a brief moment, their eyes meet. She turns back and, with a Thariosian battle cry, rushes, shield and blade raised.

The Thariosian woman gives no quarter and Nelah knows that to offer mercy is to fall to her blade. Where the others fight to defend, she fights to kill or be killed.

The warrior's attacks come rapidly. Quick strikes meant to confuse and overwhelm. A thrust to her neck, sidestepped, a shield arcs towards her face, slipped under. With her head and posture lowered, Nelah notes her opponent's footwork, understands her shifting balance, and reads her momentum. She is fierce, wild, and reckless.

Nelah rises and holds the woman's gaze, begging her to stop with a glance that warns that she is about to die and all that she needs to do is step away.

"Don't..." Nelah says.

But the Thariosian does not listen. Nelah knows that this woman has thrown everything at her. She sees her chest rising and falling in exhaustion, and for a moment there is hope in her pause. But then she lunges.

The blade descends. A high strike. Overextended. Nelah catches a wrist that was given as much as it was taken and raises her blade. The woman rushes forward, her shield slipping to the side. Why? Her face contorts in a mix of pain and relief. Her eyes widen. Nelah knows her blade has struck true. She feels the warm flow of blood over her hand as it grips a blade sunk to the hilt. Their eyes lock onto one another's, the woman's breath flees her body, and she collapses, slipping from Nelah's sword, her blood pooling onto the mud beneath.

There is no time for hesitation.

Fighting through the sadness that grips her, Nelah steps over and away from the fallen warrior to scan the field. She sees the dark-skinned man, their leader. Their eyes meet. He looks past and sees the fallen Thariosian, and the sight of her breaks him. This woman meant something to him.

Nelah then feels the closest thing she has ever felt to fear. She witnesses a rage rising in him. And for a moment, he seems on the verge of becoming a man focused more on killing than defending. She feels her heart quicken as his voice rises in despair. She braces and readies herself for his frenzied charge. But then the world slows as he calls out to his people—a call to retreat.

Valloch's warriors cheer around her as she watches his warriors retreating behind him. But as they do, he stands motionless, facing her. Facing them all, his eyes once again fall on the dying woman at Nelah's feet. His silence is haunting, and his eyes, filled with tears, rise past her to the wall upon which Valloch stands. Nelah can see the confusion, pain, and rage within him. She turns back to the wall. Sunh watches warily. Valloch smiles.

Drums echo from the wall, and the warriors of the càrn fall back into formation behind her, roaring as one voice with a singular shout that echoes through the stillness with warning.

The southland leader stands as if he hears nothing, but after a moment, he paces back, weakened by the pain of what he'd witnessed, and with each step taken, the warriors of Valloch advance. This continues for a short time, until he turns and walks away, disappearing into the pines.

Nelah kneels by the fallen warrior, picks up her blade with urgency, places it in her hands and watches as the woman stares at the sky, as if longing to see someone. Through her fixed gaze, tears roll from the corners of her eyes, and as she draws her last breath, a faint smile forms on her lips.

That night, Dothemides' followers saw grief and pain. Rage and regret, and then the kind of resignation that chilled them more than the highland winds.

Again, they came in peace, and again, they were met with teeth. An unjustified violence that cost Haphira her life.

An anger burned within Dothemides, the likes of which his most loyal had not yet seen in their king. And as he stared into the flames of their campfire, it was as if the world had vanished around him. He sat beyond blame and doubt, thinking of only one thing. Vengeance.

Haphira's body was not recovered, yet he ordered a pyre to be lit in her honor. It burned more as a symbol, and he made a vow and promise, before the Mother and Mountain, and all those who follow him, that it one day would be.

As the empty pyre burned, Dothemides set in his mind that the blackened earth beneath it would mark the place from which Dothemia would stage an attack against Valloch.

He sent Thornsten and Brynvi to take word of Valloch's cruelty to Fort Koba and to Dothemia. By his command, those that remained began felling trees and raising walls, turning the pyre site into a warcamp.

One rain-soaked morning, as the walls continued to rise, he saw her. The woman of the càrn. Haphira's killer.

She came alone, and as Bianzhi prepared to separate her head from her shoulders, the woman stood tall. She did not kneel. There was a readiness and surrender in her. Her blade fell to the mud. Her chin raised. Dothemides approached. She held his gaze. With a gesture, she was seized, bound, and brought into the camp.

"I was not granted a journal when I first stood before him. I was not granted a journal as I saw them return bruised, bloodied, but victorious.

But even after receiving it and proving my loyalty and value, I didn't feel worthy of recording my story. Shame kept me from its pages. But enough time has gone by. It is time now...

I survived the Sea of Souls and the northeastern shores of the Durajan, and I found my purpose and a people to cling to. We who had survived were taught that only the càrn mattered. Not individuals. A tribe, with souls made one by the sea. We served and lived through strength, survival, and the sword.

We claimed our lands by taking what we desired, killing those who stood in our way, and defending them with brutality. If you came to Càrn Valloch, you did so knowing you may never leave. But they did not know.

Dothemides had come in peace. But Valloch would have nothing of it.

I was a defender of our territories. And I was ordered to drive back the intruders. I faced a young woman on the field. She was younger than me. Fierce and wild. Her final charge was not madness, it was longing. I would come to know her name in the days that followed. Haphira. In the end, Dothemides and his kin retreated.

Perhaps it was his pain, perhaps it was his grief, perhaps it was his sorrow when she fell that haunted me. That still haunts me. Haphira had served him for years and lost her love, a warrior named Koba, in the Three Thanes War that bled the ground red on the steppes. Since hearing their story, I've felt that their souls still live among them.

Dothemides came in peace. But Valloch... I... gave him blood. I followed the order of the càrn and not the feeling in my soul.

On that day, something changed in me. Changed for many of us. I knew then that we had struck a blow that would come back to haunt us. I remember feeling it in my bones.

Not long after, I left the walls of Càrn Valloch and laid my sword down at his campsite.

I cannot say why Dothemides spared my life. I cannot say why he stayed the hands of his warriors who stood to cut me down. But he did. In my heart, I knew the storm and sea, even the Mountain itself, looked upon our actions with shame. I gave myself to him, to replace the one whom I had so unjustly slain.

I remember when I, and those he demanded be given to him, returned south to his city. To the place they call Dothemia. I did not know if I would live or die. But I knew I would accept his judgment and the judgment of his people for all that I had done."

Book of Nelah, Mountain's Trial 25, Year 7

My Sovereign speaks little of her past. Of those early days before her rise. But now, with peace, following so many years of war and loss...she was willing to speak of them. And so I was honored to record her words, in a book she had set down many years ago...

"It was twenty-nine years ago today. I was a child then. I had no love for my father or mother.

Nelah and Sunh were both warriors of our clan. I looked up to them. When Nelah left the càrn, she spoke haunting words, telling our elders that she believed a wrong had been committed and the gods would punish them for it. Sunh left soon after.

I observed my brother and Larastus in the meetings that followed. Secret gatherings where they spoke of the growing influence of the southland king, of the cursed choice that Valloch made, that he was told to attack them by Arican, my mother. That whatever curse was about to befall the càrn was her fault.

I remember eyes turning on me in those whispered talks, and my fear of them. I remember threats made and the motions of Agatir and Larastus to defend me against them.

They whispered of the darkened seas and of the gods' disapproval, doing so with courage in their voices. But I understood fear. The fear I saw in their eyes as they spoke of him, saying that the shamans say he will return. And he did...

I remember the chaos and the screams.

Larastus ran to defend, and Agatir pulled me away. Told me to hide. I watched from my hiding place as the dark-skinned king led an army of warriors. Faces and people I had never seen. All different yet fighting as one.

As the screams of the càrn rose, I knew they were not screams of victory. No Càrnothi dies without a final shout of defiance.

I heard many souls cry that day.

Our walls had been breached, and fire blazed across our rooftops. The forces clashed for hours, and to spare those who still stood on the field, their leader called out to Valloch. His voice carried long and was filled with so much pain.

Valloch emerged with Arican alongside him. He said his name was Dothemides. He said he came in peace and hope and was met with blood and death. He said he came this time for vengeance. He said that he learned that no challenge laid at the feet of a Càrnothi warchief can be refused. And so he challenged Valloch.

Their battle would spare lives. I watched as Valloch looked to my mother, who merely nodded. Valloch walked through his bleeding people, through the smoke and ash, and past the wounded and dying.

From my hiding place, I saw him. Tall with skin darker than my mother's and hair like long black ropes. He was strong and…so very…different. Around him were soldiers of many peoples. Among them were Nelah and Sunh. They had fought for him.

Valloch looked to Nelah and Sunh, then to Dothemides, who was cut across his body and bled from many wounds, but did not appear weak. Valloch raised his axe, and the Dothemian king was brought a greatblade.

The blade lowered, and the king charged. As he swung the blade up with both hands, his cry and the clash of weapons were all that was heard. Valloch staggered, and the king pressed. Each blow threatened to send Valloch's axe soaring from his grasp. I can still see how he fought. There was no relent, no hesitation, no mercy. Valloch staggered and looked back to my mother, who stood without expression or emotion, just silence.

Everyone watched, but none came to his aid, for no one could.

They met again, Valloch on the offensive, his axe drew blood, a glancing strike against the leg of the southland king, but that would be the first and only time Valloch would touch him.

The rest happened quickly. His blade spun, his body turned, and his onslaught began. An upward strike broke Valloch's grasp, the blade changed directions and came down, splitting the shaft in two. A second swing cut a bloodied line across Valloch's thigh. Dothemides was behind him, and the last cut the back of Valloch's other leg, sending him to his knees. Valloch raised his voice to join those who had already fallen, but his life was not taken.

The southland king spared our càrn, spared Valloch, but demanded that many warriors of the càrn come to serve him in his city of Dothemia. To repay the loss of those he loved.

He was cold and filled with grim purpose. He took many of our strongest that day, and among them were Larastus and Agatir. When they were claimed, my heart sank. Agatir, my brother whom I loved, and Larastus, a man that that little girl was deeply fond of, were two of our most proud.

When I look back now, our defeat was yet another signal of Dothemides' growing dominance, but it also left a void in Càrn Valloch. I was left behind, unprotected and vulnerable. My mother vanished, leaving the càrn in the days after the battle, and Valloch was never the same. The men of our lands were brutal, carnal, and cruel. My whole life, I had been watched. I was the *child born under the raven and storm*, and the daughter of Arican.

My brother and Larastus had been my true family and protectors. I was left to live with an uncaring father for years, and in time, when I became old enough, the wants and desires born of broken pride and lost honor had found their focus. That was the beginning of my suffering. A suffering my father allowed. A suffering he turned a blind eye to.

Though my spirit would remain unbroken, the seeds of rage and my eventual path were sown in the years that would follow."

Book of Svirva, Mountain's Trial 27, Year 36
As written by Thane Erick Longhorn

On that day, as Svirva watched the southland king take Agatir and Larastus, she saw the only family she truly knew, slipping away. She ran and was caught, pulled back by a hand that held her apart from what little joy she had left. She did not understand it. Could not accept it.

Rain fell from heavy skies, and mud pooled with blood. The hand that held her pulled. Her world was dying. She screamed his name and the sky opened. Lightning streaked across the heavens. Her scream lingered with the winds and thunder that rolled along with her cries.

The càrn stood in silence, eyes to the storm, their defeat too large for speech. She dropped to her knees in the mire, soaked and shaking as the thunder quieted. And as the storm passed, she was dragged away, but the rains would last for days.

"His letters and messages come with frequency. In them, he speaks of his love for me, for the children. He also speaks of his never-ending dream, and its costs in loss and victory.

It is a dream that keeps him far from home. There is always something. Some battle to win. Some pact to hold. Some territory to defend. I can feel the weight of his words.

I need to see him, and I have waited longer than I should have.

I've gathered a small group of scouts and warriors that I trust. I told them nothing more. Only that we head north.

Tomorrow, we ride toward Fort Koba."

Book of Samike, Mountain's Vigil 53, Year 7

"Reinforcements have been sent to Fort Haphira. We've returned to our station at Fort Koba, but the mood has shifted. The blood spilled on these lands has changed us. Changed him.

His mood was only slightly lightened when Samike arrived. We watched from the wall as the rains fell and their contingent entered. I saw it in the way that she looked at him, that she could see it in his eyes. Were it not for the rain, we all would have seen our king shed tears."

Book of Brynvi, Mountain's Vigil 65, Year 7

"The Càrnothi warriors, Larastus, Agatir, Nelah, and Sunh keep to themselves. They mind their own and keep their heads low. They are smart to do so because few trust them. But they have proven useful in the information they have about the highlands and beyond.

Somehow, Samike knows the tongue of the Càrnothi, and between them, they have provided maps of the Blackpine, settlement names, and paths up through the mountains west of the Karskathi Mountains. To the mountain range they call Volkos.

There, they say, lives a long-standing tribe who are distant cousins of the Khadari. They speak of them as being shut in, protective, and not especially warm to visitors.

Despite everything we've endured, Dothemides turns his attention there. His dream has taken on a life of its own and each ally who gives their lives for it only serves to fuel its flame. I love him, but sometimes I believe he pushes too hard.

In a few days' time, we will all ride again with him, Sunh, Nelah, and Samike, to find the Volkosi Mountains and hopefully meet its people.

I only pray we all come back in one piece."

Book of Bianzhi, Mountain's Vigil 65, Year 7

"The victory against Valloch sent a clear message. There is concern over whether or not we went too far. But I grow tired of having a hand offered in peace, only to have it bitten.

We have not been home in months. Instead, we remained in Fort Koba. I sense the concern in others. The weariness. I am as tired as they are, but I believe the Mother wills this.

We have lost, but we have gained. Where Koba fell, a fort stands in his name. Where Haphira fell, a fort now stands in her name. Dothemia's paths lead to lands once closed to us.

I believe this journey to Volkos will end in peace.

Then ... then we can go home."

Book of Dothemides, Mountains Vigil, 70

"We've made our way north and set camp just before the forest thins and gives way to the mountain slopes. I don't like this place. It feels like the ground hums with old power and some unspoken threat. But we are here. Cold and far from home...again. I am not complaining, I just hope this goes well.

Dothemides and Samike had settled in their tent. Around the fire, everyone was quiet, and I understood why. So I decided to approach their tent and step in. They never minded when I did, never saw me as an interruption. They were patient and gracious as I voiced my concerns, and he told me what to tell the others, and even invited me to return when I delivered the message. I saw in Samike's eyes that she didn't mind the idea at all. I must have blushed because they both smiled as I left.

Around the fire, I told the others what he said:

Their worries are both understood and shared. He didn't know what we would face or how the Volkosi would respond. That any who wished to remain at camp could, and that if those who continued didn't return, those who remained should return home with word of what had occurred. No one would be looked down upon for their decisions.

I knew what their answers would be. Tomorrow we will continue on together.

As for tonight? Tonight, I will sit, write, and wonder if I should have joined them."

Book of Bianzhi, Mountains Silence 85, Year 7

"We rose at dawn. When Dothemides and I emerged from our tent, we were met with knowing smiles and a bit of laughter. I suppose our passions could not be masked by thin hides and draped furs. Passions that, while pleasurable, were absent tenderness and presence.

Bianzhi smiled as well and led the breakdown of the camp, giving Dothemides and I time to plan. I knew what needed to be seen. How we needed to be perceived, so I focused on the task ahead.

It was strange how silently the Volkosi appeared. They descended with caution, their weapons ready, and watched us as they closed the distance between us.

The rumors of them being kin to the Khadari were true. Perhaps even to the Marukh as well. Most are dark skinned and dark-eyed, though among them are faces of lighter hue, hints of mingled bloodlines.

Their black or brown hair is braided or left in locks, adorned with beads or bound in leather cords. The men and women both bear the hardened look of survivors, scarred, tattooed in ash, red, or black. They wear cloth and leather with curved plates of a metal that I am unfamiliar with.

They surrounded us. Sunh didn't like it. Her hand went to her blade. Bianzhi called for calm. I met Sunh's gaze and shook my head. Sunh stood down. My love was weary of the fighting. Too much blood had been spilled already. I could see the gratitude in his eyes as we chose to handle this another way.

They asked who we were and why we were there, in a language that was Khadari, but mixed with accents of the Càrnothi and Skarn. Dothemides understood them but looked to me to speak. We agreed earlier in the morning that I would be our voice.

I told the Volkosi of our home and purpose, and the next few moments went quickly. They studied us and beckoned for us to follow. They said they would consider our words, but requested that we surrender our weapons. So we did.

When they escorted us through the village, I took in the way they lived. The influence of Skarnvald and Càrnothi was evident everywhere. And their homes reminded me of the Khadari tribes, but built for colder climes. They were circular, low, and strong, made from mortar and stone, and reinforced with clay tile roofs and wood slats.

These were not sprawling settlements, but clusters, tight and defensive. Many of them worked busily at the entrances of caves carved into the mountainside, carting quantities of ore from within.

We were taken into a large, central circular hall with three adjacent rooms, one opposite the entrance and two on either side.

Now we sit in one—no door, just two guards who remain at the entrance.

Tensions linger, but Bianzhi continues to encourage calm.

So now we wait."

Book of Samike, Mountains Silence 85, Year 7

"They have been speaking for some time. Their deliberations are tense, but it seems a voice has risen in our favor. One that urges his people to see what might be possible. I could hear from the conversation that his name is Tumahn, and that his sister, Setna, stands by him.

They've gone quiet, leaving us all to question what comes next.

I hold onto the hope that their elders will accept us and seek to form an alliance or perhaps establish trade.

And I pray to the Mother that I have not made another grave mistake in leading us here."

Book of Dothemides, Mountains Silence 85, Year 7

"It was foolishness! We hoard our gold. We guard our Umbrasteel as if it were blood. We tell ourselves it is wisdom or caution, but it is fear that guides us.

Dothemides came with open hands. He offered understanding, not demands. He saw through our suspicion, and still, he and his people stayed.

I believed, for a moment, that our elders might choose to be more, but the council refused. *Not yet.* They said.

Fah'zhela, uri!

I made my choice. I could not stay, and Setna agreed to come. We always thought as one. Our futures do not lie in the shadow of the caldera.

So we went with him. With them. To see what they had built, to know his people, and to carry a voice back to ours when the time was right.

Upon arriving in Dothemia, Dothemides and Samike thanked me and Setna for our trust and gave us empty books. At first, we were confused. But he sat and spoke to us of his dream, of those who died for it, and of the nearly seven years of struggle and toil to build it.

I saw a great many things in him. But what I see most clearly is a man that I could follow. A man in need of much rest, but also a man who will never find it."

Book of Tumahn, Mountains Silence Year 7

"The handsome one and his pretty wife were brought before our elders. I watched them speak of him, and his name, and that of his queen, Samike. She sat with those gray eyes and a belly rounding with child. She knew our tongue better than he, it seemed.

There was something behind those eyes though, that I could not place. She watched everything. And that she has traveled all this way on horseback when less than a moon away from her child's birth? That was either love or madness.

Dothemides sounded like a man of hope. The leader of a people who had been through great trials and tribulations. Yet our elders were not interested. They thought these Dothemians had little to offer despite their vision.

Khos'uk et refu! Each and every one of them!

Little to offer? They stood before us, Durajani born of Jhandai, Shadura, Càrnoth, and Skarn, as well as Khadar. How could they not see that something new was rising among them? Something that they had bled and died for.

When the council ended, Tumahn took me aside, but I was already with him in heart.

I was tired of these damned mountains, the ash, the mining, the cold, many of us were. But only my brother and I were bold enough to act. I wanted to see the rivers, rains, forests, and sands of my grandfather.

I told Tumahn that on the next day, regardless of what the elders say, I would go with him. We both believed that there was a better life to be found, and that perhaps Dothemides and his city would be the path that led us to it.

And so I write this, as the first words, into a gift that all but confirms my hopes. Dothemides wishes for me to be remembered. I feel I have made the right choice."

Book of Setna, Mountain's Silence 85, Year 7

"He is home. *We* are home, and I thank the Mother for those who remain, and the Mountain for giving us the strength to endure.

Another year nears its end. It is strange to know that what began seven years ago has become what it is today—forts, alliances, and in truth, a *kingdom*.

We are no longer the Obsidian Fortress. We have become more than *Dothemia.*

Parents of children born here say they will be born of Dothemia. Our people speak of being Dothemians. Not Càrnothi, Skarn, Thariosian, Marukhan, Khadari, Shaduran, Xeyathi, Jhandai, or Vordos, but Dothemian.

Dothemides' vision continues to grow, and the dream of a unified and thriving people is becoming clearer. He knows that challenges still loom on the horizon. Some we can see, and some that I fear see us.

I wonder how far the reach of Dothemia will extend, and I sometimes wonder how far it should."

Book of Samike, Mountain's Silence 100, Year 7

Across the Steppes, Dothemides found alliances forged in loss and suffering. In Càrn Valloch, he was met with violence and bloodshed. In Volkos, he was met with skepticism and rejection. His heart hardened to the people of the Durajan, and his tactics changed.

He now envisioned a Durajan united from north to south, as a land ruled by Dothemia. A land without cruelty, without mistrust. Where every culture would be remembered, not erased.

Those who had made their home within Dothemia, who lived in peace and protection, and cooperation had been all the proof he needed. The end would justify the means.

Those who witnessed it from outside the truth told their versions of the tale. They spoke of how the thundering of Dothemian hooves trampled over old borders and tribal boundaries. And how sacred and unseen lines alike gave way, crushed beneath the surge of Dothemia's advance. They saw a king moving without hesitation or mercy.

In his wake, trust became a rare currency, fragmenting among chiefs, tribal elders, and Thanes who resisted, watched them ride, and listened as word spread.

Still, Dothemia's reach grew, causing some to follow and abandon their old lives in pursuit of the new dream. Others fractured, torn between tradition and vision, leaving scars across the land as skilled craftsmen, fierce warriors, and wise healers chose to break away from their kin to join Dothemia's cause, leaving half-empty villages and broken families behind.

He did not see it, not fully.

His gaze was fixed on the horizon, on the dream. The realization of a united Durajan, free from the cruelty of the nations that had banished them.

Free from the cruelty of the tribes that killed before questioning and bled their own people dry with pointless blood feuds and old rivalries.

He did not see the fields left fallow, the fires left untended, the sorrow that gathered like mist in the depths of deserted homes. He did not hear the weeping of mothers who had lost their sons to ideals they did not welcome. He did not see the seeds of resentment he planted, even as he believed he was sowing peace.

To those who spoke to him of the rumors of resentment and anger that had begun to flow across the Durajan, he said this.

"Like the clearing of fields for growth, unity has a cost. It is the balance of the Mother."

Part II

BREATH

CHAPTER EIGHT

A PRINCE'S BIRTH

YEAR 8

WOVEN

They handed us nothing.

And in doing so, they gave us everything.

"I saw the boy with gold cords tied around his belt, handing out books from a basket, like fruit.

"Your story," he said, "is the only scripture we serve."

I thought it was a trick. But the cover was smooth and warm. Like sun-baked rock. Not one page was written within it.

I haven't written my name since before the brand. I hadn't even heard it spoken until I arrived here, guided by rumors across the sands.

Tonight, under the firelight, I think back on the things I loved most, and I remember my sister's laugh.

I wrote that down, and it felt holy."

Book of Elakh, Mother's Hand 37, Year 8

"I came to the market only for crushed amberroot and fire-clay, nothing more. But the city gnawed at me. There are too many voices, too many walls. I kept to the outer stalls. That's where I saw him. A young man, nervous and wide-eyed, offering not sermons or charms, but books. Blank ones.

"To be remembered," he said, holding one toward me like a cup of water.

I took it. Then another. Then, without knowing why, I took a third.

He looked surprised, but I did not explain myself. I left before Highsun.

Now, I am home, writing with one on my lap and the other two on my table of medicines. Who they are for, I do not know, but they sing with voices that rise from each in sweet song, like the pull of paths not yet crossed.

The wind tells me they are not meant for me and that someone will need them.

When they come, I will know."

Book of Nzinga, Mother's Hand 40

"Landashti. I will never forget you.

I write this now, because of the kindness of a young and fair woman, and the dream of a king.

She stood in the rain with no cloak and offered me a book like one might offer a kiss, quiet, close, and sudden. I admit, it was strange until she spoke.

"The first lie of the Nine," she said, "was that your story wasn't sacred."

Then she was gone.

I opened it, expecting poetry, edicts, and oaths. But it was empty. Not even a name inside.

That night I dreamed of my mother's perfume. I dreamed of her songs and poetry, woven in the taverns of Shadura, and I dreamed of the crowd's hush that always followed.

My mother wept when I was banished.

The last words from her lips was my name.

The first word in my journal was hers."

Book of Leiyara, Mother's Hand 46, Year 8

"I treated wounds for three days straight without pay or thanks. Then a child placed the book on my cot and vanished. Alongside it was a note.

If they forget your name, let the ink remember it.

I filled three pages with every soul I've tended since my banishment.

I do not know what these Dothemians hope to build. But if remembering is part of their breath, I will breathe it too."

Book of Aroun, Mother's Womb 60, Year 8

"I buried three friends in the salt flats. No prayers. No names spoken. Few were there for the pyre's flames.

As I journeyed to the next village, a girl followed. There, she handed me the journal as if it were bread. "So they're not forgotten," she said.

I didn't ask who sent her.

So tonight, I will write their names.

Vhatari, Rhumal, Ahran.

They laughed. They fought. They are remembered.

May they rest well in the Far Sky."

Book of Ahirah, Mother's Womb 72, Year 8

"There is joy in Dothemia. Our king and queen celebrate the birth of their son. They named him Omanessi.

They say the seed was planted during their time in the steppes. He was born amidst the growing strength of our settlement, and his arrival seems to have solidified what many see as the family's royal legacy and ensures Dothemia's lineage."

Book of Loreiaka, Wolf's Wake 17, Year 8

Chapter Nine

THE HOLDING YEAR

Year 9

WISDOM

"For two years, we have explored, fought, and suffered. But we have also gained. The Mother has blessed us with a fourth child, and with his birth, Samike and I have chosen to cease explorations. Slow the spread of our branches and deepen the setting of our roots.

It feels right. It is a time for family, ritual, healing, and strengthening."

Book of Dothemides, Mother's Hand 26, Year 9

"Nelah and I now stand by Dothemides. We know what can be. But the people avoid us. Bianzhi still looks upon us with anger behind her eyes. They say that the steppes tested him and the highlands changed him.

A slow-building tremor that causes many to wonder if he is becoming a conqueror. I have heard all the tales told around fires and camps. I know what he has endured, and I believe he should. Nelah is not so sure. Many think his anger is justified, and others consider it dangerous.

Today, alone, I found him. I told him that I would stand by him and give my heart to him and his people—our people—for what the Durajan had taken from him. With my eyes, I let him know that whatever he desired of me would be given. He took what I offered, and I was glad for it.

At first, I was worried. But in our whispered moments on that first night, he assured me that I had nothing to fear.

And I am not blind.

I saw his queen's reaction to Agatir and Larastus on the day we arrived. I will never forget her eyes as she observed them. So I stay by him and protect what he seeks to build with my life."

Book of Sunh, Wolf's Howl 82, Year 9

"This morning, as I lay between them, Larastus was the first to wake. As was often the case, he woke to my eyes taking him in, my hands wandering, and my body pressed against him. I loved his smile. He asked me why I chose him and Agatir a year ago.

And so I explained why. He listened attentively. They mean much to me, and as the first to be taken through conflict, my husband gave them no books to record their histories. But I wish for them to be remembered. So here, I will write about them. My beloved protectors, Larastus and Agatir of Càrnoth.

My husband saw them as warriors, skilled and perhaps the beginnings of a new army of Dothemia. They knew of lands he did not, and so he met with them often. I was queen, yes, but I was also his translator and interpreter.

Dothemides knew my story but not the whole of it. I had always explained it in a way that made sense.

A woman of Shaduran and Marukhan blood held captive for years in Tharios would have picked up languages. And for the companionship and pleasures I provided, I was educated by the wealth and preference of a king.

But when I began to translate the words of the Càrnothi, he was surprised, offering a pause, a handsome smile and shake of his head in gentle disbelief, as if the depth of my surprises always tickled him.

In his eyes, I saw a man who loved me wholly. A love that transcended the passions shared with his Chosen in the ways of the Mother—Bianzhi, Loreiaka, and now Sunh.

I sought no Chosen, even though it was my right in the eyes of the people who followed us. The rituals were all that I needed, until I saw them.

When my husband returned from the north, there were celebrations of the victory. He was bruised and wounded, but his eyes, his love, his embrace—it was good to feel them. Then he turned, and they were brought before me. I was told their names. Larastus and Agatir. And by the Mother, they were handsome.

Agatir stood, shaved head, eyes the color of stone, fit and strong as the lands they hailed from. Larastus had a gentility about him, not in his formidable physique, but in his eyes. When he looked at me, it was as if he trembled. I felt it too and held his gaze. I was taught to know the hearts, wants, and needs of men with just a glance, and in that instance, I knew he would be mine. And through him, his friend Agatir.

Now they are my personal guard, *my* Chosen, and my friends."

Book of Samike, Maw's Silence 76, Year 9

Chapter Ten

The Queen and the Winterborn

Year 10

THE SEAT OF DISTANCE

Maw's Silence 78

It had been a year of peace. Dothemia had grown. Its forts were secure. Over the year, Dothemides had heard stories of a people who did not feel cold, of a metal forged in flame and tempered in ice, of tales spoken of by both the Càrnothi and Volkosi who had joined Dothemia.

Larastus, Agatir, Sunh, and Nelah called them the Winterborn, but Tumahn and Setna knew them by their true name, The Karskathi.

The Karskathi lived in tribes within the valleys and canyons of the mountains named after them and were rumored to be comprised of various peoples from across the Durajan.

Believers, shamans, priests, and warriors, all driven by faith, united in worship and living beneath the shadow of The First Mountain—known to all northerners as the highest mountain in the Awakened World and the symbol of the Mountain itself.

The tales of the Karskathi were many.

Their lives were marked by rituals and trials that broke the weak and the unworthy.

Only those who made the migration through Frostfaith Pass, to their sacred site of Karskath, were allowed to remain among them.

Many tried and many died, frozen to death in the cold reaches of the north.

Those who survived were said to receive the Mountain's Blessing and were no longer affected by the cold and bitter winds.

These rumors were interesting and curious, but what drove Dothemides most were the tales of Umbral Ore and Blackwake Flux, both of which were said to be found only in the Karskathi Mountains and parts of the Volkosi Mountains.

Tumahn and Setna explained that this was why the Volkosi were so removed and unwilling to trade. When asked why they had not mentioned this before, Setna and Tumahn told Dothemides that this was the most guarded secret of their homeland, spoken of only by their rulers.

The metal produced by their combination was rumored to be unbreakable, and for Dothemides, this kind of weaponry would enable Dothemia to better defend its growing lands.

So the planning began.

Mountain's Breath 10

Dothemides led a contingent north. The journey was grueling. Southern flesh fared poorly in the northern cold. Bianzhi grumbled the entire time. Larastus, Sunh, Setna, and the others took their turns at mocking the sun-softened southerners. Samike remained quiet, always watching.

When they reached the Karskathi lands, the Dothemians were not greeted as guests or enemies but with questions.

The villages clung to the wind-swept plateaus and ridgelines just beneath the high snows. Within stood circular dwellings of stone and slanted shale roofs, layered to endure the frost winds and mountain storms. It was true that the Karskathi were a tribe of all peoples of the Durajan, but each was tall, broad-shouldered, with weathered skin and eyes like flint. As if only the strong would survive these frigid climes. All wore bone and hide, adorned not for vanity but memory, tokens from beasts they'd slain or kin they'd buried. Few spoke. Fewer smiled. And all watched.

The Dothemians learned quickly that the Karskathi did not trade in words. They measured worth in strength and steel.

One of their chieftains emerged, flanked by two priests whose presence felt carved from the mountain itself. They stepped from a round hut rimmed in mammoth ivory, the doorframe etched with runes that glowed faintly in the cold light. Their warpaints were striking—bands of gray and white cut across the face like ridgelines, with dark ochre rings around the eyes to mimic the mountain's gaze.

Snow crunched beneath their fur-wrapped feet as they approached, their mammoth-hide cloaks trailing behind them in the deep snow. Each bore a weapon unlike any the Dothemians had ever seen. They held long, black-metal spears and curved blades that caught the light like frozen fire. Setna leaned in and offered a single word. Umbrasteel. There was no mistaking it.

The chieftain took their measure with calm confidence as his gaze swept across the party, pausing on each face long enough to judge, weigh, and decide. He spoke, but not in a tongue known to most, with a voice that was low, deliberate, and echoed across the frost.

He turned first to the members of the Càrnothi delegation that had accompanied the strangers. Samike stepped closer to Dothemides and spoke of her observation: "This chieftain only speaks Càrnothi, it seems."

Sunh and Larastus stepped forward, prepared to serve as interpreters. But before they could speak, Dothemides raised a hand and then answered the chieftain himself in Càrnothi.

A silence followed. Then a grunt of approval from the chieftain. The words had landed.

Dothemides offered parley. The chieftain declined. Instead, he offered a test of spirit and strength. If they wished to speak of Umbrasteel, they would first prove they could withstand what the mountain demanded.

Each trial was trying but never cruel. They were tests of endurance, combat, and wit. Dothemides stood tall through each. As did all Dothemians who were challenged. Each one proving their worth. But as their leader, it was Dothemides who was pushed hardest. As the trials were passed, each earned grudging nods from the trial-born of the Karskathi.

As always, Samike observed. She felt drawn to these people of faith and strength. They lived untouched and free. Embarking on a pilgrimage to choose their path and be who they wished to be. Seeking nothing in return but silence and peace. There was a beauty in them beyond the physical, and she was moved by it.

When asked about her by one of the Karskathi, Dothemides declared that she was not to be challenged. That she was his queen and together, they ruled their people. Their leaders understood, the trials continued, and by the day's end, the Karskathi deemed the Dothemians worthy.

That night, the elders of the mountain shared a sacred meal with their Dothemian guests. Fires blazed in the stone-hewn feast hall, and drink flowed like thawed rivers. Samike, draped in northern furs, slipped away unnoticed by most.

Dothemides glanced around once or twice, noting her absence. But with Bianzhi and Setna discussing metallurgy, Sunh arm wrestling a Karskathi tribeswoman as Nelah cheered her on, and Larastus and Agatir swearing they'd keep Samike safe, Dothemides let his unease pass. He told himself she was likely walking among the frost shrines, finding a place to reflect.

He did not know she had other plans.

Samike had seen him. A quiet one among the Karskathi. Not like the others. Ashen skin, the cold tattooed into his bones. Silent in the contests, but undeniable. A stillness in him that felt ancient, like the Mountain's cold, had stopped to rest in his chest.

Earlier in the evening, she had spoken to Larastus privately and, through him, bore a message to Agatir, and from Agatir to this man. Samike arranged for them to find him and guide him to her tent under the cover of night. So they did as their queen bid them to.

Escorted by Agatir and his path and presence watched over and protected by Larastus, the man approached Samike's tent alone.

When he entered, he saw her. There, with furs drawn close, she stood and let them fall away, baring her perfect form before him. Desire rose immediately in him, but fear as well. She was a Queen and belonged to the ruler of the Dothemian people.

In the dim candle-lit space, his head lowered and he paused. He moved to leave, but her hand caught and held his. There was no force behind her touch, only hope, will and desire. She looked into his eyes, took his hand, then placed it upon the fullness of her chest. His eyes fell closed, his heart raced as she guided him.

Looking up at him, Samike rested her palm on his cheek, her thumb caressing. His eyes opened, and with only breath between them, she reached for him, not as a queen, but as a woman without duty or title, just the thrum of blood and breath in the stillness of that moment and space.

He had barely spoken, but his hands knew prayer. His body was litany. That night, she did not dream of kingdoms, or temples, or bloodlines. She dreamed only of the warmth and reverence offered beneath the Mountain.

His name was Stígandr, and by dawn, he was gone.

Dothemides had spent the night with their Karskathi hosts, and Samike returned to their lodge before the others rose.

No one asked where she had been. And she offered nothing.

"Our journey north was successful. I will not say that we've made allies of the Karskathi, but we proved ourselves worthy enough to trade for the ore and flux. They asked if I or any of us would undergo the trials and attempt to cross Frostfaith Pass, but to face such cold was beyond any of us. Still, they shared their knowledge, and for that I am grateful.

One day, we will return, but for now, we have what we need to defend our land, people, and territories. There's still much to be done."

Book of Dothemides, Mountain's Trial 26, Year 10

Chapter Eleven

DEVOTION AND DEPARTURE

Year 11

SOJOURN

"She was radiant. Beautiful. Captivating. She strode through Market Row. A woman of the steppes. She wasn't of Càrnoth, not with that flaming red hair. No eye could leave her. Not even mine. And I am more drawn to the beauty of my king, and the men of Khadar, Marukh, and Càrnoth than to a woman. Yet still... Her allure would cause anyone to be curious. No mind remained settled. Where she walked, heads turned and hearts raced.

We came to know her as Ailis, an enigmatic and mysterious woman of the Skarnvald people who possessed a wealth of knowledge about the Mountain and Mother. She was no stranger to combat and no stranger to the pleasures and pains of life in the Durajan.

Her presence stirred curiosity and caution in equal measure. And though she offered wisdom and a deep connection to the divine forces shaping the north, she was an outsider whose true motives remained unclear.

Her arrival marked a shift in the dynamic of the Dothemia, introducing a new influence that both strengthened and complicated our growing kingdom.

Many had a feeling that it would not be long until she caught the attention of our king.

And they were right."

Book of Shizun, Mother's Hand 27, Year 11

"Samike's pregnancy was difficult. The birth was worse. We all saw her fatigue, the strain, her pain. Her labors began in the morning, but by evening, the child remained stubborn and unwilling. When his cries rose with the following morning's light, silence filled the bedchamber.

The child came into the world with eyes that were a striking blue, hair white as snow, and his skin the color of desert sand. Samike had given birth to a son not of Dothemides. Who the father was would hopefully be known in time, but there was another, far more critical matter. Samike was motionless.

I remember hurrying to find Dothemides. He entered and sat by her. Our binders and healers did what they could. But told us all that she was in the Mother's hands now.

It took two days for her to regain her strength, and in that time, the child was fed by able mothers. She named the boy Sittrika. And we rejoiced, celebrating his birth and our queen's recovery.

Dothemides loved Samike and welcomed life, however it came. He didn't hold anything against her. But to some, the child's presence was just plain unsettling.

People are always drawn to rumors. They catch, spark, and spread like fire. Especially ones like these."

Book of Bianzhi, Mother's Tears 79, Year 11

"There is love, there is presence, but there is distance.

Yesterday, I watched her walk the halls with Sittrika cradled in her arms, looking into his eyes, smiling, and speaking whispered words between mother and child.

This morning, I glimpsed her nursing him by a window as the Wolf's cooler rains fell. She looked out as if observing a place far from here.

Moments ago, as she sat with him by the fire, I knelt by her, took her hand in mine, and kissed it. We shared a smile, and I kissed his brow and her cheek. But I saw in her eyes love and sorrow, alongside uncertainty and hope.

And in her silence, I believe she saw the same in mine."

Book of Dothemides, Wolf's Hunt 36, Year 11

"I love Nzinga. She is my all.

We live in the southern savannah. The story of our meeting... Well, it was a harrowing one.

I am a Skarnvald warrior, and was awaiting death after my hunting party was decimated by a matriarch elephant. I clutched my weapon, bleeding and broken. I closed my eyes and waited for my soul to rise into the Far Sky.

Then she found me. Nzinga of the Flame. A Khadari Shaman, with a beauty my eyes had never seen. Over time, and under her care and bitter medicines, I recovered. Her voice had power, her words wrapped in old prayers I had never heard.

She spoke to my pain and gave it meaning. Gave me meaning. A bond was forged between us that was greater than the differences of our people.

One night, as we lay under the stars, she said something strange. I had just told her how close I had come to death, and she smiled and whispered,

"The Pale Spirit must have been watching over you."

I asked her what she meant. She laughed and said, "Mganga wa Giza. Sangoma. Nganga." Her language was as beautiful as she was. "It is just a tale from my childhood... a whisper carried across the sands of a spirit said to walk the dunes and vanish within them. They say he speaks to the moon and brings rain, great winds, and storms of sand."

She dismissed it like a dream, but I remember how still she grew afterward.

Nzinga knew nothing of the Mountain, but somehow, she spoke in the ways his most devout do. I believe she was sent to me, not just to heal, but to awaken something. To remind me that I had survived for a reason.

Then she reached beside her, pulled something from the folds of her satchel, and placed it in my hand. It was a worn book. Blank, except for the first page, where she had written my name.

She told me that years ago, she traveled to a city called Dothemia during the Season of the Mother.

She said that the Dothemians are a people born of many with a beautiful message. That they handed out empty books so the forgotten could be remembered, and that she took three that day and didn't know why, until now.

She placed the book on my chest and said that I had nearly died and that if I had, no one would have remembered me or my story.

She closed my fingers around it and told me to write it, so that I wouldn't be forgotten."

Book of Jorvan, Wolf's Blood 52

"For years, I have felt something slipping. And now it has fallen so far from me that no matter how much I search for it, I cannot find it.

I fear I never will. Perhaps I never had it.

Through trials of blood and faith, we had built Dothemia together. Yet as it grows, I feel...afraid.

Afraid of its familiarity.

Afraid of its influence.

Afraid of its reach.

Afraid of being lost within it.

Confined by it.

Afraid of what I am beginning to understand."

Book of Samike, Wolf's Howl 80, Year 11

"Samike grows more distant. And in truth, so do I. It is not the child. It is what he has awakened within her.

We have spoken. Shared memories and confessions of the things we most hoped for. Discussions that gave birth to clarity.

And so now, we both love, and we both wait."

Book of Dothemides, Maw's Hunger 3, Year 11

"My decision to leave was not made lightly, nor was it without consequence. For a moment, he urged me to reconsider, but it was fleeting.

Dothemides understood. But I know the decision cut deep. And it would do so across Dothemia. There would be fracture and frustration. My children would grow with questions, pain, anger, and hatred.

I could only hope that they would one day know that I was not abandoning them, but that I was escaping the place that had become more than I ever wanted. A kinder mirror of my past.

Larastus and Agatir wanted to accompany me. But I needed to do this with only my son. To leave all of it behind. It was not sudden. Perhaps it was in the eyes of many.

But it was true. It was felt. It was known.

And it could no longer be denied.

Larastus, in particular, was the most pained. In my heart, I knew he loved me.

Bianzhi held her anger and pain inside. But I could see it in her eyes. She had stood by us for so long and protected me. But I know she will continue to stand by him.

I had been the prize of a noble once before. I could not be that again. All I wanted was to feel the sun on my face once more and to find him."

Book of Samike, Maw's Silence 78, Year 11

Books of the Remembered

"My mother said queens don't get to leave. That they must endure. But I saw her that morning. She was smiling with her face lifted towards the sun. Not proud. Not broken. Just...free. Maybe that's what makes her a queen."

Book of Morgus, Maw's Silence 80, Year 11

"I don't care whose child it was. The way she kissed his brow and whispered something before she climbed into the saddle... that was a mother. His birth changed her. Changed everything. Whatever else she was, she loved that boy more than anything here."

Book of Sinjala, Maw's Silence 84, Year 11

"Some are saying she walked out as if it were any other day. Not rushed, not cloaked in the darkness of night, just steady, with that child, tucked close to her chest.

I don't think it was shame or defiance. I think it was a choice made long before her feet reached the gate.

Sometimes, people leave because they must. Not for themselves, and not for others. Just because there's no road left where they're standing."

Book of Naji, Maw's Silence 88, Year 11

"They say she blessed this place. I say she abandoned it. Abandoned him. Abandoned her children.

The First Queen walked out the gates and didn't look back. If she cared, she'd have stayed and faced what came after."

Book of Yatahetu, Maw's Silence 92, Year 11

"People want reasons. They want the kind of story they can turn into a lesson or a warning. But I don't think her story is done. We just stopped being the part she needed for its next chapter.

That boy of hers, he'll carry the rest. Whatever it means."

Book of Fajura, Maw's Silence 93, Year 11

"*Mountain's Rise 20, Year 5*. I have gone back to my book and reread portions of that passage many times since Samike left. And in those words, I have found strength and comfort. She is gone and she is free. And in that, I find some peace.

Now, as I comfort our children and try to explain to them things they cannot possibly understand, I find myself in need of understanding. Understanding and wisdom from those who have left us.

Bakhuran journeyed to the Far Sky on Mother's Tears 80, Year 5.

He left his book and spoke of secrets to be found within the Durajan. Of the caves and hidden places. He told me to never give up on my dream.

Today, were it not for the memories that this book holds, for those who stand beneath the banner we've raised, and for the Mother who guides with balance, her departure could have caused my dream to fade from memory.

Instead, I will look for what Bakhuran spoke of. Search for these caves and resume the dream I began long ago.

I pray that the Mother will guide her steps, wherever they lead her. And I also pray that she will continue to guide mine."

Book of Dothemides, Maw's Silence 98, Year 11

Mountain's Trial 27. The Canyonlands. East of Dothemia

Bakhuran's book was a treasured gift. It contained within it many maps of the canyons and after a time of searching, one led Dothemides to what he sought.

The land outside the cave entrance was made into a camp, but not one built for war. It was built for study. Five tents were erected: for defenders, supplies, meals, scribes, and Dothemides himself.

In the upper passages, ancient paintings of Khadar origin rimmed the walls. Deeper in, the walls became damp and were laced with mineral veins and etched runes that curled along the stone. All were meaningless to any tongue that he, and those who labored with him, knew.

The Dothemian expedition investigated the site for days. Dust rose under the relentless sun, kicked up by watchers scanning for threats, the ebb and flow of supplies caravans, and the activity of Dothemides and his scribes as they explored the cave's depths.

Then they found it. One of the tunnels emptied into the deepest of chambers. Led by torchlight, they followed a slope that led to its base. As they spread around the room, standing torches were placed, eventually allowing the full room to come into view.

At its center stood stones of varied height, each one carved with endless rows of the same unknown language. The chamber breathed with something ancient. It was what they were looking for.

Word was sent to the surface, and excitement flowed through the camp as their true study began. But as days turned to weeks, the mysteries remained unsolved, and their questions unanswered.

Morning. Mountain's Trial 29. The Canyonlands. East of Dothemia

Dothemides returned to the chamber alone. To the place they have come to call the Silent Stones. For weeks, they searched, recorded, and pored over rubbings, yet still no answers came.

In the now, torchlit chamber, he opened the Book of Bakhuran and flipped to a passage. He noted Bakhuran's steady hand, sharp and deliberate:

"Faith is not knowledge. Faith is surrender. We are not meant to decipher miracles, we are meant to be changed by them."

Dothemides closed his eyes, and something stirred within him.

He closed the book and stopped searching for answers. He stopped weighing symbols. He let the silence in. Let it fill him. He thought of the Mother, and how she held both fury and mercy, how her love was never without cost. He thought of the choices he had made. The children he'd raised. The blood he'd spilled. The fortress he'd built. The kingdom he'd risen.

He thought of where it began.

Of where he was found.

A rusted cage. A prayer to the sky. Samike's face, wind-swept, tear-streaked, and lit by a sun he hadn't seen in days. A risen stone, the sound of metal breaking.

Then he thought of her departure.

Finally, he heard himself speak... "I... understand... It's alright."

He opened his eyes.

The cave was gone.

Sand pressed beneath him, warm and dry. Heat rolled across his skin. He squinted at the sky. The sun burned above. Before him, half-buried, was the cage. The same. Bent, broken, forgotten by all but him.

He looked around.

No footsteps.

No one.

Just wind and heat and the weight of something divine.

Evening. Mountain's Trial 29. The Canyonlands. East of Dothemia

In the weeks since the discovery of the Silent Stones, it had become common for Dothemides to seek time alone in the deep chambers. It was not unusual. He had done this before. But as the hours passed and he still had not returned, concern grew.

From the depths of the caves, someone called out. Cries echoed from chamber to chamber. Boots and sandals thundered against stone. Torches hissed and flared as men and women searched every crevice.

But the king was gone.

Morning. Mountain's Trial 32. Dothemia

When they returned without him, word spread quickly. Quiet at first, but relentless.

In the corridors of the Obsidian Fortress, soldiers stood tense at the gates. Blame was cast, accusations hurled.

"He's gone to find the Mother," said one elder.

"I pray the Hollow hasn't taken him," said a priest.

"He's walked into the Far Sky," said another, "just as the shamans of the sands did."

"The Pale Spirit has claimed him," said one elder of the Khadar.

Some believed the inner circle was hiding something. Others stated that whatever he found in the caves had taken him. A few believed this was punishment for his conquering ways.

The temple hymns were sung and prayers offered each morning. In the markets, people asked one another in low tones, "Have you heard?". Questions followed by no answers, only fear.

Bianzhi worked to put an end to rumors quickly, calling all to order and reason, despite her own worry. Her calm put her in a position of command, and she rose to lead efforts to find their king.

She sent Thornsten, Brynvi, Setna, and Tumahn to search the canyons and set Sunh, Nelah, Agatir, and Larastus to lead watch rotations on the eastern walls night and day.

Days passed, and fear claimed the streets. Dothemides had never been gone this long. Not without a word. Not without a sign.

Morning. Mountain's Trial 34. Somewhere in the Sands of Sifur's Breath

Dothemides wandered in disbelief. For a time, he thought the Far Sky had claimed him. But believed that if it did, it wouldn't be a place of such desolation and suffering.

The sands had changed, the dunes shifted, but he knew that the way home was east.

As days passed and nights returned, he continued to trust in the Mother. To hold faith in her guidance.

Cresting a rise, he fought the sinking feeling in his heart. The dunes stretched on, and there were countless miles to go, but the sun was setting. He found an outcropping of stone amidst the sand and slept, his mind drifting to his children, to his people, to home, and towards a voice that found him in that place between waking and dreaming, that whispered.

"Come with me..."

When he woke, the air had changed. The sands were gone. Replaced by darkness and cool stone.

He rose, confused, and looked around. He saw the runes, the Silent Stones, and the walls of the deep caves. Making his way through the familiar passages, he stepped out into the morning light, beneath a sky smudged by impending rains, and walked towards Dothemia.

At first, they didn't believe it was him. Sunh and Nelah called out.

Word reached the fortress. Voices rose from the streets. People poured from their homes and activity came to a halt along Market Row as children ran to meet the procession of guards that flanked him.

His most trusted friends were there. Their faces and his were both streaked with tears and alight with laughter. He was home.

And within the chamber of the Silent Stones, runes shimmered to life.

"He spoke that night in the temple. There was no ritual, only those wanting to know what happened. And so he spoke from his heart. He spoke of loss, endurance, and balance. Anger, shame, and bitterness. But then he spoke of purpose, dedication, hope, and understanding.

"I believe the stones moved me," he said. "And I believe the Mother guided me. Sometimes, we must lose what we hold most dear... to make way for what we most need."

When he was done addressing everyone, the room became a place of discussion and reflection. Bianzhi had stayed by him most of the evening as they walked among those gathered. Then he turned, searching, not with uncertainty, but as if guided to do so.

And then, she stepped forward.

A woman of the steppes with hair of flame, and eyes like the sky. Jewelry of bone, stone, and metal adorned her ears and hung about her neck.

She approached.

Dothemides and Bianzhi shared a glance as the woman stopped before them, bowed with reverence, then spoke as she rose.

"King Dothemides, Lady Bianzhi,"

"I am Ailis."

"I believe the Mother sent me here.

The Mountain whispered to me...that purpose was rising in the south. And when I saw him...When I saw the Dothemian King, I felt it.

He had returned to his people from a journey. The ancestors whispered of something in him. Around him. As if he had stepped through something they had not seen. Something from a time before.

He stood like the cliffs before a storm. Cracked in places, yes, but unbroken to all. But so much was hidden beneath his silence, loneliness wrapped in command, rage buried beneath resolve.

Despite the rejoicing of his people and the lightness of his heart. I saw below the surface, a man carrying too much, with no way to shed his burden. Nowhere to direct his hidden pain.

And then I knew.

The Mother teaches that pain is not the enemy, that pleasure is not vanity, and that the Mountain, through its strength and its resilience, speaks of what must be endured.

So I offered myself, neither in flattery nor in innocence. I knew what drew the eyes of kings. I knew how to be seen. When to offer silence, when to step close. I knew what to share and what to keep.

In time, he noticed. I led. He touched. He yielded. And when he surrendered, I took him, not with conquest, but with purpose.

He needed somewhere to bleed that wasn't the battlefield. And I needed someone who could go where I was meant to take them.

There were nights the pain in him would surge like a wave. So I became the shore. I let it break against me. I gave it a place to land. I bore his weight in silence, in sweat, in breathless surrender. Not to be wounded. Not to be claimed. But to heal.

Yes, the places I led him were dark. He questioned. He doubted. We endured.

That was always the path. That was always my vow to the Mother and Mountain.

And when the darkness passed each night, I smiled, I touched his face, and I reminded him...

I am not broken.

I am blessed.

He was not my captive. I was not his prey.

I go where they lead me, and I have been led here. Led to him.

And from that darkness... something sacred emerged.

This was never about power.

This was never about possession.

This was my pleasure.

This was his release.

This was our temple."

Book of Ailis, Mountain's Trial 50, Year 11

"Ailis endured so much.

And still, when I looked into her eyes, I saw no fear. No resistance. Only invitation. Only offering. Only willingness. Only want.

It was beyond lust or loyalty.

It was...in her words...*sacred*.

A devotion to the Mother. A vow to the Mountain.

A reverence for rage. For wrath. For release.

She showed me things I had never seen. Led me into places I never dared to go...not in war, not in conquest, not even in the temple. With her, I did... *unimaginable* things. And in doing so, I questioned... everything.

Even the Mother.

Was this too far?

Was this the Her will?

Each night, something rose in me, through clenched teeth and stinging tears. In tainted pleasures. In pain. In fear.

I took what she offered.

And I gave in kind.

And still, she asked for more.

She told me I had not yet been cleansed.

I left her each time with prayers on my lips, whispered pleas to the Mother...let there be another way. Let release not be bound to this crucible of flesh and fury.

Then came the night.

Her hands gripping my wrists, not to stop me... but to keep me.

Her eyes closed, not in pain, not in fear.

But in something that looked like... worship... sacrifice....

And then...

Her breath stopped.

Her grip weakened.

My pleasure ceased.

And I wept.

I pulled my hands away, ready to curse the Mother, ready to damn the Mountain Himself for this descent. I held her, thinking her spirit was gone from me.

She opened her eyes.

She reached up.

She touched my face.

And she said, from beneath me..."Now, you are free."

Book of Dothemides, Mountain's Silence 88, Year 11

"When Samike left the fortress with Sittrika in her arms, it cast a shadow over her remaining children. Kaelani, her firstborn, Omanessi, and the twins, Tananda and Kanike, were left behind, their young minds unable to comprehend why their mother had chosen to leave them.

Among the people, her departure was met with growing outrage and confusion. Samike, once revered, now faced whispers of abandonment and selfishness. This fracture may one day haunt her children, shaping their paths in ways that could ripple through the kingdom's future.

Bianzhi and I had become more than most knew.

In ritual and worship, we had found one another. And in quiet moments, we had begun to love each other as together, we watched over our king.

His heart was nearly made hollow by the First Queen's departure. We spoke, and together, Bianzhi and I decided. Dothemides would need us, and we would protect not only his kingdom, but his heart."

Book of Ailis, Mountain's Silence 93, Year 11

Chapter Twelve

PAIN'S ECHO

Year 12

THE FORGE

"Those days were difficult for our king. While he mourned the departure of the First Queen, he acted to secure the kingdom's future by marrying Bianzhi and Ailis, who became known as The Jade Queen and The Red Queen.

The two had grown to become his most trusted, and some whispered of their bond. Always together and always by his side, staying close to him in these painful times.

Aside from the pleasures that all knew they could provide him, they also bolstered his rulership with their skill in both diplomacy and strength of arms. Bianzhi was known to all the greatest warriors of the kingdom, save our king. And she imparted her skill onto Ailis, who combined them with her shamanism.

Now they have become fearsome together and have set out across the land carrying the name of their Dothemia to its far reaches to forge alliances and bring peace to neighboring tribes."

Book of Nelah, Wolf's Hunt 34, Year 12

"Our husband and King... It still feels strange to call Dothemides, husband. To see myself as Queen. To be free to love him as I always have. Part of me felt guilt. I wondered if I was glad Samike left.

I confided this in Ailis and she told me not to be ashamed and to feel no guilt. That what I felt, the anger towards Samike, and the hurt and pain that she caused, was pure and true. That was the day that Ailis and I became more.

Again, the gods have a sense of humor. I never thought I'd feel for a woman, but here I am, sharing the same furs with her each night as we lay alongside Dothemides, welcoming her touch and her warmth.

Dothemides sent us out on a mission of peace and outreach. Our objective was to ride into the sands past the canyonlands into the Khadari desert. When Ailis and I approached a particular tribe with an offering of peace, our intentions were met with suspicion.

We should have left. We wanted to leave. But for whatever rotting reason, their warriors attacked us. So we defended ourselves. Ailis and I weren't going to just let ourselves be run through.

By the end of that battle, many of them lay dead or dying. It's not what we intended or what we wanted. But that's what happened.

Then I saw her. A girl kneeling and sobbing by a man as he bled out into the sands. My heart broke at the sight of her. Ailis comforted me... said we were not the cause of this. But I felt different.

I approached her and asked her name. She was beautiful, with rich skin the color of fertile soil, long thin braids, adorned with wooden beads, and eyes the color of amber. She didn't look at me with anger or rage. She raised no weapon. She just looked back to the man who lay before her and said her name was Umaru.

I urged her to come with us... to seek refuge in Dothemia. But she refused. She said that she needed to bury the dead. Bury her Khandar, and chose to remain among the sands.

I couldn't blame her."

Book of Bianzhi, Wolf's Blood 55, Year 12

"Jorvan and I fell in love. Our bond led to the birth of our beloved daughter. We named her Azibo. Her birth sated the hunger within me to have a child and build a life with this man of the north. My Jorvan.

Her birth was a blessing. Before the flame and amidst the tribes that gathered to celebrate the children born of the sands, I lifted her and asked the Maw to instill in her a hunger to grow and become strong, and a thirst for life that no water could quench.

My love, my Jorvan, watched the rituals that day, and when they ended, we held our child and returned home together. But upon our return, we found our village destroyed. The earth had opened, swallowing it into its depths. Such was the way of the sands. Sometimes it too, hungered.

Left with no choice, Jorvan and I retreated to the canyonlands, where we have started to build a home along the more fertile lands near the tributaries, where we hope to raise Azibo in peace.

Now is the first chance I have had to write, since her birth, and I am hopeful for our future."

Book of Nzinga, Maw's Hunger 22

"I watched. I heard. I felt her suffering. Her torment. The girl once protected by Agatir and Larastus.

Svirva endured savage cruelty at the hands of our chieftain and those who served him. The cruelty caused division. But fear kept us from acting.

They were not men. They were monsters. Yet, despite their predations, her will remained strong. How did she summon the strength to fight them? How did she not break?

Each night, she would lash out against them. A fierce defiance seen by some as a mark of destiny. But it soon became apparent to those of us who were too afraid to interfere that her mind began to fracture under the weight of her suffering, even as she fought to endure.

When we could, I and other women of the tribe took pity. But through it all, she was the child who endured, the child who fought.

Looking back now, perhaps it was her purpose. Perhaps it was her path. Perhaps it was the hammer, anvil, and forge that turned her into what she would become..."

Book of Liath, Mother's Tears 82, Year 30

"She was just a girl, with amethyst eyes that caught light like no jewel ever could. I remember her smile, rare but honest, and the way she trailed after us in the snows beneath the pines, always watching, always wanting to be near.

Samike left Dothemia for the freedom of her heart. That was her path. I understood it then. But what does it say of me that I never returned to Càrn Valloch? To find Svirva and offer her the same life we now enjoy here in Dothemia.

Agatir. He is like a brother to me. I know he carries guilt, but I wonder if he sees the truth. He fears what he might find, and I fear we left her to rot in that place, or worse.

The memory of her follows me through the markets and streets of Dothemia. Sometimes, in moments of stillness, I swear I see her eyes watching me from across the river or through the trees.

I think of Svirva more than I admit. And in the silence of the temple, where no one demands bravado or steel, I let that grief sit beside me."

Book of Halumein, Wolf's Blood 23, Year 12
From the confessions of Larastus

"Her name was... is... Svirva. She is my sister.

She was always so much smaller than me, but she hit hard when we sparred. I taught her that. Showed her how to stand like the mountain, how to fall and rise again. She used to pester Larastus for attention, following him like a cub.

He pretended not to notice. But I saw the way his eyes softened when she laughed. There was something there. A lingering hope. A seed planted in frozen soil, waiting for the Mother's breath.

I believe... I want to believe... that the tribe took care of her. That she was seen and perhaps taken back in by Arican. Protected by Valloch. Separated from my father. I hope that someone helped her rise. But I am haunted by fears darker than the blackpines and deeper than the Sea of Souls.

The càrn was defeated. Our lives were spared. Valloch was spared. But King Dothemides swore to never again set foot there. Swore to never offer alliance to Valloch. In taking us, Valloch's strongest warriors, Dothemides sealed the càrn's fate. For the seasons will need to come and go many times before its strength is regained and its soldiers replenished. They will never be the same. And neither will I.

So I hold onto who Svirva was. Her laughter, her stubbornness, the way she crushed snow into balls to throw at me like I wasn't twice her size. Those are the things I keep close. The memory of her. Svirva means Survivor in the old tongue.

May she live up to her name."

Book of Halumein, Wolf's Blood 25, Year 12
From the confessions of Agatir

Chapter Thirteen

The Watchful and the Wandering

Year 13

WHISPERING LEAVES

"How do I begin? I suppose I will begin with my name. Umaru.

I was just a young girl among the Khadari tribes of Sifur's Breath. Just ten years old when I lost my parents in an attack by an opposing tribe. My father's name was Ashanir, and my mother's name was Nahndia. Their loss left me orphaned, but the Khandar who defeated my village saw something in me. His name was Matahu.

Under his protection and roof, I learned the ways of survival and combat, and he saw my gifts with the beasts as a boon to his tribe. I was skilled with them. Skilled at hunting. I held great respect for them. For they provided both protection and sustenance on the sands.

Matahu was a great warrior. One of the most fearsome Khandar's of the Khadari tribes. A man who traveled far and wide and held respect amongst peoples feared and avoided by most. But he disliked the one he called the Pretender King.

He envied Dothemia, he envied its rise, envied its strength. That was why he attacked the women he said were the pretenders' queens, when they came offering alliance. He wanted to capture them and make them his own. It was a decision that cost him and many others their lives.

I remember their offer to help. They were so different from one another.

Matahu was stern and proud, but he was kind to me. Treated me well. I needed to honor him and prepare his body and those of the fallen to be given to the sands, and I was afraid of the city along the shores. So I didn't go with them.

I thought the sand would hold me forever. I believed the wild would keep me safe, that beasts were better companions than people and promises, and for a while, that was true.

After Khadar Matahu's death, I needed stillness. The endless sky. My sand hounds were my sisters. My small oasis was my shrine. I built my life around the quiet patterns—plant, harvest, patrol, protect.

Then the winds changed. The storm came without warning. A mouth wide with teeth of sand and sky. It tore the roof from my home, ripped my fields from the earth. And worse… it took them. My sisters… my pack.

They were gone.

I found one buried and lifeless. There was no trace of the others. I stayed three days in the ruins of my broken home. Long enough to understand that there was nothing left to save. So I walked.

I told myself I would stop before I reached the walls. But I didn't. Dothemia opened before me. So many faces. So much color. The hum of voices felt like thunder after years of wind and sand.

I wandered to a place of many merchants, the place they call Market Row, unsure of why my feet led me there. And that's where she found me—Bianzhi, The Jade Queen. Her cactus-colored eyes never softened, but I saw something flicker in them when she looked at me.

She did not ask questions. She said that she recognized me and remembered my name. I was surprised when she said it, and even more surprised when she said that she was glad that I decided to come. The red-haired queen was with her, but spoke little. She only watched.

Bianzhi brought me in, gave me a room in a hall filled with many others. Some were young like me, others were older. She showed me where I could eat and bathe, and even gave me new clothes. The next morning, she approached and tossed a training staff at me, and asked if I could fight. I could. Khandar Matahu trained me well, so things came easily.

Bianzhi was not often warm, but she was precise and often funny. And I like that.

But I'll probably never forget the first time she took me beyond the gates, into the jungle.

She told me to leave the armor. I thought I had misunderstood her. I stared at her, confused. Then she said that there were beasts out there and that my mind must be sharper than their teeth.

She removed her armor, every metal plate, every stitch of leather, until only the jungle's breath touched her skin. I thought it was strange, but I followed. I had never been this far east. Never seen the jungles. She showed me how to listen. How to feel tension in the soles of your feet before danger even shows itself. How to disappear. I felt at home. Connected to the sounds and scents, and to the trails and treetops. My body bore scrapes and bruises that day. But my mind? It sharpened in that new place.

One day, as we sat on a fallen tree, Bianzhi told me that the mind is the greatest armor. She said that steel breaks and cloth burns, but the warrior who could not be broken in the mind is never truly defenseless and would always be the strongest and most fearsome warrior on the battlefield.

When we returned after training, she apologized to me for what she'd done long ago. I could see the sadness in her eyes. But I told her that I forgave her and thanked her for her words and kindness.

Later that day, the queens came to my small room. Bianzhi stepped in and handed me an empty book as Ailis watched from the doorway. She sat next to me on my small bed, looked me in the eyes, and told me that here in Dothemia, all are remembered. That remembrance was sacred. She put her arm around me and asked me to write my story.

So now, alone in my small room, I write my first words. Many of them, it seems.

I'm not sure who I am here yet. But I am alive. The future is uncertain. But I feel... I can make my place here and become a part of this great city, even if it is a small part.

Perhaps I will even one day meet the King. A man who, by building this city, must be greater than any Khandar I have ever seen."

Book of Umaru, Mother's Breath 15, Year 13

"The canyon sings today.

The wind moves through the stone like breath through a flute, and I know the Mother is watching, not with judgment, but with a soft, knowing smile.

Jorvan is mending the thatch. Azibo is asleep in my shawl, her tiny breath warm against my chest. I do not know what blessing I gave the world to deserve this peace, but I do not question it. I only breathe it in.

He is northern-born, Skarnvald through and through, all scars and resolve, a man carved by the Mountain's hardship. I am Khadari, child of heat and desert winds, raised in ritual, rooted in memory. But our hearts? They beat in the same rhythm now.

Sometimes, I watch him speak to Azibo in his tongue. Low. Rough-edged. But full of tenderness. She reaches for his beard and laughs like the sun itself has kissed her lips.

He teaches her to stand strong.

I teach her to kneel softly.

He guards.

I guide.

Together, we grow.

We could have joined Dothemia. Many would call it wise. Safer, perhaps, but land, the open sand, the red cliffs, the cool of dawn before the heat, it all feels like truth. It remembers me. And Jorvan has learned to listen to it too.

We are not apart from, or blind to, the changing winds that sweep across the Durajan. We are simply... enough, for now. This little home, built against canyon walls and shaded by the sun's path, is holy ground to me.

And Azibo?

She is the proof that the gods, my gods, his gods, maybe even ones we've yet to name, still believe in joy.

I have lived alone. I have healed strangers. I have spoken to wind and bone. But this... this is a life that speaks back."

Book of Nzinga, Mother's Hand 28

"Yesterday I saw a girl in the market. Black hair. Amethyst eyes, rare, even here. She couldn't have been more than twelve or thirteen. Maybe a year or two younger than me.

Our eyes met across the spices and silks. She didn't look away. Neither did I. There was something wild in her gaze. Not untamed like the beasts, but watchful. Searching.

Then, just like that, she turned and ran.

I waited. I thought maybe she'd come back. But she didn't. I don't know her name. But something in me hopes we meet again.

Today, I tracked a pride of lions at the edge of the Windfang Flats. One of the lionesses looked right at me. There were cubs among them, two, I think. I hope to take one someday. Not to tame, but to raise alongside me.

And maybe... maybe I will gift one to the King. Just to see him smile. I've seen him smile, only from a distance. I like his smile.

It is soft and quiet. When he smiles, it is as if he has forgotten that he is a king."

Book of Umaru, Mountains Trial 29, Year 13

She did not speak these words easily. But when she did, her voice was low, rough yet smooth, like a frost-kissed stone, a voice worn thin by memory, not weakness.

I simply wrote what she gave me.

"I... endured. I had no choice. Their torment... their hunger... their lusts knew no end. I would not let them break me. But in time... I'd had enough.

Some thought I was touched by the Hollow. That I was gone. Made empty. Just... a vessel. But while they did not break me, something did break within me.

I learned to retreat. To go somewhere else. To survive by not being there. I was not Hollow. I was filled with rage. It waited. Silent. Sleeping. And then, one day, it woke.

The monsters had left to hunt the beasts that stalk the high north, those with claws that break bone and eyes that see in snowlight.

They left me unguarded.

I ran. No boots. No allies. Just the Blackpines and falling snow. I would not linger another night there. But before I left, I took a blade from the wall. A blade of bone. Small enough for my hands. Sharp enough for its purpose.

I slipped through the village and found him. After all these years, that bastard Haegun still clung to life.

I saw him there. Alone. Retching and coughing in his cabin. It stank of his body and neglect. It was as if I were always meant to do this. I crept to his bedside. By then, he could barely speak. His eyes opened wide as he saw me and the blade I held.

He never accepted me. Never raised voice to protect me. All that was within me was my fury.

Blood soaked his furs.

Soaked my hands.

Soaked my blade.

Beneath me, he was still. Eyes frozen in fright and pain.

I remember my breathing.

The ground rumbling beneath the village.

I watched him for a moment, then I ran into the cold. Into the fangs of the north. And I did not care if the beasts took me. Better death in the wild than another night under their weight.

The cold tore at me. The wind slashed my skin like knives. But the silence... The silence was deep. It swallowed me, followed me, and watched me. I slept in abandoned dens. I drank from frozen streams. I chewed blackroot and sucked marrow from bones.

Eventually, I headed south, not because I had a plan, but because every step forward was a step away from them. Away from what they did. What they made me feel.

I was not broken. But I was changed.

The girl they took no longer existed. And the person walking south?

She would never kneel again."

Book of Svirva, Mountain's Vigil 70, Year 36

As written by Thane Erick Longhorn

Chapter Fourteen

STORM AND SHELTER

Year 14

SOULFLAME

"Svirva did not speak much when I returned. Perhaps she had said all she wished. Perhaps the memories had left her weary. But when I bowed and thanked her for her courage, for her truth, for trusting me with her history, she met my eyes.

And for once... she held the gaze.

"Thank you," she said, her voice barely above the mountain winds outside "For your persistence... in asking me to speak of those dark days, Thane Erik."

I handed her the parchment. Dozens of pages, carefully penned. Each word captured, precisely as she had spoken them.

"If you wish," I said, "they can be placed in your first journal. Worn though it may be." She was silent for a moment, then nodded. We walked to the Hall of Remembrance past the scrolls of those who had fallen. There on the shelf it sat—her first journal.

She handed it to me. The red leather cover was cracked and faded. It's binding, frayed. But the pages inside were sacred. I took it with both hands and bowed.

"It will be handled with the utmost care, Sovereign."

"The pages will be entered seamlessly. Your tale will be made whole. Your history, made complete."

I did as I vowed. When I returned it to her, she did not open it right away. But when she finally did, alone, by the low light of a hearthfire, I watched her from a distance, as her eyes moved across the work.

Newer ink. Newer parchment. Their crisp edges, a stark contrast to the older, worn pages that followed. But her story flowed through them, unbroken.

And I saw her pause. Fingers tracing the line of a passage written years ago..."

Book of Erik, Mountain's Vigil 100, Year 36

Morning. Mother's Breath 7

Across the Blackpines of the Highlands, a longtooth stalks, fleeing bristlebacks as they burst into the forest edge, narrowly escaping death.

A raven soars across the open sky of the Steppelands, over Fort Koba as if in search of something, as winds carry it with speed over the great expanse.

Below its black wings, steppeland wolves are driven back by Dothemian guards protecting a southbound caravan along a well-worn trail that leads to Hollowwind Pass.

With its feathers fluttering in the warming winds, the raven swoops down and soars through the pass as amethyst eyes are drawn skyward, catching and following its movement.

Highsun. Mother's Breath 7

A lone girl, dressed in a tattered tunic and skirt of fur and leather, walks barefoot across stones. Caught by the canyon winds, long, wild, black hair is pulled back by small hands so that she can see the trail ahead more clearly. Ahead, the pass is silent. Etchings encircle an altar. She approaches, tilts her head, and kneels, rubbing away the dust and dirt from the carved stone.

Warnings. Hollowed Ground.

The circle is large. She steps into the ring to read more, picking out the language of Càrnoth and Skarn among the many.

As she breaches the boundary, she feels something strange, like the stones are watching. She hears something and turns, but sees nothing, aside from the lit braziers that flicker and dim...just the wind.

She holds a dagger of bone in her hand. Amethyst eyes searching. She steps towards the altar. Bare feet, carrying her forward. Silent and unseen, the Unbound spirits draw close. But as she walks, they stay their advance.

Her slender arms rise as she rubs her eyes with her curled fists covered with dust and dirt. She stares back, taking in the expanse of the steppelands that she has spent days crossing. She grows tired, feeling the need to rest. She's wandered for so long.

The sound of a raven's cry pulls her back. The world returns to focus. Hooded amethyst eyes, heavy with fatigue, snap open, search, and find the raven as it takes flight.

Rising, she runs after it. Leaving the altar behind her.

Nightfall. Mother's Breath 13. The Canyonlands. North of Dothemia

Svirva followed the road south, from the canyons to the lands just north of a city larger even than the càrn. The path was lit by torches and braziers, but she stayed clear of it to avoid the eyes of those who traveled to and from the city.

She settled into the nearby hills, too afraid to enter, and too tired to leave. But tonight the canyon winds mocked her, curling and scraping through the stones like cruel laughter.

Her fire would not light. The tinder was damp. The flint refused to spark. She cursed her situation. Cursed the silence. Cursed this place, the gods, and her past.

Her hands shook as her mind shifted. She spoke aloud, though none were there to hear her. Her voice, barely a whisper.

"Stone-souled, name-lost, clutchless bastards."

"No... stop... STOP... Don't let them in again."

"You've hunted, survived... but the meat is gone."

She looked up at the distant clouds that rolled across darkening skies. Gnawing hunger sat behind her fragmented thoughts. Winds picked up. She shut her eyes against the laughter.

She thought of the city that the caravan trails led to. That she dared enter earlier that day. It was too large. Too strange. Too much laughter, songs, and smiles. No one she could trust, except...

"Try again tomorrow. Just don't stay long." She said to herself as she grew tired.

She drifted to sleep, curling inward and falling like stone past hands that reached and clawed, until she fell past them. Her descent slowed as she drifted down and landed amid whispers.

"Perhaps I will see her again... she looked kind."

"Another day of training with Queen Bianzhi. She had me running forms, barefoot again. "Feel the ground," she said. "Know it like it's part of your body." Afterwards, I was tired, aching everywhere, but when I saw her, all of that left me.

It was the girl from the canyon's edge again. She didn't run this time. She didn't speak either, but she watched with those eyes. Gods, those eyes. I couldn't look away. She was just standing there. Like a fawn that learned long ago that nothing in this world is safe, but still longs for companionship.

I walked toward her. Slow. Open palms. She didn't move. Didn't flinch. Just watched me. I came close and I told her my name. She didn't reply, but she didn't leave either. That was enough.

We shared that space for a time. The riverwills sang. The market hummed all around us, full of sound and scents and people. I smiled at her. She almost smiled back.

She was hungry and thin, but so pretty. She was staring at the smoked meats and honeyed bread behind me. I heard her poor belly growling. She clutched at it, looking angry. Embarrassed.

I was given a small amount of coin for safeguarding and patrolling the trails that led from Dothemia's eastern gates. I paid one of the merchants and asked for the food, but seeing her condition, he declined payment and gave it freely.

I thanked him, and when I offered it to her, she stepped back and looked at me. Her belly coiled again and she frowned. I extended my hand again. This time she took the food, but backed away. That was ok with me. At least she would eat tonight.

It was time for me to go, so I said goodbye to the merchant, and to the girl. When I left, I glanced back. She was still watching.

Then, she said her name. Svirva."

Book of Umaru, Mother's Breath 15, Year 14

Nightfall. Mother's Breath 17. Svirva's camp

"Umaru is a pretty name."

Svirva sat speaking aloud to the raven that stood and watched nearby. She was eating the last of the honeyed bread and smoked meats given to her two days ago.

She remembered how softly Umaru said her name. How she didn't ask for hers and how she told her anyway.

"You would like her," she said, as she thought about how Umaru stood there. Close enough for the sun to catch the sweat on her dark skin, far enough not to crowd her.

Umaru's presence was strange. Warm. She remembered wanting to run but choosing not to.

"There was something in Umaru's eyes. Not pity. Something stronger. Kinder."

"Yesterday, she found me again. This time, near the edge of the market." Svirva said as she piled the wood for her fire with worry as the clouds gathered above.

"She didn't lead. She walked beside me. She pointed out things in the city I didn't understand."

Black wings fluttered, then settled.

"The painted tiles that meant warding. The soldiers in blue, part of the western patrol. That large fortress in the distance...and the man who took my brother."

The raven twitched to the sound of branches snapped by Svirva's hands.

"I hated the sight of him. She called him King Dothemides. I wanted to say how I hated him, but she went on about how kind and gentle he was. She spoke about his queens. One red and one jade."

Svirva stopped speaking, but the memory of Umaru's words lingered. Confused her. How could they be as good as she said they were? When we hid as they walked out and she pointed, saying how kind his face was, how he smiled like he meant it...

"Were it not for how she looked at him, my hate for him would still burn. But .. she liked him and if she did..."

Svirva's words stopped, and her stomach turned strange. The memory of Umaru's smile settled behind her ribs like something caged.

"I almost reached for her hand when she closed her eyes and lifted her face to the sun to feel the Wolf's breath. I wish I had..."

Mother's Breath 20

For two days, Svirva sat beneath the southern rains, as her fire refused to catch. She had not returned to the city. She was alone with her thoughts, memories, sleepless nights and the voices that kept silence at bay.

The raven watched as she cursed the flint and the soggy tinder. Within her mind boiled as she thought about how she got here, her hatred for Haegun, Valloch, and her mother and brother.

She burned with the memory of those who tried to take everything. Their hands. Their laughter. Their stink.

Whispering their names, she asked the Mountain why she was chosen to endure so much, asked the Mother why all she felt in life was pain, asked them why she was chosen to suffer. She wonders why the first person to show her kindness in years sees kindness in this king who took everything from her.

Then the flame answered.

It wasn't a spark or an ember, it was a blaze, raw and alive, erupting from her skin, lightning dancing in her amethyst eyes.

The raven flitted away. Her breath became smoke and her thoughts and memories fractured like glass.

She recoiled, retreated, and tried to escape the flames. But she couldn't. She realized that they had somehow come from her.

She didn't understand. Was this the gods? Was she cursed? Was this real?

But the campfire burned, and as she watched it, her mind calmed, her thoughts drifted. She stared at her hands through eyes that danced with light. And as the stones shook, and the storm cleared, she sat in silence, wondering and afraid.

"The night was thick with the scent of rose and sweat. The temple rituals had left us breathless. Dothemides, Bianzhi, and I, tangled in incense and vows. The gods had been fed. And we, in turn, fed each other.

They sleep now. My king, his hand draped across Bianzhi's hip. Her breath, slow and even. Peaceful. But I could not rest.

Then I felt it. A pull.

Something raw. Untamed. A surge, as if the ancestors rose and roared as one.

I sat up without a word, slipped out of bed, and draped myself in robes. The guards bowed. The watchers along the walls averted their gaze.

I followed the traces and whispers as they led me down stone steps, through sleeping markets, past the eastern gates, and out into the night.

The land spoke. I listened. The wind led me to the canyon road, up narrow paths, and then I saw her. Curled by a fire far too large for a single soul.

Her presence scorched the stones and left the air around her raw and silver at the edges. Her hands trembled. Her breath came in stutters. She didn't hear me approach. Not until I sat beside her.

She turned sharply. Amethyst eyes, wide with rage and fear. But she didn't move. She was more than a girl. She was a storm trying to understand the sky.

I asked, "Do you know what you are?" She didn't answer.

I decided not to press.

She was new to this. And it was a thing that I had only heard of.

She was dangerous.

She was beautiful.

She let me come close. I sat with her silently, then asked her name. She said it was Svirva. She didn't look at me, she just sat, tired and afraid and angry, as the ancestors wept around her.

She asked me what my name was and I told her. Our eyes met then I saw hers grow wet with tears that refused to fall.

The sun began to rise and I had to return, but I left her with the promise that she need not be alone and that I would return to her."

Book of Ailis, Mother's Hand 27, Year 14

"I knew who she was. I saw her in the city with Umaru.

The Red Queen. Ailis.

She came to me again. She told me she cared.

She asked me if I knew what I was.

I didn't know how to act around her.

She just sat by me. Staring at me.

No one had really stared at me like that before.

Not mother, not father, not Valloch.

Then she reached into a satchel and pulled out a book, blank, bound in soft red leather, and placed it between us...asked me if I could write. I could. Valloch's shamans taught me many things.

Ailis taught me the dates and days, the passing of the years. About how the people here feel that freedom for the Durajani of this city, of Dothemia, began with the breaking of a cage.

Then she said she knew about the fire. Knew of my rage.

She said she'd teach me to not be afraid of what was inside of me.

She said she could help me understand it.

Something about it being what I was born to be.

She speaks in circles. Says things. Calls me things.

Beautiful.

Not broken.

What does she want from me?

It's dark now. Ailis left just moments ago.

Before she left, she told me that these lands have never seen anything like me."

Book of Svirva, Mother's Breath 29, Year 14

"It was a few weeks ago when I left. The sun had barely climbed above the rim of the canyon when I said my goodbyes. Nzinga didn't say much, she never does when I travel. She just placed her hand on my chest and nodded like she always does, like it's some quiet whisper of protection.

Azibo gave me a flower she'd crushed in her fist. I tucked it into the fold of my cloak. It didn't survive the wind, but I kept the stem.

The road to the Ruins of Vulfgar is long. I know every bend now. The place smells of old stone and wild herbs. It matters to me. I walk there because I must. Because Skarnvald blood doesn't wash away just because there's a river between where you were born and where you sleep.

It had taken me weeks and I stayed ten days. Listened to the rumors. Helped them hunt. It's been years since the Three Thanes War, and they are still broken and bitter. Part of me understood why.

The walk back was worse. The winds kicked up. Heavy rains caused a flash flood in the canyons. I lost a boot in the mud south of Hollowwind Pass and cursed the gods for a whole day. But I made it home.

Nzinga and Azi were outside by the cookfire. I watched them for a while. Nzinga braiding beads into Azi's hair, as Azi fussed about.

I don't know what I did to deserve them. But I'll protect them until my last breath.

This writing isn't easy though.

Nzinga asked me to keep this book. She gave it to me with that same look she gives when someone's sick and doesn't know it, like it's not a request, but a kind thing, a healing thing. So I write.

I don't know how to put what I feel into words. Not the right way. Not like she does. But I'm trying, and I guess that means something. Nzinga says remembering matters. That the Dothemians believe it. That many are beginning to believe. I think she's right.

I have found my place here. I will always be a warrior of the Skarnvald, but I am more now.

Father. Husband. Whole."

Book of Jorvan, Wolf's Hunt 49

Wolf's Hunt 62. Dothemia

Umaru and Svirva's friendship grew and deepened in the small, unclaimed hours of the day. Sitting beside streams, cooking game over crackling fires, teasing and testing each other beneath the stars. They were contrasts in every way yet bound by a friendship that deepened with each passing day.

Despite their time shared, Svirva still refused to live within the city walls, choosing to remain in her camp, which had grown to be comfortable enough for her. A simple tent, cooking fire, pots, and pans given to her by Ailis and Umaru. She preferred her there.

But often, when Umaru prepared to leave and return to the Dothemian barracks for the night, Svirva would ask her to stay, and on most nights, she did. They would speak late into the evening. Umaru's gentle presence, Svirva's wolfish smile. They would write in their journals together, side by side. Svirva stealing glances at Umaru, yet looking away when caught.

Sometimes, Svirva would wake, trembling from a nightmare she refused to speak about, but Umaru would be there, silent and steady, always offering comfort to her friend. When pressed, Svirva would only shake her head revealing a flash of something pained behind her amethyst eyes.

In training and sparring, the truth showed itself. Though smaller, younger, and seemingly fragile, Svirva bested Umaru in each test. She was swift, wild, fearless and untouchable.

When asked where she learned to fight, Svirva responded.

"In the càrn, there is only strength or weakness, breath or blood, the unbroken and the broken. Some of us...are tested more than others." Svirva slipped away to some place that was not where they both stood, her gaze fixed on a distant memory. "Some of us refuse to break."

Her words chilled Umaru.

Concerned, Umaru spoke to Bianzhi of Svirva's skill and asked if she would be interested in training her. Bianzhi accepted, and Umaru managed to convince Svirva to come into the city and see the Jade Queen.

The time had come, and Svirva followed her friend into the heart of Dothemia, where its warriors trained. Several had left on a recent mission, so the day was quiet, with few trainees around, save for a handful.

Umaru brought Svirva to the training grounds where Bianzhi stood and greeted her, and her quiet friend, as Ailis watched from the ramparts above.

"Welcome, Svirva," Bianzhi took her in and tilted her head. "I hear you are quite skilled."

Svirva's amethyst eyes rose to meet Bianzhi's but she said nothing. She looked up and around at the walls and soldiers. She found Ailis and stopped for a moment.

"I am looking forward to seeing what you can do...to see if Umaru's words are true." Bianzhi laughed, her light tone bringing Svirva back to the moment.

Bianzhi looked up to Ailis, following Svirva's gaze. Ailis looked at Bianzhi with concern but remained calm and in support of this test.

"A simple test of measure." Bianzhi finally said as she walked to a rack of practice weapons and pulled one that resembled her favored curved blade.

Svirva looked to Umaru, then walked towards a rack of weapons on the opposite side of the high-walled practice grounds. Her small hands rose and plucked two wooden daggers.

She didn't want to be here. She didn't like this.

She took a deep breath and turned, then walked towards what looked to be the designated area just a few paces away from the jade-eyed queen.

Umaru watched as Svirva looked towards her then up to Ailis and back to her once again. Umaru gave her a nod of encouragement. Svirva chewed her lip and her knuckles went white as she gripped the wooden blades.

When the call was made to begin, Svirva did not hesitate. There was no circling, no measuring, only movement. She closed the distance and when they met it was like crashing waves against rushing wind.

Svirva tucked and rolled towards Bianzhi's legs, and as Bianzhi leapt, Svirva uncoiled, her foot planted, as she slid backwards, with eyes that flashed up to the still descending Bianzhi. By the time Bianzhi's feet hit the ground, Svirva blades whirled in sweeping wide arcs towards Bianzhi's legs. Her body extending, contracting, and whipping out against her opponent. Both left and right thighs were struck, and were these blades real, Bianzhi would have suffered crippling wounds.

Svirva was serious. Bianzhi was surprised, and it was clear that something in this girl saw this as neither a game nor a test.

Bianzhi decided to press the attack. The curved blade swung towards Svirva's temple, and her black hair fell across her eyes as her daggers rose to block the attack just before it landed, absorbing the shock of the impact with a wince of determination.

Bianzhi spun backwards, her body dropping to the ground, her foot trailing an arc across the stones, aiming for Svirva's planted legs. Bianzhi's movements were quick, too quick. Svirva's legs were taken out from beneath her, and for a moment the world spun, but she rolled back, moving with the flow of the fall until she was on her feet again, crouched and lunging.

The small girl seemed to be Bianzhi's match. The training yard fell silent.

Bianzhi pressed harder. She wished to test her fully, and Svirva met the test. The clatter and clash of their wooden weapons filled the air. Svirva's ferocity left openings that Bianzhi began to read. The child was gifted, but she was raw. She was rage. Through the back-and-forth match, an opening presented itself.

Svirva overreached, recoiled, sprang, but Bianzhi flowed around the strike and tripped her, sending her sprawling. Svirva hit the ground hard, kicked up, and sprang to her feet, but her lunge was met with the same result. The third time, Svirva rose differently. Her calm turned into something fiercer. She cried out in frustration and focus, panting, preparing.

The courtyard went completely still.

Umaru felt the shift. Bianzhi held her stance, but she too sensed the danger coiling inside Umaru's friend.

Before it could break free, Umaru stepped forward and called out. Svirva froze, steadying herself. She was sweating, panting, and focused. Before her, Bianzhi saw beneath the wild hair that half-masked amethyst eyes, something almost feral.

Svirva looked to Umaru, then Bianzhi, then Ailis. She took one slow step back. Her weapons fell to the floor, and without another glance, she left the courtyard.

Bianzhi and Umaru shared a glance. Bianzhi looked concerned. When she and Umaru looked up to the balcony where Ailis stood, she was gone.

That night in the Dothemian barracks, stories would be shared of that match, with some warriors saying to those who had been on patrol that they swore the ground shook that day.

Highsun. Wolf's Hunt 74. Dothemia

The training yard of Dothemia simmered with the day's exertion. The warriors had returned from their mission. One that saw them sent to scout Hollowwind Pass and investigate the Northeast Passage to see if the Living Mountain still lingered. Among them were Nelah, Sunh, Larastus, and Agatir, who had been made lieutenants under the command of Bianzhi.

They barked drills and inspected the ranks of Dothemian defenders. From the arched gallery above, Ailis again stood with arms crossed, her expression unreadable, and glanced at the distant clouds. Beside her, Bianzhi leaned silently on the carved stone balustrade, one hand resting lightly on the hilt of her blade. Neither spoke, they only shared a smile, hands touching briefly in their shared affection.

Below, Umaru and Svirva wove between soldiers. Svirva walked slowly, eyes darting between every clash of shield and sword. She had been convinced to return by Umaru just to see, not to participate if she didn't want to.

Umaru waved to Bianzhi, who smiled back at the girl she had taken in. Svirva looked up to Bianzhi and Ailis but looked away again. Umaru turned towards Svirva, hoping to wave to their mentors together, but fell silent as she noticed her friend's pace slow.

"I'm fine," Svirva murmured, with her back to Umaru, although her friend had said nothing.

Svirva's hand tugged at the rough strap across her shoulder, adjusting the worn satchel that clung to her, pulling it away and dropping it to the stone beneath her feet. Her journal fell free of it, and Umaru hurried to pick it up before it could be damaged by the sandaled feet of the sparring soldiers.

She followed Svirva, and together they reached the edge of the central yard where among soldiers taking a break, stood two men in conversation near the center well. It was a moment to drink between training sessions as around them, the trainees paused to rest.

Through the movement, two captains were joined by two other women of similar rank and appearance. Then came the laughter. A sound Svirva hadn't heard in years, but knew instantly. The sound made her stop.

"Svirva?" Umaru asked, puzzled.

But Svirva continued, drawn across the yard as if pulled by an invisible tether. She didn't see the queens glance down, didn't see Umaru behind her. She only heard the voices.

Larastus turned first. His face paled. Agatir turned slower, and when he saw her, his expression was one of helplessness and disbelief. Nelah and Sunh straightened, for they remembered this girl.

Svirva stopped, paces away. Her voice was quiet. Too soft for most to hear.

"Why?"

Her trembling voice cut through the space between them. Larastus opened his mouth, but nothing came. She spoke again, gaze fixed on her brother.

"Why didn't you come back?"

Svirva didn't move. The sounds of the yard began to dim. A cloud passed overhead.

"You left me," she continued. "You left me with *them*." Her voice began to rise.

Agatir stepped forward. "We thought you were safe...we thought..."

"You *thought?*" Her voice cracked, raw at the edges now.

"You thought... so you left me there."

She looked at Larastus. "I called for you." Her voice trembled. "I screamed your names. But you didn't come."

The wind began to rise. A subtle shift, cool against the heat. Ailis took one step forward from the gallery edge, her gaze narrowing as Svirva's shoulders shook and her tears flowed.

"They...took everything from me. I thought you would come back. I waited! I *waited for you.*"

Larastus reached toward her. "Svirva..." His voice was a plea.

"Don't..." She withdrew from him.

Agatir stepped closer. "You're here now, Svirva. We can get through this..."

"You can't..." Her voice changed.

"You should know that I killed him...killed your father..."

She laughed through falling tears, nearly reveling in the truth she had just spoken. Her hand clenched at her side. The sky grew darker. A drop of rain struck the stone and Bianzhi looked skyward, brow furrowed. Ailis didn't move.

Agatir reached toward his sister.

"Don't...touch me."

"Svirva..." he continued towards her.

"Don't touch me!"

He reached towards her again.

Her anger rose, Svirva narrowed her eyes, then she shut them.

Hands reached for her, clawed at her, pulled, bent, and twisted her. Hands...too many hands...She drew away from them, screamed at them to not touch her, to leave her alone.

"**Don't touch me!**" she screamed.

Agatir's skin bubbled and blistered.

His arm was scorched, his face burned.

He fell back, crying out in pain, and was caught by Larastus.

The rain came heavier. Bianzhi drew her blade, stepping forward, her instinct was to defend. She had never seen anything like this, but Ailis laid a hand on her shoulder.

"No," she said quietly. "Let her be."

The air around Svirva trembled. Her eyes met Umaru's. Both of their hearts broke in that moment. She turned, eyes wide with pain, tears lost in the rain, and fled into the city's winding lanes.

From the practice ground ramparts, Dothemides watched, hearing all that had been said. His heart heavy, for he now knew the role he played in this child's pain.

Ailis watched as Svirva fled. No one spoke, but everyone felt it.

Umaru started after her, paused to look back at the fallen Agatir with something bitter in her young face, then she turned and ran after her friend.

The year was marked by the true rise of a kingdom. It was a year of building and expansion, peace and strength. The Kingdom of Dothemia was pride and purpose, made manifest.

Dothemia rose not only from the soil, but from memory, will, and sacrifice. Its black sun banner flew high, and was one of contrasts—recognized and reviled, loved and loathed, admired and abhorred.

Dothemia itself spread beyond its riverbank, climbing the hills to the north. Excavated earth became the bricks and mortar of new homes as bridges spanned the river, market stalls lined the docks, and voices from nearly every corner of the Durajan filled the air. Dothemia became more than refuge. It became a symbol. It became power.

The Obsidian King and the Jade and Red Queens were bound together by duty and purpose as much as they were bound by passion and the pleasures they shared. But no children were born between them. It was a choice made by each of them. But each had children of their own.

Dothemides spent his time with his children, Kaelani, Tananda, Kanike, and Omanessi. Kaelani, his firstborn, was now eleven, the twins Tananda and Kanike were nine, and Omanessi was five.

Kaelani and Omanessi, both born in the season of the Wolf, possessed its spirit. Kaelani was a natural huntress, taking to the bow and blade even at so young an age. She had many examples, her father, who she loved and respected. Bianzhi, with her renowned skill. Ailis, who fought with the strength of the Skarn and the ancients. Umaru, who learned beneath Bianzhi. And Svirva, who she had seen was a match for Bianzhi, even at so young an age.

Omanessi was quick to anger and hard to calm. A distance that Dothemides, despite his love, could not traverse.

Tananda and Kanike, born beneath the season of the Mountain, were quiet, calm, and observant. Holding to one another more than anyone around them. They looked up to their sister and modeled themselves after her in the way of the bow. His children were his pride, but his time with them was never enough, not for him or for them.

Loreiaka found love and settled down, moving outside of the care of her King. His name was Taroq, a Durajani born of Khadar. Their wedding was celebrated, and her husband was embraced by Dothemides and all who stood in his growing court. They were gifted with a home where they could live together with Amubira and plan their future.

Bianzhi deepened her bond with Umaru, becoming a mother figure and mentor, guiding her in the ways of Dothemia, its people and its history. Umaru would learn a great deal more in these months and found herself sometimes wondering if Dothemia would ever become more than a fortress city. It was glorious and grand, but to her, it wasn't yet a home.

Ailis strengthened her bond with Svirva, becoming both a mother figure and guide as well—someone to help Svirva channel what lay within. Ailis saw in Svirva a history of pain and suffering and a soul driven by anger and rage. Forces that she felt would consume her unless they were focused and set free. She believed in her heart that the Mother and Mountain had placed Svirva in her path, and found herself grateful that she was the one to be at her side.

To the north, Fort Koba and Fort Haphira began to expand. Both were stone and timber strongholds where, perched behind walls and atop watchful ramparts, sentinels stood day and night, and watchfires never dimmed.

Bianzhi led Dothemia's defense and, together with Dothemides, coordinated movements between Dothemia and its northern forts. Her captains were divided into foot soldiers, led by Larastus, Agatir the Scarred, Nelah, and Sunh. And marksmen, led by Thornsten, Brynvi, Tumahn, and Setna.

To some of Dothemia's citizens, the city remained a military bastion born of banishment and shaped by blood and sacrifice. But to others, it was a sanctuary. A place where the forgotten were seen, histories were written, and the branded, if they proved themselves, were not just accepted, but honored.

PART III
BROKEN

THE BOOK OF NAKARRA

Chapter 2

Verse 4

Within the silence and stillness, they surrendered themselves wholly. In sacrifice, the disciples sank into the Hollow, and like empty vessels, allowed themselves to be filled.

Verse 5

Through their sacrifice, the First Ones rose, and among them, the first of the Hollowborn, blessed with the power to humble the proud, weaken the strong, cleanse the Awakened World of arrogance, passion, pride, and greed, and allow all to be filled with the stillness and silence of the Hollow.

THE HOLLOW CREED

As written by the First Ones

"Pride is pestilence.
Love is loss.
Voice is vanity.
Borders are barriers.
The path has become our purpose,
and from the forgotten to the awakened,
our reach will extend.
We walk forward to the Time Before,
where silence is sacred,
where many are made one,
and where the Hollow is holy."

Chapter Fifteen

Vengeance, Vision, and Storm

Year 15

THE REACH

Dothemia.

A people who chose to remember. A leader who considers each person's story sacred. A king who rides, conquers, and spills the blood of his enemies. Whose reach touches the sands and canyons, the jungles and steppes, and the highlands and mountains.

The sole survivor of the Three Thanes War. The kingdom that defeated Càrn Valloch, the city that turned the brand into a banner and lures all who hear its name to its gates.

They are known. Their gods, their temples, and their rituals.

Known for their vanity and pride, and their arrogance and greed. They are a people who care only for themselves and their rise.

Something must be done to unmake the Dothemian King. Just as it had been done to Aguran and Valloch, to Rolki and Vulfgar, to Tuskspear and Bloodwolf, Sifur and Vordos. The threat of Dothemides' reign must be undone.

The Reach of the Nakarran Crusade is long, its eyes are many, and now it seems they will need to bleed into Dothemia.

Amenophis, a rising commander and warrior-priest of the Hollow Creed, is chosen to cross the seas, assess, engage, and infiltrate, as is the way of the Nakarran Crusade.

To gather names, seize captives, test the spirit of these Dothemians, and decide whether to erase them or consume them.

Mother's Hand 40. Dothemia

As seasons passed, Umaru's gifts blossomed. She trapped and tamed beasts to serve as watch hounds for the guards of the wall, savannah foals for the stablemasters, and tree-monkeys and forest-cats for merchant pets along Market Row.

Then one day, from a lone hunt, she found a lion cub, its golden fur rippling like sungrass. Upon returning to Dothemia, holding the cub in her arms, Umaru sought out Bianzhi and asked if it might be gifted to the King. Bianzhi smiled warmly and suggested that she do it herself and lead her through the gates of the palace.

Within, Umaru moved like a dreamer. It was a formidable sight. The halls, the stone, the guards in sturdy armor, the sounds of smiths and armorers ringing in the distance. It was another world entirely. She had never been inside the Obsidian Fortress, which some had begun to call the Obsidian Palace.

And at its heart, awaited Dothemides.

Presented proudly by Bianzhi, Umaru stood nervously as the King approached. When their eyes met, the world slowed. Dothemides smiled, and Umaru froze.

She found herself studying him. He was as she remembered. His skin was dark, rich, and brown, and his eyes were the color of ambers. His hair and beard were black, but greying a bit about the temples and chin, and was worn in long, thick locks, beaded with gold. The hard lines and scars of battle seemed to ease into something softer, warmer from this close. He was tall and broad, powerful but kind, and handsome yet humble. She couldn't help but smile. She wondered if she smiled too much.

Dothemides returned Umaru's smile and took her in. She was gentle, radiant and serene. Her hair was worn in thin long braids that fell about her shoulders and back in black shimmering streaks, and was beaded here and there with polished wood and carved bone. Her large amber eyes bore an innocence and softness. She was both hope and wonder. And she was captivating. Before him stood a young woman of fine features, dark skin, deep beauty and for a moment, he simply stared. He too wondered if his eyes lingered too long.

Ailis noticed and felt only calm and silence, while Bianzhi smiled because of the change in her king. Umaru could do nothing but feel the weight of his stare alongside Ailis' presence and Bianzhi's pride. Inside she shrank away in shyness, but standing before them, before him, there was nowhere to hide.

Dothemides tilted his head and laughed. Relieved, Umaru did as well. He stepped close, and as the lion cub mewled between them, Dothemides crouched and stroked his fur. He then rose and with courtly grace, kissed Umaru's hand in thanks and accepted her gift.

She blushed deeply, the warmth of his lips lingering. Ailis and Bianzhi shared a glance.

He invited Umaru to sit and talk. In the conversations that followed, Dothemides learned of her hunting, her quiet strength, her love of beasts, and marveled at how one so gifted had gone unmentioned for so long.

Later that day, Dothemides, Umaru, Bianzhi, and Ailis toured the bustling stalls of Market Row. Much to his surprise, merchants praised Umaru's name, speaking of her wild captures, kindness, and eagerness to help. More than once, Svirva's name surfaced as some asked about her, for it was rare to not see the pair together.

Dothemides asked about her too, but she was nowhere to be seen and Umaru kept her whereabouts private, as it was Svirva's wish to be left alone by all, save Ailis and Umaru. He remembered the duel between Bianzhi and Svirva as well as the power she bore within, which scarred Agatir. Few spoke her name. Many wondered if she was touched by the gods. Others wondered if she was touched by the Hollow.

Svirva watched from a nearby alley until her eyes locked with Ailis'. The Red Queen saw her, but Svirva faded back into shadow.

Mother's Womb 52. Dothemia

Dothemia had laid claim to much of the eastern jungles. Clashes with the Xeyathi had occurred, but in these days, they had become mere skirmishes, resulting always in the pushing back of the Xeyathi further into the jungles, and the claiming of more land for Dothemia's growing needs. The land remained wild and was handled with respect and reverence. They stood as blessings of the Mother to all within Dothemia.

Amidst the backdrop of Dothemia's eastward expansion, Umaru and Svirva's friendship deepened, but something changed as possessiveness grew in Svirva's gaze.

The day came when Dothemides, curious and charmed, asked Umaru to accompany him into the wild. He told her that he wished to see her talents firsthand. The city observed and, in time, began to whisper as one hunt turned to several.

Dothemides marveled at Umaru's patience with beasts, at her laughter among the trees, at her easy way with the people of Dothemia. In time, he offered her a new role, Beast Tamer of the Obsidian Fortress. And with her acceptance, her life began to change.

One evening by a campfire, Umaru told Svirva the news. It was not well accepted. What Svirva felt was not anger or sorrow, but something different. Hurt, masked as indifference. They parted quietly that night.

More hunts followed between Dothemides and Umaru. More evenings spent beneath the jungle canopy together. They came and went with increasing frequency, and as eyes followed, many began to see the change in their king. The return of his joy, the lightening of his heart, the smile on his lips, and the lessening of his burdens. But their king did not neglect his children or his people. He simply spent his time in between with the girl of the sands, who seemed to be taming the lion within him.

In the silence of the wild, Dothemides asked again about her past. Umaru spoke, piecing together the scraps of a hard childhood, her trials, and the role his queens had played in it.

By the firelight, he listened, and it saddened him, but she stated that she had moved on and held no grudge in her heart, explaining that there was a reason for all things, that it was long ago, and that she was here now. Dothemides apologized, reaching to lift her chin, and when their eyes met, something gave way.

He kissed her. It was soft, questioning. She didn't pull away. She couldn't pull away. Another kiss followed, deeper and irresistible. The world between Umaru and Dothemides blurred into one in which only breath and skin existed.

Umaru was afraid, not of him but of the impossibility of the moment and the ripple of its meaning. Yet she trusted him.

Dothemides was caught, lured not by seduction or any other intent, but by something that he could not explain, something that every shred of his being could not resist.

In the shelter of the wild, they undressed one another, reverent, trembling. Her hands traced the scars that battle had written across his flesh over decades. His lips worshiped the curve and peaks of her breasts. Their bodies found rhythm, rising, falling, the world narrowing to the heat between them. There was no time to question, no force that could pull them apart, no desire to be anywhere but in this moment. They were being moved by forces they held no power over.

When she sank onto him, her warmth embracing him, welcoming him, wanting him, they both gasped. Their passion rose like a prayer to the Mother as the canopy swayed above, bearing witness.

Something had shaken the foundations upon which they both stood, shattering it to pieces. And with the ground having given way, both fell together.

"Svirva is changing. There is a distance to her now. Not softness, not weakness. Something else. She walks heavier. Her shoulders, more burdened. The wounds etched into her linger. I see them in her eyes, in the way her hands sometimes twitch when she thinks no one's watching.

She and Umaru train, hunt, and vanish into the jungle for days at a time, returning with stories I'm not always certain are entirely fiction.

Today, Svirva came to me. Not with a question. Not with fear but with wonder. She said, "I kissed her." And then she paused and said "At least I wish I had. Maybe it was just a dream."

She laughed, but then, quieter, she said, "She only sees the King."

"Who can blame her?" she whispered, almost to herself.

I said nothing. Because even I feel Umaru's pull. The girl of sand and beasts. There's something in her that unthreads people. That takes the knots we've learned to live with and loosens them with a glance.

Dothemides smiles in a way around her that makes me feel something I should have banished long ago.

Svirva loves her. I do not believe she has ever spoken the word, not even to herself. But Umaru has her heart set on someone else.

So I watch them. I watch her, and I wonder if something is slipping through my fingers. I wonder if the Mother and Mountain will soon lead me elsewhere."

Book of Ailis, Mother's Tears 92, Year 15

"Umaru is beyond training now. She's quick, strong, and determined, and with a mind that learns without needing to be told twice.

She spends less time with me and more time with Dothemides. Ailis and I have our bond, although sometimes I question even that. But we'd both be blind to not see what's happening.

Still, it is good to see him smile again. That smile was rare for a time. Lost after Samike left. Ailis and I did what was needed, in ways that were needed. For him and for Dothemia.

No one liked seeing their king walk alone and I have been by his side since the jungles of the Xeyathi, one of the first to take up his cause. I know he loves me in his own way. I believe he always has. He once told me privately that had he not met Samike...

But what's the point in dwelling on that? I will always do what needs to be done for him and for Dothemia.

The gods continue to have their sense of humor."

Book of Bianzhi, Mother's Tears 96, Year 15

"I never imagined I'd be the one caught between such winds. It's the way she looks at me. The way her eyes linger. The things she doesn't say.

Today, she kissed me. I didn't mind, and I wasn't upset. I was just surprised and didn't know what to say.

Then she looked away. She's my closest friend. I love her and she is my sister in all but blood, but I don't feel the same.

My heart is with Dothemides.

No. I won't write his name as the one given to him by those who purchased him.

His name is Russom.

He looks at me like he already knows who I am. His eyes are fire and tenderness. His hands are strong and gentle. And gods help me, when we are alone on our hunts, when I see the want in him rise, he does not take, he gives.

But Russom is a king, and what am I? Just someone who walks through the wilds with beasts at my side and sweat and dust on my skin.

Still, he smiles at me like none of that matters.

I don't know what scares me more, that I might not be enough, or that I already am.

And things have not been the same since I told Svirva.

I know she's upset, and I've always known that there's a lot she's hiding from me. What happened with her brother made me realize there's a lot that I don't know about her. Some of those things can be frightening.

I don't want to lose what we have. Svirva is family to me, and I would do anything for her. I just hope she understands.

I think I love him, not just because he's a king, or powerful, or even because he's kind. It's because with him, it's different.

For the first time in my life, I feel like I could be more.

Maybe that's what love really is. Not the hunger, not the ache, but the hope that someone sees all of you, and still stays."

Book of Umaru, Wolf's Wake 5, Year 15

"She didn't have to say it. Her eyes always danced around the truth.

She's not mine. That's clear.

I've spoken to Ailis about Umaru, but she says that whatever happens is the will of the Mother.

She always speaks of the Mother and Mountain.

Of the Mother's wrath and the Mountain's storm.

She told me I carry both. She told me, I am both.

I told her about my dreams...shadows lurking, voices speaking, ravens soaring, bears roaring...of lightning and fire...blood and beasts.

She says they are dreams of vengeance.

"You burn..." she told me.

I told her that I can't stay. Not here.

I told her that I don't belong here.

I hate seeing Agatir, and Umaru grows closer to the king.

I told her that I needed to find them because of how they tried to break me.

For the voices they burned into my mind.

All I want is to break them.

All of them.

She told me to follow my heart. To go where the Mother and Mountain lead me. To look to the shadows and whisper to the voices. She said that the raven will guide me and the bear will protect me.

"Go be the storm."

When she said that, I felt like she was setting me free.

Then it was time to say goodbye to Umaru. She cried. So did I.

Now I walk alone. It's taken me weeks, but I made my way back north and set camp in Stonefang Pass.

The hollow-birthed wind howls like wolves tonight.

Tomorrow I'll begin to build a home.

Then the northern tribes will remember what they did.

I pray to the Mother.

I pray for her wrath.

I pray to the Mountain.

I pray for his storm.

I pray for the strength to send their souls to the sea.

And I swear, by all that is holy, they will remember me.

Book of Svirva, Wolf's Hunt 26, Year 15

"Umaru told me she needed to leave for a time. She spoke of the Khadari tradition of *Vazanti*—It means *the pause one must take*. The journey a person must embark upon when they come to a moment that could shift the course of their life. The tradition ensures that they do not move too quickly.

The desert tribes know that when you find an oasis, you do not rush to drink; you pause. You watch the water. You wait. Because moving too fast may lead you to the blackmaws beneath the water's surface. And while she knows that I am no threat to her, I understand who I am, what I represent, and what we are on the verge of becoming.

As she left this morning, many watched. I am not unaware of the eyes that follow us, both from the people and from Bianzhi and Ailis. But I am not ashamed because when she walked away, I knew it wasn't a goodbye. It was something else.

She had not turned from me; she was walking toward something. Toward clarity.

I'll need to speak with Bianzhi and Ailis soon, not as a king to his queens, but as a man to the women who have stood beside him through Maw and Mountain, giving him their strength when his faltered. They deserve the truth, for although what we are is changing, they are important to me.

They are part of me; the love I have for Bianzhi and the reverence I hold for Ailis remain, but things are changing. I owe them my honesty."

Book of Dothemides, Wolf's Hunt 48, Year 15

"Dothemia's louder than ever. Market Row is packed with traders and merchants. Soldiers gather in groups at its edges and by the palace at its heart. The city smells like too many things in too small a space, of spice, cooked meat, forge smoke, kiln ash, and boiling hides. There are too many people trying to be more than they are. We come when we must, but I'm always glad to leave.

Nzinga found what she needed today. A bundle of bitterroot, a bit of black nettle, and a jar of desert mint. Said she'll steep them for fire-itch. She's smart, steady. Always has the right thing on hand before a problem even bares its teeth. She's got a healer's hands and a hunter's spine. And I thank the Mountain every day that she chose me.

Azi ran wild today. Feet barely touch the ground. The merchants love her. One gave her dried xeyberries, another slipped her beads. She's growing fast.

Skin like Nzinga's, rich, warm like the soil after rain. But her hair's red like mine, wild and knotted. Eyes, too, my blue. Sharp and watchful. She's beautiful.

We caught a glimpse of the King today. He and his queens, the Jade and Red. Jhandai and Skarnvald. They were just passing by, but the whole market shifted when they did. I don't care much for kings, but I see the way people look at him. It's as if they want to follow him into something bigger than themselves.

Saw some Skarn faces too. A few nodded. One I knew from the old days. Said she's forging blades now, and sells them here on the row. There are more of us here than I thought.

My mind drifted to the last Skarnmoot. The way they talked about the skirmishes with the Dothemian forts, whispers of betrayal towards those who follow him. “Traitors,” some said. “Oath breakers,”.

Eyes fell on me as they spoke those words. I felt the accusation in them. I ignored them.

It wasn’t just because I live in the southlands. It was because, according to them, I was an oath breaker who turned his back on the steppes.

I’ve got Nzinga, Azi, and peace. They’ve got war songs, shattered clans, and empty bellies.

There are things I haven’t told Nzinga. Things I will never tell her. She doesn’t need to hear them, and I don’t wish to remember them.

Nzinga’s laying Azi down now. I see her through the curtain, hips swaying, waist slender, backside full and firm. Breasts heavy with the rhythm of life, of love. She doesn’t try to tempt me. She doesn’t need to.

Tonight, I’ll show her. With my hands, with my mouth, with every piece of me she’s ever healed.

She is my woman. My joy. My fire. My rest.

I’ll write again tomorrow.

After.”

Book of Jorvan, Wolf’s Blood 52, Year 15

“The savannah stretches out flat and wide. Dry, quiet. The kind of quiet that listens back. I’ve set my camp just beyond the Tharikadi Pass, near a stream that still runs strong from the canyon peaks.

In the far distance is the city of Ralmasandir.

The City of Veils and Shadows. A city whispered about by the elders. My Khandar took me there. Khandars would trade with them, goods, secrets, slaves, everything was sold there. Anything that could be purchased.

One day, a Ralmas trader circled me and asked Khadar Matahu how much I would cost...for a night or for ownership. Matahu warned, and when his words were not heeded, he killed the merchant without thought or hesitation. Such was the way of The Khandar. Some of the Ralmas drew blades. Those warriors in service of my Khandar did the same. I knew the moment the Khadari bared their teeth, blood would follow.

I didn't want to see anyone else hurt. I stepped out and touched my Khandar's arm. I was too afraid to speak. But I was more afraid of bloodshed. He looked at me, then sheathed his sword. His warriors followed.

I never returned with him to that city.

Too many predators, sharing the same small cage.

Tonight, as I settle and write, my camp is humble. It's just a simple tent and a firepit ringed in stone, but I've lived with less. I know how to be alone. And I'm good at it, most days.

Still, I think of Bianzhi. Of how she looked when I told her I needed to leave. No anger in her eyes. I know she understood. I will miss her.

Then there's Ailis. She doesn't say much, but her eyes do. And I don't think she approves of me with Russom. I can't blame her. This wasn't something I planned.

I tell myself that it's not my fault. That it's his choice as much as mine. And maybe that's true. Maybe wanting something or someone doesn't necessarily make it wrong. But it doesn't make it easy either. Not when someone else carries the cost.

I think of him, and fireflies flutter behind my ribs. His kiss still lingers. I remember the forest. His hands. His lips. The way he held me.

And Svirva. I hope she's well. I hope the world is smart enough to leave her alone. To stay out of her way. I never want to be on the other side of her rage. I say that with a smile. Mostly. But still, I worry for her.

This place feels good. Right.

It's quiet now. The stars are out. The lions sleep.

I think I'll sleep too."

Book of Umaru Wolf's Howl 78, Year 15

Wolf's Blood 63. Tharios. Southern Gates

Outside of the southern wall of the Tharios, Aeristeaus Agustus was forced backward by the tips of spears held in the hands of those who once served his father's house.

His breath was shallow as he stood, bruised and beaten. The air around him smelled of his own seared flesh.

His breastplate was tossed at his feet; the sigil of his father's house was no longer recognizable. A blue cloak followed, tattered and stained with the blood of skirmishes fought in loyalty.

Behind his former allies rose the Thariosian gates. They were worn by time and etched with fading glory. Each column, carved with scenes of a unity that no longer existed.

His heart sank. Tharios' bones were strong, beautiful even now, but the paint had faded and the stonework cracked. The wood of the gates groaned beneath iron brackets. The ramparts loomed above as silent watchers stood along the walls in threes and fours.

Former allies formed in disciplined rows, each wearing the familiar breastplates of boiled leather and rough-forged steel, but now their cloaks were dyed green, the color of House Aguran. Colors of loyalty, adopted quickly by those who turned their backs on their ruler. Tharios had long been divided, but his father's house, House Agustus, was falling.

Beyond those southern gates, life in Tharios still moved as merchants called out market prices, priests chanted beneath cracked temple spires, and women wove wool on the balconies, unaware or unwilling to see what was reaching below their city's surface.

Two more breastplates hit the dust. Hands picked them up, women's hands.

Phara and Halista were shoved forward, bare-chested and freshly branded. The soldiers watched them with the same hunger they once reserved for war. One soldier reached forward, grinning.

Phara dared him with glaring eyes.

Halista caught her by the wrist. "It's alright, Phara," she said, with quiet pride. She would not give these men their small victory.

Aeristeaus stepped toward them, placing a hand on Halista's shoulder. "Halista..." He turned, locking eyes with Phara. "I'm sorry. For all of this."

Then he looked back at the soldiers.

"We were brothers once," he said. "You can't truly believe in Aguran. Surely, you know what he is... what he serves."

A spear-tip lowered in reply.

"You are no brother of ours, *prince*," one said flatly. The guard raised his chin. Jutting it towards the valley. A final warning.

Together, they turned and walked.

Wolf's Howl 81. Somewhere beyond the Valley of Tharioc

Aeristeaus, Phara, and Halista, stripped of name, home, and the banners they once stood beneath, made their way south. For days, they walked, and in time, their feet found grass again as the savannah opened before them, smoke rising in the distance.

They followed the scent of fire and food to a camp. A chance.

They didn't know who waited there, only that their stomachs ached, and they had nothing left to lose.

"I heard them before I saw them. Their sandals were worn, and they were weary and whispering with near blistered skin, burned by the wolfsun. I caught their scent and slipped away quickly with my bow and sword to the ridge above and waited.

There were three of them, and they were Thariosian. I knew by the way they carried themselves. The man looked to be about thirty years old and bore the ornaments of their caste. I'd seen a few in Dothemia. This one wore golden beads woven into his dark hair, a beard shaped with fading precision, skin bronzed from the southern sun.

The two others were women. One had dark, long hair and deeper skin. She was proud with brown eyes filled with anger. The other was lighter with hair like sand and eyes the color of the sky at dusk. Both seemed a bit younger than the man. All three were bare-chested. Their brands told the rest of the story.

They found my tent and circled it. The man drew his blade. The women raised their bows. They were cautious, wounded, and desperate, but they didn't look ready to kill. They looked far too tired.

That's when I stood and I stepped out so they could see me. I told them I'd had them in my sights for some time, but didn't shoot. Told them they looked like they needed help, not a fight.

He lowered his sword. They lowered their bows. There was something honest in his eyes when he gave his name. Aristaeus. Then the women. Phara was the fierce one with dark hair, and Halista, the calm anchor. I offered them food, water, and a place to sit. They accepted.

Later, Aristaeus and I talked.

He told me that Tharios was split into two warring houses, led by the kings, Agustus and Aguran. He is the son of Agustus, and until his banishment, he was the defender of his father's eroding house and leader of his thinning soldiers.

In a battle against Aguran's forces, the Agustan line broke. Aristaeus and his forces were defeated. He was cut off from the retreat, captured, tried, and banished. Aguran told him that when House Agustus falls, all who serve him will have their names wiped from memory. That Tharios was no longer a place for the pride of kings.

He worries for his father, mother, and sister, and fears for all of Tharios because he believes that Aguran serves the Hollow Creed. Aristaeus spoke of how Aguran and many of his soldiers fight with no battle cries, oaths, or insults, just silence. That Aguran doesn't age like a man should, and that even after many years, he fights at the front, leads every charge, and moves with too much ease, while Aristaeus' father grows old. He said that Aguran was so devoted to the Creed that he banished his own wife and raised his son and daughter, children born of a cursed love, to fight by him as his fiercest soldiers. Soldiers that many fear.

I could tell his heart was heavy. How could it not be? He went on, and I just listened. I felt for him, for them.

He went on to say that if Aguran wins, all of Tharios will be forgotten. And before that fall comes, his father and those closest to him would be cast out, left to watch it all crumble from the Durajan, and that he, along with Phara and Halista, were just three more in a long line of others who had suffered the same fate.

He laughed at the end, like a man who's lost everything and has nothing left to grieve.

Then he spoke of a place called Dothemia, and of a man who once fought for his father before the House Wars of Tharios began, someone he looked up to when he was just a boy, and who was now rumored to be a king.

He hopes the rumors are true. That the Obsidian King is real and that he welcomes the broken and the banished.

If not, he said, maybe he'll stay out here and build something. An arena, maybe. Said it with a grin, but there was something real behind it.

They have nothing. No one to bear witness to their suffering or hear their words. So I listened, and now, make sure to write this for them so they are remembered. I think I will let them stay and help them.

But I must be careful. I won't tell him who I am. Not yet."

Book of Umaru, Wolf's Howl 82, Year 15

"It's been thirteen days since I welcomed Aristaeus, Phara, and Halista into my camp. At first, it was a bond forged more from necessity than trust. But over the days, through shared hunts and quiet labor, something deeper began to take root.

Aristaeus seemed surprised by me. Though I am barely half his age, I saw the way he watched as I moved through the wilds, how he noted my steps, and my knowledge of the land. He said little, but his respect was plain.

He once asked me why I bore no brand. I told him the truth: my parents were banished from Khadar before I was born. I was raised in Sifur's Breath by a feared Khandar. That I know every dune and thorn, every beast and burrow between the sands and the savannah. I told him that this land shaped me, and I love it, even if it tries to kill me sometimes.

I observed them too. I wondered about the bond between Aristaeus and Phara. I wonder if they are lovers. It's none of my business, I suppose.

It's clear they don't know these lands, but I guide them and sometimes tease them. Mostly to break the long silences. Laughter softens even the hardest edges.

Something is growing here. Not yet trust, perhaps. But something close."

Book of Umaru, Wolf's Howl 95, Year 15

"A bond has formed now. I'd even say a friendship.

I like Aristaeus. He's a good man, and through his insistence, he has repaid my hospitality by gathering wood and thatch to raise walls around the camp, and helping build a place I could call home.

Phara and Halista help as well. They keep watch at night and hunt whenever possible. They listen to him. Whatever rank they held when they were soldiers clearly still stands.

We now have a hut with three rooms—one for me, one for them, and a hearth in between.

Each night we sit by the fire. Phara speaks of vengeance against Aguran while Halista tries to soothe her and keep her mind in the now of things. And while they sit, Aristaeus stares into the flame, lost in his memories."

Book of Umaru, Maw's Hunger 15, Year 15

"We've begun to barter the spoils of our hunts with the canyon and savannah tribes. It's been enough for simple comforts. I miss Dothemides, but I feel more and more that I made the right choice. Everything happens for a reason. Reasons we sometimes can't see. If I weren't here, Aristaeus, Phara, and Halista may not have survived.

During a hunt in the low brush, Phara was bitten on the leg. I knew it was bad. I know the beasts that roam, the bite of the canyon hound, and the sickness it carries. But she dismissed it, saying she had suffered worse. Phara is proud. Too proud.

That was two days ago, and it was Halista who first noticed what Phara tried to hide. The swelling, a wound that wouldn't close, the tremble in her hands when she thinks no one is watching. I see it too.

This morning, I overheard Halista speaking with Aristaeus. She whispered of a deepening sickness. Aristaeus was silent for a long time and when he spoke, I could hear the helplessness in his voice.

When I approached them, Aristaeus lied and told me that Phara was ok. He doesn't want to burden me further.

I wonder if all Thariosians are this proud."

Book of Umaru, Maw's Hunger 18, Year 15

"Halista and Aristaeus were outside when I crept to the door of their chamber. Inside, Phara was trembling by the fire. Her skin was slick with sweat, and her face tight with pain as she slept. It's getting worse.

I crouched at her bedside and peeled back the bandage carefully. Both the smell and sight turned my stomach.

She is not healing. Something needs to be done."

Book of Umaru, Maw's Hunger 19, Year 15

"We're packing up and preparing to leave. Phara doesn't have much time.

I told them that the rumors they've heard are all true–that Dothemia was as real as its king and queens and that I would lead them there.

I shouldn't have waited this long.

We leave today. I only hope we make it in time."

Book of Umaru, Maw's Hunger 20, Year 15

Maw's Hunger 21. Umaru's Refuge

Umaru's words surprised him, but she didn't stop to explain more than she had to. She moved with urgency, issuing soft orders, telling Aristaeus and Halista to gather the packs and anything else they could carry.

Then, without a word, she left.

Aristaeus looked at Halista. She nodded, and he followed as Umaru stepped out past the walls of her sanctuary and looked out across the savannah, her mind racing.

She moved through the grasslands with purpose. Then saw what she was looking for.

They were just shadows at first. A herd of wild horses cresting the rise beyond the trees. The stallion at the front raised his head, watching the horizon as if he heard something. They moved with the sound and feel of distant thunder and swept across the savannah like the wake of the Wolf, made flesh.

As a child, Umaru loved to watch them as they traversed the savannah in search of grazing grounds, water, and safe cover, especially during the seasons of the Wolf and Maw. On those days, she never called out. She simply watched and let them pass. But today would be different.

Apart from the stallion, there were several mares and a number of foals. One mare drank by a stream as the stallion watched Umaru approach.

Aristaeus remained close but stiffened as he saw it, his hand drifting instinctively to his blade. But Umaru thrust a hand back, signaling him to stay, before rising from the grasses and making herself seen.

The stallion caught her scent, its hoof scraping the ground, muscles bunching, as she moved closer to the mare, slow and deliberate.

"We need your strength," she whispered. Her voice was low and steady. "We need your speed," she continued. "We need your help."

The stallion steadied, the herd paused, and the mare stood, unsettled.

Aristaeus watched as Umaru reached out, her hand brushing along the mare's face, feeling the heat of its breath against her skin. She pressed her palm reverently atop the mare's forehead, causing her to settle and lower her head, yielding.

"Thank you." She whispered, stroking its coat and mane. She turned, and her eyes met those of the stallion. Its head raised, the world seemed to breathe again, and as the stallion ran. Soon, the rest of the herd followed.

Umaru turned back to Aristaeus. He needed no instruction. He ran back to the cabin, telling Halista to gather rope and strong branches. Together, they fashioned a litter sturdy enough to hold Phara's weight, and when Umaru returned, leading the mare, Halista could only stare in open wonder.

The Thariosian cavalry knew well the price paid by those who sought to break a savannah steed. What she saw Umaru accomplish should not have been possible.

Carefully, they lifted Phara onto the makeshift litter, lashed it to the mare, and left for Dothemia.

"When we arrived in Dothemia, I led them to the apothecaries and healers that I remembered from Market Row. They saw Pharas' condition and acted immediately. There was no time for anything else.

I felt the stares. It was strange. Aristaeus and Halista didn't know what to think. Everything happened so quickly when we arrived. I was just about to try to say something, anything, when I heard my name.

It was Bianzhi. She took control. Gave me relief from the weight of everyone's eyes on me. She always seemed to know me and what I needed.

She asked questions, and I gave the answers I could. Aristaeus and Halista were next.

Bianzhi arranged for a place for them to stay while Phara was tended to.

Later, in the palace, Bianzhi left me alone so that I could speak with Russom. Ailis watched us for a moment before following her.

I didn't realize how much I had missed him. I was glad to be with him again. We spoke about my time away and about his time here. There was so much to catch up on. He asked me about every detail of my life while I was away. I told him everything, and he listened to every word, my hand in his.

It will be nice to spend time with him as Phara recovers."

Book of Umaru, Maw's Feast 45, Year 15

"Umaru returned days ago. To say that I was relieved to see her would be an understatement. The Mother has guided her safely, but I feel there is more at play than the Mother's grace.

Umaru is unlike any woman I have ever met. There is no mystery behind her eyes. There is only good, compassion, honesty, and kindness. She is wise beyond her years and has captured me completely.

This morning, she asked how I was while she was gone. I told her about the city, my children, and how Kaelani liked how I smiled when she was around.

I confessed that I was not the father I wanted to be, that my children spent more time with caretakers than with me. I told her that I worried about the lingering impact of Samike leaving years ago, and that I try to provide and care for them as best as I can, but sometimes I fear that my efforts are not enough. That they can never be enough. Not with my people's needs.

Then she asked me if what was gained was worth what it seemed to cost.

The question surprised me, but there was no judgment in her tone, only honesty.

I thought about it, then told her of the Durajan I was left to die in fifteen years ago and what it has now become through blood, sacrifice and loss—the brand raised as a banner, tribes that now join us willingly, fields that flourish, temples filled with songs in the tongues of the Nine, now shared and known by all, and of our fortifications across the steppes and highlands.

I told her that I believe that all of this is the Mother's will.

The balance she speaks of.

The balance I believe in.

Then she asked, "What of those left behind?"

The question hit hard. It surprised me.

I asked her what she meant, half knowing but wanting to hear. She held my hand and spoke of those she'd heard about. Tribes whispered of in the markets and roads. Stories of the remnants of Rolki, Vulfgar, and Valloch, people of the sands and jungles, canyons and steppes.

I knew she spoke of those affected by Dothemia's growth and conflicts. People like Svirva. People like her. Families broken and villages fractured.

I remembered my words five years ago.

"Like the clearing of fields for growth, unity has a cost. It is the balance of the Mother."

But sitting before her, I could not speak them. The words felt wrong. Cruel. Her question made me realize that a distance had grown between my dream and its realization.

And for the first time, I feared what I had become."

Book of Dothemides, Maw's Feast 47, Year 15

"When I asked him that question, I saw it in his eyes.

He realized that he had not thought of them. Of us. Not out of cruelty or indifference. He is not a cruel man.

Perhaps it was just a blindness born of hope, or a need to believe the wounds were few. To clear a path forward towards his dream was all that mattered.

I saw the conflict gather behind his eyes, the lines of worry, the strength worn down by battles he had not wanted but had fought anyway.

As he held my hand, I told him that those left behind must be remembered as well.

That's when I saw it strike him. I felt bad that I caused such conflict in him. My words hurt him. Not because I meant to, but because of the truth they revealed. He kissed me and rested his forehead against mine, shutting his eyes against the truth of what he had done. Then he kissed my hands, stood, and left. I think he needs time.

There is more to be done. So much more. He has built a place of unity and protection for those aligned with his dream, but not yet a home for all.

I found him later and told him that before I could settle here and walk these streets as one of his people, I needed to go back, find those left behind, give them hope, and show them that they have not been forgotten. Perhaps I could help heal the wounds suffered in the name of a dream too heavy for one man to carry.

I said that perhaps my sanctuary could grow. With Aristaeus, Phara, and Halista at my side, we could build a place for those left behind. Not here in Dothemia, but close enough to offer safety and a hope for a future where people could learn, heal, and remember.

Russom didn't argue. He only watched me with a kind of quiet fear.

He agreed, saying that he would give me enough coin to keep my promises and offered to send soldiers to safeguard the work to come.

I chose four to travel with me: Anaeix of Vordos, Khasun of the Càrnothi Highlands, Eligal of the Skarnvald Steppes, and Ulaka of the Khadari Desert.

We will stay together for a few more nights. Then we'll all head back home when Phara is well enough.

A home that is not apart from Dothemia. It is just a part of it that has yet to be built."

Book of Umaru, Maw's Feast 49, Year 15

"I did not expect any of this. Not Umaru. Not her camp. Not the way she moves through the world. She is sure and steady, as though she had walked two paths at once and returned knowing the way forward for us all.

When we arrived in Dothemia, I thought we would be met with suspicion, perhaps even resistance. Instead, Umaru guided us as if she belonged there, knowing every turn of the city, every stall along their marketplace, every healer who could be trusted with Phara's care. It was clear that the people were fond of her.

And Dothemides, seeing him again, was something I had not prepared myself for. Russom Balewa. He was much younger then, and I was younger still. I was just a child then, and now he has become a king. Time had shaped him, certainly, but had not broken the thread of who he had been and who I saw when I gave him the name. I was surprised he still bore it. But he wore it well, and it still rang true. A silly boy's name given to a warrior he looked up to. "He who has proven, mighty." I feel foolish at the thought of it.

I sat at a small desk in the quarters they gave us, trying to gather my thoughts, trying to make sense of how our paths had diverged and crossed again. It was then that Dothemides entered the room. I could feel his presence fill the space. He touched my shoulder, a firm and familiar gesture, and when I turned, he met my gaze with no doubt or distance in his eyes. He remembered me.

"You've grown," he said, and for a heartbeat, the boy in me answered, shoulders straightening in unconscious pride. I caught myself before it showed too clearly, rose to my feet, and we shook hands in a soldier's clasp, strong and steady.

He smiled, the weight of the crown visible but not crushing him, and told me he came bearing gifts. Three of them. He placed the books in my hands, thick volumes bound in dark leather, and said to me that Tharios may have forgotten me, but that I need not be forgotten.

We caught up on the paths that led us here. We spoke of his service to my father. The lives he had lived since. His path to rule, his children, his First, Jade and Red Queens, and of Umaru. I smiled. He was Marukhan through and through. The mention of her name showed something in him. It was a name spoken with deep affection.

I spoke of the change in Tharios. The civil war. The rise of Aguran and the hold of the Hollow Creed, and I told him of my banishment, my father's failing health, my mother's fears, and my sister's loathing of him. He took pity and told me that should the time ever come, Agustus, Photini, and Androniki would be welcomed here along with all Thariosians who were loyal to House Agustus.

It took me a moment to find my voice. That he remembered their names, my father, mother, and sister, after all these years. It struck something deep in me that I did not know I still guarded. I nodded, unable to say more. Dothemides clapped my shoulder once more and left without waiting for thanks.

That was weeks ago now.

We have since returned to Umaru's camp, though calling it a camp hardly does it justice anymore. It grows with every passing day. Many are beginning to find their way here, drawn by whispers of safety and purpose for tribes still struggling to recover. Some of the Khadari people who have settled among us have taken to calling her the Queen of the Sands. I hear it often now, murmured with a kind of fierce affection. It is not a name she has claimed, but it is one she has earned.

She organizes everything. Tasks are given, and they are done. Homes are built, simple huts, but they are homes nonetheless. Among the settlers are people of Khadar, Shadura, Marukh, Tharios, and even a handful of steppeland elders of Skarnfolk. Old wolves, as they call themselves. Left out because they were too old to fight against the Dothemian advance or too weak to wander without a clan to call home.

Skills are taught, shared, and woven into the daily rhythm. Hunts are undertaken. Meals are shared. A kind of purpose has taken root here, something I did not realize I was starving for until I saw it with my own eyes.

Umaru does not hand out journals to those who come. Such an act may connect too directly to Dothemides. Something she must tread delicately. Something which each of us understands. Yet each night, when the fires burn low and the camp settles, those of us who can, write anyway. Quietly. Privately. Continuing and learning to record the foundation of something that matters.

I have come to admire the Dothemians more than I thought possible. Strange, even to write that "the Dothemians" as if Dothemia is a nation all its own now. Perhaps it is. I find myself wondering what it might become, given time.

But I also know the truth. In Tharios and across the Nine Nations, most would give us no thought at all. Better that way, I think. Better that Dothemides be left in peace with his people, his dream, and his future queen."

Book of Aristaeus, Maw's Silence 91, Year 15

Maw's Silence 98. The Obsidian Fortress

Ailis stood atop the walls of Dothemia, the breath of the ocean sharp in her lungs, the wailing of unseen spirits thick in the air. She felt life slipping and fading like mist between her fingers. No matter how tightly she grasped, it bled away.

Blood. Love. Life. It ran freely, staining the white sands and black stones, painting the shores in cruel, vivid red.

Thunder shook the heavens. Chaos roared below. Voices rose in screams torn from the belly, raw and desperate. She fought alongside Bianzhi, their blades flashing in desperate arcs, but when she reached for her king, he was swallowed, pulled into the tide, lost.

She could not save him...

She woke with a sharp breath, heart pounding against her ribs like a war drum. Sheets tangled around her limbs, her slender form bare and pale. Beside her, Dothemides slept. And beyond him, curled in soft repose, lay Bianzhi.

The dreams had come more frequently of late. Ever since the young Khadari woman had left on her mission to heal those too blind to see the wisdom of her king.

The Skarn saw the world through the eyes of battle. Every joy a conquest, every sorrow a wound, every love a war fought to the last breath. Dreams of the heart took shape as bloodshed and ruin, and Ailis was no different. In her dreams, she was losing. Losing Dothemia. Losing the man she had once believed immovable.

Last night had proven his passions remained. His body had not strayed, but his heart... His heart grew distant, like a ship pulling from harbor in a slow, inevitable drift.

She watched them now, the two she loved beyond reason, and a cold certainty rooted itself deep within her chest.

Something would come between them.

If it had not already.

And it would be a war she could not win.

Book of Nakarra

Chapter 2

6. From this, the path to the Before became clear. If the Awakened World could not see for themselves, they would be made to. And so the Nakarran Crusade was born...

Mountain's Breath 1. The Bay of Blood. North of the Xeyathi Coast

The waters were black beneath the galleons as their hulls sliced through the fog like knives. From the shoreline, no bells rang and no cries rose. There was only the soft creak of wood against the surf and the muted splash of oars.

Amenophis stood at the prow. On either side of him moved Turadaj and Amrahi, their forms blurred in the mist. Turadaj, the Khadari shaman whose skin bore the darkness of the desert-born, walked with the quiet certainty of one who heard the Hollow whisper even across oceans. Amrahi, once of Xeyath, now a blade in Amenophis' hand, watched the shore ahead with a predator's stillness.

Their ship slowed. The others followed, the fleet converging near the fog-wreathed coastline. The forest loomed ahead, silent yet heavy with unseen watchers. From the jungle's shadowed eaves, the Durajani tribes of the Xeyathi lay in wait. Once the secret terror of the southeast, their power had withered beneath Dothemia's rise, as they were driven into hiding and bitterness. And now, another potential enemy approached their waters.

Amrahi lifted a hand and archers readied, bows drawn tight. A breathless moment passed as Turadaj shifted beside Amenophis. The shaman's eyes were half-lidded in concentration. As he listened to the land's unseen murmurs, a slow, knowing nod passed between them.

Still, Amenophis held, and his ships did not beach.

Instead, with a soft rasp of orders passed down the line, and lantern signals sent between ships in the darkness, oars dipped into the black waters, and the fleet soon veered northward. Among the Xeyathi watchers, tension and confusion stirred. This was not expected, but all were relieved.

Frowning, Turadaj turned to Amenophis in question, but the warlord smiled thinly.

"Last night, Amrahi came to me." His voice was accompanied by the rattle of oars and the creaking, groaning of the ships.

"She told me the jungle tribes hate Dothemia more than they fear death, but the Jhandai on the northern shores? There are fewer. Less prepared. We strike at the Jhandai, and use those we capture to gain the allegiance of the Xeyathi."

Turadaj nodded once, understanding. Amenophis' hand rested lightly on the hilt of his sword, the Skarn-forged blade gleaming faintly beneath his cloak. His shield, wrought in Càrnothi iron, hung across his back, a relic of conquered traditions.

"Rest and ready yourself, Turadaj. It begins at dawn."

Just before sunrise, bells rang along the Jhandai coast as villagers and fishermen gazed out from their wooden watchtowers. Cries of alarm filled the air as foreign sails emerged from the mist, fluttering like heralds of ruin.

Panic spread, boats were beached and abandoned and gates slammed shut as archers took positions atop rough-hewn walls. But it would not be enough. Amenophis smiled. His expression was almost serene as Nakarran ships of the Creed-led nation of Vordos beached, and his troops disembarked.

Amenophis and Amrahi led the charge, stepping from the longboats into knee-deep surf, weapons flashing as warriors rushed past them to engage the Jhandai defenders. Arrows whistled through the air as Amenophis' forces surged up the beach.

Shield walls protected ladder bearers, and archers provided cover, suppressing the Jhandai's defenses. Amenophis and Amrahi were joined by Turadaj, and the three walked calmly towards the walls.

By the time they approached, fighting had erupted along the ramparts. Archers lay dead, slumped over the wall's edge or lying at its base, riddled with arrows. The warriors of the Crusade were efficient and silent, acting decisively and without pause. Soon after it began, the gates opened, pushed on iron hinges by his soldiers, carving arcs into the sand that welcomed Amenophis and his commanders, like unfolding wings.

Side by side, they moved into the village, one blade singing, the other striking. Jhandai warriors met them with fierce resistance, but their courage could not match the Crusade's advance.

Fires rose. Blood soaked the sands. By nightfall, the village was silent and broken. Its survivors were shackled in iron chains and knelt, huddled under guard.

Amenophis had claimed a foothold in the name of the Creed.

Over the next few days, the Nakarran occupation of the Jhandai was complete, and it was time for the next phase of their plan.

With the village secure, Amenophis would lead a contingent south, where the Xeyathi jungles waited.

Highsun. Mountain's Breath 6. Somewhere in the Xeyathi Jungles

The heat bore down on the gathering beneath the dappled light of the jungle canopy. Every rustle of leaves, every distant crackle of a falling branch, seemed amplified in the stillness below. The forest's constant murmurs, the buzz of insects, the chirping of birds, the faint cry of a primate in the distance, served as a reminder that they were being watched, measured, and judged.

The shrill, constant chirping of insects created a dense curtain of sound, a stark contrast to the silent, disciplined rows of Amenophis' forces. Their shields were raised, and their swords and spears were held at the ready as he and Amrahi stepped out from between the disciplined rows to the front.

Ahead of them, the warriors of the Xeyathi circled like predators, faces marked with war paints of emerald green, furs of the longtooth, were draped across lean shoulders and worn as headdresses. Across bridges and walkways that spanned the tree line, archers took aim, ready to fire as those below measured the newcomers and sought to sniff out any deceit.

Amenophis spoke plainly in the language of Xeyath, telling them that Dothemia had risen too far, too fast and that the time had come for the Obsidian Kings' strength and the strength of his people to be challenged, and its walls breached and toppled. He promised that if the Xeyathi aided him, if they lent their hunters, warriors and their hatred to his cause, they would be rewarded beyond measure.

Amrahi was surprised at this, as it was not the directive given, but she said nothing. She trusted her commander and was here to serve, not to question.

What followed was the presentation of gold, weapons, and treasures from across the Nine. The Nakarran soldiers walked out wordlessly, as the Xeyathi whispered amongst themselves. For a moment, the jungle itself seemed to hold its breath. Heavy chests were laid down and opened before the soldiers took their positions once again.

Above, an archer called and pointed. The Xeyathi chieftains below looked through the Nakarran lines as a handful of Jhandai captives, bound but unharmed, spirits broken and fearful, were presented as an offering. The Jhandai were known for their beauty as well as their craft, and the slaves presented, promised both. Amenophis remained calm, allowing the promise to sink in.

Their discussion was long but their decision came. Xeyathi warriors emerged and took hold of the chains of their new captives. Others opened the coffers, marveling at the riches within. Each coffer was lifted and taken. Then emerged the Xeyathi chieftain. A man of size bearing countless scars. His skin was weathered and creased with time. His features were long and leery. Eyes sunken yet wise. He nodded and extended a hand, which was clasped by Amenophis.

It was an uneasy alliance. A risk even in the attempt. But The Xeyathi, once sovereign over these coasts, had been driven to the shadows. Fear and pride warred within them. But their loathing for Dothemia burned hotter than their caution.

With allies in place, movements were coordinated, plans made and set in motion. The next wave of ships came bearing more soldiers of the Creed. They were sleeker, faster and Amenophis welcomed them as the Xeyathi stood atop their shoreline cliffs, watching.

It was time to move. And together the uneasy allies marched toward Dothemia.

Dawn. Mountain's Trial 26. Dothemia's Eastern Farmlands

Dothemian farmers went about their duties beyond the walls of the city, tilling the fields that stretched for miles eastward, carved long ago from the dense jungles. Patrolled by Dothemian guards, the land was orderly and defended. But they were not aware of the danger along its edges until it was far too late.

They moved through the underbrush like shadows. Xeyathi archers, hidden high in the canopy, took position in the treetops. Nakarran soldiers slipped silently along the forest edge. Amenophis, Amrahi, and Turadaj stood waiting and watching.

Hand signals flew through the ranks, archer to soldier, soldier to flanks. A silent relay of precision, timed down to the second so that distance and delay would not betray the attack.

The time came.

Xeyathi archers loosed their arrows. Nakarran soldiers covered the mouths of the ambushed to stifle cries. Blades were drawn across the throats of Dothemian patrols, painting the jungle's lush green, a deep, vivid red.

Bodies were dragged into the underbrush, and the ridgeline shuddered as more patrols fell into silence, until the farmers screamed, but by then, it was already too late. Nets flew, weighted and knotted, cast by Xeyathi hands. They soared swift and sure, and the farmers fell beneath them, tangled and bound like freshly caught game.

The people scattered, and cries rang. A figure darted from the chaos, running westward, as the Dothemians that remained fled towards the city.

Turadaj sensed her movement, a ripple against the unseen. He lifted his bow, drew back an arrow, closed his eyes, and trusted the spirits. His left arm was strong, and his right hand was steady. The black and red feathers touched his ear as the bowstring bit into his cheek.

Coiled fingers loosened with a soft breath and the shaft flew, timed to her stride and pace as her feet carried her in her panic. The arrow's path sliced through saplings, brush and beneath hanging limbs. None could be allowed to escape.

A sudden trip, a fall, the impact of an arrow where only moments ago the fleeing woman stood. She looked up and saw what should have been her end. She crawled, stood, ran and slipped away, bearing her desperate news toward Dothemia.

Turadaj shut his eyes and let his anger go with a breath. The Hollow held no place for such emotions. Amrahi moved to chase but paused at the words of her commander.

“Let her go,” Amenophis added as the Dothemian captives were being rounded up.

“Let them know.”

“Let them fear.”

Along the Dothemian eastern wall, Tumahn and Setna watched a woman return. Something was not right. Her face was etched with terror as she ran beneath the gates and continued down Market Row.

Inside the Obsidian Fortress, within the great hall, where the King received audiences and held councils, the air buzzed with the day's business.

Dothemides stood with Ailis and Bianzhi at his side. A heavy wooden table rested between them, covered with maps and lists as shipments were tracked, supplies tallied, and movements of goods and soldiers coordinated.

Sunh, Nelah, Larastus, and Agatir held their stations along the walls as the children of Dothemides were tended to in an adjacent chamber.

The guards stiffened as the woman, wild-eyed and harried, rushed into the hall.

Sunh and Nelah blocked her path, hands on hilts, but Larastus and Agatir intervened, ushering her forward, their instincts measuring the fear in her eyes. Dothemides turned from the table, his expression calm, and gestured for her to approach.

Ailis and Bianzhi flanked him, the statue of the Mother looming behind them, carved in simple reverence. Three high-backed seats, shaped more like thrones than chairs, sat beneath her gaze.

The woman spoke, voice trembling, before her king, queens, and their trusted warriors, describing what she had seen.

Nets in the fields.
Blood on the leaves.
Shadows in the trees.

Confusion rippled through the room, and Bianzhi moved immediately, sharp and decisive, departing without hesitation to investigate, Agatir and Larastus falling into step behind her.

Sunh and Nelah remained with the Dothemides, who offered the woman comfort and a moment to gather herself. Dothemides looked to Ailis, and her heart sank as she felt for the first time that her dreams had been a warning.

Mountain's Trial 26. Dothemia. Market Row

News moved through the streets of Dothemia, swift and unsettling, though none yet knew the true shape of it. It flowed from the palace, not in screams or sounding horns, but in a tight, controlled stream of soldiers.

Nzinga and Jorvan stood among the merchants and craftsmen of Market Row, Azibo's small hands clasped tightly in theirs as they watched the current of unease spread. A woman had entered the palace earlier. Frightened and wide-eyed. Like an ember carried on the wind. And from that ember a flame had risen, quiet at first, but now it smoldered and spread across Dothemia's roads, leaping across people, market stalls and homes until it reached the city's outer walls.

Jorvan watched as the king appeared from the fortress, a beacon of Umbrasteel and gold, calm in the rising tension and moving with purpose. He watched the jade queen at his side, a fierce and beautiful woman of the Jhandai. Her blade, never far from her hand. But it was the third figure, Ailis, the Red Queen, that seized his breath and held it. A pride swelled in him, like a sacred duty stirring in forgotten parts of his memory, as if the blood of long-forgotten ancestors remembered her, and through her presence, called to him in ancient hymns, and war songs of battle cries and bloodshed.

As the warriors of Càrnoth surged out alongside their king and queens, Azibo tugged at her father's hand, shaking him from the moment. Her small fingers tightened around his.

"Are they under attack?" Nzinga's voice was soft as she asked.

Her sharp eyes followed the lines of soldiers now racing down Market Row as guards hurried, arming themselves with shield and blade, forming living walls across the avenues. The people whispered. Some clutched loved ones. Others retreated behind closed shutters and barred doors as shops began to close.

Azibo's face, still so young, was alight with innocent wonder. She pointed down the road at the soldiers, then she saw the Red Queen, with her wild crown of crimson hair, running at her king's side. She thought the queen must be fun, her hair was like fire, like her own. Her skin was like her father's. She saw the king too, his skin was like her mother's, like hers, rich and brown under the southern sun. She saw herself reflected back, and it made her smile.

Jorvan watched his daughter. Nzinga watched him. She knew her husband too well to not notice the war within him, the pull between fighting to defend this city and protect the innocent lives within it, and the devotion to the two souls he loved, who stood at his side.

Nzinga knew that a warrior rested within him, but also a father and husband. She said nothing and offered no argument, only a silence heavy with understanding and permission to choose.

His hand tightened protectively on Azibo's small shoulder as he watched the Dothemian rulers disappear through the eastern gate. His arm slipped around Nzinga's waist. Jorvan looked down the road again, fighting the voices that echoed in his mind since seeing the Red Queen emerge. Nzinga's palm rose to his cheek. She turned his face towards hers. Their eyes met.

"I hear them too," Her words granted him the space to decide, but told him that he must do so quickly and that she would stand by his decision.

Jorvan looked down at her as she spoke. Azibo was looking up at her parents, her face troubled and curious. He nodded to Nzinga, and she to him. No more words were needed.

He lifted Azibo, cradling her in his arms. Her tiny legs swung and clung to his waist as she gripped his vest. Hand in hand, Jorvan and Nzinga turned west, slipping through the soldiers that continued to run toward and past them as Dothemia's people ran to their homes.

Together, Jorvan and Nzinga moved quickly, fleeing the heat rising within the heart of the city, until their feet had taken them past the western walls and towards the great gates. Beyond the packed and near panicked herd of people rushing past, the gates were closing. Jorvan called desperately for them to hold.

The air was thick with choking dust as faces flooded past them. Above, guards encouraged them to remain inside for fear of attack from the west, but they continued. Jorvan's voice rising amidst the rush as his push provided a path for his family.

Moments later the looming great gates of Dothemia closed behind them with a boom. Then there was silence.

The river flowed alongside them. Their hearts thundered, their chests heaved. Jorvan and Nzinga looked back, then towards one another. They were safe. Safer here than in there. Then rose the soft sniffles of their sweet child.

Nzinga soothed and comforted her. Azibo's eyes were wet with tears. She kissed her cheek, then kissed her husband deeply. They embraced, and together they ran into the rising canyons and beyond to the west, where the shadows fell cool and deep, and the flame of the Dothemia faded behind them.

Highsun. Mountain's Trial 26. Dothemia's Eastern Walls

Following the attacks, scouts returned. Brynvi, Thornsten, Setna and Tumahn. They were Dothemides' swiftest runners. They reported a force on the move, deep in the jungles, approaching steadily. What was believed to be a Xeyathi attack had become something far more unsettling. An army marched on Dothemia.

At the gates, Dothemian soldiers took their positions. They were not accustomed to facing battle on their very doorsteps. Yet there was no panic. They stood ready and their king stood with them, not behind, but in front.

Dothemides had fought on countless battlefields, and he knew the weight of this stillness. Atop the walls, archers made ready under the command of their captains.

Bianzhi and Ailis approached, stepping to the king's side. Bianzhi bore her curved blade, the same one she'd carried for years, her jade eyes keen and steady but her heart was racing. The soldiers, young and old, awaited her signal, but she, in turn, awaited her king's command.

Ailis stood fierce beside them, a vision that no one in Dothemia had ever seen before in their Red Queen. She bore a Skarnvald war axe in one hand and a stout shield in the other. A battle skirt of leather, silk, and fur fell about her waist, split high for movement. Black warpaint darkened her eyes and fell in a single streak down her lips and chin, leaving only the blue of her gaze visible, fierce and burning. Her flaming red hair was braided wildly, a mane fit for the Mother's wrath. She was clad for war.

Dothemides watched them all, the reflection of the coming battle mirrored in his armor. The Jhandai armorer, Shizun, had long ago crafted it for him. It was a breastplate of shimmering Umbrasteel embellished with gold, made in a style that blended Tharios and Marukh. A battle skirt left his legs bare, his arms unshielded save for the bracers he wore. His breastplate bore etched depictions of his labors and his devotion to the Mother. In his hands, he clasped a longsword of Marukhan design and a shield of Tharios. Both were forged of Umbrasteel.

He whispered a prayer to the Mother. A prayer for his children, his queens, people, and his friends. But despite the prayer, his anger rose, disciplined and simmering. The thought of someone daring to attack Dothemia filled him with a darkness that he was no stranger to but did not like to face.

The sun slipped across the sky. The shadows moved, and soon, the tree line shuddered. Then, from its depths, the enemy emerged.

The Dothemian line tensed as they came into view, but there was no time to study them. Just beyond the forest's edge, Amenophis gave the signal, and Xeyathi warriors, bolstered by Nakarran discipline, charged into the open fields without war cries, without words.

Thornsten whispered a prayer to the Mountain, Brynvi joined her husband, her voice low but steady. They watched and readied, sharing glances with Setna and Tumahn. Together they lifted their bows and took aim. The Dothemian archers followed. Their longbows were thick, their archers trained and strong. They were bows of the Càrnothi and Volkosi. Difficult to pull, but made to take down the vicious prey of those brutal lands, resulting in a longer range.

Setna gave the command and fired. The Dothemian volley followed. Arrows whistled and arced into the silence, descending onto raised shields. Wounds were taken by the enemy. Some fell, but many continued.

The Xeyathi and Nakarran archers returned fire. Dothemian shields rose in response. Most arrows fell short. Amenophis swore and cursed. Turadaj's eyes narrowed.

"Calm yourself, Amenophis," he warned.

Amenophis raised an arm, a horn sounded, and the Xeyathi broke into a sprint. They were known for their speed and closed in quickly.

Another command was given, and the Dothemian arms lowered in unison, followed by the release of another volley. The Xeyathi split, forming single lines led by a shield bearer. Numerous arrows struck the ground where charging warriors once stood. The rest slammed into shields. Once the volley passed, the Xeyathi broke out of their columns and once again formed a rushing wall. Doubling their speed as they ran.

Dothemides stepped forward, his presence cutting across the Dothemian line. Bianzhi raised her blade. Ailis tightened her grip, lifted her shield, and struck the face of it with her axe. As the sharp crack rang out, she began to chant, and from the ranks, others lifted their voices to join her. The chant rolled like thunder.

Dothemides raised his shield and charged, Bianzhi to his right, Ailis to his left. Larastus and Agatir moved wide to the flanks. Sunh and Nelah pressed close alongside them, and the Dothemian vanguard followed, their voices rising together.

The weapons rose. The distance between fell away. The lines collided. They struck not as scattered warriors but as a single spear, driven into the heart of the enemy.

There was no chaos under Dothemides' command—only a fierce, cold rhythm. Bianzhi moved like water made flesh, cutting through foes with fluid, relentless precision, sidestepping an airborne warrior and lifting her blade along his exposed flank, sending a spray across the field.

The bodies of allies and enemies closed tight. Ailis lifted her shield, deflecting a spear thrust. She twisted and brought her axe down, separating the spearhead from the shaft. The backswing that followed opened the throat of the warrior whose form fell out of sight. She felt him beneath her feet as she stepped on and over him before he was trampled by the feet of soldiers who followed.

Dothemides did not fight with ease. He had seen the season of the Mother come and go fifty-five times in his life, but he fought with the efficiency of a man who had long ago made peace with bloodshed. A man who had seen numerous battlefields and lived.

The Xeyathi were reckless and wild, their movements predictable. If he was going to make it through this battle, he would need to move with precision. Reserve his energy. Watch. Wait. Strike.

A desperate lunge came at him, he turned his body sideways, and watched the spearhead slip past his chest, skimming across his breastplate's surface. Righting his position, he raised his blade and allowed the momentum of his enemy to simply fall onto it. Pulling it free, he moved on. Another strike, high and off balance, he ducked, breathed, raised his shield and stood, pressing up with his legs. The Xeyathi's legs left the ground, his body tossed and turned, until he impacted the ground behind him, and Dothemian spears finished him.

The Xeyathi, seasoned though they were in jungle skirmishes, quickly understood why their kin had lost ground to Dothemia in the south these past years. Agatir, Larastus, Sunh and Nelah lead the flanks. The Càrnothi were brutal and gave no quarter. Any foe who sought to flank the tip of the spear was put down by Dothemia's archers.

Through it all, Amenophis stood and watched. His lieutenants stood with him, untouched. And once the field was thick with blood, once the Xeyathi's charge faltered, Amenophis gave a new signal.

Retreat.

His Nakarran soldiers rushed forward, covering the Xeyathi's withdrawal, fighting enough to be seen, but never committing to true engagement. Many Xeyathi stopped to drag their fallen kin back and were aided by their Nakarran allies.

Dothemides made no call to pursue. The Dothemian line held. Ailis, breathing hard, stood red with enemy blood, her shield battered and scarred. Bianzhi remained by the king's side, her blade painted crimson.

Dothemides scanned the field, eyes sharp. Larastus was too far out, but alive. Agatir was closer, with Sunh and Nelah nearer still. Their faces were wild and bright with the blood-fury of the Càrnothi. They paced, weapons gripped tightly, fighting the urge to pursue as they roared at the retreating forces.

Sunh spoke first, her voice raw.

"Why are we letting them go? We should kill them where they stand!"

Larastus spoke next. "Sunh is right," he watched them shrinking in the distance. "We still have a chance to catch them."

From the walls came a voice, thick with the accent of the Volkosi and full of laughter. Setna called down to the Càrnothi, mocking their madness.

"There is no need to chase a dog with its tail between its legs! Let them run. Let them speak of what they saw and lick their wounds." Tumahn laughed and nodded in agreement.

Thornsten and Brynvi shared a glance, then looked out to where the Red Queen stood. Brynvi leaned close to her husband, murmuring, "She sang the old hymns. I didn't know she knew them."

Thornsten watched Ailis, radiant and alluring. It was clear he found her more than beautiful. "And she fought with a fury I didn't expect. Perhaps," he leaned towards his wife "there is more to her than the sounds we hear coming from the fortress each night..."

Brynvi smacked him across the chest, hard, but laughed. Thornsten joined her.

Through all the shared words and cheers of victory, Dothemides stood silent. He felt the pulse of his people and their triumph, but his concern only deepened. Finally, his voice rose above it all.

"This is not a victory... and we will not pursue," he said with a voice that carried across the field and commanded all ears. "They are not dogs. Their tails are not tucked. This was a test. The first winds of a rising storm." Dothemian defenders fell silent.

"The winds will rise again... and we must be ready."

The soldiers stilled, sobered by the weight of his words.

"Rest," he commanded. "Tonight, we honor the Mother in the temple." He turned only after the last of the enemy vanished into the forest edge.

"More lives will be lost before this is done. We will see that new life follows."

The field quieted. Bianzhi and Ailis came to his side, their presence steadying him as much as he steadied them. He looked to them and they to him, silent in shared understanding.

The day was won.

But Ailis knew in her heart, standing in the blood-washed field, that this was only the beginning.

"The scouts returned and left no room for doubt. This wasn't a raid or skirmish. A clutchless army from the east was on the move against Dothemia.

The scouts said the attacks came from the Jhandai coast. I had friends there. People I left behind. Catherine, Akha, Sina, Yendira, Akujin, Zenghis, and Arokoshin... So many. But each one was a stubborn soul.

They were part of the reason I didn't want to follow Dothemides when I first met him. We were living on our own, but I wanted to investigate the rumors we heard of a rising fortress past the jungles to the west. I encouraged them to come, but we had carved a life along the coastlands. We were its defenders against the Xeyathi. They wished no part of whatever it was that this fortress had to offer. I said my goodbyes and left. Aside from Arokoshin, there were no hard feelings. I just saw a future for myself that was beyond the coast.

But now this.

I won't be like Agatir, who left his own sister behind. I have to find them. So I told Dothemides and Ailis. They understood and offered to send soldiers. Ailis wished to come. But I thought it best to go alone. I know the jungle well and could slip through much more easily than a search party.

It's taken several days and several close calls, but I found their camp. A cave, deep in the Thornwilds, where we agreed to meet if things ever got bad. I used the forest call years ago, and I heard it sent back.

I found Catherine first, still beautiful as ever, still sharp as a dagger's edge. She was with Akha and Sina. It had been so long. But there was no time to reminisce. I told them we had to move and that they needed to come back to Dothemia with me, and that I would tell them everything later. If there is one thing we all shared in our pasts, it was trust.

They are packing their things, and we're about to head out. They said they know where the others could be hiding. I just hope they are safe.

Book of Bianzhi, Mountains Trial 32, Year 15

"We found Yendira, Akujin, Zenghis, and Arokoshin. Thank the gods our hiding places weren't found.

They spoke of the attack and how it came from the sea. Vordan ships. Hollow cursed bastards. Yendira said there is more to this war than the sword tribes, that there is an unseen hand guiding them.

It didn't take much to convince them that Dothemia was safer than out here.

Somehow, Arokoshin heard that I was queen. We were more than friends once, but we made our decisions. I left, he stayed, and that was that.

Tomorrow we leave for Dothemia, and hopefully we make it back in one piece."

Book of Bianzhi, Mountains Trial 34, Year 15

"We arrived this morning just before dawn. They couldn't believe what they were seeing or how people responded to me. It didn't matter. I am what I am. I have become what I've become, and now they are safe.

I brought them to Dothemides and Ailis. Both were relieved. It was good to see them. This was home and where I belonged.

And now my friends are here, like the family I'd almost forgotten, my brothers and sisters, sometimes more. It was good to know that they were now safe.

I stood tall as I spoke, offering their loyalty, their strength, their skill to Dothemia's defense. I don't usually act like that, but I wanted Dothemides to know just what they mean to me and for my friends to see what Dothemia means to me.

Long ago, when we sailed together in the service of the nation of Jhandai, I promised them I would always be there for them, even when I left.

Yen and Cat are knocking at my door. I hear them talking on the other side of it.

My friends are safe, Dothemia is stronger for it, and I am at peace despite the rough waters ahead."

Book of Bianzhi, Mountain's Trial 40, Year 15

"Another moment alone with my thoughts. Seven days ago, thank the Mother, Bianzhi returned, and with her, seven warriors from the Jhandai coast. They look to be a force, both capable and fiercely loyal to her. They are trusted by her, and so they are trusted by us all. Since their arrival, I've had a chance to speak with each and hear their tales.

The first is Catherine, a Durajani born of Skarn, as beautiful as Sunh. She says she was not born for the steppes but for the sea. She is a knife fighter with a fearlessness in her eyes, but like most Skarn, there is a quiet honor and bold spirit about her. She trekked across the highlands and traveled east, seeking the coast, and was taken in by the Jhandai. It was there that she met Bianzhi, and they have been friends since childhood.

Then there are Akah and Sina of Xeyath. I must admit, when I heard this, I was mistrustful, but again, Bianzhi's word is one thing I have never doubted. They are an older and a younger sister. Akah, the older, is protective of Sina. They know the eastern forests well, from the Thornwilds to the Woundwood and south to the Xeyathi Jungles. They hold no love for their own people and earned their brands for refusing to hunt for slaves when they came of age. They look like they have had their share of fights, side by side.

Arokoshin, Zenghis, and Akujin were the next introduced. Like Bianzhi, each was born in the nation of Jhandai. It became clear that Arokoshin held feelings for her. Something deep and long buried. They carried on like brothers, and it was clear they were close.

Yendira is striking and proud, the quiet heart of the group. Bianzhi sat close to Yendira as her story was shared. She told me that among the Jhandai, the name of Vordos carries a curse, spoken of in whispers. I've heard similar tales from Loreiaka in the past. That a pact with the Hollow tainted their lands, and those born of that nation carry that shadow with them.

The island nation of Jhandai is home to seafarers who patrol and protect their waters from Xeyathi raids to the west and Vordosi invasions to the north.

In a battle on the Vordai Strait, Bianzhi stood in command of one of the ships sent to repel a Vordan attack. The successful defense led to the capture of an enemy ship, and Bianzhi was commanded to have it burned with the crew aboard, but she refused.

In the battle, she crossed blades with a Vordan crewman. Yendira. Bianzhi said that in the clash, she saw only desperation and fear, not corruption and silence. As the commander of her vessel, Yendira was captured and brought aboard the ship Bianzhi commanded. In chains, Yendira pleaded with Bianzhi to spare her, explaining that she was untouched by the curse that had befallen Vordos and forced her to fight.

Bianzhi believed her and sought to speak to her commanders on her behalf. The order came down anyway and when Bianzhi repeatedly refused, she was branded and left on the Vordan vessel.

Those she found and brought back here were her crew, and each of them stood by her, and were cast adrift to the Durajan for their mutinous defiance. They bore the mark together, not in shame, but as a badge of honor.

To Yendira and the others, Bianzhi would always be their captain, so I do not need their oaths. They stand by her, and she stands with Dothemia. The chain of command is sacred, and Bianzhi has always held that line with honor.

She is a leader. I feel she always has been. So today, before all of our defenders, I granted her the title she deserves and one we now need, General of the Dothemian Army. She did not ask for it. She did not seek it. She simply earned it. As all true leaders do."

Book of Dothemides, Mountain's Trial 44, Year 15

"While Bianzhi organizes the defenses of the city, securing the walls, and placing her people where they are strongest, Ailis and I have turned our gaze outward. For days, we watched the walls, but there were no attacks. So we decided that the time for waiting was over.

With Nelah, Sunh, Larastus, and Agatir at our sides, we rode east into the jungles beyond the farmlands where we found a Xeyathi camp tucked within a basin of trees, their fires little more than coals. They never saw us coming.

I intended to capture at least one for questioning, but Sunh's blade moved faster than my orders. That, or she simply refused them. She struck them down without hesitation. Afterwards, as we set camp, she came to our tent.

The hour was late, and the fires burned low as Sunh entered. She did not speak at first, only knelt, her head bowed before us and waited. The Càrnothi never kneel, so I knew how deep her regret ran. She was forgiven and sent back to the others to rest.

Ailis now sleeps, and by the look of her, visions haunt her dreams. But my mind drifts to Umaru and the fact that I am grateful that she is not here to see the conflict.

I pray that she remains untouched by this war."

Book of Dothemides, Mountain's Trial 49, Year 15

Mountains Trial 50. The Jhandai Coast. Warcamp of Amenophis

Tables were littered with maps and cast aside weapons. Shed armor and clothes were left where they had fallen. Only the room bore witness. Witness to the sounds of her breath as she moved beneath him, to her dark hair spilling across the furs, to her slender waist gripped between his hands.

Amrahi sought to prove her loyalty and Amenophis sought to test it, and so it went, each morning—the rise, the rush, the release, and the calm that followed.

She watched as Amenophis moved from the bed without a word. Slipping his feet over the edge and drawing a worn cloth around his hips, he stood, walked, and seated himself at the wide table in the center of the room. His mind already moving to the day ahead. There he traced lines along the maps, weaving through the sketched rivers and jagged coastlines, marking routes that would carry his soldiers deeper into Dothemian territory.

A knock at the door. He remained focused or uncaring, Amrahi couldn't tell. She wrapped herself in a silken robe of Jhandai make and opened the door. A slave stood, not daring to speak. For a moment, she felt pity. She stepped aside and let him in. He entered, placed a simple platter of food on the table, and left without a word. Amenophis did not look up. He made no sign of acknowledgment. The life of those conquered by the Crusade was one of silence.

Amrahi closed the door behind and turned, pausing before returning to the bed, where she sat and watched him.

She would be more for him if he only allowed it. She would be fire, fury, and loyalty, all twined into one. But he came to her only for pleasure, for release, and his silence left her cold afterward. He planned and he plotted, carrying the burden of their conquest alone, but Amrahi burned with the need to be more than a moment's breath in his war.

Gathering herself, she crossed the room, lowering into a seat opposite him. Her movements were careful and measured. She chose her words with precision, breaking the brittle silence.

"I've walked among the Xeyathi warcamps along the beach and forest edge," she said, reflecting on her time among them. "They are both pleased... and impatient."

Amenophis did not look up, but she continued.

"They have taken warriors from the Dothemian farmlands, but they wish for more."

Still, he said nothing; the scratch of his dagger tip against the parchment was the only sound between them.

"They want to know when the next attack will be."

Without answering, he moved a small carved ship across one of the maps. She watched the slow, deliberate arc of his hand as the small wooden ship crossed the Wanehollow Peninsula, drifted through the Strait of Xeyath, and settled against the shores just south of the Green Reaches, east of Khadeyath Bay. He positioned it along a strip of coast where high cliffs loomed over narrow beaches.

He did not answer at first. He only half-glanced over his shoulder towards her.

To Amenophis, Amrahi was a Believer, nothing more. Faith alone was not enough. Faith could be broken, reshaped, or discarded. Faith must be tested, measured, and tempered. He found her alluring, yes, but allure was cheap.

What mattered was how long she would endure before the Creed truly took root. Until she became more. Even now, she was driven by vengeance, pride, and vendetta. Meaningless things. She was not ready. It was not her place to ask. It was his place to know.

He looked back to the map and spoke.

"The Dothemians chase ghosts in the jungle."

"Our ships have already moved downriver. A warcamp rises beyond the place the Dothemian captives call the Green Reaches. From there, the river villages will fall to us. The next blow will come from the south."

Amrahi leaned forward, her voice urgent now.

"I want to be part of it," she said with eagerness. "Not just here. Not just in this bed, Amenophis. Let me prove my loyalty where it matters most."

He had been dismissive of her since they first beached and claimed the coast. She was not included in anything other than negotiations with the Xeyathi tribes.

He lifted his gaze to her and for a moment, a thread of something almost human passed between them. A faint, thin smile curved his lips. Was it approval or amusement? She could not tell.

"You will have your chance soon, Amrahi," he said. "We sail today."

Relief, pride, and a burning determination filled her chest. She nodded, standing, almost in disbelief as she awaited further orders. "Thank you," She spoke plainly but sincerely. But he did not look at her again. Already, he was returning to his maps, his mind a thousand leagues ahead.

The dismissal stung. Her pride raged against it, but she swallowed the anger, folded it neatly within herself, and turned away. Gathering her things, she dressed in silence. She may as well have been alone in that room.

Amrahi reached for the door and turned. She was already gone from his mind. She stepped through and closed the door. As she walked through the camp, the men's eyes followed her. She ignored them all.

She thought of her past, of the kin she lost, of the blood she would avenge. Dothemia had taken much from her. Eleven years ago, her father and brother were slain. Survivors of that clash described their killers. A man of Marukh and a woman of Jhandai. Two who would become the Dothemian King and his Jade Queen. Now she would repay the debt in full. Let Amenophis use her as he pleased. He was the path to her vengeance.

And she would walk it without regret.

Mountain's Vigil 59. Dothemia's Eastern Wall

The farmlands east of Dothemia stretched wide under the grey morning sky, their edges pressed against the dense wall of the Xeyathi jungles. Patrols had been dispatched at first light to scout the perimeter, while along the three exposed flanks of the farmlands, walls of earth and sharpened stakes had been hastily raised.

Further still, Dothemides had sent others beyond the forests and ridges, to the cliffs that overlooked the Strait of Xeyath, new soldiers who had stitched themselves into the fabric of Dothemia's defense.

All were marksmen or hunters who stepped forward to defend the city: Anai and Hidraka of Shadur, Kaiba, a young huntress of Marukh, and Kikaru, a man of mixed blood, born of the Xeyathi and Jhandai. His gaze never wavered, and his bow never missed.

Together they emerged from the forest's edge, running steadily towards and past the gate and into the heart of the city. Heading past Sunh, Nelah, Larastus, and Agatir, the four entered the throne room as Ailis stepped around the table to greet them.

"What have you seen?"

Bianzhi and Dothemides moved closer to listen.

Kikaru was the first to speak. "Ships, downriver. Bearing dark sails and sleek hulls." Kaiba followed, "And a warcamp, dug deep into the cliff sides below."

The king and queens exchanged glances. Bianzhi pressed, "Anything else? How many ships?"

Kaiba continued, "Eight... perhaps ten."

"They carry a sizable force," said Hidraka.

Hearing the discussion, Sunh, Agatir, Nelah, and Larastus approached. They looked to one another, then to Nelah, who spoke for them. "Send us. Let us lead a group...set fire to their ships and camp."

Dothemides considered. The Càrnothi were not fond of sitting idle and waiting for an attack.

"To rush down and meet them in the open is too great a risk. Better to trust in our walls than risk your lives."

"I agree. We need everyone here." Bianzhi added.

Ailis stepped up. "We should clear the fields... bring in all patrols," Dothemides agreed, and sensing the unease of the Càrnothi, he continued.

"I don't doubt your courage or skill, but we will let them come to us." The four nodded.

Dothemides then looked to Kikaru and the scouts, "Thank you for this. Send word to the perimeter scouts to return and man the walls." He then looked to Nelah and the others, "Go and tell the defenders of the west gate to move to the east, and prepare."

With a nod, both groups left to carry out their orders.

Dothemides looked heavy with concern, confiding in his queens the questions plaguing him in the moment. "Why this? Why now?"

Ailis observed him. "In war, the why matters little. Only the how. How to survive. How to win." He listened as Bianzhi stepped close.

"Ailis is right. We will drive them back."

"You are both right," After a breath, he continued.

"Bianzhi, find Brynvi and Thornsten. We will still need eyes out there to bring word of the attack when our enemy is on the move." She nodded.

"Ailis, return to the front line and join the others. I will follow soon."

Before taking their leave, they paused, allowing the gravity of the situation to settle between them.

Now alone, in the quiet of the throne room, Dothemides turned to face the statue of the Mother. Umaru's words still lingered.

What of the others? Those left behind.

Her words made him wonder if his dream was the why.

What he's built...

What he's been blind to...

What Dothemia had become...

He closed his eyes to quiet the questions moving through his mind.

There was no room for doubt or fear. No place for regret or remorse. This was a war that had to be won. The Mother teaches of the balance of all things. The higher one climbs, the greater the risk of a fall. Dothemia has risen, and its enemies have taken notice. If this is a test of the Mother and Mountain, then so be it.

If the dream is to survive, Dothemia must endure.

Mountain's Vigil 60. Dothemia's Eastern Wall

That morning, the warning came.

Thorsten and Brynvi returned from their patrols, their faces grim and splattered with the dirt of a hard run. They found Bianzhi first, atop the walls, her hair braided back for war, her hand resting on the hilt of her blade.

"They're coming," Thorsten said, breathless.

"How many?" Bianzhi asked.

Brynvi answered, "More than the last time. Hundreds."

Bianzhi thanked them. They returned to their places on the wall and were welcomed by Tumahn and Setna. Across from them stood Kaiba, Anai, Hidraka, and Kikaru, whose eyes were fixed on the forest's edge.

Bianzhi turned from the wall and crossed back to where Dothemides and Ailis stood, surveying the preparations. Sunh, Agatir, Nelah, and Larastus waited nearby, their weapons ready, joined now by Catherine, Yendira, Akah, Sina, Arokoshin, Zenghis, and Akujin and others.

The defenders of Dothemia were gathered and ready.

As Bianzhi approached him, Dothemides read the news in her expression before she spoke and took a deep breath. The weight of command was heavy on his chest. His sword hand flexed once, then stilled, as Ailis, standing at his side, placed her hand over his. Her voice came softly. Words meant only for him.

"The Mother and the Mountain are with us."

Their eyes met and held for a moment. He knew today would test them. He only questioned what the cost would be.

Warcamp of Amenophis

The river winds buffeted the tents and banners, causing the fabric to snap like whips. Warriors stirred, woken before dawn by the call to arms. The air was heavy with tension as armor was strapped on and weapons were sheathed.

Amenophis was nowhere to be found among the preparations. Even now, before their march, he took his pleasures. Amrahi moved with him in the dim confines of their tent, offering herself with a passion that was as much about loyalty as it was faith.

Outside, as the sounds of Amenophis and Amrahi rose and reached their end, two guards watched as a new ship touched shore. One of them stepped in, letting Amenophis know of the approaching vessel, and was dismissed.

"Who are they?" Amrahi asked.

"Allies," he paused, "and strength enough to turn the tides of this battle. Come."

When the pair emerged, Amrahi followed, fastening the last buckles of her armor with quick, deft hands. Turadaj stood nearby, one hand lightly brushing the earth, listening to the hum of the land itself. Amenophis's closest soldiers paused at the passing of their commander and his warrior-consort, fists rising to their chests, and wearing expressions hardened by devotion.

Near the shoreline, a group of warriors gathered. At their lead, a man stepped forward, lifting his eyes to Amenophis. He was Vordan, broad-shouldered, his hair was black and trimmed short, he stood clad in steel, his face marked by war-runes that cut deep into coarse flesh. His weapon was a massive two-handed sword. They clasped hands.

"For the Creed," Amenophis said, voice low.

"For the Crusade," the Vordan answered with equal weight.

"It is good to see you." Amenophis turned and began to walk as Amrahi followed. The newcomer took her in, black eyes moving across her, void of want or judgment. Void of all feeling.

Amrahi stood unsettled beneath his presence as Turadaj stepped protectively close to her. The man looked at Turadaj and once again at her. Then, without any other form of acknowledgement, he turned towards Amenophis.

"I trust I didn't miss the battle." He asked.

"You are just in time." Amenophis responded as the two entered his tent.

"Who is he?" Whispered Amrahi.

“His name is Vragur.” Turadaj said with a pause, “And his presence and power are known.”

Amrahi and Turadaj fell into step together and entered the tent.

"First push at first light," Amenophis said to each of them, voice flat, final. “Today, we break the Dothemian line.”

The Second Assault

The battle began as the last had. There was no roar, no crash. Amenophis’ forces stormed the farmland defenses in silence. Waves of Xeyathi tribesmen emerged. Behind them came the Nakarran Crusaders. But Dothemia was ready.

Arrows darkened the sky. Spears bristled along the walls. Dothemides watched it unfold with cold calculation, calling commands with clarity and presence.

The first wave broke upon the walls like a storm surge against a cliff. Two hours of brutal fighting, neither side yielding, neither gaining.

Amenophis narrowed his eyes from the ridgeline. He raised his hand in signal, a swift downward cut through the air. Horns blared. Runners called orders, and his forces pulled back, battered but not broken.

The beach swarmed with the wounded. Yet Amenophis’s gaze was calm, already moving to the next play. He turned toward Vragur and nodded once.

The third assault would not be a simple charge. They had tested the full might of the Dothemian defense, and now, they would strike at the heart.

The Third Assault

The sun had begun its slow descent by the time the third assault came. A heavy, oppressive heat clung to the air, thick with smoke from watchfires set to illuminate the forest edge, and the copper tang of blood. Dothemides stood atop the walls, his sword resting in its sheath, watching the rows of the enemy line form anew. They were no longer a wild rush, but a focused, driven force. They advanced not as a mob but as a sharpened spear.

"This will be different," Dothemides said stoically, as he stood alongside Bianzhi and Ailis.

From behind the main line, Amenophis moved.

He had been patient. Now, with Amrahi at one flank, Turadaj at the other, and Vragur towering beside him, Amenophis signaled the push. As one, his forces began at a trot, then a run. No voices rose in the growing darkness; only their footfalls could be heard.

"It is a strange thing to see a force of such size move so silently." Tumahn listened to Setnah as they watched together.

Dothemides called out over the field, his voice cutting through. Ailis at his left, Bianzhi at his right, they moved as one, leading as the Dothemia's soldiers formed into a wedge behind them. Dothemides ran hard and heavy, and as their voices rose, roaring against the approaching silence. Time slowed for him, and for a moment, it was as if he felt everyone around him.

Bianzhi, his closest and most trusted, her curved blade rising. Ailis, her war chants echoing as her crimson hair trailed behind. Her axe held high, her shield held before her. Sunh's eyes blazed with rage, as did those of Nelah, Agatir, and Larastus.

From the wall, arrows felled foes, shot by the skilled hands of those he met long ago: Thornsten, Brynvi, Tumahn, and Setna. While warriors of the Jhandai coast charged in alongside them.

His legs burned, his blade and shield felt heavy, the enemy closed in, and darkness was falling. All around him, Dothemides felt the strength of those brought together by a dream born of hope. Their voices were a song lifted to the Mother, their battle cries were worship, and their blood was sacrifice.

Fifteen years ago, he was dying alone and forgotten, and today, though he may die, he would not die alone. He would die with those who believe as he does. Those who believe that their lives are sacred and their struggles are holy.

The forces clashed, and brutality followed.

Sunh and Nelah were locked in vicious skirmishes along the flanks, their Càrnothi blood stirring a ferocity that sent the enemy reeling. Agatir fought nearby, his shield locked tight against his body, pressing forward with all the strength he could summon. Bianzhi cleaved the raised arm from an enemy with a swift arc as Ailis' shield shattered the nose and jaw of an enemy in a single, crushing blow.

Scattered fighting erupted across the fields. Groups of enemy soldiers surged between the formations, cutting, harrying, and forcing gaps.

As the battle waged on, the enemy did not press to breach the walls. They pushed inward, toward him, seeking to draw Dothemides away from the main body, hoping to divide and disorient, but their discipline held.

Amidst the chaos, Ailis felt it first. A coolness against the skin and a pull at her spirit, as if the ancestors themselves whispered in warning. She turned sharply, her shield raised, seeking the source. The world narrowed around her, the clash of battle dulled, the roar of soldiers faded into an aching silence, and for a moment, her voice faltered as the familiar presence of the ancestors grew still.

Having slipped back behind the clashing lines, Turadaj stood, his bow drawn. The arrow loosed without a sound.

Ailis looked across the field, heart racing. Where had they gone? A single line traced through the air. The arrow whistled. The arrow struck. Ailis staggered back. She looked down, disbelief flashing across her face as she saw the shaft buried deep in her side, and her blood flowing against her leathers. She sank to one knee, breath catching as her shield slipped from her grasp.

Bianzhi cried out, rushing to her side. Dothemides pivoted; his focus was singular, but memory took over. His shield raised to deflect, his sword sank deep into flesh as enemies fell about him. His heart hammered against his ribs, but he kept his mind clear.

He looked towards where the arrow could have come from, but Turadaj had retreated into the forest's edge. Amrahi watched from the rise, measuring the enemy captains, her bow in hand, an arrow knocked, but she waited. Watching not Ailis, not Bianzhi, but the wall itself. Amenophis would be a target for Dothemia's archers. She would not allow him to fall.

Above, Thorsten raised his bow, sighted Amenophis among the enemy ranks, and took aim. Before the arrow flew, a shaft pierced his thigh, sending the shot wide. He fell to one knee, unable to stand.

Setna, atop the ramparts, shouted orders, raising her bow. Brynvi called to her, pointing. Both archers fired, and their arrows streaked toward Amenophis. They would have struck true, but one of his soldiers, loyal beyond sense or reason, stepped into their paths and fell.

Amenophis did not slow. Ailis sagged in Bianzhi's arms, her lips pressed tight against the pain. Dothemides barked commands, and defenders formed a shield around her. Sunh and Nelah fought like wild things, carving a bloody swathe through the attackers. Still, the enemy came, relentless.

And there, apart from the others, Larastus stood.

Vragur hoped to separate the Dothemian king and kill him before his army, but this one, clearly one of their most formidable, would send a message.

Larastus had moved too far, pulled away in the confusion. Once again, he fought without discipline and broke ranks in his bloodthirst, and now he faced Vragur alone.

The warlord was wrapped in blackened steel, his massive blade cleaving the air with brutal grace. Larastus braced, shield high, axe ready. When they clashed, the sound was sharp and ringing.

Larastus struck low, feinting, then struck up with his shield. Vragur evaded the attempt, caught his wrist, and twisted sharply. The resulting crack forced a cry from the Càrnothi as bone protruded from broken flesh.

A sweep of the leg, and a brutal pommel strike to the temple followed. Larastus staggered but didn't fall. He circled, breathing hard, blood in his eyes as his shield hung uselessly in his shattered arm. Through pain and disbelief, he lunged again, his axe aimed at the warlord's side, but Vragur spun with a terrible grace and delivered a crushing backhand with the full weight of his armored fist. Bone splintered, and Larastus reeled.

The final blow came swiftly as Vragur raised his sword in a high, sweeping arc, then brought it down with finality. Blood arced in a spray against the trampled earth, as Larastus fell to his knees, hands slack at his sides, and his blade forgotten. He looked up, unafraid, but silent. No roar of defiance. No cry of rage. Only a grim, hollow stillness.

Vragur raised his sword, paused, and plunged it through his chest. The sound was thick and wet. Bone cracked beneath torn flesh. And through it all, Larastus made no sound.

Soon, Amenophis sounded the retreat, a sharp call that rang through the carnage. His forces broke away in groups, slipping back toward the tree line, battered but not broken. Amrahi and Turadaj followed, bloodied but alive. Vragur stalked back with them, his blade still red.

As the Nakarran forces retreated into the darkness, Turadaj, Amrahi, and Vragur stood by Amenophis, who watched and said with a smile.

"Tonight, they will wonder who won this battle, and by dawn, they will wonder if they can win this war."

Dothemides watched the four leaders slip away into the darkness before being brought back to the silence that had fallen over the battlefield. He hurried to Ailis' side as she clung to consciousness, cradled and cared for by Bianzhi. She was pale with blood loss and gripping Bianzhi's hand tightly in pain.

Atop the wall, Thornsten lay in Brynvi's arms as the barbed arrow lay buried deep in his leg. As the silence gave way to the groans of the wounded and dying, Dothemides called to others, telling them to coordinate help.

Larastus' brutalized body was retrieved and carried back by Agatir and Nelah with a solemnity that shattered the heart. His death weighed on them more heavily than mere loss; it was the manner of it. The Càrnothi did not die in silence. They died screaming in defiance. They died with the Mountain's roar in their throats, not like this. It was a death that would haunt them, and while Dothemia had held, the cost had been high.

"Last night I stood on the battlements, watching the pyres burn across the fields, feeling the weight of the dead press down. Prayers rose to the Mother, pained voices lifted in songs meant to reach the Far Sky.

Ailis will live, thank the Mother. I stayed by her with Bianzhi until I was told that she would be alright. Bianzhi is still with her. I checked on

Thornsten. He will recover, and Brynvi remains by his side. I was told the wounded will heal, but some may never be able to fight again.

The people believe we've won. But I cannot call this a victory. Did we drive them back or just survive? I needed to think.

But as I walked alone through the streets, I could feel their eyes on me. I was their king, and I needed to be a pillar for them. I had taken on this mantle, but inside my thoughts rolled, and in that moment, I felt stretched thin.

What brought this wrath upon us, upon our city, upon my dream? Was it hubris?

There are so many that I cherish. So many that I love and honor and wish to protect.

I am alone in my chamber now. The palace is silent, but my mind isn't.
To quiet this chaos, I need to listen to my heart.
Go where the Mother leads me.

All I see is Umaru. I miss her. I miss the peace she brings. The clarity her presence provides. I need to know she is safe. I can no longer wait for our paths to find one another. Our enemy has not attacked in days. But if they come again, I could fall in the next battle.

I have to find her, ask for her hand, and pray she accepts. To wait is to risk too much.

I also know that the time has come. I have waited long enough, and I can no longer hold on to Bianzhi and Ailis. They will accept. They know my heart. I do not know if Ailis will remain after she recovers, but I know Bianzhi will. The Mother requires balance in all things. There can be no joy without sorrow. No love without loss.

I don't want to cause pain to anyone, but I have to listen to what my heart tells me.

When the attacks first began, I sent scouts north of Hollowwind Pass in the hopes of finding Samike's home. A mission no one knew about.

She'd gone north to find Stigandr, and though she is no longer my queen, I am concerned for her safety.

There is much to be done. Tomorrow, I will set it all in motion."

Book of Dothemides, Mountain's Vigil 63

Mountain's Vigil 63. Jhandai Coast. Warcamp of Amenophis

Dothemia's might had been tested. Their weight was measured. The blood soaked into their walls and soil would not soon be washed away.

Amenophis had done what was required of him. Now it was time to send word. Time to plan. Time to prepare.

"I've been living in the steppes for years now. Just Stigandr, Sittrika, and I. Away from what remains of the clans, Dothemian trade routes to Fort Koba and Haphira, and the conflicts between them. So it was a surprise to see Dothemian scouts arrive bearing a message that Dothemides wished to see me.

I agreed, of course. I didn't know what to expect. Then, days later, he came. Alone. He was dressed in armor, scarred and worn but crafted in a manner befitting a king.

But as I invited him in, I saw in him the weight he carried. A fatigue worn more plainly than the steel of his armor. I know how long he has walked this world, fifty-five turns of the seasons, and I saw the age in his gaze.

He greeted Stigandr. They clasped hands. There was no animosity. Only the warm smile of men who love and once loved the same woman, then Stigandr lifted Sittrika and gave Dothemides and I some time alone.

Dothemides told me that he was concerned for my safety and relieved to see that my family and I were well. Then he told me about the war that had come to Dothemia and the silent army that fought alongside the Xeyathi and of their black sails and sleek ships. He spoke to me of the lives lost, the warlord who leads them, and the man who killed Larastus. He told about how he died with no scream on his lips and that he fell to a wordless warrior who fought with unnatural strength.

The news, the war, the loss, Larastus' death. It shook me to my core and led me to the realization that my worst fears for Dothemia had come to pass.

I had seen such warriors before, in service to King Aguran. Hollowed out by devotion, by a doctrine that feeds on certainty and surrender. I knew then, the enemy Dothemia faced—the Nakarran Crusade.

I blamed myself. For years, I worried, but knew that nothing could change Dothemides' path. Dothemia had grown too strong. The Mother's voice reached too far, and the Creed could not allow it.

As I sat and listened, I knew I had to tell him everything. So I did.

Who I had once been, who I had served, the names, the places, the rituals...

I told him that I had walked among them, not just as a follower, but as one trusted and on the path to becoming a Believer.

But I also told him of their structure, their instincts, the hunger they mask as prophecy. I told him that I wanted to help him, to come to Dothemia and do what I could by offering my knowledge.

Dothemides didn't speak for a time. In my confession lay the answers to so many questions. Then he asked why I didn't say anything before, and I told him that I was afraid. Not of him, but of what it may mean to others. That I didn't want to cast a shadow on his dream.

Stigandr came downstairs and sat with us. He had been listening, I saw the love in him, and heard no hesitation in his voice when he said he would come. But when he said that the spirits told him that I must seek the southern sun before it is cast into darkness, I knew in my heart that it was the right thing.

My mother bore a name and a belief that led her beyond the nation's borders and into the arms of my father. Those who sought the flames of their hearts were called the *Sul'sahir*, Sun Seekers. It was as if she were speaking through him.

I asked Dothemides again to let me help, and he agreed.

Tomorrow, we will close and fortify our home and return to Dothemia."

Book of Samike, Mountain's Vigil 68, Year 15

"Together we arrived. Stigandr, Sittrika, and I. We came not as guests of honor, but as something far more complicated, necessary allies in a war that burns toward the heart of Durajan.

Dothemides gave us a home. A guarded one. A quiet structure tucked behind a well-patrolled street, and soldiers assigned to ensure our peace.

I know the truth of it. He does not command the wholeness of his people's hearts, the glances they give, and the feelings they hold deep inside. It is clear that to many, I am not welcome here. I see it in the way they look at me, like a tear in the tapestry of their memories.

And my children. They have grown so much. When I saw them, all kept their distance. All save Kaelani, who embraced me, despite the anger and tears in her beautiful eyes.

I am the mother who left her children, and the Queen who left her king and her people. But I return, not to reclaim or to apologize, but to help, and that seems to confuse them more than anything else.

Bianzhi welcomed me with that quiet strength I remembered so well, but I saw in her eyes the weight of the years between us. I was once her queen. She was once my protector. And I left her behind. She hasn't said it aloud. She hasn't needed to. I know what I took from her. Still, she welcomed me. The one named Ailis did not.

She was kind by the thinnest thread of civility. But her gaze cut like the cold northern winds. She stood beside Dothemides, proud, powerful, red as wrath, and recovering from a wound to her side. She made no effort to hide her disdain. I don't blame her.

She and Bianzhi both stood by him in the silence I left behind. That silence never suited him, and they filled it with loyalty and love. I see that now, though I feel that something frays at its edges.

Planning has begun, and we meet often in chambers scattered with maps and reports. I bring what I can, knowledge of Nakarran rituals, their officers, their instincts. Things I swore I'd buried.

The people do not cheer my name. There are no salutes when I pass. But Dothemides trusts me, and that is enough.

Let them hate and whisper. But let them remember that I came back when I was needed."

Book of Samike, Mountain's Vigil 72, Year 15

"Dothemides told us with the honesty of a man who still believed the truth was owed, even when it wounded. As he spoke of Umaru and what she had become to him, his voice did not waver, and his gaze did not lower.

Bianzhi and I both knew long ago. But I imagine it was the finality of the moment. The gentle, yet definitive declaration.

She was silent, but I saw the way her jaw clenched, the way her fingers twitched before she steadied them. But then she stepped forward with grace. She said she understood. That she would remain by his side. And she meant it.

I said the same. And I almost meant it.

We shared one last night together. Hoping to drown old scars and relive once held warmth. But we were like ghosts lying together beneath a familiar roof. Nothing but fragments of memory and echoes of spirit.

I watched them as the firelight faded. I lay awake knowing that the only wound that would one day truly heal was the one I suffered in battle. I let the silence wrap around me like a final embrace, and in the hours before dawn, I rose and readied myself.

No note or goodbye. No anger or sorrow. Only the quiet of my steps across the stones. Only calm as I let fall between my fingers, what little remained between us.

My time there had come to an end, and I left not because I was cast aside, but because the wind called me elsewhere. To the storm I released. To the dreams that returned each night since doing so. Dreams of amethyst eyes, fire, and a path of vengeance carved in blood and belief. Dreams of Svirva.

The steppes are quiet, and I am tired. The night air, calm. But the spirits welcome me. Sitting here and there alongside me, warming themselves by the fire of life that I represent, as I warm myself by my campfire.

Dothemides has chosen his future. I must now walk into mine and answer, once again, to the Mother and Mountain.

It is I who is now free, and where they lead me, I will follow."

Book of Ailis, Mountain's Vigil 74, Year 15

"This morning on the eastern wall just before dawn, Bryn and I were watching the ridgeline. We'd been up most of the night and were looking forward to some rest. There had been no movement. No attacks for days. We were thankful.

The jungles beyond were loud. Nothing like the steppes, where only the rare wolf howl or mammoth's cry was heard at night. This was a ceaseless chorus, layered, living. More alive in darkness than in daylight.

Then it shifted. It was hard to say whether something moved through the noise or whether the noise itself retreated. Like the whole wild bent to make way. A rush of wind, but not wind. A pressure and stillness that I felt in my bones. Then it passed, and the sounds returned, as if nothing had happened.

Setnah and Tumahn came to relieve us soon after. We told them to stay sharp. That something wasn't right out there.

Bryn didn't like it. Neither did I. Maybe it was just the forest and this war, playing tricks on us."

Book of Thornsten, Mountain's Vigil 74, Year 15

"Dothemides is a good man. Troubled with a heart pulled in too many directions for one person to bear. So when he told us of his intention to marry Umaru, I saw it as him setting himself free. Free to love someone who changes him each time she is near, in ways that neither Ailis nor I have or could.

But when Dothemides and I woke to see Ailis gone, we both understood. Neither of us could begrudge her. She was someone I cared deeply for. Someone I loved. But, something inside me knew she belonged more to things that I could not understand than to me or even to him. I have lost before. I will lose again. But I have gained as well.

As for his decision?

I have been by his side for eleven years, crossed the Durajan with him, fought by him, and laughed with him. For four of those years, I stood by him as queen, and now I stand as his general. Dothemides changed my life. I could never begrudge him.

But the matter at hand remained. Ailis was gone, and despite what we felt, questions lingered. We were at war with an unknown enemy, and we needed those questions answered. We needed to be sure.

Scouts were sent, and reports gathered from watchers on the walls, who were present on the morning of her disappearance. There was no sign of her departure, no trace of her passing in the wilderness.

Today is the third day since then, and the search and concerns of the people have delayed his departure to find Umaru, but I told him to focus on her. We both knew that Ailis was not coming back and that there was nothing either of us could do. He left this morning.

I went to the temple tonight and prayed for his safe return and for Ailis' safe journey. There is a strange peace in knowing she's chosen her own path and he has chosen his.

But I will miss her and I will miss him."

Book of Bianzhi, Mountain's Silence 77, Year 15

"The days have been long here. The kind of long that lives in your bones. We've built this place on laughter that often masks the ache of hands blistered from work. This was my sanctuary. My purpose. My hope. And now he stood within it.

I was in the courtyard when I saw him. Dust clung to his boots. His steed had been ridden hard. The sun caught the edges of his armor as he dismounted with Cepharion's reins in his hand. For a moment, I thought I was dreaming, that the heat and my longing had conjured him from the edge of the road. But it was real. He came to me. My Russom. My heart.

Aristaeus, Halista, and Phara were warm and welcoming. While Anaeix, Eligal, Ulaka, and Khasun greeted their king with pride and duty. Aside from them, the reception was mixed. Those who had settled here kept their distance. The weight of their wariness was clear.

I took his hand, and he held my face in his palm. We walked together to my cabin. He wasted no time. His voice trembled when he spoke, not with weakness, but with a kind of rawness I've only seen once before, when he first kissed me beneath the jungle canopy.

He told me everything. Of the war. Of the silence I'd mistaken for forgetting. I felt foolish for it.

He spoke of fear, of losing me, of losing himself. He told me of the nights he thought of me, and the mornings he feared I would no longer return. He told me of the queens, of Ailis' departure, of Bianzhi's steadiness, and Samike's arrival. But he said that although each of those things meant more to him than words could describe, what mattered most to him was me.

And then, with that same voice, rough, steady, and full of both guilt and longing, he asked me to be his queen.

I said yes, without hesitation. Not because I am naive or blind, but because I know what lives in him. I know what tears at him. I know what he's done, and what he is trying to undo. Most of all, I know now that I belong with him.

We held each other, his guilt and my hope stitched together.

The next morning, Russom shed his armor and weapons and approached those who toiled together to build our sanctuary. It was silent as he approached them. They watched as he lifted a hammer, strapped on a belt of tools and nails, lifted a beam of wood, and stood before a fence in need of repair. In the silence, his hammer struck, and he began to work.

In that moment, I hoped they would embrace him. Prayed they would stand by him. Aristaeus, Phara, Halista, Eligal, and the Dothemian guards, we all watched.

Then, someone stepped forward. His name was Ayintananga. He was a former Khandar and a man of great size. He, like many, was wary of Dothemia and their king. But unlike many, he came to my sanctuary with his tribe and with hope.

As he stood by Russom, Russom looked up at him as if awaiting judgment. A nod was offered from Ayintananga. A gesture that left Russom on the verge of tears as he returned it with humility and gratitude. Then they began to work together, and others followed.

He stayed for three nights, not in the central home but in one of the worker shelters. And throughout his stay, Russom helped mend tools, sat at fires, and listened to stories from those who dared speak. But still, not all chose to.

Eyes watched from windows and doorways. The same people who trusted me to lead them now whispered behind closed doors. They see the man who marched armies across their homelands. The man whose choices left them orphaned or displaced, and I understand. But I knew they also saw a man seeking to repair what had been broken. A man still driven by his dream.

One night, as I walked alone, I heard them. Whispers in the dark, carrying uncertainty. I approached them and chose to speak.

I told them I understood. I said that Russom understood. That he knows the cost of his dream. Knows what was left behind. That he supported me in my dream and that he carried his shame with a quietness that tore at him daily.

I let them know that he is a man who still believes in building something better and becoming someone better. Then I asked them not to forget what was lost, but not to let it blind them to what might still be built.

"Forgive him," I said. "Not because he asks for it. But because I do."

I looked each one of them in the eye and told them that I love him, and believe that what we can build now is not just for those who follow me or him, but for all of us. We are not here to forget. We are here to remember, to heal, and to create a Dothemia that is not just a fortress of stone and palace of glory, but a home of belonging where all can rest.

Before I left their quiet circle, I saw a change in them.

Russom came to me not as a king, but as a man. And I met him not as the girl from the sands, but as the woman I've become.

And now together, we will walk forward."

Book of Umaru, Mountain's Silence 79, Year 15

"Plans continue while Dothemides was away. Rumors stir, and morale is frayed with all of this uncertainty. Ailis is gone, Samike is here. Dothemides rode west in search of Umaru, and enemies could attack at any moment. It was a lot, but we had to move forward.

I was no longer queen, but I was appointed general, so I called a council. We needed to know what our enemy was planning. We knew where they were, but we needed to understand their movements. I called for Cat and Yen; they knew the coastlands the most. In addition to them, I gathered Tumahn, Thorsten, Brynvi, Setna, and Kikaru to join them. They were our fastest. We had just begun planning when Samike entered.

Whether it was her audacity, her beauty, or the sheer presence she carried, the room fell still. Every head turned as she came up the stairs and entered the throne room.

Agatir stood alongside Sunh and Nelah at the front. His expression was unreadable. Not everyone there knew that he was once her Chosen. Their eyes met only briefly. Sunh and Nelah watched her with indifference. Setna and Tumahn were tense. They didn't quite know how to feel about her. Didn't seem to like that she was here.

Samike wore a fitted leather chest plate that clung to her like a second skin, a high-cut battle cloth with armored thigh guards, bracers on her wrists, and boots worn from the road. Her arms were bare, and her hair was pulled back in braids. Those storm-gray eyes, sharp and unreadable. And her armor? It complemented every damn near-perfect curve of her body. Functional, yes. But you'd be a fool not to notice the way it both concealed and revealed, just enough to protect, just enough to turn heads. She didn't dress to be admired. She dressed to be seen and heard. And it worked.

She walked past Nelah and Sunh without a word and joined us at the table's edge. Samike was always small in stature, but the space bent around her like a tide drawn in. There was silence for a moment. Then, she spoke.

She said that she knew what we were planning. How? I have no idea, but she said that no one in that room should risk capture. She studied the map and spoke her plan without pause, to infiltrate the Nakarran camp herself. Alone.

Samike believed she could gain the trust of their commander, find his weaknesses, and exploit them in order to open a path for Dothemia to strike at the heart.

There were murmurs, laughter, scoffs, and accusations that she was trying to regain favor, perhaps the King's affection, now that Ailis was gone. That she came to unseat Umaru. But she didn't respond. She didn't need to. She stood in silence until her eyes met mine, and in that stare, I saw her resolve.

I raised my hand and told everyone to quiet down and let her finish, and she did.

She told us that she was raised among the Creed. This alone sent shock throughout everyone. I had no idea. But she gave no room for questions or debate.

She stated that she understood the Crusade and Creed in ways no one else here did and that she would use that knowledge against them. She said she couldn't wait for Dothemides to return because time was a luxury Dothemia no longer had. She would go now. When more questions rose, Samike spoke with a clarity and conviction that could not be silenced. She explained Dothemides' visit, their conversation, and her confession, using the fact that he invited her here as proof of her intent's purity.

The words carved something from me. But her eyes have always been my weakness. The eyes of a woman I had once believed in became the eyes of a woman I believed in once again. When she was done, I gave my answer. I would allow it.

By dawn, the next day, we stood on the banks of the river. Samike stood by the reedship she requested. Jhandai would never be caught dead in one of those, but it's what she insisted on having for reasons of her own.

She said farewell to her husband and embraced their son. From the shore, Tananda, Kanike, and Omanessi stood watching, but only Kaelani stepped forward. They whispered to one another, too far for me to hear. She touched her daughter's cheek, then boarded.

Agatir waded in and watched her. His feelings for her were still there. She touched his scarred hand and kissed his burned cheek before he shoved her reedship out to sea with eyes filled with worry. Then Samike settled in, raised her small sail, and looked back at us on the shore.

Our eyes met, and something tightened in my chest as she began her slow sail east.

It was always my duty to protect her. At least it had been in the past, but as her ship shrank in the distance, I prayed to the Mother that I had not just sent her to her death."

Book of Bianzhi, Mountain's Silence 81, Year 15

THE BOOK OF NAKARRA

Chapter 1

Verse 3

Nakarra saw that life always ended in sorrow and death. Beasts preyed upon man, and man preyed upon their own kind in an endless cycle of both hunger and savagery.

Verse 4

Nations rose with pride and resistance to all. A pride that would lead to bloodshed. There was only peace in the stillness Before. Peace in letting go of what drove all to such cruelty.

Mother's Hand 27

Long before Amenophis moved against Dothemia, the Creed had dispatched a parallel contingent—a secondary axis of the campaign, less visible but no less deliberate. If Amenophis was the tip of the spear, this was the haft: sent not to strike, but to steady, to hold, and to make ready what would follow.

From the time when his ships first found the Jhandai coast, before his forces first moved against Dothemia, they traveled by sea. They passed through the Xeyandai Strait, skirting the Sea of Hollows, and landed at Keyadeth Bay near the edge of the Silent City. From there, they crossed the Khadari Desert and Sifur's Breath, advancing steadily into the southern savannah to establish a forward presence in the region.

Maw's Hunger 16. The City of Ralmasandir

They arrived in the city of Ralmasandir, nestled deep in the western savannah. It has always carried a shadowed reputation. It stands as a hub, bridging the western nations with the outer reaches of the Durajan. Some say it was founded by Ralmasan, a betrayed king of Marukh, murdered by his own brother. No one knows for certain. The city does not answer questions. It profits from them.

Ralmasandir welcomes all but serves none. It maintains the pretense of neutrality, though it has long been known to turn a blind eye to the branded, so long as the price is paid. It is home to slavers and thieves, mercenaries and informants, raiders and hunters of men.

Information and rumors flow there like water through woodland rivers, flowing from the lips of wanderers who spread tales of both the Nine and the Durajan.

Here, the Crusade learned of a battle brewing in the east, where the Dothemian king faces the people of the jungles and their unknown allies, and of a girl from Khadar, Durajani-born, who is said to hold some tie to that same king.

Conversations then shifted to rumors of the northlands, where they speak of the Càrnothi being hunted and of the bodies left to rot beneath the snow.

Maw's Feast 30. The Valley of Tharioc

From Ralmasandir, Crusade forces moved north through the Valley of Tharioc and into Tharios, where they met with King Aguran. The meeting was brief and transactional.

Support was offered. A path to end their civil war and an answer to Aguran's prayers. They had come to free him. To free their city from itself and promised the fall of his brother and rival, King Agustus.

The assault came swiftly and decisively, and with the aid of the Creed, House Agustus stood no chance.

His banners were torn down. His rule was declared illegitimate. The Creed gave its blessing, and Aguran's throne was secured. One that Aguran declared himself and Tharios as now and forever devoted to the Creed.

Agustus had already suffered the banishment of his beloved son. Now he, his family, and his loyalists were driven from the capital. Among the others banished were Queen Photini, Princess Androniki, their guards, Dracca, Graccus, and Appia, and all who had once stood beside his son, Aristaeus.

Each of them was a veteran and a survivor, no longer welcome in the city they helped defend. None were spared the brand, not even their daughter.

What remained of the fallen house turned south, wandering and searching for shelter, for allies, and for any place that might welcome them.

“Halista and Phara saw them first. Figures at the edge of Umaru’s sanctuary. When we met, no words were needed. To see my father, mother, sister, and those still loyal to our house so defeated.

It hurt in more ways than I can describe. They were branded, banished, worn, and wary, but thank the Mountain, they still lived.

They told me what I already knew. Tharios had fallen, my father had been stripped of his throne, and Aguran had truly fallen to the Creed.

Thariosian banners were gone, books seized, histories pulled from their libraries. Tharios was being consumed and rewritten.

Umaru listened and asked the people of the sanctuary to bring food and water. She said little, but I saw it in her face. Her heart broke for us.

They stayed two nights. On the third, I asked Umaru if I could take them to Dothemia. All knew she was soon to be crowned Queen. I thought it only proper to request permission. She understood and agreed.

Tomorrow, we ride. I hope that Dothemides will accept them.”

Book of Aristaeus, Mountain’s Silence 85, Year 15

Mountain's Silence 98

There had been no attacks. Dothemides had departed and returned. The Red Queen had vanished, and Samike had come and gone. It was a trying time, but amidst the lingering uncertainty, the Obsidian Palace was alive with activity and preparations for the wedding of King Dothemides and Umaru.

As Aristaeus arrived with his family, the fallen King Agustus entered the city and saw things he had not known were possible. People from all nations, each one branded. Walking, working, thriving as one. Above, banners fluttered bearing the Durajani brand.

Queen Photini and Princess Androniki's eyes followed, moving from walls to guards, to market stalls and merchants. Their soldiers walked behind in disbelief as well. All of this should not have been possible, yet here, along this humble river, the city stood.

Dothemia. A city named after a young man, a mere boy at the time, who was purchased from a faltering family for a small coffer of gold coins. A man named by their son and stripped of his name by their arrogance. It was as if the very name was an act of defiance.

Now Agustus and his fallen house stood at the mercy of his former ward. His crown was gone, but a fragile dignity remained. Ahead lay the palace. Càrnothi guards approached, two women and a man. The man was scarred across his arm and face, terribly burned, yet he welcomed them with a warm, genuine smile. The women, stern and strong, beautiful and fierce, beckoned them to follow.

Inside, Queen Photini entered the court with her head high and possessed a beauty refined, not defined, by her age, with eyes the color of the deep sea and hair silver with time. She had aged but carried herself with strength. Her eyes welled when she saw Dothemides standing at the table in the center of the throne room beneath a statue of the Mother. Androniki looked around, Agustus stood stern but felt a pride well within him.

"Russom," Photini said, cupping his face in her hands as she had done when he was a younger man, and stood before him. They embraced.

Androniki, now grown, stepped forward, encouraged by her mother, and greeted Dothemides with formal grace. Though she had no memory of him, she knew the stories that had reached her of the slave and soldier who rose to build a kingdom. She thanked him for taking them in when no others would.

Agustus followed. His pride held back the tears welling in his eyes, but Dothemides could see what he held within. They stood as Agustus' family and house guards watched. Dothemides saw the weariness and the withering effects of time, struggle, and its unkind years.

Agustus blinked. His chest swelled. His lips trembled. Dothemides smiled warmly at him. Aristaeus drew close to his mother and sister. Then Agustus spoke.

"You are like a son who has risen, Russom Balewa." He paused, voice now trembling. "Your mother, your father, would be proud. I am proud...and...I am sorry."

He extended his hand, fallen king, to risen. Their hands clasped firmly, and then they embraced one another.

"Forgive me, Russom." Agustus' tears now flowed freely as Dothemides' arms enveloped him.

"You are forgiven, Agustus."

Mountain's Silence 100

From a distance, the second hand of the Nakarran Creed observed, as the remnants of House Agustus of Tharios settled into their new lives and Dothemia and its citizens prepared for the wedding of Dothemides and Umaru.

Across the four seasons, the Crusade expanded its hold and, with Tharios now under their influence, they looked north to the Skarnvald Steppes and Càrnothi Highlands.

Dothemia had opened its gates to a fallen king as the world beyond grew darker.

Tharios had fallen, and in the far north, whispers rode the winds of a girl with fury in her heart and fire in her hands.

And the Crusade began to turn its gaze toward her.

Chapter Sixteen

Wrath and Dreams

Year 16

BALANCE THE SCALES

Mother's Breath 1. Eastern region of the Càrnothi Highlands

Morning. Cold and crisp. Distant mountains rise north of a sweeping land blanketed by freshly fallen snow. Tall pines stretch on for miles as winds whistle through swaying limbs. Greatsabers hunt along the edges of highland lakes. whitewolves pace and prowl from the protection and cover of the dense underbrush, their eyes focused on their prey. By a stream, a great elk bellows, its rack wide and proud, frost rolling from its nostrils. Blood flows from its right rear flank. It is wounded and watchful.

Footsteps, harried. Breath rises in gasps. A stumble and recovery. Five men dressed in thick furs and leather race through the woods. Ivory and claws hang from their ears, necks, and belts, clattering, trophies of hunts. Strong legs carry them forward, but they do not glance ahead as they run; they glance back.

Out of breath, the party comes to a halt by the stream the elk and whitewolves abandoned moments earlier. The hunters look at each other, gasping, bent, hands on knees. Their lungs burn, and their hearts pound.

One rasps. "Do you see her?!"

A shaken head is the reply as nearby ravens fly.

"Do any of you see her?!"

None do. The other hunters look around with fear in their eyes, and their axes, spears, and bows gripped tightly.

The air grows still. Dread rises within them. Whispers carry too cleanly, too clearly, echoing through the stillness. The war-painted faces of the hunters feel it around them and within them. With practiced movements, they draw near one another, each one facing a different direction as their feet press into the thawing snow.

"We should run!" One hisses, knuckles white around the shaft of his spear.

"It's too late for that." Says another, with an arrow knocked. "Now shut up and..."

A distant twang, a whistle, an impact. The bow falls to the ground. He stiffens. His sound is guttural, panicked, pained. No words escape his lips, only the horrific sound of one drowning in his blood. He teeters, falling sideways. A companion catches him. Holds him.

The fallen hunter looks only up, past his companions, into the sky. He shudders. One approaches, and two others follow suit. The one holding the dying man roars at them with a glance, and they turn and continue to keep watch.

The angle of the arrow's entry pulls their eyes high, but they see nothing. No movement, no sound.

On the ground, a bow is placed in the trembling hands of the dying man, who grips it, waits, and continues to focus on the sky above. His mouth opens as if he wishes to roar, to scream, but he cannot. The gods cannot hear his call. Blood and tears flow from his eyes as his hands grip tighter around his bow until his chest stills and his breathing stops.

Whispers rise again; they are both close yet distant.

Another arrow whistles, then another—two impacts followed by two cries of pain. An arrow protrudes from the thigh of one and the shoulder of a second. With barely a moment to register the impact, a fourth arrow sinks into his temple. His eyes roll back, body twitching despite the soul that has already left it, and he joins his kin in death.

Three remain amidst the stillness.

A fifth shot is fired, taking the eye of another, sending him reeling back, body contorting, and crashing to the ground.

Moments pass. Two remain. Back-to-back, eyes searching through the blackpines in vain.

With the arrow still embedded in his thigh, the wounded hunter speaks. “Leave me... let her come for me... go... GO!”

There is sorrow and regret. Anger and rage. Acceptance and...a sixth and a seventh arrow, both puncture and pierce. The already wounded hunter holds his axe close to him as his weakening heart empties blood into his chest.

His lungs tighten. “The Far Sky calls to me now, brother...” His voice rises, a last cry to the heavens, amidst the pines.

Alone, the last walks with careful footfalls, slow and unsteady through the rolling fog. Eyes look high and low, left and right, forward and back. The stillness rises once again, and the whispers follow. And ahead of him, through the trees, he sees his end.

Amethyst eyes, black hair trailing in the winds, a cloak and battle skirt of bear fur, her chest covered in rough leathers. From her boots and about her neck hang bits of bone, gold, silver, and ivory. Her lips move as she whispers and watches.

In both of their eyes, there is recognition and rage.

He charges. She runs towards him, daggers in hand. Crude things of sharpened, jagged bone. She closes the distance quickly. He increases his pace, roaring, axe and dagger in his grip. Her eyes grow wild and wide, and she bares her teeth as they close.

He swings to separate her head from her shoulders. She slides beneath. With her arm outstretched. With snow and mud splashing about her knees, her dagger sinks to the hilt in his thigh, stopping on solid bone. He cries out. She rips it free.

Through blinding pain, he thrusts his dagger at her in desperation. She rolls and rises. He has given her a gift. A limb to clamp her teeth on. His outstretched arm becomes a target.

She flips the dagger, catches it, tip pointing skyward, and strikes. Fright and pain burn through him, and as he sees the jagged blade of her dagger protruding from the topside of his arm.

She feels blood flow onto her closed fist.

She twists, he cries out, she pulls, letting the blinding pain guide him. He raises his axe, she tears free, the blade slicing open his bicep like the meat of a fresh kill. Frost spills from her lips as her prey pants in anguish. One-armed and one-legged, his heart races. He cannot attack, and he cannot flee.

Sweat soaks his brow and matted hair. Froth and frost coat and cake his thick beard. Gray eyes narrow at her through dark warpaint. He drops to a knee, then falls to both.

As she stalks behind him, he whirls but is met with a blow to the head, sending his world into darkness.

Along a wall of hewn pine, a humble fortification stirs as the sun sits at its peak, melting the snows under the Mother's Breath. Watchmen peer into the deep trails beyond.

Their hunters have not returned.

The stillness rises as a horse bears a rider along, leaving a bloody trail behind. At the end of a rope tethered to the steed, a body is dragged. Hanging from the saddle are four heads.

The rider is spotted from atop the wall. Whispers echo through the still forest. They watch and peer, then their hearts fill with both dread and fear as the whispers cease.

The rider watches.

She lifts four dangling heads, held together by beard, hair, and braids. She holds them high. An archer raises a bow. His captain urges him to lower it. The rider is known. Her wrath is not a thing to be tested. The archer obeys.

She flings the heads.

They soar, land, roll, and come to rest. Each face contorted in horror and realization.

She calls out, rupturing the silence.

"Where is your tide!?"

"Where is your wrath!?"

Svirva's questions are laced with contempt.

"The god of storm and winter no longer watches over you!"

"The Mountain has forsaken you!"

She looks towards the piled heads and then to the walls, reins in hand, pointing with her dagger.

"Perhaps it is I that the Mountain now favors!"

The watchers say nothing.

"Please," she laughs.

"Continue to send your hunters and your warriors."

"I promise that I will return them to you as you see them here."

The watchers remain silent as the last echoes fade. Svirva's lips move. Her prayers rise once again.

A soft chant, learned and remembered.

She urges her steed forward, its hooves crunch through snow, and she reaches back and cuts the rope. Legs, bound at the ankles, fall limp.

She looks down at the body.

She struggles against him, the rough table before her, the firelight, shaking and shuddering, tipped tankards and spilled ale—his relentless onslaught. Her broken, jagged fingernails rake new lines across countless tears in the grain. She screams and is turned roughly. His face looms...

His eyes close as the dark room becomes trampled snow.

His cruel grin shifts into a frozen grimace.

His wounds are many and grisly.

She looks at the wall, kicks, and gallops away into the forest.

Another dead.

She will find them all.

Mother's Breath 2. Jhandai Coast. Warcamp of Amenophis

It was morning, and the meeting of Amenophis and his captains was tense. After the battle at the gates of Dothemia, the Xeyathi, having suffered too many losses, began to withdraw. Dothemia's resilience had proven too great, and the promises of Amenophis were no longer enough. A retreat back to the conquered Jhandai coast became necessary.

"Give it time, Amenophis. There must be a..." Amenophis slammed his desk in anger, silencing Amrahi's words as map markers that outlined their failing advance toppled and fell.

Across the room, she glanced towards Turadaj, whose white brows furrowed in concern and disappointment in his commander. Vragur sat nearby, polishing his blade, unfazed.

In Amenophis's mind, their position was weakening. He had observed, allied with the Xeyathi, scouted, attacked, and taken Dothemian lives, but when he sent word requesting reinforcements, the response returned with orders for him to hold and not press the attack. No reinforcements would be spared. It was not the answer he hoped for. Amenophis tasted the possibility of victory and felt there was nothing but wasted opportunity in waiting.

Turadaj stood. "These outbursts…they achieve nothing…they *do* nothing. This anger threatens your stillness, Amenophis. Let go of it. All of it. The path and nothing more guide us."

Amenophis turned, barely, but didn't respond.

Turadaj continued, stepping towards his commander. "Empty yourself of these emotions. This is the pride and vanity that plagues the Nine. They will divert you from our cause. There is a purpose behind these decisions. Trust in this and obey."

Amenophis felt Turadaj's hand on his shoulder, but he was in no mood for the high priest's sermonizing. After a brief moment, he offered a nod and calmed, but only outwardly.

With a wave of his hand, he ended the meeting and dismissed everyone. Vragur stood, and he and Turadaj took their leave. Amrahi followed and paused by the door, glancing back. The room was dark, aside from the light rising from the candlelit table. Standing alone, Amenophis began to collect the fallen markers from the floor and set them back upon the map, arranging them one by one with a calmness and precision that masked the tumult and turmoil within him.

Amrahi felt for him. More than she should, but she dismissed the thought. They held no place here. There was nothing she could say, and this was not the time. After a moment, she stepped through and closed the door, allowing the darkened room to swallow him.

As the sun rose, soldiers watched their commander walk out to the beach and stare out to sea. There, Amenophis watched the horizon, his mind filled with recent events and all that had led to them.

He remembered his commander's summons and recalled the details of their discussion with him and the responsibility placed upon him...

The history of the Nakarran Crusade was long. The faithful had lived among each nation of the Nine for countless years and taken their place within the larger tribes of the Durajan. Their purposes varied and were based on who they were sent to observe, but they were long-term, patient, and moved with force only when the time was right.

Nations took time to infiltrate and weaken. The larger Durajani war tribes of Valloch, Rolki, and Vulfgar had been under either the control or influence of their reach, and plans were in place to claim the lands and resources held by the mountain peoples of Karskath and Volkos in time.

The Durajan posed no threat until the Dothemian king slowly rose to power. At first, he was nothing of concern, but ten years ago, things changed, and a shift began.

Sacred sites were desecrated, alliances formed, clans united or conquered, and lands claimed. There were even rumors of the conquered and hidden conduits of power that once belonged to the false gods being discovered. All sensed by High Priests and Shamans of the Creed, through visions and dreams.

A power was rising, and Amenophis was chosen to observe, watch, test their strength, and send word on his findings. It was to be a last test. One that promised ascension through convergence.

He had accomplished his task, and the word he sent back was that Dothemia must fall and fall now. All he needed was more soldiers. Reliable soldiers. And Dothemia would be erased.

The Xeyathi had their uses, but their resolve was weakening. The first wave of reinforcements, led by Vragur, strengthened their position. All Amenophis needed was additional reinforcements, another push.

He could attack again now without reinforcements. He knew Vragur and his soldiers would gladly march into battle. Still, he wanted an assured victory, and the Dothemians had proven too resilient to risk falling against with another frontal assault.

As the day stretched on, the last battle against the Dothemians replayed over and over in his mind. In truth, they were more than he had expected. They were an army bound together by the banishment they shared and the brand they bore and rose as a banner.

A Marukhan king, Jhandai and Skarn queens, soldiers of Khadar, Volkos, Tharios, Càrnoth, Marukh, and Shadura—they had become a nation unto themselves. But the last battles had proven that they were not without weakness.

Amenophis remembered the command of their king and the ferocious unity of his people. He remembered their risen voices, the chants and war cries of Durajani born of all nations, melding into something entirely different.

They fought for more than the Nine had ever fought for. Something deeper. Something both beneath and beyond pride and vanity. He saw it in their eyes and heard it in their cries. They fought to be seen and would die to be remembered.

It struck him that the Dothemian king had begun a crusade of his own. Amenophis then wondered if King Dothemides even knew what he had done—the flame he had ignited.

The realization landed hard.

He would need more to win. His reluctance remained, and for a moment, Amenophis wondered if that reluctance was born of fear.

As the sun set, soldiers along the walls continued to watch their commander. Amenophis had stood alone through the day and into the night, but none dared approach him. They knew something troubled him deeply.

Amrahi and Turadaj watched him pace the sands along the shore as well, while Vragur stood guard on the beach, choosing to remain close, but giving him the distance he needed. The three shared wary glances as Amenophis returned to his cabin.

Just past highmoon, Amrahi, wrapped in robes, slipped out and walked along the creaking, wooden walkways and found the door to Amenophis' cabin. She pushed it open, stepped inside, and found him sitting. He had not slept. She entered, but he remained motionless, buried deep beneath his lingering thoughts.

Closing the door behind her, Amrahi stepped out of her sandals, stood before him, and allowed her robe to fall. Amenophis' eyes rose, guided by the slender hand that lifted his chin. She offered herself to him as she had done so many times before. Offered herself to the Crusade and the Creed. He accepted, losing himself to her pleasures.

As Amrahi slept, he remained awake. His mind on their stalled mission and on those who followed him. He glanced at Amrahi as she slept. Part of him softened as he watched her. She had given much, and he had taken more, yet still, she stood by him. Perhaps it was time for things to change. He touched her cheek, feeling the warmth of something unexpected, but pushed it away. Such feelings had no place within the teaching of the Hollow Creed.

In the hours before dawn, he rose and wrapped himself in a robe and left Amrahi to rest. Walking again, out into the sea air, he looked out across the waters of the Jhandai coastline, scanning Wanehollow Peninsula to the south, the Vordai Strait to the east, and the Bay of Blood to the north. Still, there were no ships in sight. But there was something that caught his eye.

Mother's Breath 2.
Somewhere along the Bay of Blood. South of the Thornwilds

Samike sailed for some time along the river. She thought herself mad to believe this plan could work, but the idea had taken root, and now it pulled her forward with every stroke. She believed in her heart that she could be the key that unlocked the door to the Nakarran commander and bring an end to the war that had come to Dothemia.

As she rowed, she wondered who he would be, what he would be, what she would say, and how she would earn his trust. Samike knew that it was too late to dwell upon it, too late for doubt or fear. The plan was in motion, and now only time would tell.

She decided to sail by night to avoid being seen by coastline lookouts. The cliffs along the river were high, hundreds of feet in some places, so she hoped and prayed that she would remain hidden from sight. She couldn't risk capture, so the pace of her journey was deliberately slow and, as a result, exhausting. It was taking twice as long as it should to cover the distance, but the precautions were necessary.

As darkness fell, Samike pushed her reedship out from the shore and stepped in. If the maps outlined by Catherine and Yendira were accurate, she would not be far. She should arrive just before dawn. Gripping her oars, she set out once again.

Her plan was to row a few miles east of the Jhandai coast into the choppy waters far from shore. Her reedship was simple and not meant for anything more than river travel. But there she would guide it into the large swells, further out to sea, where it would take on water, sink, and leave no evidence.

As she reached the location, the horizon rose and lowered beneath the heaving ship. Her breath caught, and her stomach churned as the cold spray and rising waters met her skin.

It was time.

Summoning her courage, she stood, surrounded by undulating swells, and balanced herself as best as she could. When she dove in, the world went silent as the tide thrust about her, and as she broke the surface and felt the ferocity of the water, she prayed she would make it to shore.

As the surf took hold of her, Samike fought panic. Despite her efforts, the shore was too distant, the waters too rough. As her limbs and lungs burned, she felt like her abandoned reedship, a thing not built for such waters, destined to sink beneath the waves. She swam, struggled, and found herself reaching up, only to fall short of the surface.

Finally, frightfully, she gasped and inhaled blackness and flame.

Amenophis's robe clung to him as he walked east along the beach, leaving footprints in the sand—prints trampled by those who walked alongside and behind him.

To his left was Amrahi, also wrapped in robes, and to his right strode Turadaj, his golden eyes taking in the unfolding scene. Behind them were a handful of armed guards, and there, lying on the sand, was a woman.

Amenophis tilted his head as he saw her. Eyes sweeping her still form. The gulls and waves echoed as the sun rose over the tides and bathed her in the morning's light.

She was exquisite.

With a gesture, two of his guards moved to check on her. Turning back to Amenophis, they let him know with a nod that she was breathing.

Amenophis stepped forward and knelt by her as Amrahi and Turadaj watched. He brushed the woman's hair from her face, took her in, and touched her cheek.

"And who might you be?" The question hung in the air, tinged with curiosity.

A sudden urge to cough. To draw breath that was not there. She sat up in airless panic, lungs burning, eyes stinging, as seawater and bile rose and spilled out onto the sand. Soon, the fire in her chest subsided, and the silent, blurred pale world found sound and color again.

Samike squinted in the rising sun, thankful to be alive. Then, seeing the figures standing before her and the man kneeling by her, she knew she had been found, perhaps by the very war leader she sought.

Through the embers still smoldering in her chest and lungs, she assessed, thought, and formulated. She remained calm and aware. Her hand rose to her chest, she coughed again, took them all in, and looked to the robed man. Then in the Alltongue of the Nakarran Crusade, she spoke.

"I thought myself, surrendered to the Silence and sea..." Her breath came in rough, her voice sandy. Her throat raw and clawed.

Amenophis's brow raised, and he responded in the Alltongue, "You are not yet bound for the blessed Hollow, it seems." He was both surprised and impressed.

She understood him perfectly. "So it seems...Commander," It was a gamble.

"What happened to you?" he asked, looking up and around, out to sea, then back to her, attempting to make connections, plot a path, and make sense of her presence.

"My ship," she said, her voice catching again, "it was lost...broken on a reef not far offshore." She struggled to shift her position, coughing again. "I barely made it."

Her body ached, but her mind sharpened as she spoke. She knew what she was. Banished from nations, unclaimed by any flag. But she also knew the Creed. Knew the prayers, the customs. Knew the way their leaders thought and how their eyes searched for weakness. She had been taught by it, shaped by it, and now she would use it.

Amenophis studied her as Turadaj's gaze sharpened, and fixed on her like a blade waiting for an excuse. Amrahi lingered just behind him, her face harder to read. There was caution in her eyes, but something else as well. Concern. Amrahi knew what Amenophis might do with this woman if given the opportunity, but she also saw her beauty and his undeniable interest.

Amenophis stepped to Samike and offered his hand. Looking up with gratitude, she clasped it and stood. He gestured for her to follow, his eyes never leaving her, and together, they walked, parting the guards as they passed between them.

With his hands clasped behind his back, Amenophis asked plainly. "So, who are you?"

"My name is Sahir," she said without hesitation. "I was born in Shadura," Samike began as they walked her up the coast. She limped slightly, playing the part of the survivor, but her breath was steady now.

"I was never one for the pride and ways of my people. Their art, their poetry, their high view of themselves...Rebellion led to my banishment, and I wandered alone for years. A child of the winds, shadows, and silent places."

Amenophis glanced at her but said nothing.

"I lived in ruins," she continued. "Abandoned temples. Lost holds. There were voices there, at first only wind I thought, then something deeper. Something I learned to listen to and in that stillness, I heard the Hollow."

They passed through the palisade, the recently erected ironwood gates of Xeyathi timber, closing behind them. The village turned war camp loomed large. She observed rows of weapons, shields stacked like offerings, and black banners snapping in the sea wind.

"In time," she said, looking back to him, "I journeyed north, up the coast and across the waters, to Vordos. There, among the cliffside enclaves, I found Believers and Priests of the Creed. I served in the lowest chambers. Washed floors. Lit braziers."

Turadaj scoffed but remained silent. Amenophis continued to listen.

"I learned the Alltongue. First by observation, then by teaching."

"You must have proven yourself humble before the Hollow to have so quickly received such teachings." Amenophis added with sincerity.

"I was searching...devoted..." Sahir continued, "I studied the sacred rites. I was not born to the Creed, but it changed me completely."

Sahir looked ahead now, her voice firmer. Amenophis walked alongside her.

"I rose. From slave to believer and now, despite bearing the brand, I carry the scriptures of the faithful within me."

This, Amenophis found interesting. And so, a test.

With quiet reverence, he spoke. Quoting sacred scripture.

"Pride is pestilence.
Love is loss.
Voice is vanity.
Borders are barriers.
The path has become our purpose,
and from the forgotten to the awakened,
our reach will extend..."

He waited and watched. Sahir listened, then spoke with equal reverence and stillness as she paced steadily through the sand.

"We walk forward to the Time Before,
where silence is sacred,
where many are made one,
and where the Hollow is holy."

The shadow of suspicion was burned away with the light of her words, and he smiled and nodded.

Amenophis led the way up the wooden stairs and down the walkway to his cabin, and for the first time, turned fully to face her. "Tell me, were you looking for us, Sahir? Do you come with news?"

"I was chosen," she said. "Placed aboard a vessel. Given no name, a map, and told to reach you. That if my faith were true, I would be guided by the Hollow. I am pleased to have found you." Her words were sincere.

"And now that I have, I can do as I was tasked and serve the commander of the advance on Dothemia."

To drive home the ruse, she continued, "To serve him and answer to him alone and no one else."

That caught him. Amenophis lifted a brow. A glance passed between him and Turadaj, and then again to Sahir. She did not falter.

"She lies," Turadaj said, voice clipped. "No one would send a single branded woman to us."

"Then explain how I'm here," Sahir said coolly, eyes shifting to meet his: no emotion, no anger, just a question.

Turadaj's lips parted, but no answer came.

Amrahi stepped forward. "She knows the Alltongue. She wears no fear. I believe her."

"You believe too easily," said Turadaj.

"And you doubt too loudly," she returned, eyes narrowing.

Amenophis's raised hand silenced them both. Then he stepped forward again, studying Sahir from inches away. She stood her ground.

He looked to the guards, then back to Sahir. "Take her," he paused. "But...no chains."

Guards moved without question, and she was escorted down a wood-walled corridor, lit by torches held in iron sconces. She was placed in a cell that was simple and clean. The door was closed, and she was left alone, save for Vragur, who watched her from the shadows.

Mother's Breath 7

Samike woke in her cell to approaching footfalls.

Amrahi returned at first light. She brought warm food, stew, dry bread, and a flask of water. She approached without guards, her steps light, her face unreadable.

From outside the cell, she watched as Sahir sat upright on the stone slab that served as a bed, her back to the wall, arms folded over her knees.

Amrahi was dressed in a light leather vest, fitting leggings, and boots. Dark hair, worn free, fell about her pretty face. Samike wondered what her station was and remembered the robes both she and Amenophis wore when she was first found. Was this woman a slave, a warrior, a protector? She stopped studying her and spoke.

"You come alone," Sahir said.

"You sound surprised. Have I reason not to be?" Amrahi replied. She entered the cell and closed the cage door behind her. The food was placed down carefully, and she sat beside it.

"Besides, Vragur is always watching, even when unseen."

"I noticed. And you have no reason not to come alone, Amrahi."

"You speak like someone who's been imprisoned before."

"I have."

Sahir took the food and nodded in thanks. She didn't ask questions, nor did Amrahi offer answers.

Somewhere in the Skarnvald Steppes

"I was once told...

The ancestors do not speak unless spoken to.
But they walk with you, if you walk in thanks and understanding.

Every path holds a name.
Every bend, a memory.

When the wind changes course or the stones shift underfoot,
it is not just weather or weight,
it is someone you have not yet remembered,
reminding you they are still here.

I whispered five names today. One came from a song, another from a grave without a marker. The rest just came to me. But I spoke them aloud anyway and then listened. They guide, and I am grateful.

This is how those who walk the path say it begins. Not with power. Not with visions, but with remembering.

If I must walk alongside the forgotten to find her, I will.
The ancestors will guide my feet, the Mountain will guide my hand, and the Mother, my heart."

Book of Ailis, Mother's Breath 7, Year 16

Mother's Breath 9

When the guards returned in the morning, no words were spoken. Sahir was escorted from her cell and led up through winding halls, past worn windows that showed the sea glinting silver under a rising sun. She was led into a private chamber, wide, wood-floored, and lit with a brazier at its center. There, Amenophis waited alone. Sahir was let in, and the guards departed, closing the door behind her.

His eyes fell on her, and he gestured for her to sit. What followed was not an interrogation, not in the traditional sense. There were no threats and no accusations. Only questions. They were soft at first, then pointed.

Verses from the Book of Nakarra.

Lines from the Hymns of the Hollow.

Quotes from the Litany of the Unbound.

Sahir answered each one, not with defensiveness, but with clarity and precision. Her memory was sharp, her tongue was fluent, and her understanding seemed complete. When he pressed harder, asking about Rituals of Convergence, meant only for the innermost circles of the Nakarran Crusade, she described them in detail.

"So you've seen them?" he asked.

"I've lived them," Sahir said. "In the Temple of First Breath, beneath the Vordan cliffs."

Again, he was impressed.

She watched him as closely as he watched her. He was a striking man—Black hair, olive skin, eyes that shimmered like desert sand. Scars trailed across his forearms, with one resting high on his cheek. He was a stern man of many battles and burning ambition, but also a man of doubt. She could feel it in his silences, in the way his eyes grew distant as he listened. He was a man pulled in two directions, torn between faith and fury.

"You have not asked why I wait," he said, after a long pause.

"I assumed it wasn't my place," she responded.

He tilted his head.

"But now that you mention it," she continued, "why *do* you wait? You've won victories and have taken ground, and yet here you sit."

His eyes narrowed. "I was commanded to."

"And you obeyed?"

"Yes...I serve the Creed."

She smiled, faintly. "And yet your hands... they twitch when you are idle."

He did not deny it.

She leaned forward, resting her arms on the table. "I've heard of your battles. Heard of what you've done to Dothemia. The blows struck against the Obsidian King."

"Why not speak of this sooner?" he asked.

"I was told to speak only to you, commander."

He hesitated. Doubt flickered in his eyes.

"I was sent to aid you," she added. "Not with swords. But with observation."

He frowned. She stood.

"I sit alone with you in your chamber," she said. "Branded. Banished. Unarmed. Surrounded by your warriors and priests."

She stepped around the table, her fingertips brushing its edge.

"How?" she asked again. "How am I here, commander?"

His eyes followed her, not with suspicion now, but with something else.

"There are ways to infiltrate and win wars that do not require bloodshed," she said.

"You know this." Sahir's presence was not unwelcome. He watched her every move as she spoke.

"More subtle ways to break and breach a wall than with brute force." She pressed.

"You want Dothemia opened to you, not just shattered, but yielded."

He rose and walked to meet her, step by step, as if drawn forward.

"And that's what you offer... Sahir?" he asked.

She didn't answer. She let her gray eyes hold his. And when he stepped forward, she didn't step back. The trap was not a snare of steel, nor a dagger in the dark. It was slower. More cunning.

That night, Amenophis did not sleep alone.

And Samike... Sahir... did not sleep at all.

"We are home now. I haven't had the time to write in many days.

I am a Queen. And I can barely believe it. We were married on the one hundredth day of Mountain's Silence.

It was strange to stand before so many. So many faces, both familiar and unknown, watched as we stood and were married before the Mother with a vow to endure as the Mountain. We married amidst the threat of war, the promise of change, the building of trust, and the grace of forgiveness. It was beautiful.

The settlers of my sanctuary had come, yet they kept their distance from the people of Dothemia. All save Ayintananga. He and Dothemides had become friends. This eased tensions, though not wholly. But I know in time tensions will fade.

The Dothemians felt countless emotions. I could see it in their eyes and smiles, and hear it in their voices. To most, I had just been a girl who had spent her time along Market Row, in barracks, patrolling the beaches, finding beasts. Many had watched as I grew close to him, but they didn't know me, nor I them. Not truly. Not completely.

Amidst the celebrations, there were reunions and introductions—soldiers, citizens, his beautiful children. I spent time with them all.

Bianzhi remains the general of Dothemia's army. She was so kind. Warm. She wrapped me in her heart and arms. The way she looked at us. I could feel it. She introduced me to Catherine, Yendira, and others from the Jhandai coast. However, I learned that Ailis had departed some time ago. I understood why.

I met Setna and Tumahn of Volkos. Her laugh made me smile, and the way she looked at Ulaka and he at her made me think they would share furs soon.

Then there were Nelah and Sunh of the Càrnothi Highlands. I had finally learned their names. Nelah was warm, almost motherly, but proud and fierce. Sunh was as radiant as she was wild, like a panther or great saber.

There was also Agatir, who, despite his scars, great strength, and his failures to his sister, was a man who was kind. I was sad to hear that his friend Larastus lost his life in battle. Watching him, I felt that he was a man living with pain, loss, and regret. Khasun and Eligal, having come also from the Highlands, were happy to see their kinfolk again. They did their best to help him smile.

Thornsten and Brynvi were a funny couple. They were filled with teases, toasts, and tall tales of battle as well as lusty stories of memorable nights and tangled sheets that never ceased to flow from them.

Then she approached me. She was proud, slender, lithe, and beautiful. She studied me with amber eyes like her father's, different from the gray of her siblings. Her hair was locked and jeweled. It was Kaelani, his firstborn. She was thirteen years old, and here I was, just six years her elder and stepping into her life as her mother. Something I knew I could never truly be.

She looked up at me as her younger sisters and little brother watched from a distance. Another, Amubira, who I learned was the daughter of Russom and the gentle woman of Vordos, Loreiaka, stood back by them. I remember most of all the look of hope in Kaelani's eyes, hope that I would not hurt her father, hope that I would be kind, and hope that I would stay.

I extended a hand, offered a smile, and met her gaze with the truth I felt in my heart. She held my hand in return. I could see that they, too, had suffered in the wake of their father's dream. And I knew I needed to be there for them, as I needed to be there for others in my sanctuary.

I embraced her, and she wept. Nobly. The siblings drew near. I embraced each of them, and in that instance, we became family.

I am home now. I know now that there is work to be done. For his people, my people, his children, and for all of Dothemia."

Book of Umaru, Mother's Hand 26, Year 16

"It has been some time since I last wrote. It's been some time since I left Dothemia behind, and bled in its name. I had given myself to his cause, his hope, and his pain.

The Mother and Mountain have guided me, and I have listened. The roads have grown colder, quieter, and I've learned to move with the land, not through it.

I know the wilds and have known them for much of my life. The stretch of the steppes, the wind-scoured highlands, the narrow, rising passes where the air grows thin. I've crossed without calling attention, slipped between places as if I were never there at all.

My camp tonight is as simple as it needs to be. A bed of moss and low fire.

Moments ago, before dusk, I noticed someone on horseback in the distance. They moved swiftly, urging their steed with intent and purpose.

I will break camp and follow before the light changes, pray that no trace remains and trust that the land will forget my passing.

If the rider leads to nothing, I'll continue. If they lead to something, I will know and I will be ready."

Book of Ailis, Mother's Hand 20, Year 16

Càrnothi Highlands. Stonefang Pass

Hooves thunder across the melting streams that lace the forest floor. Trees stand tall and dark, backlit by a setting sun as jagged stone rises ahead. The rider leans forward, urging her mount into a narrow winding path along the mountainside, splitting the earth and sending soil into the air with the passing of its hooves.

The pass twists as it climbs, giving way to a broad plateau as wind howls across the crags. Snow mottled with mud and melt clings stubbornly to the edges of the trail. Beyond, mountains stretch into the distance, their peaks like broken teeth gnawing at the cold northern sky.

The rider is a woman. Young, lithe, and strong. She dismounts with heavy steps. Boots caked with mud, she pushes through the thick wooden door of a rugged and weather-worn cabin.

She pauses in the darkened entry, tense and listening, but nothing stirs within—just silence. The silence is broken by the whisper of her breath, followed by the faintest murmur of prayers.

One by one, torches spark to life. A low fire catches in the hearth. Candles smolder then ignite, sending tendrils of smoke upward from each flame. The warm glow grows, spreading across the walls of wood and packed earth, casting its light over stones and thick hides, crudely stitched and nailed into place for insulation.

Weapons of the highlands line the walls, and armor hangs from numerous hooks. Trinkets, cloaks, and coins lay in rough piles scattered about the cabin. She steps forward, eyes scanning, until they settle on one particular pile, neatly placed.

Ink-stained fingers reach into her cloak. She draws out a small amulet and places it carefully atop the pile with slow and reverent movements. Once placed, she stands still, amethyst eyes closing and then opening again, before reaching out to reverently touch a crude effigy of the Mother that rests on a small shelf above.

To one side of the room, the kitchen is stocked with dried meats, berries, and bundles of herbs bound in twine. She lights incense with a candle, and its fragrant smoke floats up into the beams, mixing with the woodsmoke and scent of earth and pine.

With a pail in hand, she steps back outside, the cold biting at her cheeks, and descends a short path to a river near the cabin. She cracks the surface ice with its edge and fills it before returning.

Atop a short flight of stairs in an upper room, the last pail is emptied into a steaming bath. She unclips the thick bear fur cloak from her shoulders, releases the heavy belt that holds her battle skirt, weapons, and trinkets, and they clatter to the floor, revealing olive skin streaked with warpaint and runic prayers, faded from travel and caked with dirt. Arms raise and fingers work to loosen half-braided hair that falls across her back and shoulders to her waist. Beneath the wear and grime of travel, she is a radiant, dark beauty in both form and presence.

Her bare foot rises and she steps forward into the bath, sits, and sinks beneath the water's surface. There she remains, breath held, eyes open, and hair adrift in a black floating cloud.

Her bath is now cold, the room is warm, and food simmers over the cooking fire. Wrapped in a fur hide vest with a long cloth draped around her hips, she approaches a small table with a single book resting on its surface.

She sits and touches its worn red cover, thinking back to its origins in the hills east of Dothemia, years ago, and pauses before reaching for a feathered quill and ink.

"I am home.

I added another offering to the Mother, an amulet, carved in ivory and umbrasteel. It's delicate. Beautiful, even.

I find myself wondering who made it.

What hands shaped it?

What prayers were whispered into it?

I wonder if they now know that the person who they made it for has been slain.

I wonder if they know that the one who once wore it was a monster, vile and cruel.

There are others like this. Little things, cracked and bloodstained. The remains of those who took from me.

I keep them.

Not for memory.

I keep them for meaning.

Symbols.

Each one.

They lie scattered across my home.

Like bones in a cave.

I think, perhaps, I am the bear now.

But I know that I am more.

"You are the Mother's Wrath. You burn. So they must."

"You are the Mountain's endurance. You do not break, but they will."

I miss her. Her voice. Her smile. Her steadiness.

She who set me free.

And I miss my best friend. My sister in all but this...

It's been some time since I took up this hunt. Since I began to chase the names of those who once saw me as...

I wonder if she thinks of me. If she believes I will come back.

I will. But not yet.

There are still so many who must learn.

So many who must learn that I was never prey."

Book of Svirva, Mother's Hand 20, Year 16

"To be queen and yet away from him. To rise from sand and dust to stand alongside a man who dared to dream and be remembered.

My life is changing.

My life has changed.

I have been called Queen of the Sands. I am Queen of Dothemia.

Some say I am a bridge between them.

I need time—just a little.

Time alone, even if only for a day."

Book of Umaru, Mother's Hand 22, Year 16

"The people of the sanctuary work hard. Tradesfolk, laborers, and hunters each share their knowledge. They are bound by their devotion to Umaru and by their lingering mistrust and anger towards her husband.

As a child, my father spoke often of the tales of his rise. He was always eager to speak of them.

He would say...

"To rise to rule, one must make the choices that many cannot and that they must be willing to carry the weight of their choices without fail or falter."

Then he would say...

"To rule, one must be like the Mountain itself."

I hope that one day those loyal to Umaru will see this in Dothemides as I saw it in my father. I believe that in time, they will.

Earlier, I watched Umaru walk away into the canyons alone. I see upon her shoulders the weight of her choices, and pray she has the strength to bear them."

Book of Aristaeus, Mother's Hand 23, Year 16

"It was good to get away. The canyon winds, the shifting sands, and the places of the wild always cleared my mind and always showed me signs. Reminders. Today was no different.

I saw them and followed. Since childhood, I loved to find them.

To search for the story of their passing. Small things most don't see, or care about, but they were always there just waiting to be discovered, and all that was needed to be done was slow down and look around.

Faint signs, half swept away by the wind. An imprint here, a patch of fur there. Claw prints pressed at the edge of a pond. The depth that signals weight, the distance that tells of speed, and the rise and scatter that reveal the direction of movement.

As I followed, I wondered about the beasts and their grace and power. Their might and natural-born memory. Did the Time of Silence affect them? Had they forgotten? Did they, too, wake without memory as the ancestors did? Or was it a curse that only fell upon men?

I am becoming something else, but being out there reminded me always to slow down. My *Vazanti* had come and gone, and it was time now to stop thinking about where I was heading and instead focus on what was around me and what lay ahead, to consider what could be missed if I didn't.

The time alone was giving me the breath I needed.

And then I saw him.

I crouched behind a great stone. I knew many beasts, but I had never seen a beast quite like this. A lion, but different, striped. He was not of the savannah or the jungles. It's bladeteeth were far too long, and it was pale in color.

He crouched, and I listened to him. I felt him. Then he heard me and lifted his head. His eyes were white. There was such power and strength in his stillness.

I rose, held his gaze, drew my blades...I wanted him to see me as not afraid.

His eyes shifted, his body tensed, his tail went low and motionless, and his ears fell back. Something in him called to violence.

He crouched and leapt with such speed that I had no opportunity to move. But as I braced for the rake of his claws and heat of his breath, his leap carried him over me and into a pack of canyon hounds cresting the rise behind me at a full run.

I counted seven, and as he landed, one immediately died beneath his crushing bite. Four faced him, and two broke away to make their attempts at me.

The first leapt, and I dove and rolled. The other was already at my feet. I still remember its laughter. I twisted and slashed. My blade opened its side, and it fled.

Alone now, the other turned towards its pack. I looked over, and another was dead, but the lion was wounded, and they were closing in.

I couldn't bear to watch him be worn down and picked to pieces; if they won, I would be next. The rest happened quickly. When it was done, three more hounds lay dead. Both he and I survived. But not without our wounds.

I turned to him and backed away. I was glad that he lived. Perhaps that was why I was guided there. Maybe it was the Wolf that led me to read his particular story and path.

I nodded to him, and his eyes remained on mine. It was clear he meant me no harm. But my wounds needed to be treated. I remembered what happened to Phara. So I turned and went home. I was glad that he allowed me to.

When I arrived, I was greeted by panic by Aristaeus, Phara, Halista, Khasun, Eligal, Anaeix, and Ulaka. I think my condition scared them half to death. Saila and Vanti treated my wounds, and I fell asleep quickly.

This morning when I woke, I saw Eligal sleeping in a chair in my room. Aside from Aristaeus, Eligal, the youngest of those from the Càrnothi Highlands, is the most watchful of me. I've learned to appreciate his presence.

I was happy to be alive, but outside, there was a commotion. Eligal woke with a start and moved to defend me instantly. I calmed him, and as I headed out to see what was happening outside, he walked out ahead of me. Seeing something in the distance, he brought his weapon high and walked out to stand alongside the others, who had formed a wall between whatever lay beyond that I could not see, and the people of my sanctuary.

I approached and then, once again, I saw him. The lion. He followed me.

I told everyone to lower their weapons. They did, reluctantly. As I stepped past the line and approached him, his head lowered before me.

Aristaeus teased behind me and called, "Your majesty." I looked back at him and smiled as everyone laughed.

The white-eyed lion lies by my bedside now. In a place foreign to him, but no longer alone.

I believe he is home now.

I think I will name him M'kali - it means *My Peace* in the language of the Khadari."

Book of Umaru, Mother's Hand 24, Year 16

"Last night was likely one of the scariest nights of my life. Umaru returned bitten and bleeding. Wounded and weak. Everyone rushed to tend to her. All I could do was watch and pray she would be ok.

When Saila and Vanti said she would be fine...to say that I was just relieved would be like revealing just the tip of the ice shelf that hides a mountain beneath the sea.

I am the youngest of my highland brothers. They often tease me. But there is respect in their way. A toughening of the hide, as they say. Tonight, they celebrated Queen Umaru's return with drinking and wrestling by the fire. But I slipped away.

I wanted to see her and watch over her. She's sleeping now. Quiet and peaceful. Beautiful. Gentle.

I have so much to say. That I wish I could say. But this is not my story. This is not my time. All that matters is that I am here and will remain by her side.

I think I will spend the night here. Right in this chair."

Book of Eligal, Mother's Hand 23, Year 16

Càrnothi Highlands. Stonefang Pass

Svirva wakes to a knock on her door.

She sits up, furs falling away. Her feet touch the hide-covered floor within the dimly lit depths of her den as she walks to find the daggers kept nearby. Weapons in hand, she whispers, and small flames flicker and fade. Smoke rises and darkness consumes her home in shadow and the filtered gray window light of the highland morning.

Outside, Ailis feels a shift. She feels a presence within. A pulse pushes around her being, powerful in its presence. The ancestors fall silent. A sense of solitude settles over her, and she feels alone in a way she has not since the battle in which she took an arrow that almost killed her. Yet still, the feeling is different.

Ailis approaches with caution. With fingers to the door, she touches.

Inside, Svirva's bare form stands, daggers in hand and amethyst eyes shifting and alert. No one should be here. Perhaps they have come for her, perhaps they stand beyond her door.

She whispers again. The gusts wail and warn with the shuddering of branches.

Outside, Ailis breathes, taking in the scents carried on the risen winds. A hush falls over her as she leans close. Inches from the door, her lips part.

"Svirva?"

Inside, Svirva's arms tense as she grips her daggers tight. She recognizes the voice and softens, only slightly. Fingers grip the iron hasp.

Ailis both feels and watches the door. Hope rising, as it creaks open inch by inch.

Amethyst eyes peer out. Doubt and hope dance within her gaze. As their eyes meet, Ailis sees Svirva's change. Her descent. Svirva sees her mentor. Her teacher.

"Ailis?" Svirva's eyes narrow in surprise, questioning her presence, wondering if she is dreaming.

"You have become wrath," Ailis says.

"And it is beautiful,"

Ailis pushes the door, daring and gentle. Darkness is pierced by light. Svirva's arms lower as Ailis enters delicately, as if approaching a great saber in the wilderness.

Svirva looks up at her, and tears flow from Ailis' eyes. She embraces Svirva, and is embraced tightly in return.

Daggers clatter alongside boots and bare feet.

Candles and hearth spark, flicker, and return to flame throughout the cabin, filling it with warmth.

"Her eyes. There is so much pain within them. She is so quiet, so alone. Yet I sense she isn't truly. She allowed me to explore her home as she prepared a meal.

Memories fill this quiet cabin. Armor hangs, too large for her form, weapons displayed, too large for her to wield. Jewels, charms, and talismans of both Càrnothi and Skarnfolk. Trophies all, and each one, a story. A spirit. A voice. I hear them. I hear their end.

I see her possessions. Daggers and knives of bone and steel, bows and arrows, and her armor, worn and many times repaired at her simple forge and worktable.

As I walked, she whispered prayers and spoke words not meant for me. I feel at times that they are to the Mother, or the Mountain, or perhaps, some are to memories.

She has studied the land and knows it well. Crushed bone and powdered coal. Blacksap and howlroot. Writheleaf and Maw's Touch. These and more lay stored in wooden bowls, each carved by hand. Some ease pain and cleanse the belly. Some grant visions. Some weaken. Some kill.

This morning, she cooked for me, and I helped. We sat, and I held her hand across the table, seeking her eyes with mine. Her hand trembled, but in time she spoke.

She told me of her past, of what was stolen and what was lost. She spoke of a memory of Dothemides and how his hand, offered in peace, was bitten and maimed. She recalled his return, with a scarred hand bearing a blade, and the taking of her brother. The darkest of her memories was of a cruel, uncaring father and a woman who was more mystery than mother, which led to the beginning of her torment.

I learned that before finding this camp, in the first days of the Season of the Wolf, her Steppeland camp was found. They took, and still she endured.

I expressed sorrow, she shook her head, then explained that they are dead now. Her journey across the Steppelands came at a cost, but I wonder, by the look in her eyes, a cost to who?

She told me she hunts those who once preyed upon her. That they hunt her still, hoping to stop her. She speaks of laying traps, with bait and offerings. I wonder what the bait is.

I do not yet know if I am truly welcome here. Not because she doesn't wish me to stay, but because I wonder if this place has room enough for another voice among the many. But I feel there is someone she needs. Someone, in addition to me. So soon, I will return to find Umaru and lead her here."

Book of Ailis, Mother's Hand 25, Year 16

"I'd never gone this far west into the canyons, and I didn't know where she was. But I trusted those who had walked these stone valleys and across the savannah before, and in the footsteps, long faded. I searched until hers were revealed, and thanked the spirits upon seeing lights in the distance.

Her guards were understandably tense. But once surprise and shock passed, Umaru invited me to sit, eat, and tell her why I'd come.

My words were simple and sincere. When I told her that I had found Svirva, I felt her heart lift.

When I told her that Svirva both suffers and endures, I felt her pain twist in her chest.

I offered to guide her to her home, and Umaru accepted. Her protectors offered to come. They give her little space, but I understand why. She is queen now. She must be kept safe.

I told them that they could accompany her, but that they could only go so far. I would not reveal Svirva's home to anyone but Umaru.

So now, days later, I give thanks again for safe passage. I give thanks to those who have been forgotten yet still rise to guide me.

Tomorrow, Umaru and I will break camp early, leave her protectors here in the pines, and find Svirva."

Book of Ailis, Mother's Hand 35, Year 16

"Ulaka, Eligal, and Anaeix don't trust Ailis. Not openly, but it's there. In the way they watch her, how she moves, when she speaks, what she doesn't say. Her eyes linger too long. Her silences carry weight. Aristaeus watches her, too, but not the same. Less judgment. More curiosity. I understand it. She's a mystery to me as well.

With M'kali and my protectors by my side, we crossed under Ailis' guidance. I had never seen Hollowwind Pass before. Never seen the steppelands or the highlands, but I'd heard the tales. I wondered if Dothemides would worry if he knew I was here. He probably wound. But I had to see Svirva.

The land was rough in places, but the route was sound. After a few days, we set camp in a remote place. Quiet, out of sight, and safe.

At sunrise, Ailis and I left the others and made our way toward where she said the cabin would be. M'kali never leaves my side, so he came as well. She spoke more than I expected. She told me about the bitterness that she once held tightly. The battle she felt she'd lost against me. But she said that she sees me now, not with rivalry but with recognition, that we are two sides of the same coin and that Svirva needs both of us, though neither of us knows what that truly means yet.

Her words were strange, but they felt right. There was something about her. Not soft, not kind, but clear. Pure. I thanked her, and I meant it.

We stopped at highsun. One last camp before we reached the cabin. As she moved ahead to scout the path, I watched her disappear into the pines, and for the first time, I realized I liked her. Not just respected. She moves like someone who knows exactly where she is meant to be.

I don't know what to expect when we find Svirva. I don't know who I will see.

But I know that I love her, and I hope that time hasn't pulled us apart."

Book of Umaru, Mother's Hand 37, Year 16

"I have made no claims. No demands. I have shown no ambition beyond service. That is what he believes.

Amenophis trusts in what is useful, not in what is loyal. He trusts in power and sees my patience.

Amrahi tries to draw lines. Tries to assert her place through force, through presence. I have done neither. I let them speak over me. I let them question while I watched, listened, and learned. Amenophis sought counsel and direction, not division.

So now, I moved and offered him a plan.

I would return to Dothemia alone, a survivor who fled Dothemia's enemies. There, I would move freely, identify weaknesses, map the roads, routes, and defenses, and bring him back what he needed to finish this.

Amenophis said he would consider it. I knew what that meant.

He came to my quarters just after the tide began to fall. He took what he desired, and I gave what was needed. It was enough to provide me with distance from the others and space to move without question.

Before he left, I asked for ink and parchment. Tools, I told him, for the proof I sought to bring.

He agreed.

Tonight, as I write by candlelight, I cannot sleep.

By morning, I will be gone."

Book of Samike, Mother's Hand 49, Year 16

"The canyons have grown quiet. The kind of quiet that doesn't last. Days ago, we slipped into Dothemia and heard whispers of peace—an end to the attacks. But we do not trust it.

Now we are home, and since our return, Jorvan has begun to train Azi, even though she has only seen four turns of the seasons.

He trains her not as a child, but as someone meant to survive. Northern battle forms. Northern rhythms. The pace of a fight where hesitation means your end. He says he was taught the ways at her age.

Azi does not resist it. She meets the strikes. She learns the stances. She falls, but rises faster each time. Her steps are light, fast, but still they carry weight.

Skarnvald runs strong in her. The shape of it is in her posture, in the way her fists clench before she strikes.

I watch them every day. I keep the fire lit. I bring water as he assures me.

She is still young, but I believe she has already chosen the path ahead.

There is peace, for now. But peace does not root in soil like this."

Book of Nzinga, Mother's Womb 51, Year 16

Mother's Womb 55. Dothemia

Samike returned to Dothemia by nightfall, wrapped in the silence of the reedship and the weight of the news she carried. Dothemides never got to say goodbye. He was away when she left, but was now overjoyed and relieved upon her return.

Her report was clear, her words steady. She spoke of Amenophis, of his belief in her usefulness, of the way she had positioned herself beside him. She spoke of the location of his camp, the count of his warriors, and the state of their stores. She told them the plan was working.

The others listened. Dothemides stood silent through most of it, hands clasped behind his back, brow furrowed with concern. When she finished, he stepped forward.

"Samike, you've done more than any of us could have asked for. I only ask now, at what cost?"

Samike gave a sidelong glance to the fire, then back to him. All could feel the history between them—the complexity of their lingering love, but a love of a different kind, as she spoke.

"One that I will bear, Dothemides."

The following morning, her children watched from a distance. They did not run to her, but they stayed near, eyes following their mother's every step. They were old enough to understand what it meant to come and go with a purpose that kept someone far from home, but they still could not understand, accept or forgive their mother for leaving them.

Stigandr and Sittrika were the first to greet her fully, and they did so with open arms and faces lit with quiet joy. They had known her in different seasons, and in all of them, they never questioned her. They welcomed her back with love, and that love steadied her.

Others responded in their own ways. Bianzhi embraced her. Agatir looked upon her with affection, pride, and remembrance. Sunh nodded with respect. Nelah kept her distance, as did some of the newer recruits who didn't yet know what Samike had risked.

No one spoke against her. But not all could meet her eyes. Thornsten and Brynvi held her in high regard and found her courageous. They remembered her fondly, but respected her. Setna and Tumahn also held growing respect, but couldn't get past her abandonment of her children. Words passed between them that Samike could not hear, but she understood they were about her. None of it mattered. She was not there to please them. She was there to help save them.

Later, in the private chambers above the throne room, Dothemides and Samike sat alone. He thanked her, but she stopped him before he could say more, placing a hand on his. "I feel responsible," she said. "For what's coming. For all of it."

He nodded but said nothing in return.

Mother's Womb 64. Warcamp of Amenophis

Sahir, the name Samike wore within these walls, returned to the Nakarran camp days later, crossing under a moonless sky. This time, she carried news with carefully chosen words. She told Amenophis the Dothemians were planning a counteroffensive. She said this was his chance to strike first. That she would help guide the timing and location.

He agreed, though the shadows behind him grew thicker with doubt and concern. Turadaj again voiced a warning, but it was met with the same dismissal as before. Faith had already taken root, and it wore Sahir's face.

But faith in Sahir was not felt by all.

Vragur had watched her since the beginning. That night, he waited until the corridor near her cabin was clear. She had earned Amenophis's trust. There were no guards. No noise. None to witness.

As she returned to her chamber from time spent with Amenophis, Vragur grabbed without a word, one hand slamming her back to the wooden wall, the other closing around her throat. Her breath vanished in an instant. The pressure was unrelenting. Her legs kicked once. Still, his grip tightened. Her hands gripped his wrist in desperation as she kicked again in a futile attempt to shake free of his grasp. Everything spun, she felt heavy, her strength fading beneath his Hollowed grasp. Then her eyes rolled, and the world began to close in around her as her limbs weakened.

Vragur's voice came low, as he leaned close.

"If you're lying. If you've brought death to this camp," His lips lingered near her ear. "I promise that before the Hollow claims me in death, I will split you open and watch you spill onto the cursed earth beneath your feet."

Sahir's vision frayed at the edges. Her limbs failed her completely. She heard her heart drumming in her ears, and her world went dark.

When she came to, the floor was cold and damp. She gasped, coughed, and clutched her throat weakly, staring at the dark ceiling and the single line of light where her door sat open. Then she saw his boots, fading into the distance. No rush to leave. No fear of discovery. Only the certainty of his promise.

Samike lay there for a long time before she stood, dread filling her like water rising in a sealed vessel.

She knew then that this would not end cleanly. And for the first time, she wondered if she would survive.

"Ailis returned. She wasn't alone. Umaru was with her.

I saw her, and everything slowed. Not stopped. Just... quieter. Like the world was breathing softer.

I didn't expect that. I didn't know what I'd feel. I thought maybe I'd be angry.

But I wasn't.

She looked at me like I was still her best friend, still sisters in all but blood. I thought maybe we were, and maybe not.

When I saw her, I wasn't sure.

We hugged each other for so long. We didn't cry at first. But it hurt so much.

When it became too much, it was me who cried first. I knew it then.

We heard the door close.

Ailis left us alone, and Umaru's strange great saber sat near the fire and slept.

Umaru and I didn't talk right away.

Then we did.

My cave was strange to her.

My den.

She asked how I could live like this, how I was doing.

I told her that I was alive. I had purpose.

I told her that a bear needs to hunt.
And that a wounded bear never forgets its hunter.

That I sought those who once preyed upon me, and that I was well fed.

I don't think she liked how I said that.
She seemed cold after.

I whispered, and the flames grew.
I wanted her to be comfortable.

Umaru told me of her path and what she's built. What Dothemides gave her. She said she was the queen of Dothemia now.

I laughed.

She was surprised, but I couldn't help it. I told her she married the southland king. Asked her if I should bow… call her *Queen*.

She laughed and shoved me. Same as she always did. We laughed together.

I missed her laugh. Her smile. Her voice. Her eyes.
I wish she could stay. Never leave. Just so I could see them every day.

She looked around again and said she was glad to be here with me.

Our paths are too different now.

We told one another that we were sorry.
There was no need to say what for.

We talked for two days. Then she left before dawn.
We didn't say goodbye.

We didn't need to."

Book of Svirva, Mother's Womb 65, Year 16

"After all the seasons of wondering. Svirva is alive.

The home she's built is harsh, cold, carved from pain and will. But it is hers. And somehow, it fits her. Just as she once stood apart from the warmth of Dothemia's roads, she now stands apart from the world.

Fierce. Unyielding. And yet... still Svirva.

We spoke little at first. We didn't need to. Her eyes said what her words wouldn't.

So much pain. So much fury still burning in her bones. But also purpose, and however dark it may be, there is justice in it.

We are not the same.

She walks through storms.
I have chosen to build a shelter.

Her path is blades and blood.
Mine is roots and still water.

But still, when she smiled at me, that wolfish smile, so pure and real. So happy. It was like no time had passed at all. We shared stories. We shared silence. We remembered.

When it came time to leave, I promised I would return. Svirva nodded but didn't ask when.

Her eyes followed me as I walked away. There was something in them I've not been able to forget. Not sadness. Not even longing. Fear, maybe. Not for herself, but for what still lies ahead.

I turned back and saw her still standing, still and steady, watching from the high stoop of her cabin atop the ridge. Her black hair concealed her face. I wished I could see it one more time. It's an image I don't think I'll soon forget.

Ailis met me beyond the trail. I thanked her, though I don't think my words carried the full weight of my gratitude. We embraced, and I saw in her eyes the same quiet strength I saw in Svirva, but steadier, more rooted.

In Ailis's eyes, there was a promise that she would stay with her. Not just for Svirva, but for me.

Anaeix, Eligal, and Ulaka stood, relieved at my return.

I smiled, held their hands, and gave them comfort, but my thoughts drifted south. To Dothemia. To my sanctuary. To my husband. To Russom.

When I turned, Ailis was already gone.

M'kali is sitting by me now as I write. They are breaking camp and preparing for the road home across the steppes and the safe route shown to us by Ailis.

I am eager to see Russom again. To tell him what I've seen. What Svirva has become.

And yet, I carry a heaviness with me. The kind that only comes when part of your heart stays behind."

Book of Umaru, Mother's Womb 67, Year 16

Mother's Womb 67.
East of Dothemia. Somewhere in the Woundwood

The sky above the Woundwood was still dark when Amenophis led his warband through the narrow paths, just before dawn. Trees heavy with recent rains hung low over the trails, roots slick and treacherous beneath their feet. Sahir walked at his side, quiet, steady, just as she had been every day since she returned with news of the Dothemians' location...

Days earlier, Sahir and Amenophis had pored over maps, drawn by her hand and crafted by her lies.

Scouts, she claimed, had been sent ahead by Dothemides—Scouts who carried precise coordinates. If captured, they would reveal the location of the Dothemian warcamp, giving Amenophis the element of surprise.

It was a bold opportunity. One too tempting to refuse.

Turadaj again voiced his concern. Despite her knowledge, his mistrust remained. But each warning was met with the same answer. Silence. Dismissal. Amenophis believed in Sahir's precision.

Vragur believed in nothing but blood and remained fixed on her. Every move she made was watched with eyes that warned and reminded with both menace and promise.

Amrahi believed it should have been her standing by Amenophis as the architect of this plan, and the one who knew the Creed so well. But she had been replaced, and within her, contempt twisted with envy.

As the Nakarran force moved deeper into the Woundwood, Dothemian scouts were spotted, exactly where Sahir said they would be. Seeing the Nakarrans, the scouts ran.

Amenophis sent his own to chase after the women, keeping pace not far behind.

They splashed down a narrow ravine that cut through the dense canopy. Hills rose on either side, revealing a sky that cut a broad twisting line through the trees. The Dothemian scouts were swift and their footing sure. As planned, Setna and Brynvi slipped out of the ravine and into the dense underbrush beyond.

The trap was sprung.

Above, on either side of the Nakarran forces, the Dothemians stood in silence. Dothemides hand raised, his forces watching. Then the signal came.

The Dothemian forces surged from the trees. Setna, Brynvi, Tumahn, Thornsten, and Kikaru stood atop the ridge. Archers rose behind them. Arrows sailed over the descending soldiers.

Below, amidst the battle cries, the whistle and impact of arrows, and the screams of the wounded, Amenophis' forces closed ranks around their leader.

Dothemides, Bianzhi, Sunh, Nelah, and Agatir led the Dothemian charge from the southern ridge. Catherine, Yendira, Sina, Akah, Arokojin, and Yengis, from the north.

Amenophis looked around, blade drawn, heart racing. Turadaj dropped his bow and drew his weapon. Amrahi did the same; there was no time to aim, no time to fire.

Vragur cared nothing for the advancing enemy. His eyes fell only on Sahir. Dothemides took notice and raced ahead; those alongside him kept stride. Sahir stepped back and saw her end in the eyes of Vragur. She drew her blades as the forces clashed. She had no choice. Fight, or be cleaved in two.

She lunged, but Vragur stepped aside with uncanny ease. She faltered and stumbled forward, and as his elbow came down on her back and spine, her eyes went wide with pain. The world turned white, and the ground blurred before her eyes as she rushed towards it, arms splayed wide.

His knee rose into her gut, violently halting her fall. Inside, something fractured. She tasted bile and blood as her feet left the ground. Feet away, she landed hard in the riverbed. No air came as he stalked towards her. All she could do as she gasped was turn and crawl, splashing and searching for her fallen blades.

Elsewhere, Turadaj fought with unexpected strength. His broad, sweeping, Khadari blade cut through shields and felled soldiers around him. His bow was discarded, but his blade and robes were slick with the blood of Dothemian soldiers. He fought with a silence born of faith and devotion, and from his lips fell prayers in the Alltongue of the Creed as he called upon the Hollow to receive him should this be his last day.

Agatir locked on to him, struck down two foes, closed the distance, and met him with the strength and might of the Mountain.

Steel rang. The two circled, clashed, broke, and returned again in the riverbed as it began to run red with the blood of the wounded. Turadaj observed his scarred enemy through bloodied teeth.

"You serve a false king." His voice was barely a whisper. "A builder of illusions. A man of pride and vanity. I fight for something eternal."

Agatir didn't answer.

"You are nothing!" Turadaj hissed. His robes arced as he spun, with speed and grace, his blade twirling behind him, flowing from one hand to another until he gripped it high and swung in a downward cleave meant to open his opponent from shoulder to belly.

Agatir sidestepped, narrowly evading the strike and in a single, clean motion, pivoted, planted his feet wide, and drove his blade up beneath Turadaj's ribs. Deep, unflinching, and final.

Agatir could feel the blade skid against bones as Turadaj gasped, trembling, with an expression that was beyond pain.

The Khadari blade slipped from his grasp, splashed, sank, and settled on the floor of the riverbed. Amidst the chaos, Turadaj's hands clutched Agatir's shoulders in acceptance.

"Then let the Hollow take me," he whispered, eyes wide and searching for some unseen presence beyond the trees. "Let me be consumed."

Agatir leaned in close, then twisted the blade. Turadaj's mouth widened in silent agony, and Agatir pulled the blade free.

Turadaj's legs gave way. His body crumpled and struck the shallow water's surface, mouth still moving, eyes locked on something only he could see.

Vragur moved with the force of the Hollow itself, unyielding, silent, relentless, and calm. Those who came to Samike's aid fell quickly. He carved and cleaved his way, bodies falling in his wake, their strength torn from them with each brutal strike. Those who survived stumbled, minds fraying, memories unraveling.

Years ago, he had surrendered himself to the Hollow, forgetting who he was before, what his life was before, becoming only a vessel, filled with silent purpose. He was no longer just a man; he was a conduit of the unspeakable power the Creed revered. Chosen. Anointed. Ascended.

Sahir stood once again as he reached her. She turned, tried to run, tried to call out, but he was too fast. His presence smothered the air itself. She slashed at him, wild, desperate, and futile. One dagger was knocked from her hand, and the other was shattered by the sheer force of his parry.

Then he struck her again. A backhanded blow that sent her sprawling. This time, her body refused to rise.

Vragur towered above her. He raised his blade and brought it down. But Bianzhi was faster. She would forever be Samike's protector.

She descended upon Vragur like wind unleashed, her curved blade slicing low, opening leather and flesh as her steel bit into the tendon behind his knee, staggering him.

Nelah followed, and her spear struck true, slicing through the joint of his shoulder and driving him forward with her weight. He gripped the haft of the spear as its tip sank inch by inch. She twisted as she advanced. Bone cracked. Blood sprayed.

Hearing movement, tasting blood, Vragur turned. Eyes fixed and wide. Sunh crashed into him. The memory of Larastus sat behind her eyes. Her axe split steel flesh and bone as split ribs broke beneath its edge. Her dagger punched a hole in his breastplate, and before his eyes could meet hers, the axe was torn free, spilling red from the wound. The axe rose again, descended, and met his jaw with a gruesome crack. There was vengeance and pain in every swing.

Vragur turned again, body failing, strength waning. He exhaled, long and slow. He watched as Sahir pulled herself up, teeth bloodied, ribs aching. She could barely breathe. But she stood.

She had read of this. *The Last Breath of the Hollowborn*. Though none could see it, the spirits of the sacrificed left his body. Now unbound from their prison, they would be bound to this riverbed. A riverbed, made Hollowed Ground by his death.

She stepped forward. One hand clutched a broken blade, the other a jagged shard of her shattered dagger, and drove it into the flesh of his neck.

With his forces falling around him, Amenophis stood, spear in hand, facing the man the Creed had set him against.

Dothemides stood still, two-handed blade resting low in his grip. His breath was steady. His stance was measured.

Amenophis circled. The spear turned over in his hands. The water rushed by his feet. He watched for a shift, a tell, something to read.

But Dothemides gave him nothing.

When they finally met, steel on steel, blade to shaft, the impact echoed between them. Amenophis recoiled. His hands stung. The force of the blow traveled through his entire body.

He's faster and stronger than he looks.

Amenophis lunged again, leaping, driving his spear forward. Dothemides watched, waited, and slipped diagonally beneath the thrust, closing the distance so the attack sailed past his head and over his shoulder.

Before Amenophis's feet found their footing, a blow came from the shoulder of Dothemides. A blow not meant to kill, but to teach.

Water erupted in a rush with his surge, and Amenophis took the full impact on his chest and chin. His teeth clamped down, splitting his lip and crushing his tongue. He saw the sky. Saw birds fly above. Black dancing silhouettes. He stumbled back to gain both balance and distance. He tasted blood and spat as Dothemides came into focus.

At that moment, the forest around them seemed to fall away. The clash of battle became muted. Even his thoughts no longer came in complete words. Only fragments. Only echoes.

Where was the Hollow now?

He had been taught that the Hollow would fill him. That purpose would guide him, and the Creed was clarity and purpose.

But now?

He saw only a man, larger than he remembered, walking toward him like inevitability. And behind in the distance, a shadow of betrayal in the shape of Sahir.

Amenophis' footing faltered.

She had stood beside him and listened to him. Looked at him not with fear, but with understanding. He had imagined her loyalty growing. Something more than allegiance, taking root. A closeness never named aloud. Forbidden.

It had been a lie. And now the lie had led him here.

The moment was upon him. Dothemides moved with the precision of one who *knew*. He read Amenophis like the shamans read leaves. Every feint was met. Every angle, countered, every thrust, evaded.

Amenophis's arms grew heavy, and his breath came in ragged gasps. His last desperate strike came not with silence, but with a cry of fury.

Dothemides stepped across the body of Amenophis, twirling with his back to his opponent. His elbow raised, his eyes sighted his target, the torque of his body drove upward from his feet until the tip of his elbow met Amenophis across the jaw.

The spear flew from his grasp. His legs gave way, and his body plummeted. Dothemides loomed above him, blade raised. Eyes sharp, his decision made.

Amenophis didn't speak. He had no words left.

The Hollow had gone silent. Sahir was gone.

And this man… this *king* who now stood above him, had not once been touched.

The fight hadn't even been close.

Dothemides' heart raced, and for a moment, sounds trembled and gave way to the drawing of his breath. Beneath him lay the man who would see his dream turned to ash.

"Why?" Dothemides hoped he would be granted an answer, but Amenophis had no words for him. He simply awaited his end.

"So be it,"

Samike stepped between them.

"Wait…not yet," she said, her voice calm despite her pain. "You should keep him alive." Dothemides stood, confused. His eyes remained fixed on Amenophis.

"Imprison and question him so you can understand the rest of what's coming."

Amenophis looked into Samike's eyes and saw both betrayal and mercy. As her gray eyes met his gaze, they revealed both pity and hope.

Dothemides held his strike, letting the sounds of the river, the wilds, his breath, and pounding heart fill his senses.

The rest? He thought.

The blade felt heavy in his hands as he calmed. He closed his eyes for a moment to consider, then lowered it. His eyes remained on Amenophis, studying him.

"His name is Amenophis, and he knows more." Samike continued.

Looking around, Dothemides saw that Amenophis' lieutenants were dead. The Dothemian forces mainly suffered wounds. Though for some, this would be their last battle. His heart ached, and he vowed that each one would be remembered.

A woman was dragged over by Yendira and Catherine and forced to her knees alongside Amenophis. The two fighters of the Jhandai coast glanced over to Bianzhi, who approached to stand alongside Dothemides. Bianzhi nodded to them in thanks as Samike took her in. Bianzhi had saved her life once again. Their eyes met, and Samike held the gaze for a moment, unable to find words to express her gratitude, but Bianzhi understood and smiled.

"And what of her?" asked Dothemides.

Samike spoke with a strengthening breath. "Her name is Amrahi. One of his captives." Amrahi stared up in surprise. Captives? She looked to Amenophis and back to Samike, then to the imposing king.

Alongside him stood the jade-eyed warrior of the Jhandai. They were the murderers of her father and brother, and her fate was in their hands.

Samike continued. "She is worth more alive, as well."

Dothemides agreed, eyes already scanning the field. More wounded lay along the riverbed, more Dothemians would wake in the Far Sky, but they had won. Sunh, Nelah, and Agatir approached, followed by others.

Dothemides raised his eyes to the tree line. Thornsten, Tumahn, Kikaru, Setna, and Brynvi stood alongside the archers they led.

His chest rose and fell as he saw his people, his friends, his allies. They had been tried and tested, and they endured. Emotions overwhelmed him, and as tears rolled, he raised his blade, saluting them, honoring them.

Their voices rose and their cheers rang out.

Amidst the cries, he looked to Samike, and their eyes met, and her tears joined his.

"You've done it," he spoke in a voice only she could hear beneath the continued cries of victory.

"We have done it, Dothemides," she said to him with a soft smile.

Atop the hills along the river, the archers' voices rose as they embraced, laughed, and gave thanks to the Mother and Mountain.

Dothemides embraced Samike and Bianzhi, then Agatir, Nelah, and Sunh. The fighters of the Jhandai drew close to Bianzhi and hugged her, then they stepped to Dothemides to honor him as well.

In Dothemia, runners returned, calling out to everyone along Market Row that the battle had been won, and as the news spread, the city was filled with the voices of its people.

Mother's Womb 68. Dothemia

With Amenophis and Amrahi bound, and the last of the Nakarran resistance shattered, Dothemia's king, first queen, and its most renowned soldiers returned. Behind them, soldiers bore the wounded and the dead. And among them, Amenophis and Amrahi walked silently.

When they reached Dothemia, the gates were opened, and the people gathered. Word had already spread. Market Row thrummed with anticipation as the warhorses moved through the streets. Dothemides rode at the head astride Cepharion, Samike beside him. Cheers rose like thunder. Yet Samike did not raise her hand. She did not smile. Her eyes searched the crowd, but her thoughts were elsewhere.

The prisoners were taken through the heart of the city, not as trophies, but as a testament to resilience and defiance. Amenophis held his head high, jaw clenched. Amrahi remained stoic, her expression unreadable.

Later, when the sun had dipped low and the hearthfires bore witness to the daily writings of Dothemia's people, Samike visited the holding cells beneath the Obsidian Fortress, where she asked to see Amrahi.

The hall led to a dimly lit chamber, illuminated by an oil lamp. Behind its bars, Amrahi sat cross-legged, her hands unbound, her spirit untamed.

Samike brought warm food, stew, dry bread, and a flask of water. She entered without guards, her steps light, her face warm.

Amrahi sat upright on the hay-filled mattress and wooden frame that served as a bed, her back to the wall, arms folded over her knees.

Amrahi looked up. Her face showed neither anger nor surprise. Only curiosity. Amusement.

"I remember this, though not quite from this position," said Amrahi.

"As do I," replied Samike.

"Amrahi...I once believed in the Creed as you do," Samike said. Her voice was soft, but steady. "I believed it was a path to strength. To clarity. To peace. But I was wrong."

Samike paused before speaking.

"The Creed was twisted," Samike continued. "Turned something pure into something meant to control, to dominate. It punishes the broken instead of healing them. Chains them to purpose instead of giving them choice."

"You sound like him," Amrahi replied. "Their King."

Samike nodded. "It is because I love him still. I love his dream. Even though I cannot be a part of it."

"You can be free of it, Amrahi. Free of the Hollow, the Creed, the Crusade, and all that it has made you. You can be more."

Amrahi said nothing. But when Samike stood and left, the younger woman's eyes followed her until she was gone.

Mother's Womb 70. Jhandai Coast. The Fallen Nakarran Warcamp

In the days that followed, Dothemian forces, led by Bianzhi, sailed east to the warcamp of Amenophis. They disembarked from the shores of the Bay of Blood and besieged what forces remained. It was not so much a fight as it was a surrender.

The Jhandai prisoners were freed. Some wept, some bowed.

Bianzhi carried word that Dothemia came with a promise. A promise to offer protection of their villages, and an alliance should they wish it. They had homes and a community that suffered because of Dothemia's rise. Dothemia believed that they owed them this, and the people of the Jhandai coast accepted.

Mother's Womb 73. Dothemia

No one stopped her as she entered the fortress. She had earned her passage here and regained trust. Samike found Dothemides on the balcony of the chambers they once shared. Chambers that overlooked a city still alive with celebration.

"You should be celebrated," he said, without turning. "You saved us,"

"No," she replied. "We saved each other. Let that be enough."

He turned to her, eyes wet beneath dark locks, graying with time and weight.

Whatever Dothemides and Samike were, had long since faded. Their hearts had found new love and new paths, yet still they shared memories no one knew. Savior. Protector. Dearest of friends.

"Will you stay for a while?" he asked, taking one of her hands in his.

She stepped close to him, placed a hand on his chest, and stared up at him. Emotion welling in her eyes as well.

"For a time." She paused and looked out over the lantern-lit roads of the city and the activity within them.

"Stigandr likes Dothemia and its people. He finds it to have a spirit similar to the Karskathi. And he believes Dothemia's king has within him the heart of the Mountain." She said with a smile.

Dothemides could see the love she held for her husband of the north, and it pleased him.

"And what of Dothemia's First Queen?" He asked. "Samike Sul'sahir."

She smiled.

"My husband says that I must always be true to who I am. What I have become. And that, by my side, is where he wishes to be, no matter where that leads us."

"He is a good man, a wise man," Dothemides responded. "I am happy for you. Both of you."

They lingered a moment longer. Silent together. They kissed each other's hands. She stepped away, then turned.

"What will you do now?" She asked.

He looked west, up the river towards the Savannah where the sun had set just hours ago.

"I will fill the days between now and Umaru's return...with trying to be the kind of King she has inspired me to be."

They shared one more smile. They did not say goodbye. As she left, he stood in silence, the city spread beneath him, bathed in amber light.

Mother's Womb 74. Dothemia

Before dawn, Samike visited Amenophis. He stood when she entered, the chains on his wrists rattling. His expression hardened.

"You betrayed me."

"I saved you," she answered.

"From what?"

"From yourself. From the Hollow. From the Creed. From becoming what they want you to be."

He said nothing, only watched her.

"Your name is not Sahir, is it?"

"No. My name is Samike. Here, I was once Queen—the First. I helped *build* Dothemia. But I left. Because of its strength, influence, and reach. All I ever wanted was silence and peace."

"You speak as if the Creed still lives within you." He added.

Samike shook her head.

"I take what lessons life offers, Amenophis. Lessons of the Creed. Lessons of Dothemia. Lessons of the Mother and Mountain. But I refuse to be bound to any."

He remained silent.

"Freedom doesn't come from power or purpose. It comes from choice." Samike let her words hang for a breath.

"Life has offered you a lesson. Granted you a chance, Amenophis."

"So what do you choose now?" He asked.

"I choose to leave again. But this time, without running."

She turned, and before she left, she added, "I hope you choose something more than vengeance, Amenophis. I hope you finally choose your own path."

Morning. Mother's Womb 75. Dothemia

Her preparations were quiet. She did not want ceremony. But still, they gathered. Dothemides, Bianzhi, Sunh, Nelah, Agatir, Thornsten, Brynvi, Tumahn, Setna, Loreiaka, and others watched.

Each embraced her. Each thanked her. Each understood.

Her four children came last. Three stood back. Kaelani stepped forward. They embraced tightly, whispering something no one else could hear, before she returned to her father's side.

And then Samike left, together with Stigandr and her son, toward the Steppelands. Toward whatever would come next.

"I arrived in Dothemia along with Anaeix, Eligal, and Ulaka. I saw a city, changed. People who have endured. A people who had triumphed.

It was so good to see Russom again. To be embraced by him. Loved by him and to love him in return. I could see the price paid for victory in his eyes, yet also see the hope and pride of his people in his stride.

Sometimes, I feel that I don't deserve to be their queen. To be treated so differently. To be shown such love, respect, and to hear whispers of the healing and warmth my presence is believed to bring. I heard someone call me a desert rose amongst swords.

To see Kaelani, Tananda, Kanike, and Omanessi again was wonderful. We talked, ate, and when the children went to their beds, Russom and I shared our love and longing for one another.

Over breakfast, I told him of my travels. Of Ailis and Svirva. He was surprised and moved to hear that Ailis is well, and expressed worry for Svirva.

He told me of the victory, the last battle, the role Samike had played. Although we have never met, I admire her deeply. I hope that one day we can.

I told him there is no need for worry. He accepted my word, recalling the wrath he had witnessed years ago. He nodded and knew his worry was misplaced.

He's been called to the throne room to discuss the Nakarran prisoners and asked that I join him when I am ready.

I am Queen now. Perhaps it is time I stand alongside him as one."

Book of Umaru, Mother's Tears 83, Year 16

"Umaru and I have spent the days since her arrival among the people of Dothemia. When she is with me, people look at us differently. Citizens shower us with adoration. They love her and have embraced her amidst the peace we've bled for.

As we sat together by the river, she asked me how I was doing. I told her that I was grateful for our victory, hopeful for our future, and determined to do what I must to preserve it and be a better man. A man worthy of her hand. She kissed me and told me that she loved me as the man that I am—the man beneath the crown.

She asked about the Nakarran leader, Amenophis, and what I would do with him. I was not yet sure. Then she asked to see him, so I led her to him and watched as she sat and spoke to him. Even there, Umaru felt compassion.

Later, she would tell me that Amenophis was a man who was shaken and seeking. Longing for something more. Another person left behind in the wake of war. She sees the good in everyone and everything.

She plans to stay for a few more days and hopes to spend the days with me, my children, and the people. But also intends to spend a bit of time with Amenophis.

Before coming to bed, she placed a journal on the table and told me she would give it to Amenophis so that he could begin his story anew.

She is the embodiment of hope and kindness.

I have much to learn from her."

Book of Dothemides, Mother's Tears 84, Year 16

"I was sent to observe.

I abused Amrahi.

I silenced Turadaj.

I envied Vragur.

I waged *my* war.

I am emptied of all I believed I was.

Dothemides did not end my life.

Samike stayed his hand.

Umaru placed this book in mine.

These Dothemians speak of voice, balance, freedom, choice, and new beginnings.

Things that fill me now with doubts and questions.

Is my spared life and this isolation, damnation, or salvation?

Am I confined within this locked room, or is this room finally the space I need?

And this book, is this book blasphemy, or a blessing?

Perhaps I will find the answers in its pages."

Book of Amenophis, Mother's Tears 85, Year 16

Chapter Seventeen

THE RAGE OF THE RAVEN AND THE BEAR

DEATH'S THRESHOLD

Mother's Breath 7. Càrnothi Highlands

Whispers filled the high pines. Two voices moving together.

They danced and rolled, prayer and reverence entangled, echoing beneath the canopy. The trees listened. Leaves shuddered.

Far below, three men and three women knelt, blood darkening the soil. Arrows jutted from thighs and calves, crude and deliberate. None could run.

Svirva paced around them. On top of her head, she wore the bear, not merely its pelt, but its fury. The beast's head crowned hers, jaws frozen in a permanent roar, fangs framing her brow like a warning. Its eyes, lifeless and dark, hovered just above her own. Coarse fur draped over her shoulders, the weight of it turning her silhouette broad and primal. When she moved, the bear moved with her, its paws heavy, its presence formidable.

Ailis stepped into view. Her hair fell like fire, unbound, unbraided, trailing past the iron lines of her pauldrons. Eyes cold as the Mountain snows scanned the wounded without pity or pause. Her shield bore the scars of three campaigns. Her axe, darkened by blood and memory, swung low by her side.

Paint traced a single line down the center of her face, cutting from brow to chin like the blade she carried. The armor she wore was not just shaped for war, but for warning: etched with the iconography of the Steppelands, wrought in iron, stitched in boiled leather and bone. Where Svirva wore the fury and wrath of the bear, Ailis carried the cold silence felt before a highland storm.

The women among the captives recognized her. Svirva.

They had known her once, years ago. They were only slightly older than her. They remembered her torment and how Svirva survived it all. Rumors had traveled like wind through the Highland clans. She lived. She endured. And now she hunted.

The women spoke her name. They spoke of the girl they had not helped. The girl they thought had died. They did not beg. They confessed.

Svirva said nothing. A raven descended and perched on her shoulder. It watched them as if in judgment.

Ailis stepped closer, her voice low and measured. “Stand.”

The women struggled to rise, but they did.

“Leave your weapons.”

They obeyed, blades and axes falling to the earth.

“Back.” Ailis commanded.

Their feet dragged. One stumbled. Another winced from the wound in her thigh. Still, they moved in obedience to where Ailis gestured.

A nearby raven took flight.

Svirva lowered her bow, drew a blade, and without a word, she stepped to the three men who spat and swore in remembrance of her. One by one, their throats were cut, Svirva’s eyes never leaving those of her former tormentors as each execution was carried out with quiet resolve. They pitched over as they bled. She would allow no final cry.

Ailis collected the fallen weapons and bound and wrapped them, as Svirva cut offerings from the dead—rings, charms, and bone-threaded bracelets.

She mounted her horse and Ailis followed. They looked back once, to the women limping and standing in the woods with no steel and no shield.

And then they rode.

"When the women Svirva spared in the Blackpine found her home, I didn't know if they would be shown mercy again. Their torches burned less brightly than their hopes, and their sorrow bore more shadows than the night.

Svirva watched them speak. Though their wounds had not yet healed, they stood unbowed, not from pride, but purpose.

They were all Durajani, born of Càrnoth. Banished for reasons they did not speak of. Of the three, the one named Runa spoke with the most passion as she stood slender yet strong. She was beautiful with wild dark hair and deep blue eyes. Then there was Aesa, taller, thinner, likely of a family of lesser means, with dark eyes that bore a weight to them. Dersag was formidable, quiet. Short-haired, square-jawed, and broad-shouldered, she watched as Runa spoke for them all.

Runa said again that they knew who Svirva was. That they knew what she endured, believed that her fury was just, and that each of them was there to swear loyalty to her, be extensions of that fury, to protect her and fight for her. They made this vow the moment they were shown mercy.

I looked to Svirva, who still stood in silence, studying each of them.

Her raven landed nearby. The only thing that caused her to move since Runa's speech began.

She went inside without a word. I followed and asked her what she would do. Her only response was that this is not what she wanted, but I placed my hand on hers and said that this is what happens.

This is how tribes, clans, and leaders are born, and that the Mother had rewarded her fury and wrath by placing like minds in her path, and that now she must decide."

Book of Ailis, Mother's Breath 20, Year 17

"I left on foot into the wilderness alone. I didn't expect this. I didn't want it. I didn't know where it would lead. Why did they have to follow me? Did they even know?

Had Ailis seen this?

Would she tell me if she had?

My cloak, boots, and skirt were heavy with rain. It was cold. Everything was quiet. Like things were watching me.

I learned to believe there were things in this world.

Things that lingered in the quiet, the cold.

Things that watched when rain fell, and claws tore, and teeth crushed.

They were there. More than the dead. More than the trees. More than mud and leaves.

I felt them, heard them, saw them.

Sometimes I speak to them.

Sometimes they listen.

Tonight I spoke. I hoped they would hear.

Perhaps it was they who sent it to stand there beneath the rain, amidst the trees. Hunched and heavy. It turned, its paws carried its weight as it slipped from sight, then it was there again, looking back. A spirit sent to guide me.

It left, and I followed.

I walked as it led me to a waterfall, north through the high trails. I climbed its plateau and saw a great lake. Encircled by snow and trees.

It was gone. Then, behind me.

I turned back to the lake and land and saw the First Mountain in the distance, rising above those around it. Declaring itself by just being, and I understood.

I turned back, and my guide was gone. This time, he did not return.

Three days have passed. I accepted their offering.

Our tents have been pitched atop the plateau. Ailis works with Runa, Aesa, and Dersag. I will join them soon."

Book of Svirva, Mother's Hand 26, Year 17

"The cabin is gone now. We took it down with our own hands and buried the fire pit. The spoils of Svirva's hunts were moved here.

She is becoming something. Something to those who follow her and something to me. Something to the north. This girl I found huddled in canyons when I stood as the Red Queen has become more than me.

We built where she was led. The ground is hard, the wind colder, but the land listens. We set up the tents first, followed by the frames for the hall. We cut timber, stretched skins, and kept the fires burning.

And still we hunt, and are hunted. That hasn't changed.

But Svirva leads, not with speeches or plans, but with pace. She walks ahead without looking back, and we follow, not because we are told to, but because we feel in our hearts that we must.

Runa, Aesa, and Dersag fight like furies. They do not speak much. They do not need to. When they do, their voices rise in wild calls, battle cries, and the laughter born of shared victories and wounds.

Others have come.

Valka in the snow, dragging a man she had killed for trying to follow her too closely.

Gondul carried her sister's necklace in a satchel and would not speak for days.

Vaeja and Fionn came together and have not left one another's side since.

I do not know what they ran from, only that it could not have been worse than what they chose to face with us.

Roscra, Saorise, Zahona, Liath, Cassia, each one came with their ghosts, their scars. None were turned away, and all earned their place, not through words, but by watching each other's backs when the darkness pressed in.

Sometimes Svirva rises, leaving abruptly. I know why she does. I feel it when I look at her. Pains of her past converge and clash with the truth of today and the uncertainty of tomorrow.

I tell them to leave her alone. That she needs to quiet the things we cannot hear.

So we wait for her, we fight with her, and we stand by her."

Book of Ailis, Wolf's Hunt 26, Year 17

"The longhouse holds heat now. Smoke hangs thick above the rafters. Furs line the walls and floors, and blades rest on the hearth. It is no longer a camp. It is something else.

I am no longer a bear in her den.

I remembered the lesson. I remember when I was given my book.

The same must be done here.

But the things needed are harder to find. I spoke with Ailis and told her my intentions. The gifts I hoped to give to them.

We collected soot, ash, tallow, and fish oils for ink. Used scraped hide bound to rods of carved wood, tipped with bone. Then rolled and stacked them.

They did not ask; they only watched and wondered.

I worked by firelight, long after the others had fallen asleep.

The scrolls took shape.

When the last one was ready, I placed them in the corner, bound and stacked.

They are not for now. They are for after."

Book of Svirva, Wolf's Hunt 45, Year 17

"Svirva gathered us. Showed us what she had made and told us why. She spoke of a man. A southland king, husband to her sister in all but blood. In her eyes and voice, I saw and heard a loyalty to this queen named Umaru that would outlast and overshadow each of us. I wondered what kind of woman held such meaning for Svirva.

I wondered if she deserved it.

This king believed in remembrance. He believes that each person's life is sacred. That their stories were holy.

She told us that she believed ours were as well. Each one was worth remembering. The hide scrolls she had fashioned were given, and she told us to fill them.

Fill them with the dreams that guide us, the nightmares that wake us. She told us to write with the wrath of the Mother, knowing that in doing so, our memories will endure like the Mountain.

I'm starting to see now that what I feel for Svirva isn't just admiration. It runs deeper than that."

Scroll of Runa, Wolf's Blood 52, Year 17

"Tonight, I watched Svirva become a leader. She gave those who came for her something to carry. Something to outlast them.

I said nothing. Just watched.

Later, I woke from a dream.

A raven soaring beneath a sky alive with lightning, rain, and thunder. It did not cry out. It did not fall. It flew straight into the storm."

Book of Ailis, Wolf's Blood 52, Year 17

Mountain's Rise 7. Across the Steppes and Highlands

Another hunt. The last is slain. Her wrath, once wild, becomes tempered, shaped by purpose, no longer driven only by pain.

By the time the last of those who tormented her falls, her enemies are far and wide. She had become a force of reckoning. She has become more than a name.

But with vengeance comes retaliation.

A shadow for every fire she lights. A hand raised for every one she cuts down. Each strike dealt was remembered, and not all in fear.

They gather.

They speak her name not with dread, but with anger.

With strategy.

With intent.

Vengeance marked her.

Now, retribution follows.

Across the Steppes and Highlands, a new blood feud burns. In the hearts of those who have lost sons, vengeance stirs.

Rumors drift. Some among the Skarnfolk seek shelter behind Fort Koba's stone walls; others from Càrnoth slip into Fort Haphira in shame. They do so out of fear.

They speak of the Raven and the Bear, and the Wrath of the Mother, her Furies, and the Red Shaman who rides with them.

They say she no longer travels as a lone huntress.

They say her followers grow.

They say she has become a wartribe.

And that the sons of the north are her prey.

Light of step and steady of breath, unknown scouts and runners move beneath the open skies of the Steppelands and the dense forests of the Highlands. Their long strides and quiet determination carry them night and day to the lands of broken thanes and remnant chieftains.

Watchers atop weathered walls, settlers around firelit camps, thinned villages, and wary hunters all turn to see as the messengers approach. In each encounter, a missive is delivered, and each bears the same message:

The southland king of Dothemia, the survivor of the Three Thanes War.

The Wartribe of the Raven and Bear, hunters of the sons of the steppes and highlands.

They have claimed our lands, fractured our people, bled our villages dry of their protectors, hunters, and laborers. Forcing the weak and the broken to flee behind their walls for protection.

I've sat in the Skarnmoots of the Highthanes. They hoard their own and continue to bide their time. To wait and watch.

Mine was the only voice among them that saw the truth of things. I did not sit in silence; I made my voice known and demanded it be heard.

Yet still they do not rise.

I know you feel it. Desperate and discouraged. Knowing in your hearts that the Mountain has forgotten you and the Wolf no longer howls for you.

You are right. We have been forgotten. And if we do not act. If we do not find unity. If we do not rise and cleanse our lands, we will be wiped away.

The time has come to drive these Dothemians back south, break their forts, and reclaim our lands. The time has come to hunt down this War Tribe of The Raven and Bear her Red Shaman and her Furies, and slaughter those who butcher our sons.

If you believe in the words you read, if you feel the storm rising in your hearts, come to the place marked on the map you hold in your hands, on the one hundredth day of Mountain's Silence, a day that marks the end of things, a day of judgment.

"I received a missive today. I never saw the runner. Azibo handed it to me before running off toward Nzinga. As she ran, all I could do was scan the canyons, watch the ridgelines.

What the message says was just as concerning. I am wanted at a meeting of the northern clans of both the steppes and highlands—something about rising against Dothemia and a highland war tribe.

Stranger still, whoever wrote this called me *Thane Bloodwolf*. A mantle I lost years ago when Vulfgar raided my father's village and forced those he did not capture or kill into the Savannah.

When I heard Vulfgar fell in the Three Thanes War, I was half glad for it, but when I heard it was to the Dothemian king, I knew there would be trouble ahead.

If I am to believe the promises written, I have an opportunity to rise again and rebuild.

Empty words. Still, I'll go. And I'll listen."

Book of Jorvan, Wolf's Blood 60, Year 17

Mountain's Silence 100

They arrived. Some were alone, others in groups, all were hardened by loss. They gathered in the quiet valley known to smugglers and oath breakers, now chosen for this uneasy meeting.

No names were given. No banners flew. Only a memory passed in secret, a summons with no sender. All who came sought answers.

Tension held the air taut. Questioning glances flickered behind guarded eyes. Each suspected the other. Remnants of Vulfgar, Rolki, and Bloodwolf sat alongside dissenters of Llothvik and Valloch and many others.

And then they heard the hooves.

Riders emerged from the western wood line. Mist trailed them like cloaks. At their head rode a man as broad as the bristlebacks of Càrnoth, with hair the color of wolf hide, dyed crimson, and a gaze sharp as steel.

Among those gathered, Jorvan, hood drawn, sat alone, hoping not to be seen or recognized. Then another sat alongside him. His skin was dark, his hair black, and his beard coarse. Charms hung about his neck, carved in the holy likeness of the Wolf.

Jorvan studied him. He did not recognize the painted symbols that adorned his tanned and weathered skin, or the manner in which his hair was braided and shaved. He wondered who he was but said nothing.

The horses stopped. Jorvan's eyes turned to the procession's leader. It was a face he knew.

His voice carried as he reined in his mount.

"I am Bjorn Tuskspear," he announced, the name falling heavy among them like a thrown axe. "And I thank you for coming."

His armor bore the mark of Skarnvald. Yet at his side rode a Thariosian, grim and well-armed, his helm etched with faded family sigils of Aguran. Another bore a scarred shield of Vordos. Behind them rode five more. Each was draped in cloaks too fine for common men and bore weapons gleaming in ways that made even the most seasoned among the assembled pause—Ralmasan mercenaries.

Bjorn continued, ignoring the rising murmurs.

"The gods have forgotten us," he said. "We fight, we fall, and we are left with nothing."

"We watch the Dothemians rise. We fear the blackpines and the war tribe of the Raven and Bear that stalks them."

"We run, fetch, and cower behind the walls of Koba and Haphira like tail-tucked, toothless pups."

Some nodded. Others frowned.

"How long can we sit and cower? How long will we lower our heads and accept?"

Bjorn paused.

"I have found new allies." His gaze shifted to those who flanked him.

"Allies who promise an end to the chaos that consumes our lands."

A hush fell over the gathering as Bjorn now walked and spoke among them.

"From the west, they came, not to conquer, but to join us. To bring order where even the gods have failed."

Jorvan's eyes narrowed. This is what he had come to hear. The man alongside him leaned in. Jorvan noticed and looked back to Bjorn.

Bjorn did not flinch. "I bring men who have seen what we suffer. And who would help us end that suffering? Not all who follow the Hollow do so out of a desire to see all things wiped away. Some seek purpose and order. No different than the rest of us."

Voices rose in anger. A woman from the highlands spat to the ground. "Nakarran, then?! You dare bring the Hollow into our midst?"

A long silence followed. Among the crowd, one elder raised a hand. "And at what cost, Tuskspear? What price must we pay for such...*order*?"

Bjorn's gaze hardened. "Only what we've already paid...our names, our homes, our own damned gods."

Jorvan's heart sank. Bjorn looked toward him, and by his eyes, he recognized him, even cloaked. Bjorn stepped through and towards him and stopped. Jorvan stood, and eyes nearby fell upon them.

"You came, old friend." Said Bjorn.

They clasped hands, and Jorvan nodded.

"Though I cannot believe what I am hearing, Bjorn."

Bjorn released his hand and turned, responding both to Jorvan and to the assembled, his voice rising over the weary whispers.

"Believe only that a storm is rising! And you all must either rise with it or be swept away by it. This *must* be done."

Bjorn then glanced at the man alongside Jorvan and placed a heavy hand on his shoulder, welcoming him. The man turned, and Bjorn studied him.

"Yours is a face I do not know. A name, traveler." Bjorn waited expectedly.

"I am Nashoba. Like the others, I am here to listen and learn."

"Welcome then. It is good to see that even a stranger seeks to hear the truth spoken."

Nashoba offered only a faint smile as Bjorn turned and made his way back through the assembly.

They had fought too long. Lost too much, and though the Nakarran Crusade was a poison in the eyes of many, the thought of *something*, anything, that could carve meaning from their suffering, stirred a bitter hope.

In the end, they did not embrace Bjorn's allies, but neither did they send them away.

It was not allegiance that formed on that day. It was a grim acceptance—a pact born of fading endurance.

And as the riders settled among them, and night began to fall, none noticed the cold that crept into the wind. Or how the wolves no longer howled.

EPILOGUE

Dothemia

Dothemides sat and took his journal in hand.
His mind on Umaru, his children, Dothemia's peace.

He turned to it without realizing at first.
A single page, perfectly fitted.

How long had it been here? How did he not notice it?
He had written in his journal for seasons, yet here, the page sat, written not in his hand but in the hand of a woman who knew him more than any other.

Samike.

She knew the rhythm of his journaling.
She knew he never missed a day.
She knew the exact day he would reach this page.

Today was Wolf's Howl 76.
As with all phases of the seasonal moons, the day comes with meaning.

Echoes of victory or warning.
The gathering of tribes.
When lines are drawn.

Surely, she had chosen this day for a purpose.
And as he read the words, a dread settled upon him.

Dothemides,

You have achieved greatness. You have built something rare: beauty, wonder, belonging, remembrance. But it sits on a blade's edge.

Dothemides. My friend. My first love.

Understand this: The Creed and Crusade have not been defeated.

They have walked among the Nine and the Durajan since the Awakening, and they remain, still.

Hidden. Embedded. Whispering.

Amenophis was only the beginning.

They will come again. Be vigilant and be ready, for I believe the war has only just begun.

DRAMATIS PERSONAE

The following appendix contains information that reflects the full events of Book One. Readers who have not completed the story may wish to finish the book before proceeding.

Dothemia

Dothemides (*Doth-eh-MY-dees*) – Child of the Nation of Marukh, King of Dothemia, once a soldier and slave, now builder of a fortress forged from memory, battle, and vision—husband, father, and leader of a people shaped by loss and rising purpose.

Samike (*Su-MEE-kay*) – First Queen of Dothemia, born of Shaduran and Marukhan blood, branded, banished, and risen to shape the course of a kingdom. Tactician, mother, and survivor, her voice disarms, her presence redefines, and her choices change nations.

Bianzhi – Friend, lover, queen, and general. The most skilled warrior of the land. Her bond to Dothemides is defined by loyalty, love, and duty.

Haphira — Tharios-born, marked by early gentleness and fierce resolve. Bound to Koba in love, and to Dothemia through memory and hope.

Koba — Banished from Marukh, drawn to Dothemia by conviction and clarity. A fighter, a recorder of truth, and beloved of Haphira.

Loreiaka – Vordan-born consort of Dothemides, mother to Amubira. A quiet presence, observant and faithful, often tending the children during times of war.

Umaru *(Oo-MAH-roo)* – Khadari-born tracker and knower of beasts. Called the Queen of the Sands by those she aids, shelters, and leads. She moves with quiet certainty between wilds and rising kingdom, and walks a path of compassion and healing.

Kaelani *(Kay-LAH-nee)* – Firstborn daughter of Dothemides and Samike. Given the title of Princess in the earliest days of the Obsidian Fortress. She embodies the promise of a new people—unbranded, yet born of banishment, the first light of a nation yet to rise.

Bakhuran *(Ba-KUR-an)* — Centuries-worn mystic, Khadari by blood and Durajani by heart. A chronicler of the hidden truths of the land who passed his final knowledge to Dothemides.

The Wanderers

Jorvan – Once a warrior of the Skarnvald, now a father and quiet protector. Torn between the love of his family and the call of the north.

Nzinga *(En-ZING-gah)* – Khadari healer and shaman, wife to Jorvan, mother to Azibo. She trusts her instincts to guide her into a future not yet seen.

Azibo *(Ah-ZEE-bo)* – Daughter of Jorvan and Nzinga. Raised among the red cliffs and wilds of the canyonlands, where strength and wonder grow side by side.

The Steppelands

Ailis *(AY-lis)* – Enigmatic shieldmaiden, shaman of the north, whisperer of the ancestors. Fierce and unwavering, Ailis is guided by the Mother and Mountain to stand alongside the destined.

Brynvi *(Brin-vee)* – Sister of Llothvik, huntress of the steppelands, keen-eyed and quick with her bow. Joined Dothemia to scout, to serve, and to watch. She stands by Thornsten in battle and in bond.

Thornsten – Husband to Brynvi, watcher of paths and quiet sentinel. A marksman who stands not before, but beside the dream of Dothemia. He holds reverence for the old hymns and carries humor that endures even in war.

Thane Llothvik — Thane of Skarnvald, sharp in judgment, measured in speech, and embroiled in steppeland blood feuds. He offered Dothemia shelter and allied with them as their purpose unfolded.

The Highlands

Svirva *(Sveer-vah)* – Born of Càrn Valloch, forged in torment, fueled by fire, and driven by vengeance. She wears the bear, commands the raven, and leads her Furies with unrelenting purpose. Her wrath became a wartribe and a path others now follow with blood on their blades and her name on their breath.

Agatir *(Ag-eh-teer)*– Brother to Svirva, warrior of Càrn Valloch, steady and loyal. His silence hides his shame, and his strength is shaped by guilt. His heart is bound to both Dothemia and the sister he failed to save.

Larastus – Loyal and brash. A Durajani born of Càrnoth. Chosen by Dothemides alongside Agatir to serve. Known for his skill, his strength, and the trust he earned among those who stood the line with him.

Haegun – Branded fallen warchief of Càrnoth, father to Agatir, unbending in pride and hardened by war. Turned his eyes from Svirva's torment and lost more than he ever understood.

Arican *(AH-ree-kon)*– Mother to Svirva, born to no banner, she moved through chief and clan as smoke and ember. Wherever she walked, desire and shame followed, and none who touched her life remained unchanged.

Valloch *(Val-ock)*— Warchief of the northern highlands, shrewd and unyielding. Feared more than followed, he ruled through dominance and built a legacy of cold obedience and fractured loyalty.

Sunh *(Soon)* – Fierce and fire-hearted, once a warrior of Càrn Valloch, now a blade sworn to Dothemia. Her loyalty is unshakable, and her skill in battle is unquestionable.

Nelah *(Nee-la)* – Warrior of Càrn Valloch who once raised her blade against Dothemides, only to lay it down in remorse. She offered herself as recompense and now stands among his trusted.

Stigandr — Karskathi priest and eventual husband to Samike. Stoic, spiritual, and loving he walks the Mountain's path and stands by her always.

Sittrika — Son of Samike and Stigandr, marked from birth by whispered doubts, yet held by his mother with fierce and unshakable devotion.

Runa — Banished blade of Càrnoth, bold of voice and steady in purpose. She was the first to kneel to Svirva, and the first to rise as Fury.

The Thariosians

King Aguran – Seemingly ageless warlord of Tharios. Feared by his enemies, untouched by time, and bound to the Hollow Creed. His rise shattered House Agustus and turned Tharios into a battleground of power and belief.

King Agustus – Ousted sovereign of Tharios, brother of Aguran, and once served by Dothemides, he now stands dethroned by creed and blood. He walks with dignity among the Durajani, still bearing his crown in silence.

Aristaeus *(A-ris-TAY-us)*– Son of Agustus, prince of Tharios, forged by loss and burdened with failed leadership and bound by loyalty to Umaru.

The Volkosi *(Vol-KO-see)*

Tumahn – Brother of Setna, archer, and a quiet voice among the Volkosi. He chose trust when his people clung to caution.

Setna – Volkosi-born and sister to Tumahn. Observant, steadfast and wry, her arrows find their mark, and her convictions run deep.

The Creed

Amenophis – Priest of the Crusade and warrior sent to unmake Dothemia. Torn between purpose and doubt, his path fractures when shown mercy by those he meant to destroy.

Amrahi – Believer in the Hollow, who stands beside Amenophis. Devoted to purpose, yet shadowed by envy, pride, and ambition.

Turadaj — Sorcerer Priest of the Creed, zealot of its rites and silence. Advisor to Amenophis, he fought with fervor and prayer, invoking the Hollow with blade and whispered breath.

Vragur *(Vra-Goor)* – Hollowborn warrior in the service of Amenophis, a towering shadow of brutality and belief. His blade does not simply kill; it drains, leaving ruin in body and mind.

THE CALENDAR OF THE AWAKENED WORLD

The rhythms of the Last Gods measure time in the Awakened World and echo the arc of life. From birth and growth, to struggle and sacrifice, to loss and reflection, the calendar is not just a reckoning of days, but a mirror of becoming.

Each year is divided into four Seasons of one hundred days.
Each Season is divided into four moons of twenty-five.

Each season is used in rites, formal records, and the histories of the Nine Nations. But within the Durajan, something new was born.

Dothemides revived something more profound, the personal record.

Among the banished and the broken, he placed journals in their hands and urged them to write, not just for posterity, but for presence. For remembrance. For proof that they lived.

In doing so, he gave the calendar new meaning, not just a divine rhythm, but a map of the soul. Each season became a stage of becoming, each phase a breath in the long story of what it means to survive and remain.

What follows is the calendar of Durajan and the Awakened Lands:

Season of the Mother

She who gives, heals, and weeps.

The Season of the Mother begins with renewal as life stirs, and the land exhales. Her hand brings birth, growth, and healing, guiding the planting of seeds and dreams. Beneath the soil, life is nourished by hope and ritual. As the season closes, joy and sorrow intertwine in quiet reflection.

- **Mother's Breath**
  (Days 1–25) The world exhales after winter. Life begins again.

- **Mother's Hand**
  (Days 26–50) Her hand nurtures and guides—a time for planting, building, and healing.

- **Mother's Womb**
  (Days 51–75) New life grows unseen. Hopes deepen. Rituals of fertility abound.

- **Mother's Tears**
  (Days 76–100) Joy and sorrow mingle. A time of birth and loss. Reflection before the hunt.

Season of the Wolf

He who hunts, protects, and howls.

The Season of the Wolf begins with the rising call to readiness as hunters stir, and warriors hone their edge. Boldness follows, as strength is tested, action demanded. Blood is spilled, and bonds are forged. As the wolf howls, victory and warning echo, and the people gather to face what comes.

- **Wolf's Wake**
  (Days 1–25) The wolf rises. Hunters prepare. Warriors sharpen their blades.

- **Wolf's Hunt**
  (Days 26–50) Boldness, strength, and trials define this time—the season of action.

- **Wolf's Blood**
  (Days 51–75) Heat and risk dominate—battles rage. Rituals of endurance test the people.

- **Wolf's Howl**
  (Days 76–100) Echoes of victory or warning. Tribes gather. Lines are drawn.

Season of the Maw

That which consumes, transforms, and silences.

The Season of the Maw begins with both hunger and offering, as harvests are reaped and preparations are made. Then comes the withering, a time of rot, decay, and release. At last, silence falls, sacred and still, as all prepare to endure what follows.

- **Maw's Hunger**
  (Days 1–25) The season begins to devour. Offerings are made. Crops start to fade.

- **Maw's Feast**
  (Days 26–50) Plentiful harvests and solemn sacrifices. A time of reaping and remembering.

- **Maw's Wither**
  (Days 51–75) Decay and rot set in. Rituals of surrender mark the waning of the year.

- **Maw's Silence**
  (Days 76–100) All things fade—a sacred hush before winter.

Season of the Mountain

That which endures, judges, and remembers.

During the Season of the Mountain, the cold returns and the people steel themselves for what lies ahead. In its stillness, stories are shared, actions are remembered, and judgment is rendered. It is a time of vigilance, reflection, and the silent end before rebirth.

- **Mountain's Rise**
  (Days 1–25) The cold stirs. The people steel themselves for what's to come.

- **Mountain's Trial**
  (Days 26–50) The harshest tests of all: cold, famine, and perseverance.

- **Mountain's Vigil**
  (Days 51–75) A time of stillness. Stories are shared. Elders are remembered.

- **Mountain's Silence**
  (Days 76–100) The end of things. Deep judgment. Time to reflect.

So moves the calendar of the Awakened World, not only through the land and sky, but through the lives of those who walk it. Its seasons mark not just time, but truth: that to be born, to fight, to endure and to let go is the cycle we all walk. And in remembrance, we live again.

GLOSSARY

Càrn

Settlements of the Càrnothi people, more than villages, each càrn is a fortified stronghold built upon war, bloodline, and honor. Ruled by chieftains, càrns are the lifeblood of Càrnoth culture, each one steeped in legacy and bound by clan rites. The most feared of them is Càrn Valloch, seated in the northwest and named for its brutal chieftain.

Càrnoth

One of the Nine Nations, Càrnoth lies in the far northwest of the Awakened World, sharing its southern border with the nation of Skarn. A frigid land of tundra, crags, and storms, Càrnoth is shaped by war and hardship. Its people, forged in frost and fire, are ruled by kings who fight as much among themselves as they do with their enemies. Their might is unmatched, though their numbers are thinned by the unforgiving cold and the wilds that surround them. Were it not for these natural barriers, they might have already conquered the West.

Hollowborn

Individuals who have undergone Hollow Convergence and become living anchors of the Hollow. They speak little, show no emotion, and fight with steady will and blackened eyes. Their weapons drain strength, resolve, and will. Victims are not killed but subdued, then brought for spiritual judgment. To be struck by a Hollowborn is to begin to fade, inside and out.

Hollowed Ground

Places thick with residual Hollow energy and inhabited by the Unbound. Marked by unnatural silence, dim light, and a pressing weight in the air, these lands erode strength and clarity over time. Prolonged exposure causes confusion, hallucination, and collapse. The fallen may become vessels for the Hollow, reborn as forgetting all, even pain.

Jhandai

Located in the southeast seas of the Awakened World, the island nation of Jhandai is home to elite sailors and swordfighters. Proud defenders of their waters, they rebuff all who would exploit or defile their shores, particularly the cursed Vordans.

Karskathi

The Trial-Born, stoic, ascetic devotees of The Mountain who have survived sacred ordeals in the northern frost. Their rites and rituals are dedicated to the mountain frost and the Umbrasteel and Blackwave flux found within. Like the Volkosi, Karskathi are skilled at forging umbrasteel.

Khadar

Situated in the southern expanse of the Awakened World, the nation of Khadar borders Shadura to the west and faces Xeyath across the Keyadeth Bay to the east. A rugged desert land, where survival hinges on precision. Khadar's people are nomadic hunters and archers, masters of distance and movement. They value peace, but defend their lands with silent force.

Marukh

The nation of Marukh lies in the southwest, bordered by Tharios to the north and Shadura to the east. A wealthy land of fertile valleys and stone-walled cities, Marukh is known for its dynastic traditions and rigid caste structure. Its people are disciplined and graceful, bound by bloodlines known as the Sajhiran.

Nakarrans

Zealots of the Hollow Creed. They are not bound by blood, race, or homeland, but by unwavering belief. Found across the Awakened World in secret cells and silent strongholds, they infiltrate every level of society. Diverse in appearance and speech, they erase lineage and ego in service of a singular truth: all must be emptied to be filled. Their society is structured around spiritual devotion, ritual conquest, and transformation through Hollow Convergence.

Shadura

Positioned between Marukh to the northwest and Khadar to the east, the desert nation of Shadura sees art in all things: combat, mourning, and memory. Ruled by a queen called the Zahirat, Shadura's people revere elegance, storytelling, and the beauty of creation as divine truth.

Skarn

Skarn spans the northwestern forests of the Awakened World, a nation hemmed in by Tharios to the south and Càrnoth to the north. Defined by hardship and vigilance, Skarn's clans are bound by honor and constantly tested by ambition, raids, and inner discord.

Skarnvald

The wolf-clans of the northern steppes of the Durajan. Hardened, fiercely independent, and bound by blood oaths, they walk the path of endurance, silence, and judgment beneath the gaze of the Wolf and the strength of the Mountain.

Tharios

Found in the western heartland of the Awakened World, the nation of Tharios shares its borders with Skarn to the north and Marukh to the south. A militarized and deeply structured society, its noble houses are locked in perpetual rivalry, trading in wealth, power, and war.

The Hollow

An ancient, consuming force, neither purely physical nor entirely spiritual, that erodes identity, memory, and will. It is not merely death or void, but a purposeful unmaking. Those who follow the Hollow seek to cleanse the world of burden and self, preparing vessels to be remade by the Nakarran Creed.

The Hollow Creed

The guiding faith of the Nakarrans. It teaches that individuality, memory, lineage, and emotion are burdens that must be surrendered. In emptiness lies purpose; in surrender, transformation. Through Hollow Convergence, the self is shed so that the Hollow may inhabit and reshape it.

The Hollowed

Those who fall in battle against the Hollowborn and are taken alive. Weakened in body and mind, they are brought before Nakarran Priests to be Weighed. Through interrogation, their truths are laid bare. Those who submit may rise, reborn as Believers or even Hollowborn. Those who resist, even as they waste away, are sacrificed in future rites. Their fates are considered sacred steps in the spread of the Hollow.

The Unbound

Unstable, disembodied remnants of the Hollow, created when Convergence rituals fail or powerful Nakarran are slain. They linger in sites of death and sacrifice, unable to anchor to a vessel. Though they have no form, they can influence thoughts, emotions, and memories. Their presence turns sacred sites into dangerous territory.

Umbrasteel

A rare, black-metal alloy mined in volcanic regions and deep mountain veins. Coveted for its strength and rumored to sing in battle, it is sacred among smiths and warriors alike.

Volkos

Descendants of the Khadari who migrated northeast to the volcanic lands, the Volkos are fierce, isolated, and deeply distrusting of outsiders. Skilled miners and smiths, they are known for their forging of umbrasteel and their deep ties to fire and stone.

Vordos

To the northeast lies the island nation of Vordos, a fallen land plagued by the Hollow and driven to desperation. The world shuns its shores. In their isolation, they seek dominion by force.

Xeyath

The southernmost of the Nine Nations, Xeyath is wrapped in jungle and mist, untouched by direct borders. Keyadeth Bay separates it from Khadar to the west, while the Xeyandai Strait lies between it and Jhandai. Its tribes value stealth, strength, and slave-taking over coin or conquest.

ACKNOWLEDGEMENTS

To my test readers, thank you. You gave your time, your thoughts, and your honesty. This book is sharper, deeper, and more complete because of you. Your encouragement helped me believe this story was ready to be shared. I'll always be grateful.

With appreciation:
Anne, Mireille, Mike, Kareem, Colin, and Marc.

I hope you've enjoyed Book One.
Book Two of The Durajan Series is coming.

Visit Alania Press

The world of Durajan doesn't end here.

Explore the Awakened World

Visit: https://www.alaniapress.com

Dive deeper into The Durajan and the Awakened World with maps, faith, art, calendar, characters, language, and more.

Also keep up with news, the author blog, press kits, FAQs, updates, and what's coming next.

Follow A. H. Lewis on Instagram

https://www.instagram.com/ahlewisauthor/

www.ingramcontent.com/pod-product-compliance
Lightning Source LLC
Chambersburg PA
CBHW020935310726
48980CB00007B/779/J
9798998845840